Books by B. V

Visit BVLarson.com for more information.

Demon Star

by
B. V. Larson

Copyright © 2015 by the author.

ISBN-13: 978-1516920792
ISBN-10: 1516920791
BISAC: Fiction / Science Fiction / Military

-1-

I watched as a squadron of Demon ships hovered in what they assumed was full stealth. They were parked in open space, partway between their home planet and my ship.

Normally, a group of motionless warships would be boring. But there was an intruder closing in on them. I could tell they weren't sure what to make of the curiously designed craft that had suddenly appeared in their region. Neither were we, until our long range optical sensors showed us seven tentacle arms protruding from its underbelly. I could only wonder how the craft looked to them. It didn't have any weapons nor did it seem to be a merchant vessel.

The snooping vessel was, of course, Marvin's *Greyhound*. Marvin was probably the most interesting member of my expedition. He was a robot who'd built himself out of spare parts—but he never seemed to finish the job. *Greyhound* was a fast space yacht that Marvin had become one with, rather like hermit crab crawling into a shell and taking up residence.

"What are they going to do?" Adrienne asked me, stepping up to massage my shoulders. She was wearing nothing but a smart towel—which I found intriguing. Due to self-knitting nanofibers, the towel stayed up, covering her critical zones with aggravating effectiveness.

We were in our shared quarters aboard *Valiant*. Recently, I'd begun to fill what was supposed to be my sole place of rest with numerous pieces of equipment. I was still debating the wisdom of that move. How could a captain ever relax if he was tied in electronically even in his stateroom?

"I don't know," I said, watching tensely through a scope that led to a remote optical pick up. "They play cat and mouse out there with the other worlds all the time, and I guess it's all part of a cold war to them. But they can't be happy about some alien ship uncovering their stealth."

After about three minutes, the Demons made their decision. A single missile leapt toward the intruder.

Marvin seemed to be well aware of the silent fleet that thought of itself as invisible. I could imagine his excitement. His tentacles must have been whirring around the cockpit taking in all sorts of information regarding this new species of alien.

He initiated evasive actions. Just as the missile was about to strike, he engaged thrusters causing it to miss and swing around in order to retarget.

Seeing that their first shot had gone wide, the Demons proceeded to fire two more missiles in quick succession.

"That crazy tin-plated machine…" I muttered. "He's not even running yet."

"Let me see," Adrienne urged, tugging at me.

"You'll have to wait. I'm not sure if we're going to have to intervene."

"How could we do that? We're too far away."

She was right, of course, but I kept watching anyway.

Marvin dodged again, but then he finally turned and started to run. I guessed that three missiles were interesting enough. He directed his tiny ship toward open space and poured on the speed.

Leaning back from the scope, I grabbed Adrienne's small hands. They were still on my neck, and she was breathing hotly into my ear. I knew her interest was only in the events going on in space, but that stuff was pretty far off. I'd been sitting here for hours digesting all available data on this new star system we'd dubbed Trinity, and I could use some R&R.

"Don't even get started, Captain," she said, struggling lightly and slipping from my grasp. "My shift starts in ten. What happened to Marvin?"

"I don't know. He's running around with missiles chasing him. I'm switching over to general monitoring."

I tapped until the smart wall nearest my hand displayed a large set of red contacts that moved like beetles looking for dinner.

Adrienne didn't leave. She eyed the display quietly.

"I thought you were going on duty," I said.

"First, why do you have our ship's personnel up on the integrated display system? I thought you were researching Trinity and its three sentient races."

"Lieutenant, did you know that a lot of physical activity can be accomplished in the span of ten minutes?"

"Just tell me who you're tracking," she demanded.

"These contacts aren't personnel. They're not even human—at least I don't think so. They're the aliens who inhabit the third planet, and according to Marvin they speak a weird bubbling language he doesn't yet understand. We're calling their planet Ellada."

"Why Ellada?"

"It's part of Greece—some think they resemble classic Greek people."

"But I thought you said they were aliens...?" She came around the table, moving closer to the display.

Now I knew for sure I wasn't getting a break—especially the kind I was looking forward to. Once she had her curiosity up, she could be just as bad as Marvin.

"Their civilization shows all the marks of a parallel to Earth's." I tabbed the display and brought up some shots of their cities and parks. They looked like fantastic science-fiction artwork from back in my dad's day.

Adrienne studied them intently.

"Cody, these aliens look like Mr. and Mrs. Universe from Earth. All of them are drop-dead gorgeous. How is that possible? Look at that male there! What's he wearing—or rather, not wearing?"

"Hey now..."

"What? Are you jealous? You will always be my captain."

She eased into my lap, and for the first time, I began wishing that smart towels were not so smart. Hers kept sliding in between her skin and my hands.

"This could be the break we have all been needing, Cody. Exactly what you and I have been needing. A real…"

"What? A real home? That's what I'm afraid of. What happens when the crew sees this? What will they do when they have the opportunity to trade a life of hardship and danger for a place in paradise?"

I eased Adrienne to her feet and stood up. Our mood had been dashed by real problems again—that had been happening a lot lately. I turned off the display and wished I'd never let her see it.

Adrienne pursed her lips. "What makes you think that these 'aliens' will invite us to stay? We thought the Pandas were cute and cuddly too, remember? Back before they ate all our officers… Hopefully these aliens will think we're ugly and won't want anything to do with us."

"I almost hope you're right."

She sighed. "Well I don't. I want it to be paradise. Hope is all we've got right now. What if it could work on this world? Have a life, raise children…"

Seeing the look on my face, she grabbed up a handful of my tunic. "We'd continue to try to find a way back to Earth, of course. But we would have a base, a home base with abundant resources, and not having to feel so…so desperate all the time."

"It scares me is all," I said. "It reminds me of what happened to the crews of early European sailing ships when they encountered the idyllic South Sea Islands. It wasn't long before easy lifestyles and willing women led to mass desertions, a breakdown in discipline, and even mutiny. A lot of the crew isn't Academy-trained. The odds they'll hold together is slim."

"Is that what you think of us?" she demanded. "Is that what you think of *me*? Just because we didn't go to the same school you did doesn't mean we're just a bunch of illiterate sailors forced by press gangs into unwilling service? That we would desert at the first chance we get? That *I* would desert? We're

4

Star Force, by God, and we're not going to go rogue. I'm no deserter and...and I'm late for my shift, Captain."

I knew I'd done it again. What is it about keeping my big mouth shut that I just don't get?

She dropped her towel to the deck as she donned her uniform, giving me a full view of what I was not likely to be having for a long while.

"Listen Adrienne, I hope you're right about our crew at least, but I've hung out with marines and crewmen enough to know how the line-dogs think. They're brave and resourceful in a tough spot, but they also don't see much beyond today—their next meal, their next drink, their next hookup. They can't afford to, because they might be dead tomorrow. When presented with enough temptation..."

She just glared at me in return. Then she saluted sarcastically and turned to leave the cabin.

"Wait..."

"Is that an order, Captain?"

"Does it have to be...? Fine, yes, it's an order."

She stood there waiting, her back still turned to me. She was pissed.

"The details on this stuff need to stay between us. In fact...Valiant..."

When I addressed the ship, it responded with an acknowledging tone. It was always listening, but generally didn't care about our personal affairs.

"Ship," I said, "who has accessed these files besides Marvin and me?"

"Lieutenant Commander Hansen did so most recently," Valiant answered promptly in a feminine voice. "Lieutenants Bradley and Sakura have viewed files within the last two weeks."

"Forward them private messages that I'm restricting access, commissioned officers only. Oh, plus Kwon, too."

"Restriction enabled. Messages sent."

"That won't stop the crew from finding out," Adrienne said. "If there's one thing I've learned in the last year, it's that scuttlebutt moves at light speed."

5

"It's just to slow it down and keep the crew from replacing their pics and vids of home with pics and vids of Ellada."

"Will that be all, sir?"

"Adrienne I...yes, that will be all. You're dismissed."

She left in a huff. Damn, I didn't always understand women.

I had to get to the bridge, and I needed time to puzzle things out. Not the part about Adrienne, I was sure that would just take time. But these aliens? Could they really be human? And if so, how? Convergent evolution might result in some similarities, such as the bipedal form, but it sure couldn't account for the perfect congruence between our kind of human and the Elladans. Then there was the fact that they spoke a weird language...that didn't fit.

The only easy explanation for why we looked so much alike was alarming. Could Ellada have been seeded by our planet—or was it the other way around? Given that Earth had only had space flight for a century or so, I'd bet credits to crullers the transfer had been from them to us.

The implications were staggering.

Earth had always had those who believed in "ancient astronauts" even though I'd never been one of them. Faced with such similar beings, however, I felt forced to reconsider.

Depending on how long ago they'd visited us, who knew what their relationship to Earth humans might be?

My own private theory was that an alien race such as the Blues or the Ancients had come along at some point and moved some humans from one planet to the other. They carried us along and then, like the famous case of a dozen rabbits being released in Australia—we Earthlings had jumped ship.

It could have been more sophisticated and purposeful, of course. They could have tinkered with the DNA of our primates to turn animals into humans. The evolutionary jump from apes to Homo Sapiens had never been clearly explained, and had occurred with relative suddenness within the timeframe of natural history.

I told myself to get a grip. None of these theories mattered much now. I had decisions to make, and I suspected that my curiosity was going to win out.

We would meet with the aliens. And why shouldn't we? I mean imagine returning to Earth with the answer to one of the oldest questions in creation: the origins of mankind uncovered at last.

For some reason I thought of my father, Kyle Riggs. To my knowledge, he'd never discovered anything so dramatic.

I smiled to myself.

Top that one, old man.

-2-

My musings were cut short when I reached the bridge and took over my watch, relieving Bradley, a meaty fireplug of a man.

I'd ended up deciding not to change horses in midstream by confirming Hansen as my XO. He was the most competent commander besides myself. But competence wasn't trustworthiness, and I still had a few doubts about Hansen and his motives. Not many, but enough that I'd rather keep his duty schedule and mine in synch so that I could observe him and not give him free rein in my absence.

That's why I'd ordered Bradley and others to rotate through bridge duty when we were off. As a side benefit, the new people were developing a sense of responsibility faster without Hansen or me looking over their shoulders all the time.

"Situation report, please," I ordered after I'd relieved him.

"No change, sir," Bradley replied. "We're sucking up data like a sponge, and we haven't had anything directed at us yet—no coms or any indication they even know we're here—which seems kind of odd."

"Why's that?"

"Well, you'd think with three sentient races in this system that at least one of them would keep this ring under surveillance, or even guarded."

"We're one hell of a long way out, which might explain it. At least as far out as Pluto in our own Solar System. That's what, six or seven light-hours?"

Bradley nodded. "Roughly."

"And the brown dwarf star where the scary-looking aliens live is farther than that, right?"

"Yes, sir. About six times as far out, forty light-hours from the system core. Hoon's preliminary report says that if it were any closer, it would probably destabilize the triple star in the center. A brown dwarf is the smallest stellar body possible— this one is only about eighty times the mass of Jupiter. Some scientists dispute whether they should be called stars at all."

I nodded approvingly. "You've been studying up."

"I was always interested in astronomy, and now that nobody's trying to kill us, I'm passing the time by reading the latest files." He lifted his eyebrows to me. "All the latest files."

I nodded, understanding that he was referring to Marvin's now-classified report on the alien races and my recent message. "Then you understand the need for discretion," I said with a lowered voice.

"Yes..."

"Good." I turned to the holotank and adjusted it, waving him over. "Any indication of more rings, other than those near the alien worlds, and the one we used to get here?"

"No more yet, sir. I had Benson start a gravitic scan, since that sensor system didn't get damaged in the fighting. The scan is still running. As dense as the rings and stardust material are, that might be the best way to find anything made by the Ancients."

"Good thinking, Lieutenant," I said, slapping Bradley on the shoulder. "I can see you're making the transition to being a commissioned officer well, taking the initiative and maintaining a wider view. Keep it up."

"Thank you, sir." Bradley glowed with pride.

"Anything else to add that I can't learn from your logs?"

Bradley chewed his lip, but eventually said, "No..."

"Then you're dismissed. See you next watch period."

"Sir?"

"Yes, Bradley?"

"If there is...I mean if this could be a chance...a place to take a break...even if it's not paradise? Speaking on behalf of the crew, well, we could sure use one about now is all. A break, I mean."

"Thank you Bradley, and noted. Now, get some R&R—you deserve it."

"Thank you, Captain." He gave me a sharp salute and left toward the cantina.

What was it Adrienne had said about hope? Looks like she was right and I was going to have a lot of apologizing to do. Again.

Getting back to business, I looked over our logs. We were down to five ships—*Valiant, Stalker, Greyhound* and two Nano frigates.

"Ship, patch me through to Captain Kreel on *Stalker*," I said.

"Channel open."

"How are your repairs coming, Kreel?" I asked.

All of our ships currently floated in close proximity to a cluster of asteroids, with a mixture of marines, crew and Raptors—minus Marvin—working at full speed to mine and process raw materials into desperately needed parts.

"Slowly, Captain Riggs," Kreel said. "Lieutenant Turnbull has allocated priority to *Valiant* in most instances, as is proper."

"Sorry about that, but given the location of our sole Nano factory, she's correct to do so. It's better to have the most vital ship fully repaired as quickly as possible."

"No apology is necessary, sir. I merely state facts."

"Have you had any luck getting the Nano ships to produce spare parts for you?"

"No, the machine intelligences are not cooperative."

I sighed. "Their factories have to be programmed in detail by someone with expertise in cybernetic systems, or you'll never get what you want. Do you have anyone like that?"

"No. We're all warriors."

"Damn." I thought for a moment, but I couldn't see any easy options. "Unfortunately, Nano ships don't like it when strange people come aboard, especially if they're of different

10

races from their own command personnel, or I'd send over some human technicians."

"Perhaps the sentient robot could reprogram them," Kreel suggested.

"I've already tried that. The Nanos like him even less than biotics. I think they view him as some kind of deformed Macro."

"Then the Nano ships shall continue with their standard replication protocol."

"Agreed."

I'd ordered the Raptor command personnel on the Nano ships to give them instructions to autonomously mine the asteroids and build copies of themselves using their own internal factories. It would take weeks to produce even one more ship, but given years of time and materials, they could build a new fleet for me. It was the best we could do right now.

"I'll talk to Lieutenant Turnbull and try to get you some more spare parts for *Stalker*, Kreel," I continued. "We're going to sit here and rebuild until we're either at full strength, or something forces us to do otherwise. Any other concerns?"

"No, sir. We live to serve."

"Glad to hear it. Riggs out." I let out a long breath after I closed the connection. Dealing with aliens, even friendly ones, made my brain hurt. I suspected I was in for more headaches ahead.

Two hours later, I turned out to be right.

"I'm receiving a message from species number two," the ship's AI said.

"Which one is that?"

"The gas giant dwellers, of course," the AI replied with a hint of testiness.

"Don't you dare go all Marvin on me, Valiant."

"Command not understood."

"Never mind. Let's call them Whales from now on, shall we?"

The aliens that inhabited the Jupiter-like world had tentacles in various parts of their bodies, but otherwise resembled their namesakes.

"Rename successful."

11

The ship's brainbox hadn't been updated since we'd fallen through the Eden ring, and it had been slowly developing more and more personality as it drifted further and further from its baseline. I figured the reasons for this were obscure, and I'd already decided not to inquire too deeply.

"What are the Whales saying?" I asked.

"Unknown. Processing power has not been dedicated to translation databases."

"Then dedicate twenty percent of your neural chains to the task. How long will it take to translate with that level of allocation?"

"Approximately thirty hours."

"For one message?" I demanded incredulously.

"That includes all the time to populate the vocabulary and syntax databases. Afterward, translations of text should approach near-simultaneity."

"Right. What if Marvin helps?"

"Far less time will be needed. Marvin's translation capabilities exceed mine."

Was it my imagination, or had bringing up Marvin caused a hint of peevishness to enter the ship's voice?

"Get Marvin on the line, then," I said.

"Captain Marvin here," came the robot's voice a moment later. "I'm very busy, Cody, so let's please make this discussion a brief one."

"I'm going to make you even busier, Marvin—and don't start whining about it."

"It's impossible for me to be busier as I'm already working at one hundred percent of my physical and neural capacity. Unlike biotics, I don't become fatigued, need breaks, or withhold reserves in my efforts. It's also impossible for me to whine."

"Not true," I snorted, "you don't have a nasally tone, but you are definitely capable of whining."

"I'm naturally displeased by alterations to my plans. I make rational prioritization judgments based on—"

"Okay, okay, forget about that," I said. "I need you to reprioritize and dedicate twenty percent of your neural circuitry to building translation databases and subroutines for the

12

Elladan and Whale languages. Work with Valiant and make sure that she's able to function as an interpreter as well as you are once you're finished."

I didn't want to make the mistake of relying purely on Marvin again. After all, the first time we'd encountered a biotic race, his faulty translation had gotten *Valiant's* original captain and officers eaten.

"I thought ship repair was my top priority."

"It still is, Marvin. That's why I'm only asking for twenty percent. I'm leaving you eighty percent to devote to fixing everything. By the way, did you manage to outrun those missiles I saw chasing you…?"

"Reprioritization complete. Marvin out."

"…Marvin?"

He'd cut the channel, and my repeated attempts to reopen it failed. We received only automated responses indicating communications were currently impossible. Thinking this over, I wondered if he'd taken my percentages literally, putting twenty percent of his processing power into translations and the rest into repair efforts. It could have been that, or it could have been he was dodging me—quite possibly, it was some combination of both.

I'd wanted to ask him more about the missiles that he'd teased into chasing him, but I figured it was pointless now. He'd report on that topic when it suited him. Maybe he was planning to run the missiles out of fuel or jam them so they couldn't detonate. Then he could take them aboard and dissect them. It wouldn't be the first time.

"Valiant," I said, "let me know when that Whale message is translated to a high degree of certainty. Say, ninety-nine percent."

"Understood. Estimated time to completion, fifty-one minutes."

"Much better."

That was interesting. A little high-school algebra in my head told me that Marvin must be more than thirty times as effective as Valiant when it came to translation.

I occupied my time by reviewing what our still-degraded sensors had collected about the complex star system. Ellada, the planet populated by humanoids, was remarkably Earthlike in every detail. It even possessed a moon of similar size to Earth's, only a few percentage points smaller.

One of the interstellar connection rings orbited at a stable Trojan point ahead of Ellada's single moon, but there didn't appear to be any traffic in or out of it. No fortress guarded it either. In fact, other than a few communications arrays, nothing floated nearby.

To me, that meant the ring wasn't functioning. It might be under the Elladans' control, and they only turned it on when needed. But as Marvin was the only being I'd ever known to actually get a ring to do what he wanted—sort of—it seemed more likely that they didn't know how to make it work.

The situation dampened my hopes that their ring would provide us an easy route back to known space. However, maybe Marvin could use it to communicate, or even get it working again, if he would apply himself to the problem.

Ellada's similarities to Earth made me decide to attempt to communicate with them first. If they didn't know how to get back to Earth, they at least might be interested in learning about a twin planet in the same galaxy. As soon as we'd affected repairs, we'd head to their world.

I spent the next fifty minutes examining Ellada in detail. A fleet of at least a hundred cruiser-sized and larger ships occupied the Trojan point retrograde from their moon. The area was a natural parking lot, a stable place where only the tiniest of station-keeping corrections were needed to prevent an orbit from decaying. I presumed these vessels were warships as freighters or passenger liners would be constantly shuttling around rather than simply waiting.

In fact, we'd detected plenty of commercial traffic to and from Ellada's moon and among several asteroids parked in orbit. When our sensors were repaired, I was pretty certain we'd find shipyards on those natural satellites as well.

The Whale planet, designated Trinity-9, was like most gas giants. The massive world was circled by dozens of moons. Three were substantial, and the rest were the size of asteroids. The big ones had installations of some kind on them, and some of the small ones did too, probably for resource collection and defense.

Because Trinity-9 was much closer to us and the Whales built things bigger, I easily found a fleet of perhaps two hundred warships in orbit there too. These weren't "probable" as I could clearly see weapons on them in the imagery.

I found it interesting that both inner races had substantial military forces. I wondered whether they were enemies or allied against the monstrous race we'd begun to call Demons who lived on a planet near the brown dwarf. It seemed intuitive to believe that the Demons would covet the inner planets and their resources.

Most alien races, I'd found, seemed to want to dominate their neighbors and take their stuff if they could. Not so different from humans, I supposed.

Unfortunately, the brown dwarf was so far away that we could barely see the main planet that closely orbited it. What we could make out was a world larger than Earth by half, with smaller seas.

"Translation complete," Valiant said, startling me out of my thoughts.

"Run it."

Text appeared on-screen:

Friendly and peaceful greetings, visitors, in the name of the (untranslatable—name—rendered as "Whales") Combine. We have many questions and answers to exchange with you. Unfortunately, this star system is in a state of war. We and the (Elladans) are threatened by a race of insectoid creatures we call (Demons), driven by their mad god to attack all within their reach. Take defensive measures to guard yourselves. Depart your current location before nineteen days seven hours pass. We await your reply with open skulls.

I pondered this for a few minutes. "Well, if the Elladans look like Greek gods, I know what to call the brown dwarf. Valiant, designate it as Tartarus. That's the Greek mythological Hell."

"Stellar subsystem designated."

I was about to schedule an officers' conference to discuss the message when the ship's voice spoke again.

15

"Weapons fire detected."

It always struck me as strange how dispassionate the computer could be when describing its own possible doom. Valiant was pissy when asked to juggle resources, but when she announced a coming battle, she was as a smooth as glass.

I rushed to the holotank, putting my hands on the cool walls of it. I stared at the shifting lights, but I couldn't pick out the source of the launch against us. The computer wasn't showing any trace-lines back to the point of origin.

"Where's this attack coming from?" I demanded.

The watch-standers on the bridge sat forward and began querying their consoles, but no klaxons wailed, so I forced myself to wait calmly, doing my best to display the proper bearing of a captain.

The image zoomed in until the ninth planet and its moons filled the holotank. Icons appeared—yellow for Whale ships and red for the dozen unknowns that appeared to be firing. Missile tracks reached out from the crimson markers, arcing toward installations on the moons and asteroids, as well as some of the single ships plying the lanes between.

The main Whale fleet orbited on the opposite side of the planet, and though I saw drives flaring as those ships got underway, it seemed clear that it would be quite a while, perhaps even hours, before they could intervene. Circling a gas giant takes time from a standing start.

It also seemed clear that whatever was hitting the Whales had taken them by surprise.

"Valiant, get Hansen up here," I said.

"Executive Officer informed. He's on his way."

"Send Kreel a feed of what we're seeing then give me some active sensors."

"Active sensors are still degraded to thirty-six percent."

"Do what you can," I replied. "I want to make damn sure nobody's sneaking up on us." I doubted they could be, we were so far out, but it was better to be safe than sorry.

A moment later, ship's AI reported. "No anomalous objects detected."

"Ping with actives every hour or so from now on."

"Protocol set."

I didn't like using active sensors as they announced to everyone we were here. At this point, however, I felt I had no choice. We couldn't afford to be taken by surprise.

Hansen hustled onto the bridge, smoothing his smart-cloth uniform before stepping to my side. "What's up, Skipper?"

"Something's hitting the Whales."

"Any danger to us?"

I shook my head. "This is five hours old, we're far enough away, but I had Valiant do an active sensor sweep. We came up with nothing, so I'm pretty sure we're fine for the moment."

"Then why am I here?"

My eyes narrowed. "Because you're my XO. Would you rather I left you out of the loop until the situation is critical? You're not just a warrant officer anymore, Lieutenant Commander. Being a commissioned officer means you work harder than anybody below you."

He turned to look deliberately at the holotank.

"Keep me in the loop, Captain."

After a moment, my gaze followed his, easing the tension. Maybe I was getting too jumpy.

"You can see the tactical plots," I said. "The Whale main fleet is out of position."

"They're standing still in the middle of a fight?"

"They're underway now. They were hit by surprise by these guys here," I pointed at the cluster of red icons. "The Demons have launched a missile strike on a bunch of Whale installations."

In the holotank, over a hundred missile tracks curved toward as many targets.

18

"That's gonna hurt," Hansen said. "Most of those seem to be nonmilitary vessels and installations, and if the missiles are nukes..."

"Yeah." Distance and shielding were the only good counters to nuclear weapons. No material I knew short of stardust could resist direct hits. "I hope they have good defenses. We just got a message from the Whales that warned us the system was in a state of war, so it's not like they're unprepared."

"Message?"

I gestured toward a side screen where the translated text was still displayed.

Hansen read it. "What's this about nineteen days seven hours?"

"No idea. You know, those missiles sure are going fast."

"Yeah. Way faster than something launched from the ground should be."

I zoomed in. "I'm running the plot on one of them, back to the origin. Let's see..." After rewinding the record, I ran it forward again in slow motion until the missile's engine flare appeared, but I couldn't see a ship. It must be stealthed for a surprise attack. "Valiant, what's this missile's speed at launch?"

"Approximately two thousand miles per second."

"Whoa. Pretty fast." I rubbed my eyes. "Extrapolate its back-vector and plot."

"Plotted."

I zoomed out farther and farther, until the red line pointing opposite to the missile's launch vector reached 300 AU in length—very near to the brown dwarf. "A stealthed Demon ship, cruising fast. Valiant, at that speed, about how long would it take to travel from Tartarus to Trinity-9?"

"Disregarding acceleration time, roughly two hundred days, plus or minus ten percent."

I chewed my lip. "And how long until a ship, moving that fast, reaches Ellada?"

"Approximately five days."

"We have to warn them," Hansen said. "If the Demons hit the Whales, they'll probably hit the humans too."

I shook my head. "No."

"Why the hell not! They have five days."

"Two reasons. Figure them out."

Hansen scowled. "Why are you playing Academy games with me in the middle of a battle?"

I sighed. "This battle is five light-hours old is why, and we're days away from the gas giant even if we left now at maximum speed. We're spectators." I lowered my voice. "I know it bugs you that a guy twenty years younger is lecturing you, but you're going to have to start thinking like a captain if you're ever going to be one. Part of that is soaking up the theory as well as the practice."

"Me? A captain?" He laughed.

"Why not? If Star Force confirms your rank, and if I have anything to say about it, you'll get a shot at your own ship when we get back."

Hansen's face smoothed. "I never thought of that."

"Well, I have. You've got the guts and you certainly have the experience, if you want it bad enough. Now, play along. Have you figured out the reasons I'm not bothering to warn the Elladans?"

Turning back to the holotank, Hansen's brow furrowed. "I guess if the Whales are really their allies, they'll have sent a message immediately. Either that, or the Elladans will simply see what's happening, no doubt better than we can, as they're closer."

"Hmm, okay. That's one reason. What else?"

After a moment of thought, Hansen shook his head. "No idea."

"Ellada is about two light-hours farther away from us than Trinity-9. In about," I checked my chrono, "one hour and fifty minutes, give or take, I'm pretty sure we'll detect the same sort of surprise attack aimed at them. So you see, no matter what we do, either these two races got it covered, or it's too late for us to do anything."

"Sending the message might show our good will, though," Hansen said.

I thought about that. "Good point and good thinking, but I'd rather wait. We're taking things at face value here. We

20

don't know that the bad guys are the Demon critters from Tartarus, or that the good guys are the ones that look like us, or like friendly sea creatures. You can't judge an alien by his form. We don't want to end up on the wrong side of things. I do not want to risk upsetting the wrong alien. The last thing we need in our current state of repair is another enemy."

Hansen looked skeptical and whispered, "Not taking sides might be easy for officers at the top like us, but the common crew will always have a strong opinion one way or the other—especially regarding a race that looks as human as we do. I don't want to be on the wrong side of that, either."

"You're probably right, and that's an excellent observation." My words weren't empty praise. I was very happy my XO was starting to distinguish himself from the crew and think like an officer instead of merely a pilot. Sure, that was elitist, but if a leader doesn't believe he is the best man for the job, why should he be in command?

Of course, it didn't pay to say that too loudly in front of subordinates.

We turned back to the displays. "Let's see how this goes. It's going to tell us a lot about what we may be facing."

"Okay." Hansen leaned forward to rest his hands on the holotank platform and put his nose against the smart glass that held the magnetized, glowing nanites inside. "The acceleration on their missiles is no better than ours, once you discount the speed of launch. I also don't see any direct fire. If I were conducting a surprise attack like this, I'd have mounted some railguns and fired them at fixed targets before I ever launched the missiles."

"Maybe the Whales have defenses against railgun salvos. They do have active detection systems going all the time. Perhaps they're good enough to spot incoming clusters."

"But not the launching ships?" he said with a hint of disbelief.

"The ships must be heavily stealthed. They might even have some kind of cloaking technology."

Hansen snorted. "That's a pipe dream. No one's ever come up with anything like that."

21

"Marvin's working on it. I wouldn't bet against him. And if there's one thing I've learned in the last year, it's that high technology makes the impossible possible. Look at the Ancients' teleportation abilities." I reached a finger up to point at the display. "The first missiles are about to impact."

In the holotank, tracks began winking out as they reached their targets. I zoomed in on one and looked at the associated readings of the energy yield, spectroscopy and so on. "Big nukes, as I suspected. Very dirty, too. Massive radiation, maybe specially enhanced, like the old neutron bombs."

"Valiant," Hansen said, "can you project damage to targets?"

"At this moment the battle has already occurred," Valiant said. "There's a ninety-nine percent probability that all of the nonmilitary ships have been destroyed. Military vessels will have received light to heavy damage. Ground installations vary from no damage to being completely destroyed. I'm still collating my analysis of the variables. Do you wish to prioritize processing power for this purpose?"

"No," I said quickly. "Repairs are still your top priority. Let me know when your analysis is complete."

"That was a nasty surprise attack," Hansen said. "The Whales' active sensors failed to detect their attackers. We need to find out why and configure our systems to give us warning within the next nineteen days."

"The Whales' warning deadline?" I glanced at my XO's thoughtful face. "You think they expect an attack at that time?"

"Yes. I think they saw something coming toward them, nineteen days away. Maybe we need to look for it." Hansen tentatively manipulated the holotank, moving its view outward and along the back-plot I'd calculated.

"Somewhere in here would be my guess." Hansen said, marking a stretched sphere that delineated a pretty large chunk of space. The area represented about one percent of the two-hundred-day distance out to Tartarus, or two days' travel.

I nodded. "Work on that manually to spare Valiant's processing power. Get a sensor tech to help you if you want. Let me know when you come up with anything important. I'll be in engineering or logistics. You have the bridge."

22

"Right," he said absently, fiddling with the holotank controls.

I left him there and strolled down to engineering, one of the ship's two central spaces. Logistics, which held our busy factory, was the other. Sakura was standing in front of her bank of consoles with her arms crossed, looking unhappy.

"How's it going, Lieutenant?"

"Never as well as I hope, sir, but not too bad," she replied, without looking at me. "I hear there's some action at the Whale planet?"

"Word gets around fast. Yes, a surprise attack by the Demons—that's what we're calling the insectoids that live near the brown dwarf I've designated Tartarus. The battle is too far away to affect us, though."

Sakura grunted, still staring at her consoles and readouts. "It would be optimal if we didn't see any action for at least a week, preferably a month. Right now we have ample materials and a lot of repairs to perform. Even Marvin seems to be keeping out of trouble. He's consistently creating system improvements from onboard *Greyhound,* so at least I never have to meet with him in person."

She said this with real irritation in her voice. I knew she didn't like the robot messing with her systems without her direct oversight, but I wanted Marvin to dig me up some evidence on who had tried to kill me several times, under cover of repair efficiency.

"And you don't want to disrupt things before we're back to full strength," I said. "I get that."

Sakura was definitely the classic engineer, the type who liked to keep organized and on schedule rather than wing it. In this instance, I was in wholehearted agreement. I hated the fact that my little force was less than one hundred percent ready.

"My mark on the wall is when the Nano ships finish their first two replications," I told her. "It may be a couple of weeks from now. Then we'll decide to either have all four working on reproducing again, or to do something else."

Finally she turned to look at me with only a slight change of expression, perhaps a look of worry. "It would help me a lot if we could put a small factory aboard one of the Nano ships to

23

use in making parts for *Valiant* and *Stalker* rather than reproducing more outdated frigates."

I almost told her that was impossible, and then I thought of something. "Nano ships will usually only accept one commander. If you think it's important enough, you can give up an engineering tech to become a biotic component for the Nanos. That way, they'll be able to directly access and script the factories the way you want them."

Sakura's eyes narrowed. "The Nanos took heavy casualties in the last battle. Engineering techs won't make good command personnel, and I'll need them back here."

I shrugged. "Once they're installed in a Nano, they're difficult to remove without them dying. You think about it and let me know what you want to do, based on your needs as my chief engineer." I forced myself to clap her on the shoulder just as I would any other officer, though something about the woman made that an uncomfortable gesture for me. Maybe it was because she never seemed to loosen up in my presence the way the others would.

Sakura nodded, ignoring my hand. "I'll think about it, sir. Will there be anything else?"

That seemed to be a hint for me to go away.

"Good job so far," I said. "I'll do my best to give you all the time you need to put our ships back in order. Thanks for your hard work." With those platitudes delivered, I took my leave.

Next stop was our logistics chamber and the factory, Adrienne's territory. I hoped I could keep from saying something stupid again and just play captain...

I stepped through the smart metal doors that were in place to dampen sound and provide a vacuum seal when creating more delicate equipment. Adrienne was seated at her console facing the chugging, clunking manufacturing device, her furrowed brow showing me she was hard at work keeping the parts flowing from the production end. I did my best not to think of smart towels and long showers.

On the opposite side, Marines in battlesuits doubled as human forklifts, carrying steel crates full of ore, minerals and ice between the cargo airlocks and the factory. They set down

24

the quarter-ton containers in rows and picked up empties to take back.

A couple of machinist's mates in powered exoskeletons checked readouts on the factory and selected the right materials to lift and dump into the various hoppers, based on the needs of the moment.

While much of the specifics of what went on inside was mysterious, generally speaking, a factory could be programmed to produce just about anything, and it would tell those running it what it needed. If something wasn't available, it might be able to substitute one material for another, but the more complex the item, the less likely that was to work. It was one thing to make a deck plate out of a different grade of steel or even change to aluminum or brass, but if you wanted, say, a nuclear warhead, only a few radioactive isotopes would serve.

I stepped into Adrienne's field of vision and leaned my elbows on the back of the console in front of her as if standing at a bar. "Two beers, please," I said.

She smiled. "Sorry, beer is low priority right now...but I have hydrofluoric acid coming out soon. Want some of that?"

"Is it drinkable?"

"Anything's drinkable...once."

"I'll pass—and Adrienne, I get it. About needing hope that is. I'll do all I can to see that relations work out with the Elladans. Other than not having beer, is everything on schedule?"

"Yes, Captain Riggs." She smiled. "Just keep the ore flowing for a couple more weeks and we'll be fine."

"That's basically what Sakura told me."

"She's a smart woman."

I frowned. "Any idea why she can't relax? Around me, I mean? We've been working together for long enough that she shouldn't be so uptight anymore."

Adrienne shrugged, only half listening as she continued programming. "You've never shown her the kind of attention that you've shown other women, like Kalu—or me. Maybe that's bothering her. In fact, some women might never let a thing like that go."

25

I fought not to roll my eyes. She gave me a look indicating that I'd better not even think about crossing such lines again. Before we'd really gotten together, I'd had moments with Kalu—and Adrienne had never forgotten it.

"That was so long ago. I mean, why would that bother anyone?"

"So you're saying that you never once considered taking Sakura to your cabin? Just Kalu?"

This was going south fast. No matter what I said I was doomed. So, like every male in the same situation, I just let my jaw hang down and tried to come up with something to say, which of course made me seem even more idiotic. Paleolithic caveman grunts and groans were all that managed to come out.

"You're so cute when you're flustered. The great Captain Riggs, speechless. Listen, I believe you, but that doesn't alter the fact that Sakura might secretly like you and you never gave her a second glance as a woman—not that I expect you to start now. You'd better not, in fact. But I sure know how I would feel. Cody, I think you're a great captain. I am sure she thinks you're a great captain, too. But as far as women are concerned you're clueless, and you'd best just leave it at that."

I decided to retreat while I still could. "Thank you, Lieutenant. You've been very helpful."

"Any time, Captain," she said. "Will you be taking lunch in the wardroom today?"

"I suspect I shall." I imitated her British accent to try to lighten the mood, and I might have seen a slight smile in response.

"I'll see you then." She turned pointedly back to her work.

Walking back to the bridge, I felt a bit bored. Here we were, stuck far from the action, with nothing to do but make repairs. I found myself itching to move, to make progress toward our goal of going home, but told myself sternly that we needed to be fully ready.

Of course that is exactly when Murphy's Law hit—or should I say Marvin's Law?

"*Greyhound* is approaching our position at excessive speed," Valiant said calmly. "The ship is being pursued by a group of nuclear missiles of unknown origin."

"Marvin...? Valiant, connect me to Marvin, right now."

"No response," the ship's feminine voice said calmly.

Thinking hard, I decided to assume the worst.

"Valiant, activate emergency fleet battle protocol and keep trying to contact Marvin."

I scrambled to the bridge. By the time I was back in my chair, emergency lighting had dimly illuminated the entire ship. Crewmen were racing to their battle stations and the ship was pulling a hard turn to starboard.

Finally, my com light went on inside my helmet, which I'd crammed over my head. I opened the channel request.

"Captain Marvin here."

"Marvin where were you?" I demanded. "No, never mind that. Do you realize that you have enemy missiles on your tail?"

"Yes."

"Do you realize that they're carrying nuclear payloads?"

"Yes."

"Enough to wipe out my entire fleet if they were to go off in close proximity?"

"That would match my own estimates of their potency."

I recalled stories of my dad beating his command chair to a dented wreck after talking with Marvin. Today, I understood his state of mind.

"Please," I said, "tell me that you have some kind of plan to rid us of these missiles that does not cause the loss of all biotic life in this region of space."

"Yes."

"Yes...as in you have some kind of plan? Or yes you're going to tell me?"

"Yes."

"Marvin if you say yes one more time, I swear..."

"Captain Riggs, Hansen here. These missiles—they're like the ones we've been observing from long range. They're very fast but they do have an obvious weakness. Due to their extraordinary speed, they lose the ability to maneuver efficiently. If they do not catch a target immediately, as in the case of *Greyhound*, Marvin may be able to continue to dodge the missiles long enough for them to be intercepted."

"You mean *Greyhound* has to play the role of the hare in this situation?" I asked, frowning.

"Exactly, Captain.

"Great work, Hansen," I said. "Marvin did you catch that?"

"The resources necessary in order to fully understand how my functioning as prey animal will solve the current problem would no longer allow me to continue to provide evasive actions and maneuvers."

"Marvin…"

"My assigned mission was to analyze and assess all alien technology," he continued. "Especially technology of military origin and design. I'm continuing to study the missiles from the Demon planet. They've exhibited not only speed but stealth capabilities."

"Marvin…"

"I shall make a pass near *Valiant* so that her more advanced system sensors can further extrapolate my findings."

"Wait! Marvin? A pass near my ship? With nuclear warheads?"

Just then, outside the port windows, several missiles shot by in a blur. This must have been what fighter pilots used to call a fly-by, which would upset their officers to no end due to their recklessness. Of course, they weren't trailing live nuclear warheads around. Marvin was definitely making me understand things from the officer's point of view.

My helmet crackled. "Riggs? Hansen again. I believe if Marvin were to pilot himself into the gravity well on the far side of the largest asteroid, even as slight as that rock's pull might be, we might get out of this. The missiles following him may be forced to crash into the rock due to the length of time it would take them to correct trajectory and continue to follow the robot back out into space. We could also have some point defense in order to shoot them down in case they are able to rise back out of the asteroid's gravity."

"Let's try it," I said. "Get a couple of Nano ships into position. Marvin, you heard Hansen's plan. Go for it."

The Nano ships had the best chance of surviving any nuclear fallout should anything go wrong. I hoped for all our sakes nothing would.

"Valiant, keep me appraised of the situation. I am heading to the command center."

"*Greyhound* will be entering the gravity of the asteroid on the far side in less than ten minutes," the ship answered.

Upon arriving at the command center, we observed through the Nano ships' communications relay as the scene unfolded. Marvin was ducking and weaving *Greyhound* through space and the missiles had to make much wider corrections each time in order to continue following and with each correction they would lose a little ground. Finally the Nano ships were in position on the far side of the largest asteroid and Marvin made his descent towards the surface.

For a brief moment we could see nothing but exhaust flares reflected in the resulting dust clouds as the missiles followed *Greyhound* towards the surface. Then an explosion occurred as at least one of the missiles impacted the asteroid and sent up a cloud obscuring our sensors.

At first, there was no sign of Marvin or *Greyhound*. But one of the three missiles became visible above the nuclear cloud. It just hovered there as if seeking a target. The other two must have temporarily disabled its tracking by detonating.

And then, just as suddenly, *Greyhound* pulled straight up out of the cloud and back into space. The missile reacquired *Greyhound,* but it was too late—the Nano ships were waiting.

As the final missile began to accelerate from the radioactive dust cloud, the Nano ships fired. The explosive backlash rocked the ships, even though they were supposed to be at a safe distance.

"Marvin! Are you okay?"

"No."

A feeling of cold dread went through me. I wasn't sure what I'd tell my father if I ever got back to Earth with the news I'd lost Marvin.

"What's wrong? Are you damaged?"

"The loss is a terrible one," he said. "One of my Microbe colonies has been destroyed and the other may suffer severe mutations. Fortunately, I was prepared for this and my third colony is shielded within a lead sphere. Overall, despite the difficulties, I'd have to say my experiment was a success."

Microbe colonies? That sounded like Marvin all right. He'd been fascinated by microbial life since the first day he'd constructed himself.

Shaking my head, I breathed out a sigh of relief. "Congratulations, Lieutenant Hansen, you saved the day."

I gave Hansen a much deserved salute. He returned one sharply, along with a smile that I had rarely ever seen.

"I guess I did sir—but no, I stand corrected. I guess *we* did, sir. It was a team effort."

"You see?" I asked. "You do have the mind of a commander."

Hansen moved back to the holotank. A look of concern shadowed his face.

"Anything else to report?" I asked him. "Now that one more near catastrophe is over?"

"It's Ellada, sir."

I joined him at the holotank.

"Ellada got hit by a sneak attack at the same time as Trinity-9," Hansen explained. "But we saw it later of course…"

"Poor bastards," I said, looking over damage readouts.

"You were right," Hansen told me. "A warning wouldn't have helped them."

"What about your theory concerning a larger attack?" I asked.

He pointed at a pulsing red icon. "It's fuzzy, but there's a Demon fleet out there, coasting in, aimed at Trinity-9. Marvin picked up his missiles from that same outlying squadron of ships. There are at least three hundred big mothers—battle cruisers or battleships I'd say."

"Three hundred?" I grunted as if punched in the stomach. "How far out?"

"A month or more from the Whales, slightly closer to us, on an angle. They'll pass us some distance away, but it wouldn't be difficult for some of them to peel off and fly by here—to attack us or at least do a recon in force."

"How long until they can get here? To us, if they saw us, I mean."

Hansen cocked his head. "You mean if Marvin hasn't totally screwed us all? At current speed, just over eighteen days."

"So that's not what the Whales were warning us about, I guess. As far as Marvin is concerned, I completely agree with you regarding what he did. It was reckless. But at the same time if it has provided us with intel that could prevent those stealth fighters from getting past our sensors, he may have indirectly saved us all—as much as I hate to admit it.

"The Whales may know something we don't, sir. Probably best to be gone before the time limit they gave us runs out. That way we're safe either way."

"Agreed." I fiddled with the holotank until it displayed the whole system again. "The Demons have been on their way for months, if their speed is comparable to their stealth attackers. Three hundred ships isn't a fleet, it's an invasion. They mean to wipe out the Whales or even conquer them."

My XO turned to face me fully, looking down on me from his superior height with a frown. "I guess we'll have to pick a side soon. Either that or let the situation choose for us."

-4-

The next two weeks passed quickly after I ordered everyone to go on double shifts. That not only got things done faster, but it kept everyone too busy to do much more than work, eat and sleep. Marvin's fly-by with the nuclear missiles, if nothing else, got everyone motivated and working without complaint. We'd flown through the ring right into a war zone, and I was sure that it was only a matter of time before we would have to choose sides—or they would be chosen for us.

I had Marvin install several new RQTEA units. They were quantum radios, or "ansibles" for short. We placed a unit on *Stalker* and one on *Valiant*. We already had matching units on *Greyhound* and in my suit.

Marvin grumbled a bit, as apparently certain parts for the devices were made of exotic materials and took a lot of time to produce in his tiny factory, but I insisted. The value of faster-than-light communication devices was obvious. They also might provide backup if normal coms went down.

With the Whales' mysterious deadline and the Demon invasion coming up, it was imperative to get going soon. Did I want to get into the fight? Yes and no. I disliked the thought of casualties, but even more, I hated to miss out on a chance to make some allies and do some good in the universe. Despite what I'd said to Hansen, everything we'd observed indicated

32

that the Demons were the aggressors and the Whales were fighting a defensive war for survival.

The Elladans on the other hand were an enigma. We'd sent a number of messages to them, already translated into their odd language. We even included pictures and vids to show them we were human, but so far we'd received no replies.

One thing we did observe, however, was the movement of about half the Elladan war fleet to the vicinity of Trinity-9, while the rest spread out around their own planet. That made sense to me. That was the way they should've arranged their forces to meet the attack.

Poring over the data from the aftermath of the initial conflict, I decided they'd taken significant damage to their infrastructure, but it wasn't enough to cripple them.

I thought perhaps the surprise attack had been meant to shake their morale and to force them to guard their home and thus send fewer ships to meet the Demons at Trintity-9. If so, it had succeeded.

We exchanged more messages with the Whales, who sent us details of the Demon ship classes. I spent the day before we were due to pull up stakes and head sunward, looking these over. I carefully modeled the tactical situation in the holotank.

Generally, Demon ships were shaped like cylinders. They were ugly and graceless, with drive engines of equal size and number at both ends, which I thought was an odd configuration. Still, it would make them quite maneuverable, since they wouldn't have to flip over to change from acceleration to deceleration. They'd also be survivors. Getting your engines knocked out in combat doomed any spacecraft. If one set of their engines was damaged, they still had the other.

Their weapons were mounted on the sides, rather like old sailing ships with their cannon broadsides. Weapons placement hardly mattered for missiles, of course, but for the direct fire stuff it affected their tactical employment.

The largest model they had was a battleship which was easily twice the size of *Valiant*. This ship mounted a dozen heavy missile launchers and about the same number of big lasers. As one would expect, it was heavily armored.

Behind the battleships came assault carriers, nearly as large as the battleships, with multiple launch tubes for scores of fighters. Thankfully, they displayed no heavy weapons of their own.

The third and most numerous type was a cruiser a bit smaller than we were, but much larger than our Nano frigates. This kind of vessel mounted four missile launchers and four heavy lasers.

"Nasty bastards," Hansen said as he came up beside me at the holotank.

"Yes, but do you see what they're short of?"

Hansen nodded. "Point defense. Only a few small lasers here and there. They must rely heavily on their fighters."

"Fighter cover and dodging," I said. "With engines at both ends, they can change direction faster than we can. But there's one other thing I don't see much of."

My XO thought for a moment. "Marines?"

"Right. Or more specifically, the assault craft that Marines would need. Of course, they're probably not going to try to occupy the gaseous environment of Trinity-9 with its floating cities. As we know, there are solid-ground facilities on thirty or forty moons that you'd think they'd want to capture intact."

"Maybe they decided to simply wipe them out and mop up later," Hansen suggested.

"Maybe."

"You sure their carriers don't have landing boats?" he asked.

"The launch tubes are too big to deploy missiles, but too small for landing craft holding more than a handful of critters. I'm not saying they couldn't conduct an assault operation, but it would be far smaller than one would expect, given the size of the ships."

"What if they have some other way of deploying marines?"

I shrugged, chewing on that one.

The com speaker pinged once, and Marvin's voice spoke. "Captain Riggs, I am detecting a slight increase in the nearby ring's energy state."

"Have you been fiddling with it, Captain Marvin?"

34

"I fail to see what a musical instrument has to do with the current situation."

"It's an idiom," I said.

"Idioms consume processing capacity."

"Not nearly as much as you want me to believe. Marvin, have you done anything to the ring since I told you not to?"

"Of course not, Captain Riggs," he said. "Now that I've been promoted to the rank of Ensign in Star Force, I would never disobey a direct order."

"Sarcasm must consume processing power, too, but you're using it."

"Speaking of processing power," Marvin said, "I'm running low. Perhaps we could return this discussion to the relevance of the increase in the rings energy state?"

"Fine." I forced myself to quit trying to beat Marvin in an argument and took a deep breath. "What do you think is the significance of the ring's change?"

"I don't know."

"That's it?" I demanded. "That's all you have to say?"

"Yes."

"Marvin, don't irritate me pointlessly. Is there anything else that you can tell me?"

He hesitated. It was a small gap, but a noticeable one. When dealing with Marvin, you had to pay attention to such things.

"Yes," he said finally.

I surmised that he wasn't going to tell me whatever it was he had to say next without a struggle. "What is it about this ring, Marvin? Out with it!"

"I can tell you what it is *not*. It isn't network resonance communication such as we or others have used before, and it isn't the energy increase immediately prior to a ring transit."

Frowning in dissatisfaction, I pressed on. "Do you have any theories?"

"I do."

I waited for more, but the channel fell quiet.

Clearly he was going to force me to ask, so I resigned myself to stroking his ego again. "Fantastic. I'd love to hear them, Captain Marvin. No one else understands this stuff the way you do."

"Thank you, Captain Riggs. It's good to hear that you comprehend how vital I am to this mission."

I gritted my teeth and said, "Absolutely. Now that we've established your importance, what's your theory?"

"We know the rings provide transit and communication. If I were designing the network, I would build detection capability into them as well, in order to observe each star system."

"So you think the golden machines are taking a peek at what's going on in this star system? The Ancients?"

"Or some other entity who has more control over the rings than we do. That's one possible theory, yes."

I looked at Hansen, who shook his head. "I don't like it, Skipper," he said. "Feels wrong."

"Agreed." Like him, my gut was telling me to get out of our vulnerable grounded position and into open space, ready for battle. And, if one of the slabs decided to come through, it seemed like raw distance was the only thing that might provide a measure of safety. "Valiant, relay this to all hands and ship commanders: I want to lift off in twelve hours. Marvin, keep me informed about any more significant changes in the ring."

"I will do so. Captain Riggs, I would like to attempt to access the ring resonance network. Establishment of communication with Earth or some other known space system could be achieved."

I thought about it. "You can do that once we're underway, Marvin, but not before. Just make sure you know who you're talking to before you give them any information. No releasing malware into the network!"

"I resent the characterization of my hacking attempts as malware," he complained. "No harm was intended."

"But harm was done, Marvin. Clearly, the golden slabs were interested in you. I'm still amazed we got out of there at all."

The golden slabs were large vessels of unknown alien origin. They tended to sniff around, moving with such speed they seemed to teleport from place to place. Many of us thought the slabs were related to the Ancients who'd built the rings—but that was just conjecture.

"In the future, I will include larger margins for error in my risk calculations."

"You do that," I said. "Anything else?"

"Not of significance. Marvin out."

Hansen chuckled. "You seem to be handling him better lately."

"Don't count on it. I think he's just more aware of the many threats in front, behind, and all around us. That makes him more cooperative."

"Maybe for the first time it's sinking into his thick brainbox that he needs us as much as we need him."

I shook my head ruefully. "I hope so. Now back to work."

Hansen nodded and moved off to manage the command staff. Changing the ship's routine was always hectic and took four times as much supervision as one would think.

I was just turning back to the holotank to continue familiarizing myself with the Demon ships when Hoon lumbered onto the bridge in his water-filled suit. I suppose I should be thankful that he was aquatic, or he'd be up here more often. In agitation, he waved his mouth-parts, which served him as hands.

"Captain Riggs, I object to your sudden change in schedule! I have several delicate processes that will take longer than twelve hours to complete."

"Sorry, Professor, but that's the way it is. We've detected a change in the ring's energy state that concerns me."

"Let me see the data."

"Marvin has it. Ask him."

Hoon shuffled his body and his various appendages. He looked at me with a stance I'd come to recognize as suspicion. "Why did you say 'we detected' if it was the robot that actually noticed the anomaly?"

"Because we're a team, Hoon," I said. "We share. It's what starship crews do. Competition may strengthen us as individuals, but it's the cooperation of those individuals that has allowed us to survive."

"Your cultural and linguistic conventions are of no concern to me, young Riggs. Be more literal with your communications in the future." With that, the steer-sized lobster scurried off, his motions oddly precise for a creature of his mass.

For the next twelve hours I continued to deal with my key personnel, mostly stroking egos and getting people to work with each other. Hansen did a good job of running interference for me and resolving things, only kicking decisions upward that he felt were worthy of my time.

I managed to grab a four-hour nap. When I returned to the bridge shortly before we lifted, everyone had taken their stations.

"Bradley, launch some more recon drones with active sensors and get half our armed Daggers out there for combat aerospace patrol. It will be good practice for your people and provide us with extra security." I'd never stopped thinking about the Demons' stealth ships or whatever had launched the surprise missile attack. No matter how unlikely it was that they'd be able to divert some toward us as far out as we were, the consequences of such a strike made the extra precautions necessary.

"Aye aye, sir. Launching now."

Before long, we had thirty of our sixty Daggers spread out around us, a dozen of them recon versions blasting away with their active sensors in all directions.

"Valiant, tell the Nanos to lift and hold station," I said.

The four frigates rose from the asteroids where they'd been resting. The two new frigates had Raptor command personnel aboard. Sakura had declined to offer up her people after all, apparently deciding better factory utilization wasn't worth the disruption to the ship's operations.

I agreed with her decision. When it came down to it, I'd frankly rather have two out of two-hundred-plus Raptors in the unpredictable Nano ships than a couple of my sixty remaining humans.

I noticed Marvin had lifted without orders, so next I told Kreel to move *Stalker* into space. Then I nodded at Hansen, who flipped on the repellers.

I sighed with relief as I watched our asteroid cluster fall away beneath us. We were mobile again, with all systems near one hundred percent and nothing around us but empty space. I felt much less vulnerable.

"Set a course for Trinity-9 and easy does it," I told Hansen. "Let's not look too eager or show how fast our ships can really go, but get us there well before the Demons do."

"Roger, sir," Hansen replied. "Course laid in. ETA is about a week. We should arrive with several days to spare."

"Excellent." I turned to the holotank. "Valiant, is there anything artificial at all out here within, oh, a couple light-hours? Even a hint?"

"Nothing anomalous detected. All minor bodies have been identified as natural."

I chewed my lip. Something was nagging at my consciousness. "What's your set percentage threshold for certainty right now, Valiant?"

"Ninety-five percent."

A jolt of adrenaline shot through me. Back in the golden planet system, I remembered telling Valiant to set her certainty percentage lower than the usual ninety-nine percent in order to get her to let me decide about the remaining five percent.

The flip side of this setting was that if I asked the ship to be *sure* about something, one out of twenty times she'd be wrong.

"Change setting to ninety-nine percent and go active on all sensors. Relay to all ships to do the same. Display any objects that don't meet the new certainty threshold."

In the holotank, the sphere of the light speed sensor pulses—radar and lidar of various wavelengths—expanded outward around our fleet, showing me in real time the limits of its range.

"There!" I exclaimed as a group of yellow icons lit up. Distance and vector data appeared a moment later, showing the bogeys were traveling toward us at the same high speed the Demons' surprise-attack vessels had been.

Within one shocked second, I calculated that we were already too close to run from them. The problem was inertia. We were heading toward them and they were heading toward us. You can't just turn a spacecraft around on a dime—well, not unless you were flying one of the Ancient's golden slabs.

"Designate those contacts as enemy!" I snapped.

Instantly, they turned red. We were soon to be engulfed in a sea of them. I took a moment to curse computers everywhere for all time, then opened the general command channel and initiated the override. Effectively, I was talking over everyone in the fleet.

"All ships turn ninety degrees from your inbound vector. Take a new heading spinward along the plane of the ecliptic. Apply maximum acceleration while maintaining formation. Bradley, launch the remaining Daggers to form a screen behind us. Valiant, soft-launch a missile salvo and get it moving slowly toward the bogeys for defensive use."

In the holotank, I could see *Stalker* moving to a position lagging *Valiant* somewhat, covering our six. I didn't countermand the maneuver because the Raptor battleship was more heavily armored than we were and had a highly effective point defense phalanx in her tail. It was good to see Kreel taking initiative without orders.

"Damn, they're moving fast," I muttered. My ships were like marines running laterally as jet fighters came in at supersonic speeds. The only thing helping us was the fact that they were still at least an hour out, and we were going sideways, moving faster all the time. The enemy appeared to be adjusting course, but the closer they got, the more their speed would work against them. They should overshoot us and be forced to double back.

The bogeys lit their fusion engines as they detected our active sensor pulses hammering at them. Their positions resolved from fuzzy anomalies into eight bright pinpoints of light. I compared their engine power with their change in vector to get a rough estimate of size. They appeared to mass considerably less than the Demon cruisers, so what I was seeing were smaller ships, even smaller than our Nano frigates. I designated them "stealth corvettes."

I adjusted the holotank to display their predicted path. I was relieved to see the end of their path begin to diverge from our position about ten minutes later. This showed that their course changes couldn't overcome their great speed. It was just like a supersonic fighter plane from old Earth. It had limits to its turning ability, so did the Demon ships, and as we accelerated, we were exceeding them.

Before I could get too happy, Valiant spoke. "Missile launch detected," the ship said with its damnably calm voice.

Apparently, the Demons had done their math homework, too.

-5-

As I'd expected, missile tracks appeared, matching the ones we'd observed in the surprise attack on the Whales and Elladans. Of course, missiles could maneuver at much higher G limits than ships. The predicted weapon plots quickly intersected us and clung stubbornly even as the corvettes' paths continued to diverge. Thanks to Marvin, we were prepared for them, but we didn't have an asteroid this time to provide cover and an alternate target.

Hansen glanced over with a question on his face. For the benefit of everyone on the bridge, I spoke up. "Their ships can't turn fast enough to catch us, so it looks like they're not trying anymore. They'll sail on past and probably continue toward the inner planets."

I took a second to glance around, seeing worried faces everywhere.

"Unfortunately," I continued, "we've still got sixteen heavy nukes tracking us that will be here in about thirty-five minutes. Odds are we won't be able to out-turn them, so everyone get ready. We need one hundred percent kills, people."

I could feel the tension build as the minutes ticked down. Our missile spread, the first line of defense, interposed itself between us and the enemy weapons. With difficulty I kept myself from reminding the controllers to take the high velocity into account—I had to trust my people and not micromanage them.

Explosions blossomed as our warheads detonated in the enemy's path, trying to catch their weapons as they flew through. Three Demon missiles disappeared, and another seemed to lose tracking, going ballistic while still accelerating into empty space.

"Good job!" I announced, despite the fact I was disappointed in the kill ratio. "Four down, twelve to go."

The Daggers engaged next, blasting at maximum Gs to match course and speeds with the incoming nukes. Instead of trying to take them nose-on, the drones were setting up to shoot as they fell in behind the enemy missiles, which were making themselves easy to spot by the fusion engine flares of their constant course corrections.

Each drone only got a couple of shots, though, before the distance increased again. Hits were scored, but it wasn't clean. We lost a Dagger when one nuke sensed a passing target and exploded itself.

Our small ships had laser cannons that were too small to reach far, and the missiles rapidly outdistanced our Daggers.

"Five more missiles down," I said. That left seven coming in at us. "Fire with our mains as they come into range. Valiant, signal all ships to open up with beams."

"What about more missiles, Captain?" Bradley asked.

"Not yet. Prep a spread for final defense, but I'm hoping not to use up any further nukes."

He looked concerned, but he turned back to his staff. I knew what he was thinking—that it was much better to expend missiles than lose ships—but I had to balance the probabilities of the moment with the needs of the future. Missiles we didn't fire now might save our lives later.

"Remember, everyone, Marvin already gave us a test run on their missile capabilities. We've had plenty of time to practice in simulation, which is more than we've ever had before. Keep sharp and we'll nail this."

Rolling barrages of long-range heavy laser fire knocked out one more missile, and then *Valiant's* secondaries opened up at the midranges, which was where she shined. The medium-sized beams hit hard enough to kill a missile in one shot and were accurate enough to pick them off, given time.

43

The enemy weapons began to corkscrew as they approached, apparently to mess up our targeting. Hopefully that would make them less accurate as well, but three missiles remained when they came into point defense range. One aimed at *Stalker*, one at *Valiant*, and the last at one of our Nano frigates.

Stalker presented her tail and easily clawed the first missile out of space with a blaze of point defense beams, but the other two shot past too quickly to track. At these speeds, anything not coming directly toward a target became near-impossible to hit.

Half a second later, *Valiant's* combined weapon suite slagged the one locked on us.

Then, everything changed. The missile that had been locked onto the Nano ship dove right down into *Valiant*. Everyone held their breath as our point-defense cannons swiveled with fantastic rapidity, locked on and fired dozens of intersecting beams…

The missile, sensing its own demise and the nearness of its target, detonated early.

In space, there are no shockwaves, but the energy released along with a gush of hard radiation struck *Valiant*. The power went out and the troop deck went red on my displays. They'd hit us in the gut.

For a moment, everything flickered black, including my brain. Radiation, EMP effects and a physical jolt knocked me to the deck.

My arm was pinned for a moment, and I had to roll an unconscious staffer away. Picking myself up, I realized my arm was more than pinned, it had been broken and hung limply at my side. I tapped desperately at the console with my good hand. Blood trickled from my scalp down into my eyes, and I blinked it away. It stung.

"Kwon, report!" I demanded.

There was only a crackling sound. Were communications out? Or was he dead? I wasn't sure.

"Sir," Hansen said, looming at my side. He helped me to a fully standing position. "We've got one dead on the bridge. Six below. What are your orders, sir?"

I looked at him. "You were right, Hansen. I should have fired every missile we had. I thought we had it handled."

Hansen's mouth worked, but he said nothing. Finally, he spoke again. "What are your orders now, sir?" he repeated.

"Find Kwon. Dead or alive, I want to know his status, and that of his marines."

"Right—on it."

Hansen left the bridge. The lights flickered as if they were going to come on fully—but died down again into a dim emergency-red glow.

Sucking up the pain of my broken arm, I helped tend to the wounded.

I'd fucked up, and everyone on the bridge knew it. That was the hardest thing to take.

I vowed to myself not to underestimate the Demons or their smart weaponry again.

"Continue maximum sensor sweeps," I ordered when we had the fires and the wounded under control. "Don't lose track of the enemy ships. At this point I don't care that we're lit up like Christmas trees. I don't want as much as a speck of dust anywhere near us without knowing about it. The Demons have proven themselves hostile, so there's no need to act neutral anymore."

Hansen returned in time—without Kwon. "As far as we can tell, he was blown out of the deck. There's no signal, but he could still be alive…"

We exchanged glances. Hansen was telling me the worst, but he was doing it gently.

"Hansen, reduce acceleration," I ordered. "Send the Nano ships back to search for our lost marines."

While he complied, I turned my attention to the incoming stealth corvettes that had launched the missiles. All I could think about was Kwon. It seemed wrong that the big man had accompanied my father on countless campaigns and I'd managed to get him killed by being arrogant and cocky. Internally, I was seething for revenge on these Demon ships.

Gauging and extrapolating, we plotted their likely courses over the next hour. They should pass us at long range. I had to make a quick decision. Should I take a few shots at them and watch them blow on by, or change course to put ourselves in their way again in order to take them out?

I decided on the latter. They'd expended one salvo of what must be a limited stock of missiles, given the small size of their ships, and there were only eight of them. Our seven ships and sixty Daggers outclassed them by at least a factor of ten. The only advantage they had was speed, now that we had good sensor locks on them. By taking the fight to them, we could not only win an easy battle, but pick up more information on our enemies.

The tickle and burn of nanites reknitting my broken arm caused me to sweat, but I didn't ask the medics for any relief. I needed every ounce of brainpower I had to defeat this enemy—cleanly this time.

"Hansen, bring us around on a converging course," I said. "Valiant, pass orders to all ships to maintain formation. We have a huge advantage in firepower, so I want to maximize our chances on offense, which means we need to sidle up to them as they overtake us."

"We can't catch them once they do, Skipper," Hansen said. "They've built up too much velocity."

"I know that. I just want to increase the time they spend in our weapons envelope."

"Got it." Hansen aimed *Valiant* in the same direction as the approaching Demon ships, angled inward, and smoothly increased thrust to maximum. Once the courses of our other ships had matched ours and stabilized, I had a thought. "Bradley, can your Daggers sow some mines in the enemy's path?"

My CAG shook his head. "No time, sir. All our drones are out, and it would take too long to recover them, load mines, launch and get them there."

There was no accusation in his voice, but there could have been. I'd wanted maximum anti-missile coverage so I'd deployed every drone we had, but that had given up our ability to quickly launch anything new. I filed that lesson away for later.

"What about missiles?" I asked.

"The Daggers are all clean for defensive work, sir. No missiles. We can launch a spread from *Valiant's* tubes."

"Do it. Fire one per. Maneuver them in front of the enemy and park them. Use them like mines. Maybe we can catch some in the blasts."

Eight green tracks in the holotank showed our missile salvo curving to take position ahead of the rapidly closing Demon corvettes. It would be interesting to see how they handled the challenge, given that the specs on the other ship types showed substandard point defense.

Adjusting the holotank further, I finally began to get some good optics on the corvettes, making sure to record. They appeared as black cylinders similar to Demon cruisers, but of course smaller...much smaller than I'd expected. I didn't see any weapons at all on them, in fact. The missiles they'd launched must have been externally mounted.

My supposition was confirmed as I watched them maneuver during the final seconds before they ran over our waiting missiles. The eight small tubes arranged themselves into a circle, ends pointing perpendicular to the center point, and then performed a starburst maneuver, scattering in all directions. We detected no point defense fire of any kind.

Our last-ditch attempt caught six of them in explosions triggered immediately before they arrived. At such speeds in space, split-second timing was critical, but our controllers were veterans and triggered the detonations so that the corvettes flew directly into the blasts just as they peaked.

Two of the enemy ships managed to partially avoid our trap, but both were carried tumbling outward by their velocity and were significantly damaged.

"Put me through to Marvin," I said. I had noticed Marvin had carefully positioned *Greyhound* in the lee of *Stalker* and her powerful point defense phalanx, undoubtedly calculating that to be the safest place around.

"Captain Marvin here."

"You've got by far the fastest ship, Captain Marvin. Can you chase one of those damaged corvettes down and recover it?"

"That would result in significant fuel expenditure, Captain Riggs."

"Granted, but wouldn't you like to examine the Demons' technology firsthand? Wouldn't our chances of survival increase significantly if we had details on what we were fighting?"

"That is true. Will *Greyhound* be refueled when I return?"

I sighed. "I give you my word I'll make sure you have enough fuel, just as I would for any captain and his ship."

"Define 'enough.'"

"Dammit, Marvin, every second the damaged corvettes are moving farther away. I'll make sure you're taken care of—just get going!"

"Command accepted. Captain Marvin out."

Hansen looked over at me. "You shouldn't let him get under your skin."

"Don't you have some damage reports to check on?"

"Command accepted." Hansen replied, and he turned back to his display.

I turned to the holotank, watching as *Greyhound* accelerated to maximum on her three outsized engines. Marvin's ship had started out as Adrienne's father's space yacht, and the name had been no accident. She was fast. Maybe even faster, now that Marvin had modified her.

"Hansen, bring us around easy, repellers only. Get us back onto a course for Trinity-9. Once you're done, meet me at the holotank."

My XO nodded, beginning the maneuver. Using only repellers would save fuel and mask our change of direction if the enemy wasn't tracking us closely. When he'd finished, he returned control to *Valiant's* brainbox and stepped over to me at the holotank.

"What did that attack tell you?" I asked.

"That they don't like us?"

"Obviously. But why don't they like us?"

"Why would they?"

I made a sound of exasperation in my throat. "The Whales have established relations with us. They've sent useful information. The Elladans at least haven't shown themselves to

48

be hostile. Why did the Demons attack us without even talking?"

"Because they're an aggressive race that wants to take everything for itself. They're bugs, Captain. Most bugs on Earth defend their territories and try to take over more. They don't negotiate."

"These bugs are intelligent enough to build starships. Your explanation is that they're acting on mere instinct? I don't believe that. Any alien this technologically advanced must understand basic politics and strategy. Why attack a newcomer and make enemies immediately before attempting negotiations? In order for those ships to have arrived when they did, they would have had to divert those eight corvettes from their main fleet when they first saw us arrive through the ring. Instead of talking, they dispatched a strike force."

Hansen turned to stare at me and lowered his voice. "You're a thinker, Captain. I get that. But sometimes you over think things. Did the Mongol hordes try to talk every time they encountered a new village or castle? No, they had a policy: surrender or die."

"But they didn't ask us to surrender. That's my point. They simply attacked." I rubbed my neck, trying to work through the situation in my head. "I think you're right about one thing, though—policy. Whoever's in charge of the Demon fleet is following a policy of destroying everyone else. Maybe like any military leader, he has political masters back home. If their command structure is particularly rigid, he's not going to deviate much from his orders. So..."

"That's a lot of conjecture," Hansen replied skeptically.

"But the Whales' intel confirms it. Their messages said the Demons have been attacking them for decades. Every year, they send a bigger fleet than the last."

"Then why aren't they better prepared?"

I shrugged. "Maybe the stealth corvette surprise attack is a new development. If the Whales thought they had more than a month before the Demon fleet arrived, they'd become complacent doing their final refits. Crews would be taking leave, stuff like that. You can't keep warships at high alert for too long."

"Yeah. Speaking of that, I think we should go back to normal operations and shut down the active sensors. They're like beacons announcing our exact positions all the time."

"Agreed. We'll stay at battle stations for the rest of this rotation, and then stand down. Use repellers only to change course enough that we aren't predictable. We can rotate a few recon drones out for constant coverage."

Hansen nodded and resumed his position at the pilot's console. I checked on Marvin and saw he had a long time before he would be able to overtake the damaged Demon ship, probably a full day or so. Good thing everyone was heading generally in-system.

"Sir," Hansen said suddenly. "The Nano ships you sent out to look for our lost marines have returned."

I looked at him, trying to get some clue what he was hinting at. He had a poker face, and I assumed the worst.

"Kwon's gone, isn't he?"

Hansen broke into a grin. "Not quite. Let me pipe the channel through to the bridge speakers."

"—that was total bullshit! You tell Riggs that!" Kwon's voice boomed. "I don't like to die. Especially not in space. Bullshit!"

"Kwon!" I shouted, grinning. "You're alive!"

"Only barely. I think my dick was blown off. Your doctor-boxes had better have a way to grow me a new one, dammit."

"I'm sure we can do that, Kwon. Did your men survive?"

"Nah—well, two of them did. We lost three. They got torn apart and fried. I was lucky because I was up against the blast doors, ready to fly out if needed. When the deck came apart under my boots…that was quite a surprise."

"Yeah, sorry about that. Glad to hear you're still breathing. My father would never have forgiven me."

"You're right about that. He never would have. Kwon out."

I heaved a sigh and leaned on the console, sweating. My broken arm throbbed, shooting lances of pain along the ruptured nerve endings. Why did the nanites always repair nerves first? Why?

-6-

After we'd all recovered from the immediate aftermath of the battle, I moved to the ready room and called Marvin. My left arm was still out of commission, but the nanites in my system were sewing it back together as quickly as they could. It burned and tingled like a limb that had gone to sleep and still could barely function.

"Now that you're not actively repairing our systems," I told Marvin, "I presume you've got some spare capacity to give me a report on your investigations?"

"About the Demon ships or the threats on your life?"

I frowned. I'd been thinking of the enemy fleet, of course, but Marvin had reminded me of another topic we'd been concerned with. Why? Was this his odd way of hinting he had information concerning the assassination attempts?

"Tell me of your internal investigation, Marvin."

"I have discovered many interesting things. For example—"

I sensed he was going to get into gossip and distractions. I didn't have time for that today. "Get to the point, Marvin. Did you discover further evidence?"

There was a hesitation. I waited him out in silence.

"Yes," he said at last.

"Who does it point to?"

"Professor Hoon."

"What?"

51

"Did my transmission come through garbled?"

I took a deep breath, mind racing. "No, I'm simply shocked. What evidence do you have?"

"I've discovered a number of vestigial and partial files in the system indicating he altered yours and Kwon's suit telemetry, as well as the med-bay programming, and he created the video of you mating with Sergeant Moranian."

"Fake video of our virtual clones mating, you mean," I snarled. Of all the attacks on me and my authority, that had actually been the cleverest and most effective, and I found my temper rising once more. "Dammit, Marvin, why didn't you tell me this before?"

"You set higher priorities on other activities such as repair, translation and our current battle strategies."

"You couldn't take five minutes out of your day to inform me?"

"Every time I exercise my judgment to deviate from your orders, you castigate me. As a consequence, I've recently decided to comply strictly with your obsessive prioritizations."

I was steaming, but I tried not to let it show. "All right," I said. "That's how I want you to keep doing it. But you should have reported on these findings. That was your charge."

"I don't recall you asking for a report during the last two weeks."

"We were so busy, and I assumed you'd tell me if you came up with something!"

"I ran across a saying recently in my research on idiomatic speech, which states that when you assume, you make an ass out of—"

"Yes, I know that one, Marvin... Dammit! Never mind!" I was getting sidetracked again, and I found my mind burning anew with the desire to find out the truth about why Hoon had been undermining my command and trying to kill me. "Talk to you later, Marvin. I have to get on this."

"But Captain Riggs—"

I selected the "ignore" option, squelching Marvin's prattle. Storming out of the ready room and through the bridge, I headed for the damaged troop pods. I found Kwon in the dayroom, which had survived the destruction. He was bench-pressing at least five hundred pounds on a resistance machine, and he had a heavy bandage wrapped around his groin region.

That surprised me, I'd thought all that talk about having his dick blown off had been marine-talk, but now, I wasn't so sure. I decided not to say anything about it.

"What's up, boss?" he asked.

"Get in your armor. We're going to talk to Hoon in his quarters."

"In battlesuits?" Kwon stepped into his suit and sealed up, activating his short-range private com-link and synching it to mine. He did seem tender when his bandaged region sank into the crotch of the machine, but he said nothing. He only winced.

I suited up alongside him. "The conversation might get a bit heated," I told him, "and we'll be under water. I don't want to be the victim of an accident."

"Welcome, Cody Riggs," the suit interrupted as I closed it around me.

"Thanks, suit. Now shut up."

"Command accepted."

"I don't get it," Kwon said, reaching automatically for a laser rifle. "You think Hoon's dangerous?"

"Marvin just told me he uncovered evidence Hoon was behind the attempts to kill us—he tampered with the suits and the autodocs."

"But he's not even human."

"What does that matter? And put down that laser. The suits will be enough."

"How do we know what he has in his quarters and lab? Have you ever been in there? Maybe he has weapons."

That stopped me. "You're right, Kwon. I haven't been in his workspace since the refits." I switched channels. "Valiant, have you ever recorded Hoon possessing any device aboard powerful enough to pose a significant threat to an armored marine?"

"No."

"There you go. We'll risk it." My anger simmered, but I wanted any rage to be under my control. Kwon had a tendency to shoot first and ask later, which was fine in combat, but not so good inside the hull of our own ship.

"Okay," Kwon said, reluctantly setting his rifle back on the rack. He surreptitiously checked the suit's integrated laser. This was a short-range utility beam, usually used for work rather than combat, with approximately the power of a pistol. I decided not to worry about that right now.

"Let's go." I lumbered out of the armory, marines in the half-wrecked passageways scattering before us. The troop deck had been slathered with constructive nanites, and the walls had the look of melted metal quickly shaped into a patchwork.

I could hear some of the troops calling out to Kwon, asking what was going on. He told them to button it and get back to their business, and then he followed me.

Kwon and I stomped down the passageways toward Hoon's quarters. Soon, I was inside the water-lock and pounding on the lobster's inner door. I could have issued a command override, but I was getting angrier by the minute as I contemplated confronting the annoying creature and finally obtaining some answers.

After water had flooded the lock and the inner door had opened, I barged in past Hoon to stand in the middle of the room. The water was crystal clear, of course, and the light was bright. For some reason I'd expected a dim, murky environment.

"What's the meaning of this, young Riggs?" Hoon said, once again waving his mouth parts in an agitated manner. I found it odd to see the Crustacean naked, without his pressure suit, making him seem even more alien than usual. "Why have you intruded on my privacy?"

"You will address me as Captain, Professor. As I am the captain, aboard my ship, I can go anywhere I damn well please. I've never inspected your spaces, so I decided to pay you a little visit."

Hoon scuttled closer to face off with me.

"Captain Riggs, I find this 'visit' highly irregular, and my superb translation software tells me that you are agitated and expressing yourself even more discourteously than usual. I accept your putative authority, but I demand you explain your actions. I am a diplomatic representative of my race and will not be treated this way."

"Diplomatic immunity goes only so far, Hoon. I haven't checked my law books lately, but I bet it doesn't cover attempted murder of a Star Force officer or sabotage of a Star Force vessel."

"Your words convey no meaning I can connect to my situation. Are you implying I have attempted to murder someone or sabotage this ship?"

I stepped forward, raising my armored fist. "I'm not implying anything, Hoon. I'm flat-out accusing you. Marvin found evidence you tampered with Kwon's suit and mine. Further, you hacked the autodocs and faked sex vids that got me into so much trouble."

Out of the corner of my faceplate, I could see Kwon's hands working, as if he wanted to grab something and tear it to bits.

Hoon backed away from us. "Your accusations are preposterous. I have neither the motivation nor the technical expertise to commit such crimes."

"You've bragged to me many times about how smart you are, how many academic degrees you hold and how much faster than humans you learn. I don't see how it would be all that hard for you to teach yourself about our cybernetic systems during the time you've had aboard."

"In that, you are correct, Captain Riggs. I could acquire those skills, but I have better things to do. You are welcome to examine my meticulous research logs and determine for yourself that I simply have not taken the time away from more important tasks."

"I doubt you logged your crimes. You've had plenty of time to do these things, being a clever lobster."

"I cannot prove a negative, but under your own laws, I do not need to. I am innocent until proven guilty. Besides, what possible motive would I have for performing these actions? I am one Crustacean stuck among you disdainful humans. My life is sufficiently miserable right now that I logically have no desire to make it worse by interfering with your semi-competent attempts to return us to civilization. In point of fact, I have more motivation than anyone to get home, in order to rejoin my kind and get away from you humans."

I stomped my heavy foot on the deck, creating a pressure wave in the water and causing Hoon to flinch. My voice rose, translated by my suit and spoken in the Crustacean language by the external speakers.

"You lobsters act so superior and rational," I said, "but you hold a grudge as well as the next biotic. I've read the histories. I've even reviewed some communications between you and my father. You blamed him for what happened to your home worlds when it was clearly your own damn fault for changing sides every time it seemed to be to your advantage. Your people betrayed biotics everywhere instead of standing shoulder to shoulder with us. When I showed up, you saw a chance to take it out on me."

Hoon scuttled half to the left, and then back half to the right. He was like a sheep looking for escape from wolves. "The first attempt on your life occurred long before we met, Captain Riggs."

"Depends on what you mean by 'first.' I had some very odd and rather deadly things happen to me long before I graduated from the Academy, things that wouldn't be that hard for a lobster with brains and money to arrange."

"Grim bigotry!" Hoon declared. "Is your dislike for aliens so great you've lost your mind?"

"No, Hoon, I'm seeing things very clearly today."

"I insist upon a formal court," he said. "I must say at this juncture that the situation appears clear to me. *You're* the one holding a grudge. Following the treaty between our peoples, I'll presume this visit constitutes notice that I'm under investigation. I therefore invoke my right to counsel and refuse to say any more."

I took a step forward, with Kwon following suit. I wanted to find the culprit who had killed Olivia and who had tried more than once to kill me. If it had just been me that would be one thing, but the fact that Olivia and others were considered collateral damage was beyond irrational. It had to be the work of someone not wholly human. Alien in fact as far as I was concerned. I could feel the rage I'd kept in check for so long boiling to the surface.

"Laws and regs are pretty thin out here, Hoon," I said. "If you come clean right now about anything you're involved in, I promise not to invoke the death penalty. If we end up proving your guilt, though, we might have to manufacture a whole bunch of butter-flavored sauce for your funeral."

Yeah, I was that mad. I admit it.

Hoon's tone finally began to take on some humility. Perhaps it was starting to sink in how close he was to becoming a crew-sized pot of lobster bisque. "Your disgusting threats to consume my flesh have no additional power to frighten me as I don't believe in an afterlife. Nor do I respond emotionally to your taboos. However, as I do not wish to be unlawfully tortured or executed, let me assure you that you're completely mistaken. I am innocent of all crimes. Consider the source, Riggs. If there is evidence, it has been falsified or manufactured."

I blinked at him thoughtfully. "Why would Marvin lie?"

"Why does the robot do anything? He has his own purposes. Perhaps he is mistaken. In any case, as I said, you're free to examine all my records and correspondences in detail."

"Of course I'm free to do that. I don't need your permission," I growled.

Despite my anger, Hoon's steadfast denials were starting to cool me off. He was right about due process, too. If I turned into a tyrant in this instance, I'd end up paying for it later. A captain didn't have the luxury of being a hypocrite in front of his crew. They might start to ask themselves what would keep me from chucking the regs if one of them became a suspect, and why they should follow the rules when I didn't bother to do the same.

"I stand ready to assist in any way I can," Hoon said. "I will provide all codes for my encrypted files, but I insist that Warrant Officer Cornelius be assigned to monitor the investigation."

Hoon's request made me wonder if the hooch-swilling chief of the gun deck, whom I'd recently promoted from senior noncom to warrant officer, was somehow part of the conspiracy. Then it occurred to me that Hoon would want to keep any co-conspirators as far from himself as possible.

Maybe he thought that Cornelius' alcoholic tendencies would make her ineffective.

Then I decided to quit wondering and ask him. "Cornelius? Why her?"

"Because she debunked the false mating videos. To me, that proves she is either impartial or on your side. You will not suspect her of shielding me. And because I have nothing to hide, she will make an excellent witness in my defense when the time comes for the formal hearing."

He had me there. I couldn't see any reason to deny his request, unless I was missing something. But I wasn't about to be out-foxed by a lobster, or by anyone else for that matter. "Fine. Cornelius it is. Valiant, lock down all of the computer systems Hoon has access to and don't let him make any alterations. Hoon, provide the AI with your access codes right now so she can make complete copies of your files."

"Of course, Captain Riggs. I will do so immediately."

Fear seemed to have made him compliant, which was a sensible response for any highly intelligent species, but now that I was calming down, I wondered what it was going to cost me later.

"I'll leave you to it, then. Come on, Kwon." I stomped out of Hoon's watery quarters, dissatisfied. I'd hoped to find something out by confronting the lobster in his lair, so to speak, but he hadn't fallen apart. Did that mean he was telling the truth, or simply that he had long prepared for this day?

My gut had begun to doubt Hoon was guilty—at least, guilty of trying to kill me. Maybe whatever Marvin had found was evidence of some lesser meddling, or maybe it really had been faked the way the lobster claimed.

Once the water had drained away and left me in a dripping battlesuit, I opened my faceplate to rub my eyes. I wished that for once things would become clear.

With a flash of insight, I realized that this was why I often felt eager for battle. It was the clarity and simplicity of combat that I was drawn to. Distances, speeds, weaponry, tactics, winning and losing. None of this murkiness, the guessing of motivations, looking for traitors among my crew.

I imagined my sentiment went double for Kwon.

Military service wasn't supposed to be like this, dammit. I'd gobbled up life at the Academy like a ravenous tiger, digesting everything I'd been taught in order to turn myself into the model officer. I thought I'd done a decent job until now, especially thrust into the role as captain so soon, but sometimes I felt as if I was drowning in a situation that simply didn't fit the way things ought to.

My usual response to self-doubt was to knock back a few cold beers and talk things out with one of my closest confidantes—Adrienne or Kwon, depending on the subject matter. Both had their insights, and I really needed someone to bounce my thoughts off of right now.

As Kwon was handy and informed, I decided it was time for a chat with my most trusted subordinate and, dare I say it, friend.

"Come on," I said as we got out of our suits in the armory. "Let's grab a couple of brewskis in your quarters."

"Always a great idea, boss," Kwon replied eagerly.

I wanted to hang out in his cabin because the marines were used to seeing me come by and talk to him. Going anywhere else might get people wondering. Hell, they were probably already wondering why we'd visited Hoon in full armor, but there wasn't much I could do about that.

Once the door was shut, I guzzled two bottles out of a six-pack of the mediocre factory beer Kwon had set in front of me.

"Not knowing who tried to kill us is driving me crazy. I'm starting to suspect everyone. I told Marvin to look for evidence, and he told me he found some, but..." I rubbed my forehead. "What do you think?"

"We talkin' about Hoon?"

"Yes."

"I'd sooner trust the lobster than Marvin."

He'd already drained the first two of his own six-pack and then slammed down another.

"But Marvin has no reason to finger Hoon, and Hoon has every reason to lie."

"Unless Marvin has been lying all along and he's the one trying to kill you."

I shook my head. "I've considered that possibility several times from every direction and it doesn't hold up. Marvin maneuvered the original captain and officers into being killed by the Pandas so that I would end up in charge. If he wanted to kill me all along, that makes no sense. No, he's saved us many times over. It's not Marvin."

Kwon finished his fourth bottle, belched, tossed the plastic empty into a corner for the smart metal floor to recycle and reached for another. "Even though you're sure it's not Marvin, that doesn't mean he's right. He's been wrong before, especially about biotics. He's not human, so he doesn't really know what humans think."

I raised a finger and then paused with it in the air. "Damn, Kwon, that's true. I thought he'd make a good investigator because he was objective…but maybe I need someone else."

"But who else can you trust that's brainy enough? And don't look at me." He said this with an utter lack of self-consciousness. Kwon was a man who knew his place in life, and that was a rare thing.

"Don't sell yourself short, Kwon. You're not stupid, but I get what you're saying. It's not your thing. I need to find a biotic with the free time, the brainpower and the motivation to keep digging until he finds the truth."

Kwon laughed. "That sounds like Hoon. Maybe you could have him investigate himself!" He slapped his knee and finished off his fifth bottle.

I gave up even trying to match him drink for drink, but I drained my third and opened a fourth.

"Who else could I get?" I asked. "I'm pretty sure I could trust Cornelius, but she's overworked as it is, and she's not really a technician. She'd have to get help from one of her people, which would undercut any chance of confidentiality."

Kwon leaned forward, putting his massive arms on the small table that held our beer, making it creak. "Take it from an old chief who's been leading grunts for thirty years. You don't have to trust everyone. You only have to know what makes them tick. Like, if I got a guy who can't stay away from whores, I don't try to make him."

I looked at him thoughtfully. "What do you do?"

"I just make him tell his squad leader which cathouse he's in, so we can find him if he doesn't answer his com-link. I also tell him to report back to me if there's any funny business, like if our people get robbed there. You gotta give guys like that a job that lines up with their flaws, so they stay on your good side. Like you did with Hansen."

I sat back, crossing my arms while holding onto my bottle with the tips of my fingers. "See? You're wise, Kwon. But how do I apply that to the current situation?"

"Boss, you gotta use someone that wants to find out the truth just as bad as you do. Someone who has the skills and the time."

I sighed, exasperated. "There's no one left."

Kwon shrugged. "What about Kalu?"

I choked. "Are you crazy? She hates my guts."

"Only 'cause you blew her off when she tried to hook up with you, but not as a captain. Everybody in the crew hates her for the way she acted with Sokolov. The only place she can go without catching shit is the science lab and her quarters—or Ensign Achmed's. That guy's getting himself some good squeeze every night." Kwon leered and made lewd motions with his hands. "But what if you were her? You'd want to get everyone mad at someone else for a change."

I thought about what Kwon said. "That actually makes a lot of sense. She has the technical skills, and I'm as sure as I can be that she wasn't behind the attempts to kill us." I clapped the big man on the shoulder. "I knew this was a good idea."

"Beer's always a good idea, boss." He finished off the rest of his six-pack and glanced at mine.

I pushed the two I had left over to him. "All yours. Thanks. I need to go see Kalu."

"Better put your battlesuit back on first!" Kwon guffawed and belched.

"Thanks for the advice," I said, throwing Kwon a mock salute. "Later."

My first stop was on the gun deck, where I gave Cornelius the outline of the situation. I assigned her to work with Hoon and ordered her to focus on the lobster and his possible role in anything nefarious. I didn't tell her about Marvin's parallel investigation or the possibility of Kalu joining in. I figured the more hounds I had independently sniffing at this trail, the better.

62

My second stop was the logistics chamber, where I found out Adrienne was on her lunch break. I checked my chrono and realized I'd missed our usual appointment. Cursing myself, I checked my appearance in the nearest head mirror, took a leak and hurried to the wardroom.

The glance I got from Adrienne could have flash-chilled a bottle of champagne, so I put on my best contrite expression and stepped over to her to plant a kiss on her cheek.

"Sorry," I said. "I got held up."

"Yes, and you smell like you were ambushed by a beer lorry," she said.

"I was brainstorming with Kwon. Seriously. Thanks to him, I have an idea."

"Kwon? An idea?" Her British sneer was extreme.

"Hey, he might not be the sharpest tool, but he knows a lot about people. Talking to him helps me think."

"And it conveniently provides you an excuse to drink at lunch."

"I only had three beers," I said. Then I frowned and squinted. "Maybe it was five…I forget. Anyway, now I need your help."

Adrienne softened somewhat. "Oh, now you need my help? All right then, but it's going to cost you. The price will be named later. So, what service can I render my esteemed Captain?"

"Besides the obvious?" I grinned.

She looked annoyed, but she was flattered. "Yes, besides that. I'm not just a pretty face, you know."

"There is the gorgeous body. And, you're a great conversationalist. Not everyone knows about that part. Let's not even mention—"

"Oh, do shut up." She laughed, and I knew I'd slipped out of the minefield.

As I broached the next topic, I realized I was entering a new danger zone, but I felt I had no choice…

"I have to give Kalu a task," I said, holding up a hand as I saw her face turn sour at the mention of that name. "That's why I came to you, so you'd be sure nothing funny was going on. Not that I'd want there to be…"

The look on her face told me I was failing. I pressed on, not knowing what else to do.

"Anyway, look," I said. "Kwon pointed out that we don't really need someone we like or trust to help find out who's been doing us dirty. We only need someone with the right motivation—and Kalu is in a big deep hole with the crew. She has the skills and the desire to point the finger at the real culprit. If she finds something..."

"The heat comes off of her," Adrienne finished. "I see."

Her eyes narrowed in thought, not in anger.

"All right," she said after thinking it over. "What do you want me to do?"

"Come along with me to talk to Kalu. Be my wingman."

"Be your chaperone, you mean."

I held up my palms. "If that's what you want to call it. Look, we have so few people. If we can get Kalu working for the team instead of against us, everybody wins. And, as I'm sure you know, she and Achmed are keeping each other plenty busy. He's coming along in his studies. I'm hoping she'll be satisfied enough with his status."

Adrienne nodded, relaxing. "Okay, Captain. Your logistics officer will accompany you during all interactions with Doctor Kalu—for purely professional reasons, of course."

I grinned and stood. "Let's go."

Adrienne gripped my hand and let me draw her to her feet. "Aye aye, Captain, sir. Lead the way."

I admit I was slightly giddy as we walked arm in arm down the passageway, and I forced myself to put on a serious face as we approached the laboratory.

When we entered, Doctor Benson bustled over to us, his round face concerned. "Good day Captain, Lieutenant. What can we do for you?"

I glanced past him to see the sexiest portion of Benson's team adjusting a scanning microscope with one hand while holding a sandwich in the other. "I need to steal Doctor Kalu away from you for a few minutes," I said pleasantly.

"Oh, is something wrong?"

"Not at all. It's an administrative matter, not a scientific one."

Benson seemed puzzled, but nodded. "Of course, sir. If you'll excuse me, I have work to do." He turned away.

Adrienne had already stepped forward to tap Kalu on the shoulder, startling her. My girl leaned down to say something I couldn't hear, and then the two women walked out of the lab.

I followed. We ended up in a nearby conference room with the door closed tight. It appeared that Adrienne was taking charge, so I decided to keep my mouth shut and see what she could accomplish.

"Doctor Kalu, we need your help," Adrienne began, putting on an air of command I'd seldom seen from her. Maybe she was channeling her aristocratic side, as if back on her estate.

"I'm listening," Kalu said with a sulky look.

"I'm listening, *Lieutenant*," Adrienne snapped with a flat stare.

Kalu's mouth worked as if she was sucking on lemons, but eventually she forced a calm expression. "All right, Lieutenant Turnbull. What's this about?"

"This is about improving your life, if you care to. Do you care to, Doctor?" Now that she had established her dominance in this little verbal catfight, it appeared she was going to twist the screws a bit.

I didn't mind. Whatever Kalu got from the crew, in my book, she had coming.

"Of course I care," Kalu said with a burst of annoyance. "I'm sick of only being able to go three places on the ship. I'm sick of the looks the crew gives me. But I've confessed to everything I'm guilty of, and I had nothing to do with trying to kill anyone—or even those vids."

"I know that," Adrienne said, idly running a finger along the table in front of her as if inspecting for dust. She lifted her hand and examined it casually. "That makes you the perfect person to find out who did." Raising her eyebrows, Adrienne fixed Kalu with an expectant look.

With a deep breath, Kalu replied, "I'll do it. Whatever you want. Anything to clear my name." She held out her hand to Adrienne as if to shake on the deal.

Adrienne put her hands deliberately behind her back and stared down her nose at the extended limb as if it were dipped in twice used waste lubricant. "Shaking hands is a sign of mutual respect, Doctor Kalu, and you haven't earned mine yet. Come up with something solid and perhaps you will."

By this time the alcohol in my blood left me struggling not to laugh at Kalu's discomfiture and Adrienne's roleplaying, so I turned away. I tried to watch them in the reflection of an inactive wall screen. It wasn't as if I thought Adrienne didn't actually mean what she was saying, but I'd never seen her treat someone with such exaggerated firmness before—except possibly for me, that is.

Maybe she was growing into her role as an officer. What was it they said? "Fake it till you make it"? I'd certainly done a lot of that myself, so I couldn't fault her.

Kalu dropped her hand, looking as distressed as I'd ever seen her. I struggled not to feel sympathy, telling myself that she'd earned all the crap coming her way. She swallowed and said, "I'll do my best, Lieutenant Turnbull. I'll need the restrictions removed on my access to computer systems."

Adrienne glanced upward, as most of us seemed to when addressing the ship's brainbox. "Valiant, grant Doctor Kalu access and copy permissions to all ship's files and computer systems, but do not allow her to make any changes whatsoever."

"Command confirmation required. Captain Riggs, do you concur?"

"I concur."

"Protocols updated."

The two women eyed one another for a moment more before Kalu sighed.

"Thank you, Lieutenant," she said.

"Don't mention it, Doctor," Adrienne replied immediately, speaking all the while as if she were sipping sherry at a social event.

Kalu took a deep breath and walked out of the room. Somehow, she seemed both deflated and more relaxed. It must be a great relief for her to have found the beginning of a path back to the inside of our tiny society.

When your entire world consists of sixty people in a metal box the size of an old seagoing cruiser, every social and psychological event seems magnified.

-8-

Late the next day, *Valiant* relayed a channel from Marvin to me in my quarters—voice only. Adrienne had gone back to the logistics chamber after dinner, so I'd been staring at the wall screen, which showed an overview of the system. I was trying to spark insights into our current strategic and tactical situation.

"Hello, Marvin. No video?"

"I'm using the ansible, which allows near-instantaneous transmissions, but it also has drawbacks. In particular, this sub-standard unit I've been issued has a much narrower bandwidth and lower information carrying capacity than the standard com-link."

I chuckled. "You can always find something to complain about, can't you, Marvin?"

"I detect unwarranted sarcasm."

"Sorry," I said, although I wasn't sorry at all. "What do you have to report?"

"I've grappled a Demon corvette-class ship, and I've begun to analyze it. In accordance with your express wishes to receive regular updates, I thought I would take five minutes out of my day to clue you in."

"I detect unwarranted sarcasm."

"Sorry," Marvin said, clearly not sorry at all.

Damn the robot, he was picking up on idiomatic speech faster than I'd expected. Maybe pushing him toward more

68

natural conversational modes wasn't such a great idea. It might make him harder to handle.

"That's an impressive use of slang, Marvin, but you can save your processing power," I said casually. "What have you found out so far?"

"The ship contains one biotic controller, now deceased. It possesses no weapons aside from two external racks for missiles, already expended. Its hull consists of materials designed to absorb or deflect sensors, commonly termed 'stealth.' None of the ship's technologies, such as engines, sensors or communications, appear to be more advanced than ours. It possesses no ansible or magnetic shields."

"All good news. Great job, Captain Marvin!"

Marvin's voice hesitated slightly. "While my observations are highly preliminary, I did find one apparent anomaly. The interior capsule occupied by the biotic was lined with a thin layer of anti-bacterial fluid."

"What? Something like soap?"

"More like the lining of phlegm inside human lungs."

My face twisted up in disgust. "They coat their ships in snot? Why?"

More hesitation followed, and when Marvin replied, I thought he seemed distressed, perhaps even annoyed. "I have no idea," he said eventually.

"That bugs you, doesn't it?"

"Is that a joke based on the insectoid nature of the Demons?" he asked. He seemed genuinely uncertain.

"Not at all. I only meant that puzzles intrigue you, the more mysterious the better."

"That's true."

"You don't even have a theory?"

"Not at this time."

I leaned back in my chair and laced my hands behind my head. "Some kind of natural product of the occupant, perhaps?"

"Not that I could determine. I examined the possibility the coating might supply warmth or comfort, but nothing is confirmed. As far as I can tell, the slippery coating only makes the ship more difficult to operate. That's a significant disadvantage."

I blew a long breath out through my nose and closed my eyes, trying to germinate an idea, but couldn't. "Feel free to consult with Benson or anyone else about it, Marvin. I'm no scientist. When you come up with a theory, let me know. How long until you rejoin us?"

"Approximately three days. I must reverse course and overcome the outbound inertia of both my ship and this corvette. My estimates show *Greyhound* will retain less than twenty percent of her fuel capacity when I do."

"We'll top you off," I told him, "I promise. Anything else?"

"Not at this time. Marvin out."

Marvin's report was both reassuring and unsettling. I was glad to hear that the Demons didn't seem to have any super-weapons or technology beyond our capacity to understand, but the unexplained layer of snot had to mean something. What was it meant to do?

Hopefully, some of our big brains could come up with a reason it was there. Until then, I filed the information away and returned my thoughts to the star system.

For the next few days, Hoon sent me hourly queries asking when his restrictions would be removed. The lobster was nothing if not single-minded. I told *Valiant* to add the queries to the log but not to otherwise notify me.

Cornelius spent her time looking through Hoon's computer records, which were separate from *Valiant's* brainbox, and Kalu combed the ship's systems. She was allowed to look but not touch, so to speak.

Shortly before Marvin rejoined us on our long journey in toward Trinity-9, I called Cornelius to my quarters. We took seats in the corner that served me as an office.

"Drink?" I asked, pulling out a bottle of the best Scotch analogue Adrienne had been able to make in the factory.

"*Natürlich, Herr Kapitan*," she said with her usual rosy-cheeked good cheer. "I presume you would like a report on the lobster?"

"Of course."

"I have found absolutely nothing out of place in his separate records system. Of course, I'm not a cybernetics

70

expert. I do have a good eye for detail though, and everything seems in order."

"Hoon is very smart and very meticulous. He could have covered all of his tracks."

Cornelius held up her glass of Scotch-like drink and looked at it closely as if trying to find a defect. "If he's so skilled, why cover his tracks in his own systems but leave evidence in Valiant's?"

"Presumably he's not as familiar with Star Force cybernetics as his own. He screwed up."

She shook her head, and then drained her glass. "Mm. No, Captain. If you want my opinion, someone is trying to frame Hoon."

I let my chin sink to my chest in thought. "Unless Hoon is so clever that he's running a double-bluff. He knew we'd eventually find traces of his meddling, so he deliberately made his efforts look clumsy and fake, hoping we'd discount them for that reason."

Cornelius shrugged and set her glass down near the bottle, a deliberate hint. I chuckled and poured her another. She sipped, and then said, "Of course, that is possible, but I do not believe it is in character for Hoon to risk himself and his research so far from home. If he were to make some attempt, I would expect it to be when he had a reasonable chance of getting away with it."

"Unless he's starting to become mentally unstable," I said.

She merely shrugged, and I took her meaning. We could speculate all day. What I needed was evidence, and she had none.

"Well, thanks, Chief. You've been a big help, if only to eliminate possibilities." I stood and opened the door.

Cornelius tossed back the rest of her glass and rose to her feet, throwing me a casual salute. "Always happy to share a drink with you, sir."

Once she'd gone, I called Adrienne to join me. When she'd arrived, I messaged Kalu to report to me. I wanted no chance of the sexy scientist arriving first.

I didn't offer Kalu a drink. Instead, I sat behind my desk, with Adrienne off to the side, and gestured to the chair in front of me. "Have a seat, Doctor, and tell us what you've found out, please."

Kalu took a data stick out of her lab coat pocket and slid it across my desk with a scowl. "This is my report. I composed it on a separate computer in the lab, so only you and I have a copy. Not even Valiant has access."

"Explosive?" I said it lightly, but my pulse had quickened with the hope that I would finally learn something solid.

"Yes. But the problem is, with all the fakery and framing going on, I can't be sure…"

I interrupted her. "Assume you've found the truth. What about Hoon?"

"I believe Professor Hoon is innocent of anything to do with the investigation."

Adrienne leaned forward. "Does that mean he's guilty of something else?"

Kalu squirmed in her seat, avoiding Adrienne's eyes. "I wouldn't say 'guilty,' but he is an alien, and he has his own agenda, rather like Marvin. It appears he routinely tries to hack *Valiant's* systems. Sometimes he's able to get in and view files, but I don't think he's ever been able to change anything."

"Why haven't I ever heard anything about this?" I asked.

Adrienne cleared her throat. "Sakura and I knew about it, Captain," she said stiffly. "I reported it to Hansen long ago, and he told us to keep an eye out but not to bother you…that you had enough on your mind already."

I raised an eyebrow in amazement and irritation. "I'm the captain! I decide what's relevant and what's not. What else have people been keeping from me?"

The two women exchanged glances, and for a moment, I felt as if I were on the outside looking in, as if despite their animosity they shared something I never could.

"Dammit!" I said, standing up. "How the hell am I supposed to command this ship with everyone keeping secrets? Both of you need to come clean with whatever you know."

Adrienne held up a hand. "Cody, we don't know anything…and it's not even about ship operations. It's social."

Kalu nodded with downcast eyes.

72

"Given our situation," I snapped, "everything is about operations. So what is it?"

"It's nothing," Adrienne insisted. "Just that Sakura and Hansen aren't seeing each other anymore. Lover's quarrel. Bound to happen sometime."

I relaxed. "Well, it's good to know the basics, but you're right. I don't need that kind of detail. Now, about this data…?" I picked up the stick and looked at Kalu.

Nervously, she answered, "I came at the problem in a different way, Captain. More rigorously and scientifically. Rather than simply looking for things that were out of place and chasing the evidence like a detective, I performed an analysis of each anomaly's first occurrence and tried to cross-correlate everyone's access logs and whereabouts. I thought that, no matter how clever someone is technically, the timeline should reveal the culprit."

Still standing, I placed my hands flat on my desk and leaned toward her. "Get to the point! Who is it?"

Kalu licked her lips. "Sakura. She's the only possible source for all the changes, hacks and fakes."

"But you don't have real proof? No smoking gun?"

She shook her head. "I know it seems thin and circumstantial, and you probably think I made it all up, but you can have anyone you like check my analytical methods. Marvin could validate it, or *Valiant*, or even her." She jerked her head in Adrienne's direction.

Adrienne picked up the stick. "I'll do it," she said, glancing at me. "If there's a flaw, I'll find it. If not, we'll know for sure. Until then, Captain, I suggest we take no action. There have been too many unsubstantiated allegations flung about already."

"Damn straight," I said drily. "Getting everyone paranoid is one more way to undermine us all." Then I slammed the flat of my palm on the desk, leaving a hand print that slowly filled back in as the smart metal did its job. "Did you take this information to Hansen first? Is that why he and Sakura broke up?"

"Yes, and no," Kalu said, lifting her head defiantly. "Hansen is more objective about me than either of you,

Captain. I wanted to make sure proper procedures were followed, and that someone else of command rank knew what was going on."

I wanted to snarl and rage at her, but she was a civilian, and I hadn't told her specifically to report her findings only to me, so technically she wasn't out of line. Still, I thought it was a dirty move.

Unexpectedly, Adrienne spoke up in support. "Hansen's your XO, Captain, and he's supposed to handle crew discipline at his level if he can."

"You're lecturing me about procedures now?" I said, my voice rising. "Hansen can't be objective if the evidence points to the woman he's sleeping with! When did you tell him?"

"This morning. You said you wanted a report by today, so I didn't see the harm."

"And then Hansen broke up with Sakura?"

"No, that happened yesterday," Adrienne said.

I shook my head in puzzlement. That timeline didn't fit my preconceptions. "Okay, fine, forget the breakup then. What did Hansen say?"

"He said thanks," Kalu replied, "but indicated he'd sit on the information until you saw it."

That reassured me. Hansen and I had our differences, but it seemed like he was playing things by the book. "Okay. Doctor, you're dismissed."

Once she'd gone, I turned to Adrienne and sighed. "I have a headache."

Adrienne walked around behind me to massage my tight neck muscles.

"Steady on, old chap," she said, mocking herself a little. "I'll check Kalu's conclusions. If Sakura really is guilty, we'll force her to confess. But I still can't understand why she'd do it."

"Me neither," I said. "I simply can't believe it. I just can't. She's our top engineer and she's vital to our chances of getting back home. I can't think of a worse situation if it proves true. I am just going to have to trust that whoever the assassin is, they will want to get back to Earth as much as the rest of us do and will wait till that happens before they make another attempt,

74

especially if they know we're onto them. I sure as hell can't be an effective captain if I am walking around paranoid all the time not knowing who to trust."

"Well, I know what helps me to clear my head." She eased her way into the sleeping chamber and started up some soft music. The sounds floated out from behind the door that she hadn't managed to quite shut.

I looked at the door and wondered if the saboteur could be Adrienne? I mean, I'd accidentally gotten her sister killed after all, and...no, no, that was just crazy thinking. I had to stop or I would go insane.

Adrienne's head popped out from behind the door. I noticed that she wasn't wearing her uniform.

"Come on," she said, "we don't have all day."

I guess if Adrienne turned out to be the assassin, there was no better way to go. I had my uniform off before I even reached the door.

After we'd enjoyed ourselves and dressed again, I got a call to the bridge. When I got there, Hansen gestured at the main screen instead of the holotank. On it was displayed a close-up of a golden slab.

"A Golden Slab?" I asked. "Have we discovered something new that I should know about?"

"Yeah, one showed up a few minutes ago, near the ring we came through."

"Damn, so it came through behind us?"

"Not in the conventional way. It just appeared, as they tend to do."

I rubbed my neck, still a bit stiff. "And now?"

Hansen glanced at a sub-screen and then held up a hand. "Three...two...one...pop." The slab vanished. A moment later, the screen jumped and showed the golden agent of the Ancients again.

I moved to the holotank and adjusted it to display the space around the ring and ran the record backward and forward until I got what I wanted. "The slab appeared its standard jump distance from the ring, waited a few minutes, and then jumped again. But where's it going?" I said this last without expecting a genuine answer, as the plot extending in its direction of "travel" reached out into empty space.

"I don't think it's going anywhere. Look where it went next."

I fiddled with the holotank for a minute without finding it. The odd thing was, we were looking at the past. Since light travels at a steady speed, when something was at a great distance we could only see where it *had been*, not where it was now.

With normal ships, this wasn't such a problem. They were following a course, and you could predict where they might be an hour later by watching them. But when something big just popped from here to there—well, it was disturbing. The thing could be looming over us seconds from now, taking us totally by surprise.

"It's at the asteroid cluster where we mined materials," Hansen said helpfully.

"There it is... But why?"

Hansen shrugged. "It did show up right on time. Nineteen days seven hours, more or less, as the Whales said. That's why I had all the passive sensors aimed there, but nothing active. I didn't want to attract undue attention."

"Good thinking." I glanced back and forth between the holotank and the screen, chewing a lip.

Abruptly, the slab vanished again. A couple minutes of searching couldn't locate it. I said, "Well, whatever it was here for, I guess it didn't find it."

Hansen shrugged again.

-9-

Greyhound rejoined us in the middle of the ship's sleep cycle and took a position near *Valiant*. The damaged Demon corvette was grasped in the Nano-style tentacles Marvin had added to his small ship. I'd left instructions for *Valiant's* brainbox to wake me because I wanted to talk to Marvin right away, full video.

Closing the door to the bedroom where Adrienne lay sleeping, I activated the screen in front of my desk. When the two-way vid-link was established and the robot became visible, I jumped right into the details that had been bothering me for hours.

"Marvin, about Hoon. We're investigating him, but I don't think he was the one that did it. The evidence must have been faked or planted."

"I agree."

"What! When last we talked, you told me the indications pointed to him."

"That's correct, but you ended our conversation before I could explain that I didn't believe the indications."

I tried to recall the details, but I couldn't be sure Marvin was right. Had I cut him off and sought out Hoon to confront him? Maybe…

"Ah…" I said aloud as my memory of the conversation returned. I'd squelched him mid-conversation, ignoring him and rushing off.

"I remember now," I said. "Damn."

I could've saved myself the trouble by simply staying calm and listening. I'd discarded one of the cardinal rules of leadership, which was to gather as much information as possible before making a decision.

In other words, *don't jump to conclusions*.

"Is Hoon still alive, Captain Riggs."

"Yes, fortunately," I said and sighed. "Okay, Marvin. I should have listened to everything. So, is there anything you need to report right now about the ship or anything else?"

"Not at this time."

I rubbed my eyes, still groggy. "Fine. I'll talk to you in the morning."

"It's 0213 hours. Technically it *is* morning."

"Technically, you're right," I ground out through gritted teeth. "I'll talk to you after I've *technically* had breakfast, Marvin." I cut the link and went back to bed.

After getting up and having a cup of bad factory coffee, I ordered Doctors Chang and Benson to suit up and take a look at the Demon corvette. Hoon requested the same privilege, and after a bit of thought, I allowed it. Probably it was best that they and Marvin were all there to monitor each other. Maybe someone would notice something out of place.

Sakura wanted to come along and I almost said no, but realized that might tip her off that I was onto her. If in fact it was her. This could all be just another fiasco like the one with Hoon. This was seriously interfering with my command. I had to set it aside and focus. All intelligence that we could gather about the Demons was priority.

Unfortunately, other than the strange layer of slippery stuff inside the hull, there was little to distinguish the Demons' technology from our own other than style and emphasis. They had brainboxes, smart metal, fusion engines, repellers and other modern tech.

That should have told me something, but at the time I had too much else on my mind. Only later would the significance become clear.

On the last day before we arrived at Trinity-9, we finally made real-time contact with the natives. I'd been expecting an in-person conversation with one of our two potential allies once the light speed transmission delay fell to less than ten seconds.

My small fleet was decelerating but off-center. When we came into orbit, we were still well outside of weapons range of any other warships or planetary defenses. Idling the engines also allowed us to communicate more easily, without having to transmit through our fusion exhaust or repeller interference.

I'd programmed my smart cloth uniform to Fleet dress mode, although I left off the one award I had—for Academy graduation. Better no ribbons at all than a pathetic single. I also made sure that the video pickups were focused solely on me as I sat in my seldom-used bridge chair. I had no other crew or consoles visible in order to give away as little as possible just in case either of these aliens ended up being hairless versions of the Pandas or sharks in whales' clothing.

When an answer finally came, it turned out to be the Elladans that contacted us first. I had expected the Whales to call as Trinity-9 was their home planet, but perhaps they were letting humans talk to humans.

Or humanoids.

"Greetings, lost children," a regal man on the main screen said in a translated voice, which was totally out of synch with his lip movements. "We have awaited this day for eons and welcome you to your ancestral home of Ellada!"

Dressed in a single floor-length garment, he wore a silver medallion at his neck, which I assumed was a communications device. His salt-and-pepper hair was perfectly shaped on his head. That hair didn't look quite real.

I'd studied up a bit on alien cultures within the last few days, and so I knew I had to tread lightly. Anything might be misunderstood. What most impressed me so far was that they were translating our language rather than the other way around. That meant they were advanced linguistically, and perhaps had a computer as powerful as Marvin on their side of the fence. That was something to remember.

"Nice to meet you," I said, giving him a steady smile. "I'm Captain Riggs of the Star Force ship, Valiant."

"I'm Senator Diogenos," he replied. "I speak for the Elladan people. Please inform me as to your intentions here in our space."

I raised my chin, my hands resting on the arms of my chair like a throne. "Thanks for your welcome. I command the squadron of ships you see in orbit, but we come in peace. I look forward to meeting you in person as you appear to be our biological cousins. I have many questions that require answers."

"Excellent responses, Captain Riggs. I can see you're a man of dignity and presence. We've studied your ships and crews. I'm impressed by the way you keep the lower orders in their places, as is proper."

"Uh…" I wasn't quite certain who he was talking about when he said "lower orders." Our alien allies the Raptors? Brainboxes? Or was he referring to other humans?

Having no idea what he meant, I pressed on. There was no sense in getting upset over a possibly faulty translation.

"I'm sure our cultures must have some similarities," I said. "We look so much alike…but I'd rather discuss practicalities. These Demon creatures that are on their way here, for example. I presume they're intent on conquest?"

"Of course, Captain. They're creations of the mad Ancients. Their sole purpose is to extend the force of their will over us and eventually over the rest of the universe."

"The whole universe?" I said, trying not to chuckle at this guy's overblown declaration. "What's stopping the Ancients from attacking you themselves? They can teleport wherever they want."

Diogenos scowled slightly. "You speak lightly of a millennia-long struggle."

"Sorry…but let's talk about the insectoids we call Demons."

"An apt name."

"As you probably know, the Demons attacked us as well, and we have a saying…the enemy of my enemy is my friend."

"I am happy to hear this, Captain. I eagerly await our first meeting in the flesh. But now, I must go. Please come down and visit us in person." He lifted his hand in farewell.

That hand…it looked odd to me, just for a second. It blurred and shifted as if not quite solid—but then it looked perfect again, and I chalked it up to transmission anomalies.

I wasn't quite ready to sign off yet. Too many questions bubbled through my mind. "Before you go, I have a question, Senator. We captured a Demon ship, and we found it was layered with slimy fluid. Do you have any idea why?"

Diogenos hesitated, as if uncertain what to tell me. "I am not a technician, but we have many here that will discuss such specifics. Until we meet." The screen went blank before I could say more.

"He dodged that question," Hansen said from his pilot's chair.

"He did indeed," I replied.

"And what the hell was that crack about the lower orders?"

"No idea. But my mother's people in India still struggle with the remnants of the old caste system. Maybe that's what he meant—some kind of social class."

Hansen turned control over to *Valiant* and stood, walking to the holotank. "I guess it's a good thing we look like them, more or less."

"I suppose it can't hurt. But don't worry. We're not about to adopt their customs."

"I'm not worried about adopting their customs," Hansen said, "but I am worried about them adopting us."

"What do you mean, adopting us?"

Hansen led me over to the holotank. I knew he'd appointed himself devil's advocate long ago, and it seemed he was trying to make a point here. The view in the holotank was one of the average street scenes we had been seeing since we had been able to get sensor readings.

"Okay, Lieutenant, what am I missing?"

"The collars, Captain. Notice that nearly all of them are wearing collars. If those collars represent anything like the ones from Earth's history—I've got no desire to be wearing one myself. I don't know who the lower classes are here, but I sure don't want to be finding out the hard way."

"Hmm," I said thoughtfully. "You're right. Do you think we'd be helping the wrong side? The side of some kind of enslaving race?"

"No, sir I don't," he said, "but I thought *you* might think it's a big deal. I think we got far more critical things to worry about. These guys could be cannibals for all I know—like the Raptors and the Pandas, remember—but unless they try to eat us, we need to find a way to work with them if we want to get home. No matter what their quirks, we aren't going to change their society, but you're idealistic enough to want to try."

It felt like the start of an argument, but he had a point. My job was to get us home, and to do that. Our new allies had to stay allies. That meant dealing with our common enemy, the Demons, first. The rest could be negotiated afterward. It still made me wince and rub my neck, looking at what I had first seen as merely part of the local dress.

"You're right, XO. First, we kick these bugs' asses. Universal peace and harmony will have to wait until later."

I made sure everyone had a good rest before we approached our parking orbit a million miles out from Trinity-9, one we'd chosen for ourselves. No ship-mounted laser I knew of would more than tickle us at this range, though the surface installations could probably do us some damage.

"Valiant," I said, "you're to control our shields until command personnel tell you otherwise." I lounged in my chair waiting for our allies to contact us. "Snap them on at the first sign of any attack."

"Protocol updated." A moment later, the AI went on, "Incoming transmission in full video."

"Put it on."

I'd expected Senator Diogenos' picture, but instead I was treated to the face of a Whale. Because of the transmission lag, I had a few seconds or so to stare at it.

Blunt nosed with a centrally located round mouth, it possessed four eyes equidistantly placed around the forward edge of its head. I presumed this allowed for parallax vision within its front 180 degrees of arc.

A fringe of a dozen fine tentacles sprouted from what would be the neck on a terrestrial whale, apparently to serve it as hands. This Whale clutched several things in those appendages as it floated in front of its video pickup, holding the devices of unknown use well within its own field of vision, much as a human would.

It maintained its position with a selection of larger, flattened tentacles that sprung from its middle and nether regions. These seemed to function much as those of a jellyfish or octopus, for propulsion and station-keeping, as it floated in the middle of a room. Because I had no reference for scale, it seemed to me as if it were the size of a dolphin, but I was certain that was only a trick of the vid, as the Whales usually ran at least a hundred yards from nose to tail—if they had noses or tails.

Its translated words were spoken in the ship's voice. "We greet you, Captain Riggs. We are called Farswimmer, and have been appointed as liaison to your squadron."

I raised my eyebrows. "Pleased to meet you, Farswimmer. Our translation issues seem to be a thing of the past."

"The Elladans worked with us to optimize our language databases and transmission systems in order to more easily mesh with yours."

As it "spoke," I could see nothing that indicated how—no mouth movements or other telltales. I'd have to ask *Valiant* or Marvin about that later.

"Good," I said aloud. "Avoiding misunderstandings between our two peoples is a high priority for me. By the way, do you or the Elladans consume other sentient creatures for food?"

The Whale jerked as if it'd been hit with an electric prod. "Absolutely not. Our diet consists of plants and tiny sea creatures. We're a nonviolent species and only wish to be left in peace."

"Yet you have ships of war."

"An unfortunate necessity that has been forced upon us. When sharks attack, the pods must defend themselves."

He must mean pods of whales, like schools of fish or flocks of birds. Our translation software was doing a fine job. I wondered if Hoon would make a good liaison to these creatures. Then I remembered these Whales weren't really aquatic. They only looked that way. Actually, they functioned like living airships floating in the thick soupy atmosphere of their gas giant home. I supposed they had some kind of internal bladders to control their buoyancy.

"I completely agree, Farswimmer, and we're glad to fight by your side against our common enemy. Can you provide us with more intelligence data on the Demons?"

"We have prepared a package to be transmitted on your signal."

"Go ahead and send it now." *Valiant* already knew to check the data for malware, so I went on, "Tell me, how much of your technology did you develop yourselves, and how much did you acquire from the Demons or the Elladans?"

"The Elladans blessed us with the knowledge of machinery thousands of years ago, when we were but nomadic primitives."

I stroked my chin, my eyes unfocused. "So where did *they* get it?" I mused.

I hadn't intended it to be a direct question, but Farswimmer replied. "It was bequeathed them from the Departed Gods, those who made us."

"Made you? So you don't believe you evolved from lower life?"

The Whale's tentacles waved in a complex pattern, and a moment later the translation software provided the sound of laughter. "What a curious idea. Forgive us, Captain Riggs. We do not mean to impugn your religious beliefs, no matter how unscientific."

I stifled laughter myself. I guess one guy's religion was another's rational belief system. "Likewise, Farswimmer, but...you said some kind of gods made you? That seems like religious belief as well."

"We understand your confusion, Captain, but the eldest among us remember those times quite clearly. The Departed

Gods appeared unto us before they left. This is not a matter of belief but of fact."

"They remember back ten thousand years?" I gaped. "How long do you people live?"

"We live until we are killed. We do not run out of life as you unfortunate humans do."

"You mean you only die from violence, or perhaps disease?"

"Exactly."

Wow. Immortal beings. Or at least beings with a lifespan measured in thousands of years, which might as well be the same thing. To them, we were like bugs that hatched in the spring and died at the onset of winter.

"Um...back to these Departed Gods. What did they look like?" My obvious working theory was that Farswimmer was talking about the Ancients, and if these Whales possessed firsthand knowledge of them, I wanted it.

"None could look upon one directly and live, but they appeared as living fire dwelling within the stars."

"Within the stars? Valiant, are you certain that is an accurate translation?"

"Yes. Certainty parameters are currently set to ninety-nine percent."

I held up a hand, hoping the translation software would interpret the gesture while my mind whirled through the implications.

"So about these...powerful creatures," I said, unwilling to call them gods. "Let's term them Ancients, if you don't mind."

"That is a reasonably accurate designation."

"Okay, so...they were made of fire and lived within stars. You say they created you...how?"

"According to them, they altered our planet and seeded it with organic life—life which they'd designed for the environment. At first, the life was microbial. From these beginnings, they engineered ever more complex creatures to populate the ecosystem. We're their crowning creation upon our planet as the Elladans are upon theirs and you are upon yours."

I glanced over at Hansen and Bradley who, like the rest of the bridge crew, were listening intently, their eyes wide.

"Valiant, mute me for a moment, will you?" I asked. Once that was done, I turned away and said to my crew, "This is fascinating stuff, but it's not necessarily true."

"But it *could* be," Bradley said eagerly. I could see that the man was taken with a tale that explained human origins so neatly, but without evidence, that's all it was: a tale.

"Let's all stay skeptical, all right? Keep our eyes open for anything out of place. Remember, every one of the alien races we've met—the Pandas, the Lithos, even the Raptors—has deceived us or tried to kill us at one time or another, not to mention the golden machines and Sokolov."

"Right, Skipper," Hansen said heavily, glaring around at the watchstanders. "This is a war zone, people. Don't get complacent."

I nodded to Hansen and snapped my fingers, turning back. "Valiant, unmute the channel."

"Done," said the ship.

"Farswimmer," I said, "do you mind answering more questions about your people and the Ancients?"

"Not at all. It is our purpose as liaison to foster communication. We do have some queries of our own."

"Of course. Let's talk about the Elladans. Why do they look like humans?"

"Because they choose to do so. Just as you all wear uniforms, they do the same."

I frowned. Clothing wasn't what I was getting at. Maybe clothing was a significant thing to the Whales. They didn't wear any except for a few adornments and technological devices.

"All right then," I said. "What about the Ancients? How exactly did they manipulate your planet's environment and the creatures there?"

"By means of machines."

"Did the Ancients ride around in ships, then? Is that how they left their stars?"

"They could not leave their stars until they learned to manipulate space. Even now they usually send machines and control them from afar."

This was beginning to sound familiar. The Blues had done something similar by creating the Macros and the Nanos to explore beyond their gas giant home while they themselves were largely trapped within the gravity well of their own planet. In fact, Earthlings had done much the same thing when we started to explore space by using robot probes more often than manned missions.

But that was before the Macros came and changed everything.

"But...how could creatures of fire, beings that dwell within stars, make *machines*?" I asked. "I mean, what kind of materials could stand up to that kind of heat and pressure?"

I couldn't tell you how, but I got the impression Farswimmer smiled. "Our scientists have debated this question for many years, and they have theories. The most popular explanation is the use of precisely controlled magnetic fields. But it really doesn't matter. Their science is advanced so far beyond ours as to seem supernatural, though we know it isn't."

I realized he was right. Our scientists were no different. I imagine all scientists were the same in that regard, debating the possibilities all day long. But as Captain, I didn't have that luxury. I had to get us home, and for that I needed answers. "Do you think the Ancients are dangerous?"

"If they wish to be," Farswimmer said. "They are individuals. At times, they come out of their lairs and do what they wish with lesser beings. Think of them as farmers or gardeners. If they're bored with their garden—they might choose to make drastic changes."

"Hmm," I said thoughtfully. I didn't like the idea of being a farm-animal—or worse, a turnip to be plucked or plowed over. "How do you fight a star dweller?"

The Whale made a motion I interpreted as a shrug. "We do not know. Some of the more radical among us have proposed creating weapons to attack the brown dwarf itself, but the time scales to build such projects range into the millennia."

"Yeah, I don't think that's only a Whale issue," I said with grim amusement. "Humans have a way of ignoring their problems until it's almost too late, too." I drummed my fingers on my chair arm and thought while Farswimmer floated patiently on the screen. "What about the golden slab machines?" I hoped that would translate well enough to understand what I meant.

"The Cubics?"

"That's a good name. We'll use it from now on."

"We believe they're a remnant of the Ancients' machines, but they have begun to malfunction. Their visits have become more erratic, and lately they have acted unpredictably."

"For example?"

"They've stolen various pieces of machinery from space near the far ring—the one you arrived through. Probes, observation satellites, even one crewed ship. We and the Elladans now give the ring as wide a berth as possible as do the Demons. The Cubics are simply too powerful to deal with, and we've never found a way to change their behavior."

I smiled. Farswimmer seemed like a decent guy, so I didn't mind sharing a technique with him. "We found a way," I said. "At least, one rogue human did. He planted a fusion bomb in the Cubics' control center which knocked them out for a while."

"Humans are resourceful creatures!" the Whale said. "Perhaps you're a superior breed—like the Elladans."

I sat back, putting my hands behind my head. For some reason, Farswimmer's agreeability and willingness to subordinate himself was beginning to make me suspicious, so I decided to needle him a bit just to see what the result would be.

"Doesn't it bother you to think we're somehow superior?" I asked.

"Every species is better than others in some areas. Elladans are better at war, at technology and at exploration. Ketans value other things, such as art, song and harmony. We are what we are, and you are what you are. We only wish to end this conflict and return to our peaceful ways."

Ketans…that was a new term. I figured it was what the Whales called themselves.

88

"Right," I said. "A sensible attitude."

Well, if Farswimmer wasn't lying to me, these guys wouldn't make any trouble for us. I hoped they could fight, too, however. I had the feeling the Demons were resourceful and unlikely to cease their aggression.

"But when we defeat this latest attack," I said, "the Demons will only build another fleet, and another. Do you guys have any plans to counterattack? To defeat them and win the war?"

"Given the distances involved, that's very difficult. Attacking fleets have many disadvantages. They cannot resupply with personnel, fuel or ammunition, and they cannot withdraw. They must either remain at speed to conduct one attack, or they must expend fuel to slow down and fight to the death. The defense, on the other hand, can resupply from stores, use moonlets as weapons platforms, and can see the enemy fleet approaching. Also, given that we hold two worlds, even if the Demons devastate the defenses of one, the other can counterattack and relieve its ally. Thus have we coped with the Demons for the past decades, and we will do so today. We are confident."

Damn. I chewed my lip. The Whales seemed committed to a purely defensive stance, which was probably fine for now...

But the fact these Demons launched an attack fleet every year... Eventually, something had to break.

"Thanks, Farswimmer," I said. "You've given me a lot to think about. I need to consult with my officers and call you back later, okay?"

"Of course, Captain. We're at your service."

I sat a while after the screen blanked, eyes unfocused, musing. There was so much to digest.

-10-

The sound of a throat being cleared broke my ruminations on all Farswimmer had told me, and I glanced over to see Hansen jerk his head at the ready room door. Nodding, I stood and went in. He followed me, leaving Bradley with the watch.

When the door had shut, Hansen turned to me. "Pardon me, Captain, but we're getting off track."

"How so?"

"It's not our job to win this war for our new allies. You didn't even ask about their rings—whether they worked, where they went? What if we can simply move on?"

"We can't leave these people at the mercy of genocidal monsters."

"Why not?"

Hansen had probably meant that to be rhetorical, but I pulled out a semi-bullshit answer anyway. "Because eventually they'll come after us. It's always better to stop a threat early."

"But early is relative," he argued. "Okay, I can see us helping with this battle coming up to gain their goodwill, but after that, it will be another year before the Demons attack. In that time, we can get home, then Star Force can get involved for real. Once they know about these new threats—the Lithos, the Demons, the Cubics—they'll have to get off their asses and start exploring again. But none of that's gonna happen if we don't get home."

I could hear the plaintive note in his voice, and it resonated. I wanted to see Mom and Dad again and friends I'd left behind, not to mention simply to walk a planet in peace. I longed to have Adrienne by my side—maybe on some beach somewhere…

But another part of me was afraid, I realized—not of anything physical, but of losing my command. What if Star Force decided I didn't deserve to skipper a ship any longer? I knew I'd find it damn hard to work under someone else after being the top dog for so long, but I also knew that too often organizations followed the "rules" instead of common sense. Despite the evidence, they might think that I was too green to be the boss again.

Then again…maybe the flood of new intelligence would convince Dad to come out of retirement, and with his influence…

Feeling a bit ashamed, I pushed my own concerns away and forced my mind back to the here and now. Hansen stared patiently at me, waiting for an answer.

"You're right, XO. I was getting caught up in finally having a lot of questions answered. Tell you what, talk to the officers and senior noncoms, and make a list of their most vital concerns relating to our current situation. Summarize it, and bring it to me. I'll use it next time I talk to Farswimmer and Diogenos. That will help me stay on track, okay?"

Hansen nodded. "I'll get right on that."

I followed the XO out, leaving the bridge. We went in opposite directions in the central passage.

"Valiant, where's Marvin?" I asked the ship aloud.

"Aboard *Greyhound*."

"Put me through." I continued down the passageway, walking toward the armory.

"Marvin here," came a voice from the walls nearby.

"Captain Marvin, dock *Greyhound* with *Valiant*, will you?"

"I do not think that is a good idea, Captain Riggs," he replied.

"Why not?"

"We could be attacked at any moment, and doing so would limit both ships' freedom of action."

"Good point. Bring her alongside then, and I'll jet over."

"Complying."

He didn't sound happy, but I didn't care. I slipped into my battlesuit, but I didn't bother taking a beam rifle.

"Greetings, Cody Riggs," said the suit.

"Hello, suit. What's cooking?"

"Question not understood."

"Never mind. Systems check."

"All systems nominal. Fusion cell warming up. Batteries at one hundred percent."

"Good. Close and activate."

The suit wrapped itself around me and the niche clamps released. The servos begin responding to the sensors touching my body, and within moments I felt as if the armor were a part of me again.

"Just like riding a bicycle," I said aloud.

"Comment not understood."

"I mean, this feels familiar."

"Comment ignored."

The tiny brainbox I was interacting with didn't make it easy, but I kept making small talk with the suit. It was part of my ongoing tests. I had a theory that the brainboxes of our equipment became slowly smarter, and they also were more and more responsive to their individual users over time. After all, Marvin had said the brainbox which became *Greyhound's* controlling AI, my old suit core, "liked me better" than him. It was only a small piece of evidence, but I figured that I might be onto something.

Normally, brainboxes were reset to standard parameters when they received updates and upgrades, but these days we were beyond contact with the Fleet. We'd been operating without those routine patches. I figured anything that made our AIs smarter and gave us an advantage was worth looking into.

To conserve air, I used the standard airlock rather than the assault version. It was just big enough for one battlesuit to stand inside comfortably. When the external hatch opened, I gazed out into the starlit void with the sense of wonder that always hit me. Looking at the universe with your own eyes, with nothing but a piece of smart glass between yourself and

92

the vacuum, was completely different from even the most detailed holotank representation. It always took my breath away.

A ship slid noiselessly into view. From my vantage point, it seemed like a wall covered with a thousand bizarre fittings and bits of machinery, sensors, heat exchangers, emitters, repellers, thruster nozzles and a lot more I couldn't identify.

Greyhound had arrived. She braked with a jet of gas and floated directly across from me.

I could see the ship's open airlock, so I stepped out into space. Long practice allowed me to ignore my inner ear, which was convinced I would fall into an abyss. As soon as I was free of the gravplates, I floated straight outward, adjusting my trajectory slightly until I was able to grasp the handle next to the entrance.

Once I'd stepped inside, the airlock cycled and opened inward revealing a narrow passageway barely wide enough for an unsuited human—or Marvin's cylindrical central body—to pass. I'd mandated that *Greyhound* remain minimally usable by humans. However, no way the suit would make it through, so I cracked it and stepped out after making sure the atmosphere was breathable.

"Marvin?"

"I'm in the forward compartment."

When I reached what used to be the control cockpit, I found Marvin had opened up the space around it to make a workroom. The cockpit itself was intact, though surrounded by equipment.

Half-identifiable gear lay here and there. I thought I recognized scanners, analyzers and microscopes as well as a 3D fabricator and a cryo-chamber. His tiny factory held a place of prominence high up on one wall. Marvin had cameras pointed at and tentacles manipulating something that looked like a steampunk ant farm, though I could see no creatures inside. One of his "eyes" pointed my way as I entered.

"What ya working on, Marvin?" I asked brightly, hoping to jolly him into letting something slip. He was usually cagey about his many experiments.

"I am examining the cellular structure of the body I recovered from the Demon corvette," he replied.

"Found anything out?"

"Of course."

"What's the best way to kill them, then?"

Another camera joined the first, giving him a binocular view of me. "Lasers and nuclear weapons seem effective."

"That's not very helpful. Tell me something of significance that I don't know."

"These creatures don't need an atmosphere to survive."

I raised an eyebrow. "That's interesting. So, no life support?"

"They use hydrocarbons and water to sustain life, but they ingest those rather than breathe. Their adaptations have advantages and drawbacks."

"Such as?" Letting him lecture me was a way of making Marvin happy and storing up goodwill for later.

"They can operate in a vacuum, protected by their exoskeleton and supplied by internal stores. They can even consume more materials to resupply themselves, with no requirement for air of any kind. Thus, they need no suit, no oxygen tanks, and unless the temperatures are extreme, no heating and cooling or extra protection from radiation. They are also nearly impervious to chemical or biological weapons."

"So they're damn tough critters."

"Yes. Not as tough as machines, but for biotics, they're impressively designed."

"I wonder what designed them..."

A third camera shifted to me, but then I lost it again. I must not be all that interesting. "I have theories," he said.

Then I remembered that Marvin still had a live tap on *Valiant's* coms. He didn't know that I knew about his spying. That was the way I wanted it for now.

"Tell me about that slime inside their ship. What have you learned about that?"

Four cameras aimed my way briefly, then it went back to two again after a brief moment's study.

"It serves multiple purposes. There are cilia inside the hull of their ships. These move the material around. Waste and sustenance are moved to the aliens."

I almost shuddered. A digestive system inside each ship? It was disgusting—but then, so was the interior of any human's gut.

"You said multiple purposes. What are the others?"

"Waste removal."

"And?"

He hesitated.

"There appears to be an anti-bacterial effect."

"Ah, interesting. So the slime is like our own internal organs—except the bugs have it on the outside. Disgusting, but intriguing."

"Why should these biological functions repel you?" Marvin asked, awarding me with a record-breaking bouquet of five cameras.

"That's part of human instinct. We're repelled by things that are strange and possibly dangerous."

"Interesting."

"Okay…" I said. "You're sure now that they're insectoid, right?"

"Technically no, but functionally, yes."

I rolled my eyes. "What I'm getting at is maybe they have different kinds of bugs? Workers, warriors, queens, technicians—like the Worms? This specimen would be a warrior, not a worker."

"That seems reasonable," Marvin said cautiously.

"So we need some bug spray…metaphorically speaking. Something better than brute force."

"Biochemistry is not my strongest field of expertise. I suggest we include Professor Hoon in this enterprise. Hoon also has an exoskeletal body similar to the Demons, and we may be able to gain particular insights with his help."

I cocked my head at Marvin, who cocked his cameras right back. "Are you saying Hoon knows more about biology than you do?"

"By no means."

"Good, because I seem to remember you doing pretty well with the Microbes. Isn't that biochemistry?"

"Let me clarify my proposal," Marvin said, uncoiling himself and sliding closer to me. Cameras dipped low and swooped high, getting different angles on my face, so he could read my responses. "The best case scenario doesn't have to involve Doctor Hoon directly. Perhaps he has an abundance of offspring to contend with. If he would be willing to spare a dozen or so, I could easily fabricate a lab to address this issue."

Staring at him, I got a sick feeling.

"What are you...?" I asked, then I got it. "Marvin, I'm not allowing you to turn Dr. Hoon or his children into specimens for your death-sprays. You can just forget about that right now. It's bad enough that I accused him of trying to kill me, but to then suggest that we test the bug spray on his children? He would probably try to kill me for real this time."

"An inconvenient possibility."

"Marvin, just see what you can come up with using the Demon that we have and I'll check with Kalu and Bensen."

I made my way back to *Valiant,* but I had the feeling I was missing something. I finally made it back to the bridge and found myself in front of the holotank. I just stared into the display. My gut was twisted in knots. What was I missing? The Demon fleet was three days out from Trinity-9, and I was pretty confident we had good tracking on all of them, because the Whales were hammering the incoming enemy fleet and its area of space with a blizzard of electromagnetic waves.

This allowed us to pick up the reflections on our passive sensors without adding to the active pings, in the same way that the human eye sees in the glare of floodlights. The Demons' stealth technology we'd found on the captured corvette could be overcome by the application of enough illumination, and everything in the holotank and on the screen was labeled with a high confidence factor.

So what was bugging me? I began to pace around the holotank.

I slammed my fist onto a console. "Yes! *Valiant*, calculate a prediction for the Demon fleet's turnover and deceleration, assuming they intend to slow enough to take up orbit around Trinity-9 without overshooting."

"What's the maximum G-force parameter?"

I racked my brain for a moment then decided I didn't need to come up with the number myself. "Reference Marvin's exploitation report on the corvette and the Demon corpse to estimate."

Valiant thought for a moment. "Combined ship and biotic G force parameters estimated at twenty-two."

"Ouch. Twenty-two Gs is heavy duty, even with gravplates to counter the forces inside the ship. Let's assume that's the most they can do. When will they need to begin deceleration?"

"Negative two days, twenty-one hours."

"Negative? You mean it's too late?"

"Yes. As you specified 'without overshooting,' sufficient deceleration is now impossible using the parameters given."

I leaned my forehead against the smart glass of the holotank and tapped my knuckles gently on it, thinking, looking at our allies' deployments.

The Whales had set up a gauntlet for the Demons to run. A cone of battle with its narrow end pointing directly at the enemy. The tip consisted of automated fortress-asteroids bristling with beam weapons, some railguns and missiles. As the attacking fleet destroyed these sacrificial installations and advanced, they would encounter continuously thickening defenses until they ran into the main Whale force of about two hundred heavy warships.

The simulations showed that the Demons would beat the Whales, but only barely. The hundred fifty or so Elladan ships that formed the reserve would tip the scales in our allies favor, and I hoped my little squadron could do its part as well without getting ourselves killed.

But now, the Demons had passed the point at which they could slow down enough to actually conquer the planet and its system of moons, unless they were to overshoot and come back. Would that be an effective tactic? I put myself in their place.

Overshooting would make the gauntlet far less bloody on both sides. At high speeds, hit probabilities would be low. Then, they could reverse course and come back.

But I didn't need a machine to calculate that in the time it took the Demons to come back to the fight, the Whales and Elladans could easily shift forces to meet them. Unless I assumed our enemies were idiots, there had to be something I was missing.

Though I hated to ask for help in matters of tactics, I decided to call Hansen and Bradley to the bridge. Once they'd arrived, I explained the situation to them.

"The force with speed has the advantage in combat," Hansen said in a tone that implied I should know this already. "Their missiles and projectiles will come in faster and hit harder, and once they get close, they'll be tough to target—at least from the side."

I nodded. "Sure, but in this case, it also limits their ability to maneuver. They're in a pipeline and even if they blast sideways starting now, they can't avoid our allies' defenses. The Whales might be pacifists at heart, but they're doing a decent job at setting up a kill zone."

"Maybe the enemy has some kind of secret weapon," Bradley said.

"Like what?" I made a come-on motion with my hand. "Go ahead, speculate. What if you were them?"

Bradley chewed his lip. "Well, the hardest thing to stop is hardened mass going fast. If I were designing this attack, I'd have as many cheap bullets as I could in front of me, like a shotgun, to overwhelm the defenses and clear everything out."

"But there are no cheap bullets, unless the enemy ships launch them…and according to the Whales' intelligence reports, they have missiles and beams, side mounted, totally unsuited to these tactics."

"Not totally," Hansen said. "Their side-mounted beams are good for zooming past, shooting as they go."

"But at these speeds, nobody's going to hit much," I replied. "That's why we're trying to figure out what they're up to.

I could see my CAG was still chewing on something. "Bradley, talk to me."

"Well, what if the Whales are wrong?" Bradley asked. "That is, what if the Demons changed-up their usual weapons mix or even the way they plan to use them?"

"Okay, so what would you do if you were the attackers? Remember, they refight this battle every Whale year or so, it seems, whenever the planets line up favorably."

Bradley tapped at the holotank controls for a minute. "I'm setting up a crude simulation, but I think it will be explanation enough." After a few moments more, he pressed the key to run it.

The display zoomed in to show the Demon fleet approaching Trinity-9 and its defenses. The simulation and ran at fast-forward speed to compress hours and minutes into seconds.

As the enemy neared the cone, ten big ships split apart into a hundred or so chunks each. The pieces, still coasting at two thousand miles per second, slammed unerringly into defense fortresses and ships, wiping them out.

"Of course, in the real world, not all of them will strike, but you get the idea," Bradley said.

"Trading ten ships—big, cheap suicide ships actually—for about half the Whales' combat power. A good deal."

"This is a wild-ass guess, though," Hansen objected.

Bradley wasn't the argumentative type, so he only frowned.

"In the details, maybe," I said, "but I think he's correct in principle. They've built up all this wonderful kinetic energy. They'd be stupid not to use it for more than mere travel."

"So that explains why they're not slowing down, but they're still going to be fighting an uphill battle when they stop and come back to Trinity-9."

I walked around the holotank, looking at it from all angles. Suddenly, I saw what I would do if I were them.

"It's because they're not planning to go back home."

Running my fingers over the controls, I set up a different sim. "What if they do this?"

This time, instead of coming back, the Demon fleet kept on going after their slashing attack on the Whales, curving gently but inexorably toward Trinity's central stellar pair.

And toward Ellada.

"Shit," Hansen rumbled. "With half their fleet helping the Whales, the Elladans are gonna get smeared."

"What are we going to do?" Bradley said.

"You two talk strategy. I need to speak with Diogenos." I entered the ready room and told *Valiant* to put me through to the Elladan liaison.

Diogenos' overly handsome face soon appeared on the screen. "Greetings, Captain. What can I do for you?"

"It may be I can do something for you, Senator. I'm sending over a couple of files with simple simulations that I hope you can adapt to your computer systems, but I'll explain anyway. The Demon fleet doesn't seem to be slowing down for an assault on Trinity-9—the Ketans' planet—we think they're going to hit and run past, aiming for Ellada. Half your ships will be caught hopelessly out of position."

Diogenos' patrician face turned gray with realization. "That is grim news, if you are correct. Our strategy has always been to use the Ketans as faithful phalanxes and bulwarks to absorb the Demons' firepower."

I raised an eyebrow. "That seems like a brutally cynical attitude."

Diogenos shrugged. "We're the superior species. We taught them technology long ago and encouraged their evolution. Without us, they would still be like the whales of the oceans, bright animals only. Besides, their planet is enormous. With no solid surface, it's generally immune to strategic strikes with large-scale weaponry. Their floating cities can maneuver, even submerge beneath the clouds for a time, and their people can disperse, feeding as if in the wild. We Elladans, by contrast, are vulnerable to attacks on our city-states, our agriculture, and our industry."

So much for being the superior species! I kept the thought to myself. "Philosophy aside, what will you do about the Demons?"

100

Diogenos' eyes stared past the vid pickup, as if into the distance over my shoulder. "I have relayed your insight to our military. They will decide such matters. Now I must speak with the Senate. Thank you for the warning, Captain. We welcome any further aid from our faithful allies."

"No problem, Senator. Riggs out."

Allies, eh? I guess we'd been upgraded from "children." But I wasn't sure what other aid we could lend.

Then I remembered that we were also in the Demons' path, although we still had time to move out of it.

-11-

"Valiant, connect me to Farswimmer." I didn't want to rely on the Elladans to explain to the Whales our predictions about the Demon attack.

When Farswimmer appeared on the screen, I told him about our conjectures.

His tentacle motions conveyed dismay. "Our ship commanders wondered about the lack of deceleration but believed that the Elladans would come up with an explanation and a course of action."

"The Elladans? You're relying on them to do your thinking and run the battle for you?" I wasn't sure if my incredulous tone translated.

"Of course. They're much more adept at the conduct of hostilities."

"And who takes the brunt of the casualties?"

"In terms of ship losses, we do—as is fair. It's our own planet we defend, after all. But in terms of lives lost, the Elladans suffer more than we do."

"I'm surprised the Elladans take any losses. As I understand it, the Demons have always attacked your planet rather than Ellada."

"Creatures such as yourselves and the Elladans are small and require large crews of individuals to serve your warships, correct?"

"Sure, mostly, though we do have some small ships with only one person aboard and even unmanned ships. But we find that there are advantages to having more people aboard—redundancy and flexibility, for example."

"Exactly. Each of our ships contains only one body. Therefore, fewer lives are lost."

I sat back thoughtfully. "Of course. That makes sense. Each of you takes a lot more life support than a human."

"We're also much more adept at multitasking, given our physiology."

"Physiology?" I wasn't at all sure what he meant.

"Of course. One of us is like a crew of humans."

"Huh?" Clearly, I had missed something somewhere.

"Did you not peruse the files we sent?"

"Uh," I said cautiously, "I skimmed over some parts. What are you referring to?"

Patiently, it seemed to me, Farswimmer said, "Each of us has several brains, adding more as we grow. When too many occupy one body, we divide into two beings."

"Multiple brains…yeah, I saw that, but I thought the extra ones were to help control a very large creature. Are you trying to say that you actually have more than one mind living in each body?"

"Of course."

"Then who am I speaking to now?"

Farswimmer laughed. "All of us, as we're all interested in newcomers. If you were an Elladan, for example, probably half of our minds would be preoccupied with their own peculiar interests."

I force my slackened jaw to close. "Well, it's going to take some time to get used to that idea, so for now I'm going to treat each of your bodies as one being, okay?"

"That will not offend us, Captain."

"Good," I muttered, still thrown off. Well, the best I could do was follow my own advice, so I decided to simply go on as I had been. "In any case, you might want to start reorganizing your defenses."

"We will consult with the Elladans. Thank you again, Captain Riggs. We depart." The screen blanked.

103

What a bunch of happy-go-lucky creatures. Didn't they feel the urgency in all this?

I knew that they'd fought similar battles with the Demons on many previous occasions, but I didn't think the Whales should be so complacent. I wanted to grab Farswimmer by the tentacles and shake some sense into him—or her, or them…whatever. It especially bugged me that they seemed to defer to the Elladans in everything. I wasn't even sure why it bothered me. After all, it was better than if they tried to lord it over us humans.

I left the ready room and joined Hansen and Bradley in running tactical sims in the holotank.

It was all well and good to ponder multi-brained whales and oddball humanoids with delusions of grandeur, but we'd never get where we were going if we didn't live through the next few days.

* * *

The Elladans and Whales took our warning seriously in the end.

I watched in grudging admiration as the Elladan commander, whoever he was, immediately turned his fleet around and blasted back toward the inner planets on the most efficient course possible.

Projecting the Elladan and Demon fleets' paths, it became clear that the defenders would get to Ellada late, but only by a little. This presumed the Demons would decelerate to assault the planet.

If they cruised on through instead, they could do a lot of damage, but then they'd be in the same position we predicted for Trinity-9—having to turn around and come back for a serious assault.

I ordered my little squadron to take a similar but separate course that would have allowed the Demons to overtake us, but place us at long range. We could apparently accelerate faster than the Elladans, a fact I found interesting.

We couldn't be sure of their ships' limitations, though, as neither ally had provided specs on their respective ships. I couldn't really blame them. I wouldn't have given info like that to a bunch of new people that popped into the Solar System either. Still, I would think that if the Elladans could move faster, they would be doing it in order to get home in time to fight.

The Whales shifted their defenses too, placing their warships behind their moon fortresses, setting them up as shields against kinetic strikes. It was the space borne equivalent of digging foxholes, in case we were correct in our guesses. From their chosen positions, they could strike with beams as the Demon ships went by.

Hansen stood next to me at the holotank as the timer ticked down. "Almost there," he said unnecessarily. I could see the situation as well as he could.

"Yeah," I replied. "Good luck, Whales. Now we'll see if Bradley was right. Glad we're a long ways away." We were far ahead of the Demons, of course, on our way to Ellada, though the enemy was coming after us like a speeding freight train.

In the tank, we watched as three hundred red pinpricks suddenly blossomed into thousands and began to maneuver. Contacts broke apart and separated.

"A missile barrage," Hansen said. "There are more than a thousand new contacts."

"Targets?" I asked.

"Plotting. It'll take a few seconds to determine their trajectories."

It was my guess they were firing at the Whale ships as they flew by. I couldn't help but feel a little uneasy. They'd probably spotted us by now as well.

While the enemy couldn't alter course much, they could spread out, both sideways and front to back, and that was what they were doing. Now, instead of a compact fleet, they became an expanding and moving sphere.

The leading edge of the globe of Demon ships touched the Whale defenses. Red and green pixels winked out by the dozens. I zoomed in on the action and slowed down the recording, intensely curious about what exactly was happening in this titanic confrontation.

Increasing the resolution to maximum, I focused on one enemy. It turned out to be a needle shape, about a hundred feet long and two wide, like a very narrow missile body. It had no thrusters or repeller vanes that I could see, though perhaps it was too distant for such detail.

I followed it in as it struck a Whale orbital asteroid fortress, where it gouged out an enormous crater. Several others slammed into the same installation, and in short order the base had been turned into a smoking wreck.

"Bradley was right, more or less," Hansen muttered. "Cheap kinetic missiles." He pointed. "The Whales are taking some out, but they're so slim that they're hard to hit from the nose on, and even if they do…"

"There's no real mechanism to damage. They have to be melted and forced off course by the heat and laser pressure, or they're going to hit anyway."

"At least the Whale warships won't be taken out."

I saw he was right. The Ketans' cruisers were either shielded by their asteroid moons, or they were maneuvering to get out of the way of the Demons' ballistic darts. With space so vast, it was actually quite easy to dodge non-maneuvering projectiles.

The Demon warships were another matter.

At such high speed, the battle took place within the space of minutes. In the end, the Whales had lost most of their relatively immobile fortresses, but only a few ships.

"What about this flock of contacts here?" I demanded, pointing out a swarm that had moved separately, past the rocky moonlets.

"Plotting. There—ah, that's bad."

The missiles weren't heading toward the whale forts or their ships. They were headed toward the planet.

"They're doing a civilian strike," I said, watching grimly. "Do we know where they'll land?"

Hansen shook his head. "We can figure out the coordinates, but not what's down there in that soupy atmosphere. Let's hope it's not a bunch of Whale elementary schools."

Helplessly, we watched these missiles plunge toward the gas giant. The Whale warships, sensing the threat, moved out from behind cover to intercept. Beams slashed out, taking a few of the missiles out—but the range was extreme and most of their shots missed.

"They can't stop them," I said. "But they feel they have to try. They're out of position, and they're going to get hurt."

"That's probably why the Demons did it, to draw out the Whale warships."

The strategy was working. Dozens of Whale warships were hit and destroyed once they were out in the open.

We continued watching with tight-lipped concern as the missiles slammed down into the Ketan home world. The impact explosions brightened the atmosphere like lightning seen from above a cloud.

By this time, the Demon fleet had been reduced to half its original size, but most of that was due to their own design and strategy. Their slim ballistic missiles hadn't been launched, but rather, they'd been split off. In other words, some of the enemy ships had been composed of nothing but a control mechanism and a bunch of darts stuck together to create a ship. When the time came, each traveling body disassembled itself, leaving nothing but an engine and a framework also aimed at a Whale fortress.

"Do you think they've saved more of those kinetic bundles for Ellada?" Hansen asked.

"Probably," I said, "but our side will have an advantage for the next battle."

He looked at me, questioning. "So, we're going to get involved?"

"Don't you think we ought to? They just struck civilian targets before our eyes."

Hansen looked at the holotank but said nothing.

"The next wave of ships will have to decelerate at Ellada to fully engage," I continued. "That will let us catch up to them. Unless I miss my guess, we're going to create a lot of scrap for our factories."

Hansen's eyebrows went up even further. "Really? How?"

107

I smiled. "When I give the battle orders, XO, keep your eyes on the holotank."

-12-

I spent the remainder of the day thinking. I'd almost decided to confront Sakura about what Kalu had dug up, but I now had decided against it. With us going into battle soon, she was vital to ship operations. Even if she had it in for me personally, there was no evidence she was a traitor to Star Force or wanted to sabotage the mission as a whole.

As long as I was careful and gave her—or whoever it was—no easy opportunities to get rid of me, it made more sense to let sleeping dogs lie.

I did drop by Hoon's workshop in armor again. Suiting up in armor was a pain compared to wearing a spacer's jumper, but it made me feel safer.

Hoon didn't remark upon my equipment. Maybe a critter with an exoskeleton naturally assumed those without were happier when armored.

He wasn't entirely wrong.

"Professor," I began, "it seems you're in the clear again, at least as far as anyone is."

"Apology accepted, young Riggs. Now, I have much work to do." He gestured toward the air-water-lock I'd only just entered.

"I didn't apologize," I growled, but then relented. "Whatever, if it makes you happy. I'm actually here to discuss

109

any theories on the slime we found inside the Demon ship. And, I'd appreciate being addressed as 'Captain.'"

"I'm sure you would. The slime is obviously shielding of some sort."

I ignored his irascible commentary. "That's what I thought...but for what?"

"The robot and I have two theories, but they're farfetched."

"Farfetched is better than none at all. Indulge me by speculating."

"I'm not certain you could comprehend the mathematics."

"Then leave it out and explain in layman's terms."

Hoon sighed, or at least that's what came through my translation software. "Very well. As one of the less idiotic members of your species once wrote, eliminate the impossible and what remains, however improbable, must contain the truth."

"You're quoting Sherlock Holmes? You know he was a fictional character, right?"

"I'm quoting Sir Arthur Conan Doyle. Are you not aware that the author is actually the one who created the quote? Fictional characters cannot create."

I threw up my hands. I should have known that putting Marvin and Hoon in the same room together was a mistake. "Argh. Go on—the slime is shielding?"

"If you want me to explain, you would do well to cease distracting me with irrelevancies."

I kept my mouth shut and waited, teeth grinding.

"You do realize that slime, as you put it, has the purpose of preventing biological infections?" he asked.

"Yes," I replied. "At least, that's what it does for humans."

"Very good. But as far as we can tell, these Demons aren't disease prone."

"So...the slime prevents something else from getting through?"

"There is hope for you yet, young Riggs."

"Sure, Hoonie-boy."

"I find your mode of address entirely too informal."

"Ditto, Professor."

"Very well...*Captain*."

110

What was with all these fat-brains that made them feel so superior? If they were genuinely so smart, they'd have figured out that scientific capability wasn't the only measure of competence. "Please, Professor, cut to the chase."

"That's it. The mucus layer is designed to prevent the intrusion of biological agents. What kind and for what purpose is as yet unknown."

I tried to scratch my head before I realized I was in armor. "I was hoping for more clear answers."

"We all hope for the best, Riggs. We settle for realities and long periods of study. Now, if you don't mind, I'd like to get back to my work."

"Fine," I said, and left.

Out in the hallway, I found myself cursing Hoon. He was smart and useful, but his attitude was extremely irritating.

"They've passed us, Captain," Hansen said as I strode onto the bridge to get the latest update. I'd dropped off my suit at the armory.

"Got it," I replied. "I had a notification trigger set with Valiant."

In the holotank, I could see that the Demon fleet had overtaken us, far off to the side, and they were beginning to curve inward toward Ellada. From now on, we would be on converging courses, with our ships still accelerating to match speeds with the enemy.

We were a few hours from Ellada. Assuming the Demons were going to start braking soon, the plots we'd calculated predicted we'd catch their fleet by the time we reached the target planet. This would put the Demons between two forces—ours and the defenders, with the Elladans' expeditionary fleet—the one that had been at Trinity-9 and was now running for home—also converging from the flank. They would be hours late to the party, but better late than never.

"There they go, right on time," Bradley said from his usual position standing behind his drone controllers. He stared at the wall screen nearest him, which showed a simplified version of the situation.

I saw that he was right. Most of the Demon ships had begun to decelerate. Those that did not, Valiant marked as kinetic bundles. We wouldn't be overtaking those. The Elladans would have to deal with them.

Tensely, I watched as our rate of closure increased. With us still accelerating and the enemy decelerating, we began to catch up faster and faster, even as we slid in behind them.

"Missiles?" Bradley asked.

"Not yet."

"Daggers?"

"Just wait, CAG," I said. "We've got this."

As usual during battle, my mind had gone into overdrive, and I didn't like people asking me questions. Then I relented a bit in order to explain. "If we launch drones or missiles now, they have to use their own fuel to keep accelerating. The longer we wait, the longer their range or patrol radius. It would be the opposite if we were decelerating."

Bradley nodded, clearly worried that we had no drone support placed around our ships, but the range was still extreme. Because the enemy was slowing, they had the same problem with launching missiles or fighters. We were "uphill" from them. The longer they waited, the better their weapons would perform when launched backward at us.

Over the next couple of hours, as we came in from the side to take position behind the Demons, I watched the display. The arc representing the maximum effective range of *Stalker*'s big laser finally reached the rearmost Demon ship. "Valiant, tell Kreel to open fire."

A moment later, a line of green stabbed at the enemy. "Damage?"

"Moderate."

"Tell him to keep at it. Put me through to Cornelius."

"Cornelius here, Captain," the muscular woman's crisp Teutonic voice replied a moment later.

"We'll enter long range for our lasers in less than an hour, Chief. This will be a pure beam fight until we overtake them, so the gun deck is going to get a workout."

"No problem, sir. We're ready."

"Glad to hear it. Stand by, Riggs out."

The Demons began to alter their motion, wiggling their drives slightly to make their individual paths less predictable

112

while still lined up along their overall deceleration route. This made them harder to hit, but decreased the efficiency of their maneuvers with wasted motion and forced them to spread out as well. All this was good for the Elladans and for us. I'd take anything that multiplied the enemy's problems.

Over the next half an hour, three enemy ships flared and were marked destroyed as *Stalker*'s massive beam cannon slammed shot after shot into the rear of the enemy fleet despite their evasive maneuvers. Our assumptions proved correct— they were highly vulnerable from this angle, because the Demon ships were designed to fight from the broadside, not from the stern or bow.

While putting an engine in each end allowed for unorthodox maneuvers, it also meant that from this direction, their armor was thin. They had little more than a clamshell that slid over the fusion exhaust port. They didn't seem to have shields or screens.

But what they did have was more than two hundred big warships, not counting the kinetic bundles. If we hadn't been approaching Ellada and in a time crunch, I would hold the range open and keep sniping, but we couldn't do that if we were going to help our fellow humans. We had to get in closer so that our midrange weapons would come into play.

Unfortunately, that would allow them to do the same. I would try to finesse things, though, creeping closer and only doing battle with a few of their ships at a time. It would be a delicate dance under pressure.

"Mains firing," Hansen said. I hadn't given the order, but Cornelius knew her job.

Our four heavies lanced across the distance to converge on the rearmost enemy. A moment later, that icon showed slight damage. The Chief had fired at the longest range possible.

We knocked out several more Demon ships which drifted ahead of their decelerating fleet. I noticed Marvin stayed far back in *Greyhound*, but the four Nano frigates were edging out ahead of us. They could accelerate faster than we could, though they had orders not to.

"Dammit, get me Kreel."

"Kreel here, Riggs."

"Captain Kreel, tell your people to get those frigates back behind us. They don't have the firepower or armor to fight so many Demons in close, and they don't have the range to shoot from here."

"I acknowledge, sir, but my pilots are having difficulty controlling them."

"Nano brainboxes are willful. Have your people order them to form up around *Greyhound* and protect Marvin until they receive further orders. That will make him happy and keep them from throwing themselves away."

"Understood."

"Captain Kreel, you need to turn your brain on. Riggs out." I really didn't have much to complain about with the Raptor captain, except that he lacked imagination and creativity which might be a good thing in some cases, given he controlled half my squadron's firepower, but dealing with the nano ships was like dealing with first timers right out of boot camp wanting to play hero. He was going to need to rein them in.

Eventually, the frigates fell back toward *Greyhound* as ordered, leaving *Stalker* and *Valiant* to hammer the Demons. For a while, we were in the perfect position, able to hold the range while the enemy couldn't close it.

But that had to change as we continued to overhaul them, and they kept on slowing down. This became clear when the three rearmost demon battleships rotated to present their broadsides.

"Cease acceleration! Shields up!" I snapped.

A moment later the ship thrummed with the impact of several enemy beams.

"Damage?"

"None," Valiant replied.

"What if we'd been hit without the shield?"

"Damage would have been moderate."

"Damn." I stared at the three battleships which had rotated back to continue their deceleration.

This maneuver left the other Demon ships as their rearmost guard. The pause in their deceleration caused them to drift forward along the rest of their fleet's course. Then several of

114

the now-closest ships turned to present their broadsides, and I understood their strategy.

"They're going to keep a rolling barrage on us, rotating ships to fire and drift forward while others keep decelerating," I said for the benefit of the bridge crew.

I chewed my lip. We'd destroyed thirteen enemy ships—an amazing kill ratio considering we'd taken no damage at all. But if we kept moving in closer, their superior numbers and firepower would quickly reverse the situation. They'd gotten tired of being pummeled.

"Cease acceleration. Use repellers to hold the distance open and steady our course. Keep us at maximum effective range—and Valiant, snap the shields up any time we're targeted."

"Acknowledged."

The dance I'd anticipated continued, each side sniping at the other with little effect, now that we were both taking countermeasures. The best we could do now was provide a distraction and lower their effectiveness. Well, I hadn't expected our harassment to be decisive. Not with seven ships against hundreds.

Hours passed. I took a quick nap in the ready room and made sure everyone rotated with their backups and assistants for meals and rest, even Hansen. He had a young kid named Lazar training to fill in as ship's pilot, a former drone controller.

So we were fresh and ready when the Demons began to engage the Elladans near their home planet.

By this time, the enemy fleet had slowed enough for a straightforward fight. If they won, they'd hold the high ground above Ellada—and they were going to win, at least temporarily.

Half of the Elladan forces, over a hundred ships on their way back from Trinity-9, continued to curve in from the side on the most efficient course. It was clear they would still arrive late. They could have opted to speed up, but if they had, it would have meant overshooting after one pass. It must have been an agonizing choice for them.

I thought about the beautiful cities and landscapes of Ellada, an idyllic world, and knew things wouldn't look so pretty when this fight was done.

The enemy kinetic bundles had already split apart, spread out and ripped through the Elladan orbital fortresses. The immobile platforms didn't have the ability to dodge or the firepower to destroy all the darts coming at them.

Soon it would be ship to ship, and the Demons outnumbered the defenders by almost three to one.

First, the Demons launched a blizzard of fighters from their assault carriers—over a thousand of them. The Elladans put up almost as many, some rising from bases on their moon. That seemed like good news, anyway.

Then the Demons launched their missiles. We counted a full spread of more than five thousand. It was a nightmarish, awe-inspiring sight—the largest concentration of firepower I'd ever witnessed. The swarm would begin to close on the Elladans in about an hour.

The only enemy vessels that held their ordnance back were the twelve ships of their rearguard, apparently assigned to keep us at bay.

Instead of sending the missiles in first at the Elladans, which is what a Star Force commander would have done, the Demon fighters charged ahead.

"What the hell are they doing?" I muttered to myself. It seemed a damned expensive tactic. Manned craft were far more valuable than one-shot missiles, not to mention the lives at stake.

But the Demons didn't seem to care about lives.

The Elladans launched missiles as well, but only a paltry few hundred. Their graceful ships seemed to be configured mainly with beams and railguns, though they hadn't provided us with specs. I guessed most of their missiles had been stationed on their fortresses. If I'd been in charge, I'd have soft-launched them before the installations had been smashed and left them drifting in space to be used later.

I checked the positions of the defending Elladans and their reinforcements racing to the fight. I knew that if we were going to help these people now was the time as the battle was soon to be decided. Maybe the Demons' command and control would make some mistakes with so much going on.

"All ahead full," I told Hansen. "Valiant, let Kreel know to lead us in and open fire with his primary cannon."

Stalker was more heavily armored than *Valiant*, and we'd fitted her with shielding.

"Message delivered," said my ship.

"CAG, deploy forty-eight Daggers."

"Aye, aye," Bradley replied, and soon we had a screen between us and the enemy.

In response, the Demon ships turned their broadsides toward us and began to return fire. Right now, it was ineffective as *Stalker* outranged anything they had.

They also began launching fighters from their assault carriers, three sets of twelve, all at once. Instead of carrying them in an internal flight deck like ours, Demon carriers had a dozen each in individual launch tubes. They were much larger than our unmanned drones, with four small lasers and four counter-missiles each.

The rest of the space inside the assault carriers was taken up with landing craft according to the intel the Whales had provided. I'd been a bit puzzled by their design as the unarmed shuttles and pinnaces didn't seem suitable for battle, only for transport, but it didn't matter right now.

Stalker pounded on an enemy battleship, one of the three nearest us. Between shots, she raised her shield. I could see that giving the Raptor battleship its own Star Force brainbox had improved her battle efficiency.

Broadside, the Demon battleship and its two fellows fired back intermittently rather than in volley. They managed to maintain a constant barrage. Their six rearguard cruisers stayed farther from us, and the three assault carriers were farther still.

When *Valiant* came into range again, we added our mains to the mix. "Concentrate fire on the same battleship that *Stalker* is hitting," I ordered.

In response, our target began using their end-mounted engines to twist and turn like a mad pinwheel, reducing the effectiveness of our lasers to partial hits. The ability to easily move sideways to the arc of fire was one advantage of their setup that we didn't have.

I kept a close eye on their fighter screen and ours. I was pretty sure that, ship for ship, theirs would be stronger, but ours would be much faster being smaller and unmanned. "CAG, I want you to feint with your Daggers toward them and try to get their fighters to follow, to draw them toward us."

"Will do, sir." Bradley issued orders to his controllers, and soon I watched as our screen swooped forward, fired beams at ranges far too long to damage the enemy, and then turned to run.

"Keep doing that, closer and closer," I said.

"They're burning fuel, sir," he replied.

"Let me know when they get to fifty percent."

"Yes, sir."

On the fifth and closest feint, we lost a Dagger—and then three more blew up in rapid succession. I cursed and bared my teeth.

Then the enemy cruisers turned and fired their mains in a volley. That told me what I wanted to know. "CAG, have the Daggers launch their anti-ship heavies. Target their fighters with one missile each, and lay the rest on their ships."

Each drone carried two external packs. One contained a heavy nuke missile and the other a rotary counter-missile launcher. I was hoping the enemy didn't look too close, as only the heavies were being fired now, holding the CMs in reserve.

Forty-seven missiles leaped toward the Demon squadron, and in response, the enemy fighters advanced to meet them. This was standard tactics for fighters trying to kill missiles, because the longer they waited, the harder it would be to hit their targets as the rockets gained speed.

"As soon as they start picking our missiles off, blow the nearest ones at your discretion," I told Bradley. "I want a smokescreen between us and them, at least for a little while. Valiant, launch one volley of our own missiles, aimed at their battleships."

Although our beams were less effective against the dodging enemy, their ships had given up the ability to move easily toward or away from us. "All ahead full. Now that they're busy with our missiles and Daggers, we'll move in closer."

"On it," Hansen replied, and *Valiant* surged forward. *Stalker* followed a moment later, with *Greyhound* and her escort of four Nano frigates farther behind.

The Demon fighters were already shooting at our leading missiles, coming closer and closer in order to do it. In response, our Daggers sniped at the enemy, knocking out a couple of them.

A volley of fifty or so missiles launched from the Demon ships, but from my point of view, their timing was poor and badly coordinated. I chalked that up to them not realizing that the second pack on each Dagger wasn't a nuclear missile, but a counter-missile launcher with a dozen seeker rockets in it.

When we'd lost three or four missiles to their fighters, Bradley's controllers began detonating the warheads, creating clouds of plasma and brief EMP whiteouts that fuzzed sensors. This complicated everyone's targeting, hopefully allowing more of our weapons to sneak in closer.

In response, the Demon fighters moved forward even farther, trying to close with our weapons and take better shots.

"Bradley," I said, "I want you to blow a bunch of our nukes and launch half the Daggers' counter-missiles toward their fighters. Time it so that when the smoke clears, they'll be surprised and facing a shitload of fighter-killers."

"Yes, sir!" Bradley replied, and barked orders to his controllers to set up my ploy.

A moment later, twenty of our missiles detonated at once just in front of the Demon fighters. At the same time, our Daggers fired over two hundred counter-missiles from their 12-packs. The tiny rockets accelerated at high speed behind the screen of plasma.

Bradley timed it well. Once the hot gases began to clear, our salvo was too close for the Demons to avoid it.

The enemy knocked out more counter-missiles than I expected. I could see why they relied on their fighters for point defense. Each craft's four lasers fired independently and with surprising accuracy, but there were simply too many weapons aimed at them—approximately eight for every Demon.

Combined with the confusion from the nuke detonations, they couldn't keep up.

Within thirty seconds, thirty-two of their fighters were swept from space, leaving only four. They turned tail and ran for their carriers. Half our Daggers were gone, but I accounted the battle a victory anyway.

Cheering broke out on *Valiant*'s bridge, and I let them whoop and holler for a moment. "Rotate out the rest of our reserve drones," I said, "bring in the damaged ones for repairs, refueling and rearming."

"On it," Bradley replied. Four Daggers fired off their remaining counter-missiles at the oncoming Demon missiles and then turned to run back to Valiant.

Those enemy missiles advanced in a wave over fifty strong, but now they had no fighter screen to escort them in. Our Daggers made short work of them. Any that couldn't be brought down with laser shots were killed with counter-missiles.

"Nice job, everyone. We have space superiority," I said. "We have fighters and they don't."

Even though their three battleships and six cruisers outgunned us, our shields gave us an enormous advantage. We fired salvoes and snapped on our shields between volleys, and so were vulnerable for less than one second out of every ten.

They countered by spinning their ships around their axes. They continued to pinwheel and thereby spread the damage. Also, they pulled back their most heavily damaged ships. That kept their fresher vessels forward taking the hits. It was a grinding battle, and even though we were winning, I didn't like what it was costing us. There was a lot of generalized damage to our forward hull. Several lasers, missile launchers and a lot of sensors had been taken out by shots that hit us when our shields were down.

"All Daggers rearmed," Bradley reported. "We have thirty-one still operating, but we've exhausted all our capital missile stores. Everything we have left is on the Daggers."

"Understood," I replied. I'd been using up our nuclear missiles at an unsupportable rate, but we'd managed to clear away their fighter screen. Now we would see if my gamble would pay off. "Send in the Daggers now. As soon as they start taking hits, launch all their missiles and have half follow them in, keeping the other half near us in reserve. Suicide the attackers if you have to. I want those bastards smashed and the way cleared. The Demons will have to form a new rearguard, or we'll crawl right up their tails."

I watched in the holotank as the two dozen Daggers swung around on looping attack runs, twisting in three dimensions to try to confuse the enemy as they advanced. They got quite close before the first one was destroyed.

When the four remaining Demon fighters moved in to do what they could, our Daggers launched their big nuke missiles, two each, creating more than sixty targets.

"All ahead full," I ordered. "Relay that to *Greyhound* and the Nano ships. We'll continue the general assault to finish off whatever survives the nukes." I didn't expect Marvin to take many risks, but he might do some good, and if he held back too much, I could use evidence of his cowardice against him in some future negotiation.

That's how I had to think with Marvin, always looking for an edge.

With poor point defense and little in the way of a fighter screen, the Demons were doomed. They did everything they could to stop the incoming missiles and Daggers, which only allowed us to fire our beams more freely at them as my squadron closed in. I ordered the capacitors emptied, using the power-hungry anti-proton weapons as well as lasers to do maximum damage in minimum time.

It turned into a slaughter—as I'd hoped. Half our missiles died, but that left more than twenty to slam directly into Demon ships.

The three assault carriers and six cruisers were wrecked outright, but their battleships were damned tough. I had to give them credit for ruggedness as they survived three or four direct fusion strikes each before finally succumbing.

"Slag them with beams," I ordered as we moved in to optimum range. Soon we were giving them the coup de grace, blasting anything that showed a significant power signature.

Marvin held back, of course, but the Nano frigates attacked with evident gusto, buzzing around like angry bees.

I had reason to curse my overconfidence then, as *Valiant's* voice abruptly blared.

"Boarders detected. Assault imminent. Implementing anti-boarding protocols."

-13-

"Anti-boarding protocols approved!" I snapped to Valiant. "Hansen, you have the bridge."

I had no idea what was going on or how the Demons had infiltrated so near to us before triggering the alarm, but I wasn't going to sit on my ass while it happened, despite Hansen's strangled protest.

"Warn all the other ships!" I ordered Valiant as I ran for the armory. "I want to know where they came from. Why didn't we detect them earlier?"

"External sensors rely on radar and infrared laser pulses," Valiant answered promptly. "The Demon boarders return no radar signature and only minimal infrared as they are wearing no suits. Also, the battle-space contains thousands of pieces of wreckage."

"In other words, they had a lot of clutter to hide in."

"Correct."

"No sealed suits," I muttered, recalling that the Demons didn't need atmosphere. "They must have deployed into space once they realized their ships were doomed—especially the hundreds of Demon marines on the assault carriers."

"Your unproven assumptions have failed the ninety percent probability test."

"Eighty percent is good enough on this one, Valiant. Dammit. We should have stayed out at long range and moved on."

Valiant remained silent. She never criticized my command decisions, for which I was grateful. I wasn't so easy on myself, though.

Entering the armory, I threw myself into my battlesuit.

"Welcome, Cody Riggs," said the suit.

"That's me, suit. Seal and prep for full combat mode." I reached for a laser rifle with one hand and plugged in its power cable, and then picked up my Raptor axe in the other. "Switch my HUD to tactical mode."

Inside my faceplate, I saw a diagram of *Valiant* with icons scattered through her interior. Several angry red splotches showed where boarders, presumably Demon marines of some sort, had landed and begun damaging the hull.

"Display marines," I said as I strode out of the armory toward the nearest enemy location. Several clusters showed up immediately, each near a splotch.

"External feed. Give me a look at what's attacking us."

A window opened in front of my eyes, showing slick, shiny motion around an airlock. Though difficult to resolve, I was able to make out the limbs and carapaces of various bugs.

One type looked like the things I'd seen in the specimen boxes of the Cubics' planet, vaguely humanoid in size and shape. Others seemed larger and looked like scorpions with twin tails.

The third type I'd seen before. They were huge beetles with horns a yard long projecting from their heads. The type that had chased Marvin all over the square. We'd also seen a bunch of them within the Cubics' planet. Until then, I hadn't realized they were part of the Demon forces. I wondered if they were a variant of the same race or a separate creation of this mad Ancient in Tartarus. That is, if what the Elladans said was even true.

The Demons seemed to function as a team. They focused on taking out the turrets. Once again, I was glad that I'd installed the additional point defense to combat the Lithos. The low beams were doing a lot of damage as they sought to land. I couldn't tell how many had been killed by those weapons as the dead had probably already drifted off into space.

I rounded a corner to spot a handful of my marines waiting, weapons pointed toward the airlock, the weakest spot in this area of *Valiant*'s armored hull. One turned toward me, and I could see it was Sergeant Moranian, Adrienne's most hated rival.

Great.

"Stay back, sir," she said, but I ignored her words, clomping up to join them.

"It's the Demon bugs," I told her. "Some are like those beetles we fought before, on the Square."

"Any idea of their armaments, Captain?"

I took another look at the display within my HUD. "Looks like the humanoids have guns in their hands. The beetles will probably fight with their organic weaponry as before. There are also scorpion-types with two tails. No doubt they've got something nasty in their stingers."

Just then I heard a pounding on the deck-plates and turned to see a large group of Raptors running up. "Command us, Captain Riggs," their leader said over the short-range com-link.

To augment our dwindling supply of marines, I'd had sixty Raptor warriors inducted into Riggs' Pigs and stationed in one of our cargo bays in hibernation, armed and armored for just such a situation. Valiant had activated them as part of the anti-boarding protocols, of course. Now I patted myself on the back for my foresight.

"You Raptors honor us with your efforts," I told them. "Spread out by squads. Use your HUDs to locate any breaches and kill anything not friendly. One squad, stay here."

They took off in all directions, except for one squad, as ordered. I didn't have the time to micromanage them, so they would have to function independently to slow down any attacks until marines could reinforce them.

"Valiant, open firing loopholes on each side of the airlock. You and you," I pointed at two marines, "get in position to fire through them. The rest of you take cover at the corner."

All told we had only six marines—counting me—and ten Raptors. I never had enough troops. It crossed my mind to wonder whether I could recruit some Elladans to join us—

especially more women to balance out the crew. It was a pleasant thought, but it was misplaced today.

Without warning, the airlock blew open.

"Pour it on!" I roared, holding down the trigger on my laser for long searing bursts. My faceplate dimmed to black to preserve my sight as Demons pushed forward into the corridor, but our ambush slaughtered them in the confined space, especially with the crossfire from the two marines I'd placed to shoot through the holes in the side walls. Automated defenses joined in from *Valiant*'s internal turrets installed in the overheads.

Soon the passageway filled with smoke and the steam of boiling bodily fluids, making our lasers far less effective. A scorpion leaped out of the gases toward me and knocked me flat.

It was on me, filling my vision with churning mandibles and dripping saliva—the thing was hideous up close. I'd never been a big fan of scorpions, and this one was all over me. Its twin stingers rasped and leaked venom over my suit. The curved tips were seeking a way in, trying to punch through the armor.

My faceplate was hit multiple times, making me wince away and cry out. I expected the visor to star—but it didn't. A syrupy yellow splatter of venom obstructed my view.

Roaring and making sounds of disgust, I wrestled with the thing. Then an axe swung out of nowhere and chopped away two legs. Another swing of the axe, and the bug was cut down. I was hauled to my feet.

All around me, a mass of struggling chitinous creatures battled with marines. If it hadn't been for our armor, we'd have been slaughtered. Already, two of the Raptors had been overcome and weren't moving.

There were too many Demons.

"Fall back to the next intersection and use active sensors! Moranian, haul ass to the armory and pick up as many rocket launchers as you can," I ordered.

Anti-armor weapons weren't standard issue for repelling boarders in *Valiant's* enclosed spaces, but now I wished I had some, as they wouldn't be affected by the concealing fog.

"Aye, aye, sir!" she yelled as she turned to do as I asked.

"Valiant, vent the atmosphere to clear the air where you can. We need clean vacuum for the lasers to be effective!"

"Venting."

Retreating to the crossing of two passageways saved our butts, but it also allowed more of the things onto the ship. Smaller beetles and scorpions pressed toward us, dying hard to our massed fire, but their sacrifice allowed humanoid Demons to dart into the lateral corridors in the rear and begin rampaging within the ship. These bugs were armed and appeared to be more intelligent.

The crew had armed themselves and barricaded all the doors and hatches, but I knew they'd be no match for the enemy. The bugs were beginning to run wild inside the ship.

The close confines worked against us as we retreated deeper into the vessel. The armored beetle-types blocked us from counterattacking even as they died. They were holding us back just as much as we were them.

Fortunately, I had a solution.

The ship's corridors were laid out in circles, with connections running from the center to the hull, so all we had to do was fall back further, then move laterally to intercept the enemy. As soon as Moranian came back with an armload of rocket launchers, I distributed half to our troops and ordered the other half set on the deck.

I pulled aside two marines. "I need you to hold this position," I told them as we set up camp in front of the power coupling chamber. "Use rockets when you need to, and I'll leave two Raptors to back you up. Moranian, take one marine and four Raptors back and move to the starboard side of this deck. Intercept the bugs moving to flank us. I'll take the rest and go to the port side."

Without waiting for acknowledgement, I clanked all the way to the hull of the ship. There was another passage there that circled the deck.

Armored boots pounded on the deck behind me. Riggs' Pigs were all veterans now, and the Raptors followed orders to the death, so I was confident of my backup.

As soon as I reached the next passageway, I turned left. This one had a long arc with a contoured wall that followed the outer hull of the ship. Small automated laser turrets had been set up at the intersections. They tracked us restlessly, each equipped with its own simple brainbox and orders to shoot any detected enemy. Today, I was very glad we'd installed them, despite the risk of placing automated weaponry under full AI control.

I turned left again at the next passageway leading outward. Ahead of me, I could see the blazing green of our lasers mixed with orange return fire—apparently the result of Demon firearms. These were the more sophisticated troops that carried weapons.

"Valiant, what kind of rifles are they using?"

"The Demon infantry is firing a pulsed plasma array," Valiant replied.

"Will our armor hold against a direct hit?"

"Battlesuit armor should be proof against several shots before failing, except for the faceplate."

No surprise there. Faceplates were always the weak spot. The only way to get around that would be to do away with them and use cameras mounted elsewhere on our armor, but experiments like that always resulted in lowered combat efficiency.

I slowed as I approached the ruckus in front of me at the next intersection. Even using my HUD, I couldn't tell exactly what was going on.

Suddenly, my four Raptor marines darted past me, followed by the lone marine, a private named Smith.

"Stay back, sir," Smith said. "We'll handle this."

I was about to overrule him when I realized I was doing what Hansen always accused me of. I was becoming too involved in the details of close combat. Yes, we needed every battlesuit, and yes, the open-space battle was over for the moment, but getting myself killed would be a stupid thing, and not only for me personally.

After all, if Marvin was willing to get all the other officers killed and eaten because he calculated I had the best chance of getting us home...well, who was I to argue?

As the Raptors switched to their battle-axes and leaped to attack a half-dozen Demon infantry from behind, I hunkered down and shifted my focus to my HUD.

"Suit," I said, "tactical overview, display the entire ship."

A 3D diagram appeared in front of my eyes, and I manipulated it with a combination of eye movements and voice commands to see what I wanted. The Demons had broken through the hull in six places, including the four standard airlocks and the two drone launch tubes. With the heavily armored beetles as battering rams, they'd chewed their way much farther in than I'd hoped.

Friendly green icons surrounded most of the incursions, but the red blotches were still spreading in some places. I tried to figure out what the problem was by examining the situation deck by deck.

In the upper area, mostly occupied by the drone storage and handling deck, it appeared that the enemy was well contained. Someone, possibly Bradley, had organized the systems there to put up a stiff defense. The many Nano-style tentacles, usually used for repair and rearmament, held heavy tools and flailed at Demons. Parked Daggers with activated lasers fired using reduced power causing a lot of collateral damage but blowing handily through the creatures.

It looked like we'd have one hell of a lot of repair work to do, but at least the enemy was being slaughtered.

On the main deck, where most of our marines and Raptors were, we were pressing them back from all sides.

Frowning, I noticed a region without green contacts where a nest of red icons kept disappearing from view. Where were they going?

The answer became obvious when I moved the "camera" to display the lower deck. The Demons must have cut through the floor and were attacking downward into areas of lesser resistance.

I located Kwon's icon on the other side of the main level and keyed a direct com-link. "Kwon, they're cutting through the deck to the lower level. Get everyone you can down there, now!"

"Roger, sir," Kwon roared, and he cut out as he switched to short-range to give orders to the forces near him.

"Suit, short-range noncom channel," I said. When the com-link icon changed to the desired freq, I spoke to the squad leaders. "This is Captain Riggs. We've got to keep the enemy contained, Pigs, but I need you to send everything you can spare to the lower deck."

Without waiting for a reply I switched channels yet again to speak directly to Cornelius. "How're you doing down there, Chief?"

"Not good, Captain. I have several casualties, and the enemy is damaging my guns."

"Screw the beams, Chief. We can make more. Save the personnel. Help is on the way."

"Got it."

On my HUD, I could see clumps of friendlies working their way toward the lower deck. Most used the ramps and ladders, but there was a simpler, faster way for those with command privileges.

"Valiant, create a hatch directly to the lower deck, right here at my feet, and keep it open," I said.

"Not advisable. Enemy is present in strength beneath you."

"I'm counting on it. Now do it!"

"Command not accepted. The preset danger levels—"

"Override!" I shouted, staring down at the deck between my feet.

"Override accepted."

Below me, the smart metal of the deck rippled and withdrew, exposing the bare ribs of the structural nanosteel-alloy supports. The material wrapped itself around conduits and pipes, leaving a hole barely big enough for me to fit though in my bulky suit.

"Geronimo!" I yelled, stepping into the hole. My weapons held above my head to keep them from catching on anything.

All three tons of me slammed down atop a scorpion, facing backward. The force of my landing crushed its back, but it kept struggling anyway.

The twin tails snapped reflexively toward me. I threw myself sideways and chopped at the nearest stinger with my axe.

It bit deeply, but couldn't sever the armored tail. I rolled onto the deck, jerking the axe free. I fired my laser directly into the thing's softer underbelly, and ichor boiled out of the hole in its chitin.

Something knocked me sideways a moment later, and I somersaulted into a handful of Demon infantry, sending them tumbling like bowling pins. Lashing out with my axe and firing wildly with my laser, I created as much chaos as I could…until something grabbed me by the foot.

I had time to see a beetle clamp its mandibles around my ankle before it picked me up and whipped me like a rag doll bashing me against the housing of a medium laser. I could feel my entire body bruise, and I saw stars, but forced myself to skitter sideways, taking cover. I dialed an injection, a hero's cocktail of stim and painkiller, and a moment later I felt the discomfort fade as my heart pounded so hard it felt like it was about to explode.

Orange plasma bolts splashed near me, and I realized I'd lost my axe. Picking up the laser rifle dangling from its cable, I stuck it around the corner and triggered a burst to keep the enemy at bay, hating to think of the damage all this was doing to the interior of the gun deck. Fires raged here and there as a result of all the hot energy we were throwing around.

Reinforcements began to pour in from the doors and ladders, and I could see small green beams sizzle through the smoky gas. Those would be shots from laser pistols. A group of friendly crewmen were holed up in the machine shop off to my right defending the doorway.

"Hang in there, people," I called over my short range com-link and rolled to my feet, lifting my rifle to fire a long burst at a beetle trying to chew its way inside. The laser pistols hardly bothered it, and plasma bolts striking near me kept me from concentrating my beam long enough to burn through its tough exoskeleton.

"Warning: battery low," my suit suddenly said into my ear.

When I ducked back into cover and checked, I could see it was true. My battlesuit capacitors were down to five percent. I needed to wait and let the fusion generator recharge before I had enough excess to use my power-hogging laser, but I had no time. The gun crew was about to get an unwelcome visit from a beetle.

I slammed the rifle into its stowage clamp and eyed my fallen axe lying a few yards away in the open. Taking a deep breath, I charged out and scooped it up as I ran. Taking it in a two-handed grip, I swung it laterally like a pool bat and cleaved a Demon infantryman in half.

The monster next to it fired at me point-blank. I could feel the heat of the orange blast singe my knuckles through my gauntlets, one of the thinnest parts of my suit. I kicked out, knocking the weapon out of the Demon's hands and then slashed it with my axe.

Cat-quick, the bug leaped back and pulled long knives from its battle harness. A moment later, it attacked me with a whirl of blades. I countered by punching at it with my broad double-bladed axe and blocked the blades with its hard metal handle. I'd never bothered to analyze what the Raptors had made my weapon from, but it was tough stuff, at least as hard as nanosteel.

I very much wanted to dispatch my opponent and get back to trying to relieve the gun crew holed up in the machine shop, but this Demon must have been one of their champions because he fought me to a standstill—an impressive thing considering I had the battlesuit and he had nothing but two short swords. If the Devil himself had designed these things, he could hardly have made better combat troops.

I backed up, trying to work my way around the room, when suddenly a huge figure loomed out of the choking smoke supported by two Raptors. He leveled a laser rifle. "Duck, boss!" Kwon roared, and I threw myself behind a laser housing.

Green beams caused my faceplate to darken as I rolled to my feet, turning my back on the Demon champion that Kwon and his flankers were gunning down.

132

The beetle had widened the door enough to force its way through to the gun crew. Pounding across the deck, I raised my axe over my head and brought it down with all my might on its shiny brown back. The blade bit deep but then lodged in the thick chitin. Enraged, the beetle spun, but I clamped my hands onto the haft of the weapon and hung on.

Now I was riding the thing like a bull with no saddle as it hopped and tried to twist to reach me. Using the buried axe as a solid handle, I remained beyond its clutches as it danced and crashed into workbenches sending tools everywhere.

Warrant Officer Cornelius and her people stood at one end of the long narrow room and fired their weapons, some hitting me as they tried to damage the beetle.

"Careful, dammit!" I roared as the bug thrashed. "Aim for its legs!" This would have the dual benefits of slowing the thing down and missing me, I hoped.

A dozen thin beams popped and sizzled low, having no effect that I could see, but at least doing me no damage. I kept trying to plant my feet, but the carapace was too slippery for my boots to grip. It was all I could do to hold onto my weapon's handle like an arctic climber clutching an ice axe against a mountainside, waiting for reinforcements.

Kwon appeared in the doorway as I'd hoped he would. Assessing the situation, he clearly realized he couldn't go blasting away with his heavy laser without endangering our lightly armored people in the room. "No beams!" he yelled to the two Raptors with him. "Attack!"

The warriors leaped, their spiked and armored tails complementing the axes in their hands. They struck and bounced upward, using their superior jumping skills to ricochet off the walls and then onto the beast. Each time they landed, they gouged out chunks of beetle armor.

In response, the twenty-ton, combat-vehicle-sized creature tried to scrape me off by slamming me against a bulkhead. This half-stunned me, but my armor was tougher than the wall so I only had the wind knocked out of me. I lost my grip on the axe and slid down onto the floor.

As I crawled along the edge of the wall toward the gun crew, I looked beneath the beetle's thrashing legs and saw

Kwon jump forward to seize my axe handle. Though he wasn't actually stronger than I was, with his armor he was considerably heavier. Between his weight hanging off the handle and all the other damage it was taking, the big bug had begun to slow.

I checked the charge on my suit and saw it had crawled up to twelve percent—enough for a few laser shots, so I stood up in front of the crewmen and unslung my rifle. Sighting carefully, I fired at the thing's head. My fourth shot boiled one of its compound eyes, and its relatively coordinated struggle turned into a thrashing death frenzy, the pain making it crazy.

Kwon finally ripped my axe free and slid down to land on his feet. He chopped at the beetle, the Raptors joining in. With all of us together, we managed to bring it crashing down.

-14-

"Nice work, Kwon," I gasped, looking around the wrecked machine shop at the truck-sized carcass on the floor and the dozen gun techs putting away their weapons to begin setting things right. "Now get back out there and mop up."

"You stay here then, okay boss?" he said.

"Yeah, Kwon. I'm done with marine stuff right now. Go." That assurance freed him from his desire to constantly bodyguard me. Frankly, if I wasn't needed out there, I was fine taking a quick break from the hand-to-hand fighting. My cracked ribs ached when I breathed, even with the painkillers.

"HUD, switch to ship-wide tactical," I said to my suit, and was relieved to see that most of the red blotches had been wiped away. "Valiant, damage control status?"

"Serious damage to gun and drone decks." That made sense as those were located top and bottom, immediately inside our hull armor. "Standard airlocks inoperative. Other internal systems degraded, but repairable."

"Casualties?"

"Two human crew and two marines KIA, seventeen wounded but likely to survive. Twelve Raptors killed, thirty-nine wounded."

"Damn. Put me through to Marvin."

A pause. "Marvin is unresponsive."

"Keep trying every five minutes. Where's *Greyhound*?"

"Docked with the wreckage of a Demon battleship."

135

I growled. Marvin was off exploring alien tech, which was all well and good, except that repairing *Valiant* was my highest priority. The robot was hell on wheels when it came to rebuilding machines. I got the feeling he regarded that function as akin to doing unpleasant chores, though, and so avoided it when he could.

Switching my com-link to the bridge, I said, "Hansen? What's it look like in space?"

"Clear around us. The Nano frigates are hunting down the last few live Demons floating in the wreckage. What's your feeling on prisoners?"

I thought about that. "If one of their humanoids can be taken, I wouldn't mind capturing it for interrogation, but don't go to extraordinary lengths."

"Okay, well…"

"What?"

"I think I can get you one, but I have to move fast. Hansen out."

I shrugged. I'd wanted to find out about the battle between the Demons and the Elladans, but the holotank would tell me everything I needed to know soon enough.

Someone tapped my armor, and I turned to see Cornelius in a crew suit. Her faceplate was open to show her red cheeks. I opened my helmet and sniffed the air. I smelled chemicals, smoke and an indescribable metallic stink from the dead bug that occupied half the deck.

"Thanks, Captain," she said. "I believe we will have to change our underpants, but not until we get the weapons in order, yes?"

"Yeah," I replied. "Bust your asses, Chief, because the day's not over with."

I turned and left Cornelius to her work and headed for the armory.

I took a quick detour into the factory room and waved at Adrienne. It appeared she'd sealed up tight, and no enemies had gotten in.

"You good?" I asked as I clomped over.

"Brilliant," she replied, grabbing my shoulders and lifting herself off the floor to kiss me through my faceplate. "You look like hell."

"I made a mistake," I replied. "I assumed the Demons had been beaten, and I forgot they don't need spacesuits. They abandoned ship and boarded."

"How?" she asked.

"What do you mean?"

"How did they reach *Valiant*? I mean, with no suits, how did they maneuver to attack us in open space?"

"Good question. Find out and we'll both know," I said, putting her down carefully. "I have to go."

"Stop by the infirmary first," she said, pointing down the passage with a long-nailed finger.

"I'm fine, and I'm sure they're busy with the seriously wounded."

"That's why you need to stop by. Show you care. Press the flesh. Good for morale."

I chuckled. "I'd like to press some flesh with you."

Adrienne smiled. "That's just the adrenaline talking. Now go on, off with you." She sat back down at her consoles. "I have a lot of parts to make."

I resisted another sexual joke and left her to her work.

Withdrawing my gauntlets into my suit, I clapped a busy Doctor Achmed on the back as he set a marine's broken leg. Speaking encouragement to everyone around, the wounded cheered me. I felt guilty because it was my mistake that had put them there.

I left the infirmary as soon as I could.

The armory was already beginning to fill with marines servicing their weapons and dropping off their suits to recharge. Relieved chatter mixed with rough jokes, and a grim mutter of greeting sounded when I arrived.

I saw Moranian sitting on a bench in a corner, staring at a gauntlet held in her gloved hand. When I'd backed my suit into its niche, I walked over to her.

"You did good work today, Sergeant," I said.

She looked up at me, short red hair plastered on her skull and her eyes haunted. "Thank you, sir."

"Your first combat leading troops who didn't make it?" I guessed.

She nodded. I pressed my lips together considering her distress. "I don't have any easy answers, Rosalie. We take it one day at a time and we make it through."

Hefting the gauntlet, she turned it over, and it dripped blood onto her knee. The color was a surreal near-match to her vivid locks. I realized that the gauntlet wasn't hers, and it wasn't empty.

Someone's severed hand remained inside.

"This was Rayburn's," she said.

I dredged the man's name out of my memory. He was a lance corporal, a good man...and one of the KIAs.

"He had a family back home," she said. "Now they don't have him. He came so far—but didn't make it. Doesn't seem right." She slammed the metal gauntlet on the bench beside her. She looked like she was fighting an urge to vomit.

Post-combat reaction could do this to the strongest of us, I knew. Biology didn't care about decorum or embarrassment. Stuff like this was one reason marines drank so much.

I wanted to put a comradely arm around her and comfort her, but I couldn't risk it. Considering the history between us, it might reignite Adrienne's jealousy.

Spotting Gunny Taksin, I grabbed his elbow and whispered in his ear, steering him toward Moranian. He nodded and sat down, talking her through it.

I wished I could have done it, but I kept myself at arms' length from everyone except Adrienne, so I wouldn't be wrecked every time someone died.

That necessary distance denied me many of the common mechanisms my people had for coping with tragedy. They had to see me as larger than life in order to believe in me...in order to believe in getting home against overwhelming odds, in order to keep from cracking.

After every battle, my little band diminished, grew more fragile. With no replacements to our community, no reinforcements, everyone was worried. Especially the marines who stood on the front line.

Something had to be done, something drastic and maybe dangerous. An idea occurred to me once more, an unorthodox idea, but it would need time to implement. I put it on hold for the moment.

I made a quick round, slapping backs and speaking words of praise to my dwindling cadre of Pigs. After that I washed my face as a poor substitute for a shower, grabbed a beer to take the edge off and headed for the bridge. Everything still hurt, but I could feel the fizz-in-the-blood sensation that told me my nanites were working to heal me.

I dropped the squeeze-bottle into a corner for ejection through the deck before touching a wall and turning it into a door.

Hansen nodded to me as I joined him at the holotank. Lazar was sitting in the pilot's seat, looking nervous. There was no need for him to be edgy. We were floating in space—or technically, still traveling toward Ellada, but as everything held position together in a free-fall, it was a minor distinction.

The rest of the bridge was deserted, with only the minimum number of watch crew. The rest were helping with repairs and damage control.

"What about that Demon prisoner I wanted?" I asked before Hansen could speak.

"It's in the brig," he replied.

"I'm going to see it."

"Now?"

"I might learn something vital."

Hansen growled and turned away.

"Valiant," I said, "have Kwon meet me at the brig."

When I got there, I found Kwon waiting.

"We have a prisoner, Kwon. Want to see it firsthand?"

Kwon chuckled. "Why do you always want to talk to the enemy? Just kill them."

"Because there's always a chance we can find something out that helps us win."

"Whatever you say," he said with a shrug.

"I say back me up, but don't say anything, okay?"

"Okay, boss."

I closed up my faceplate and entered the outer brig, a small room with a couple of desks, lockers and screens for guards to occupy. A Demon-shaped helmet and battle harness lay in a heap on a small table, along with one of their pulsed-plasma rifles.

The two marines there saluted me. I returned the courtesy and said, "Give me a view inside the cell." A screen lit up, and I saw a humanoid Demon squatting awkwardly atop the metal chair bolted to the floor. It appeared to be injured, with one upper limb broken and dangling, dripping ichor.

"Open it up," I said.

The ship created a dilating doorway, and I stepped into the opening.

"Kwon, leave the rifle outside. The two of us in suits can handle him. Corporal, close the door behind us."

When we'd gone inside, the door vanished. We barely fit in the room with the Demon backed up into a corner, holding up its unbroken limb.

"Valiant, do we have any translation software for Demons yet?"

"Yes. Marvin provided a partial data set before his priorities were diverted. I have since refined it as I was able. It should suffice for basic understanding."

"Good work. Translate then, and project my words to its ears…or whatever. Does it have ears?"

"It has sound receptors."

"Good. Creature, do you understand me?" I asked.

"I hear," came the flat-toned, translated response.

"Why do you attack the humans and Ketans?"

"We do what we must."

Hmm. This thing specialized in vague answers. "Why are your ships lined with slime?"

"I'm not permitted to provide information regarding the technical capabilities of our war vessels."

"Fair enough. What was your role in the battle?"

"I do not understand."

"Were you a pilot? A technician? A passenger, a marine?"

"I repaired machinery."

"What machinery?"

140

"All machinery."

Okay, maybe they didn't differentiate by specialty. Maybe I could approach this from another angle, because this bug didn't seem very sophisticated. Maybe, if he was hive-grown and programmed, he wouldn't know much about bullshit, sneakiness and interrogation.

"What would happen if the slime coating inside your ship stopped flowing?" I asked.

"I would repair the regenerative organs."

"Why would you repair it?"

"To avoid crew efficiency degradation."

"How might they be degraded?"

"Crew effectiveness suffers when the lining is breached."

I reached up to scratch my chin, but my gauntlet bounced off my faceplate. I wanted to crack it open, but if this prisoner had any chance of hurting me, it would be through an open visor, so I resisted the urge.

"Okay," I said thoughtfully. "What if the lining were entirely stripped away? What would happen?"

"The crew would mutiny. But you know this already. Why do you ask me, a lowly repairer unit?"

"You're the only one left alive to ask," I said.

"You're not Elladan, are you?" the bug asked me. "This ship is not of their design. This I know."

I didn't answer. After all, I was supposed to be interrogating him.

"We're not Elladan," I said. "We look like them, but we're independent."

"I believe you are trying to deceive me," it said. "You fought with the Elladan as allies. The battle briefings warned against the deceptiveness of Elladans and their allies, so unlike the honesty of True Ones like ourselves. You're as pathetic as I was told. I will say nothing more."

True to his word, he wouldn't talk after that. I considered breaking off a few extra antennae, but ruled it out. Who knew if he would even care? When we exited the cell, I was surprised to hear Kwon start laughing.

"What a stupid guy," Kwon said. "Doesn't know his ass from a hole in the ground!"

That made me think. "Yes, you're right. But he gave me hints despite his stone-walling."

"What?"

"Never mind." I checked my chrono. "No more time, but this has been interesting. Let's go."

On the way out, I told Kwon to provide the critter with water and whatever food or material Valiant said it could eat. I still wanted to talk to it later, but right now I had too many balls in the air. I decided to head for the bridge.

"What?" I asked Hansen as I arrived.

The holotank displayed the Ellada-moon planetary system, including their orbital fortresses and warships. The time stamp showed half an hour in the past, so Hansen had obviously set the view to get me up to speed on what had happened during the battle for Ellada—a battle that must be mostly over.

"They redeployed based on the expected kinetic attack to preserve some of their fixed assets," he said, gesturing.

"I see what you mean." The Elladans had formed their slow-moving forts into several groups, and then lined them up along the enemy axis of approach, with the largest of them set as shields for the smaller ones. There was even a group that had been moved behind their moon.

Hansen touched a control, and the view advanced, fast-forwarding.

"There are the bundles, breaking up." The fake battleships, which had never decelerated, shattered and spread out into kinetic darts. "They have thrusters and control mechanisms to aim them at different targets within a narrow arc, but they're going too fast to truly maneuver."

"Right." I watched as the darts approached the fortresses lined up in front of the Elladan warships. They looked like too many children hiding behind too few trees. "How does it turn out?"

Hansen looked grim. "Best to watch, Skipper."

I growled impatiently and ratcheted up the play-back speed until the darts began slamming into the closest fortresses. Mines detonated just before the darts landed, destroying some and knocking others off course—but there were too many going too fast. They tore the guts out of their targets and blasted on through.

Fortunately, the impacts changed their trajectories enough so that most of them missed the fortresses hiding behind, but a few impacted the next in line, and one even struck a third.

"What's this bundle doing?" I pointed at a group of a dozen darts that were taking a different course.

Hansen's face turned grim. "You'll see."

I watched as the group flew unopposed, diverging slightly toward…Ellada.

"Crap."

"You said it."

At the last minute, Elladan warships raced to intercept the kinetic missiles, but it was too late. The metal bolts plunged down into the atmosphere, transforming briefly into bright fireballs before stabbing into the hearts of twelve Elladan cities.

"Damn," I breathed.

"Yeah. They had to suffer millions of dead, unless they evacuated. Even then, the economic damage…"

"The Demons suckered them," I said with sudden realization. "They did the same thing to the Whales. They deliberately drew the Elladans out of position then went for the civilians. When the Elladans set up to counter the attack, they left the planet itself vulnerable. I'm actually surprised they didn't get hit harder."

"Maybe the Demons want something left to conquer," Hansen replied.

In a few more seconds, the holotank display slowed down to a real-time view of the battle. I forced myself to forget about the obliterated cities and concentrate on the military situation.

All told, about half of the Elladan battle stations survived, and all of their warships, of course. Still, between the stealth attack a few days ago and this, they'd lost at least half of their defenses. Combine that with the fact that half their mobile fleet—the best, most effective half, I strongly suspected— would arrive late to the battle. They were about to get hammered by an attacking force at least twice their strength.

"This is ugly," I said.

"Would have been worse without our help."

I looked at Hansen's haggard face. He'd aged in the last year. He was in his forties, but right now he seemed to be a decade older. "Still think we should stay out of it?"

Slowly, he shook his bald head. "When it was the Whales…well, hell, they're not human, and their planet could swallow a thousand Earths. They weren't at risk of genocide, just being knocked back to the stone age. But these people are human, and Earthlike planets…"

"Are small and fragile, by comparison," I finished for him. I raised my voice enough for everyone to hear. "Also, if the Demons win here, we're screwed both ways. If we can't get back to Earth, we will have lost the only other planet we're ever likely to feel at home on. And if we can get back to Earth, that means the Demons can reach Earth, too. Then we'll regret we didn't help our allies stop them here, even if that takes more sacrifice."

Hansen nodded, realizing instantly what I was doing. Speeches were most effective when they didn't sound like speeches, when the crew thought they were getting accidental insight into their leaders' minds.

"Damn right, Captain. We're behind you one hundred percent."

I almost choked but kept a straight face. I guess Hansen knew how to bullshit too. Hopefully, there was some truth mixed into that cow manure.

Valiant spoke then. "I have Marvin on the com-link, audio only."

"Captain Marvin! I need you back here fixing *Valiant*."

"I thought you wanted me to create a weapon to use against the Demons. You used the idiom 'bug spray.' To create such a thing, I needed to examine their technology and biology in detail."

He was right. As usual, I had too much for him to do, so it was my role to set his priorities. "How close are you to coming up with something?"

"I need several days at least, perhaps weeks."

"Then I apologize, but I need you to help get *Valiant* combat-ready again. We have to help the Elladans win this

144

battle. Once that's done, we'll see about taking the fight to the enemy using your bug spray."

I could tell by the sound of Marvin's voice that he wasn't happy being diverted from a technical challenge, what he considered fun. "It is not efficient to disrupt my research at this time."

"Maybe you'll stay an ensign forever," I said angrily. "Promotions in Star Force aren't automatic, you know. But I have a further incentive for you, Marvin. A technical challenge that's right up your alley, one even more interesting than the bug spray."

Even though we were on audio only, I could imagine his cameras and tentacles perking up to stare at me. "What kind of technical challenge?"

I had his full attention now. "I'll give you the details after *Valiant* is repaired—in fact, after all our ships are repaired. The faster you get that done, the sooner you'll hear the details of this challenge."

Clicking and metallic rasping sounds came clearly across the com-link, probably his tentacles coiling over each other.

"I'm on my way. Please inform biotic personnel to limit their interference in my operations."

"Will do. Riggs out." Once the channel had closed, I said, "Valiant, put out a general announcement that Marvin will be helping with the repairs and to stay out of his way."

Then I turned back to the paused holotank view and started it going again.

Demon ships continued to slow, spiraling inward toward Ellada, with thousands of missiles and hundreds of heavy fighters leading them. I didn't understand their tactics, sending such an enormous salvo ahead. If I'd been in charge, I'd have kept things together so that while the Elladans were trying to fend off the nukes and small craft, my battleships and cruisers could take a bunch of free shots.

In other words, I'd try to overwhelm the enemy all at once rather than coming in waves.

On the other hand, if they had enough to win the battle, this might minimize their casualties. But they didn't seem to care so much about casualties…so it didn't make sense to me. I couldn't help feeling there was some critical element to this whole situation I was missing, that if I could just figure it out, everything would suddenly become clear.

The Elladan home fleet did their best to preserve itself. Instead of trying to defend the planet and its population, they abandoned any attempt to intercept the nuclear missiles.

The Demons seemed to be playing along. None of the nukes were targeted at cities on the surface, though about five hundred of them arrowed downward toward planetary defense installations. Lasers reached up from the ground and speared most of those, but about fifty of them made it through to raise mushroom clouds into the upper atmosphere.

"So they put up with this every year?" Hansen said from beside me.

"No. The Demons have always hit the Whales before, which is why the Elladans fortified them. Looks like this year the Demons wised up and changed their tactics. Speaking of tactics…"

We watched as the cloud of missiles chased the Elladan fleet around their planet. The Elladans had adopted our intel and kept ahead of the demon missiles picking them off as they sought to maneuver. The Elladan fleet allowed the Demon missiles into medium range and did its best with beams, knocking down at least a thousand. Then they ran, diving down into the planet's atmosphere on the back side, where more, untouched, planetary defenses could assist them.

At the end of it, all the Demon missiles and most of the heavy fighters were destroyed. The only Elladan ships to survive had slammed themselves into their oceans and hid themselves deep under the water, out of sensor range, where the nukes couldn't follow, leaving the Demon fleet in possession of the planet, its moon and its ring—for now.

-15-

A few hours later, as the main body of the Demon fleet approached Ellada, I met with my command staff. They had haggard faces and serious expressions, but they were listening to me closely. No one liked what they'd witnessed the day before. This endless war between three races had taken a grim turn.

"So far, the Elladans have done better than I thought they would," I told the group. "Like the Macros, the Nanos and the Lithos, these Demons are tough, but they're not all that flexible or smart. That seems to be a failing of hive-type beings, if I can generalize from only three examples."

The holotank recordings were all caught up to real time, and I racked my brain for ways to help our allies. "How soon until we're in range?"

"At our current speed, about four hours," Hansen replied.

"And…" I adjusted the holotank. "The Elladan relief fleet will get there in about three. So we need to speed up."

"If we speed up, we'll have to slow down later," Hansen said quietly. "You know how it works."

"I don't want to make the same mistake as the Demons have—splitting our forces in time, if not in space. Ideally, I want to get there ten or fifteen minutes after the Elladans do, so the battle will be fully joined, and we can figure out where we want to throw in our weight."

Hansen snorted. "We have seven ships—only two of which are heavy enough to fight without getting fragged in one blow."

"Plus our drones and the missiles on them," I added sternly. "Worst case, we'll take our shots, whip on around and return to Trinity-9. There, we can join up with the Whales."

"And leave these humans to get wiped out?" Hansen asked.

I frowned at him. He was full of objections today.

"The Demons won't wipe them out," I said. "If they intended to do that, a thousand kinetic darts would have been aimed at the planet. No, they want to seize Ellada. Unless I miss my guess, they want to conquer Ellada. If they do, the weak-minded Whales will eventually fall."

Hansen remained unconvinced. "We need to kill them, Captain. That's my opinion as your XO. We have to kill the Demons."

"I get that, but we have to play it smart."

"We have to *kill* them!" he shouted suddenly.

I stared at him for a second, and he stared back. Was he feeling battle-fatigue?

"Take a break, Hansen," I said. "That's an order. Get a beer, get laid, take a hot shower or grab a nap—whatever. Lazar can handle the cruise inward the next couple of hours. Come back fresh and ready to kick some ass."

"Yeah. Okay—sorry sir." Hansen got up and walked heavily out of the ready room.

I broke up the meeting and spent my time checking the ship and encouraging the crew. I made sure to look in on Sakura to see if I could detect…well, anything. Suspicious behavior, signs of cracking, whether or not she and Hansen had made up? I didn't notice anything, but she was very hard to read.

The repairs were going well. In fact, the crew seemed as energetic and focused as they'd ever been. I ordered the Raptors back to their cargo bay, but not into hibernation. They would be all right for a few hours.

I noticed the marines helping with the heavy manual labor, as usual. What I didn't expect to see as I rounded a corner were a couple of my Pigs taking swings at each other in full armor.

As I didn't have my suit on, I didn't try to get between them. "Valiant, vector the nearest four marine noncoms here in full armor, ASAP, and relay me on a short-range com-link, max amplification."

"Marine noncoms on the way," said the ship. "Com-link activated."

"Stand down, you two!" I roared.

They should have stopped, held fast by the sound of my voice in their helmets. I yelled again but gave up after it became clear they were unlikely to harm each other. They were doing more damage to the walls and floor, actually.

Internal laser turrets twitched and tracked the two, and I told Valiant to put their stupid brains to sleep before a mistake was made. I wished I could do that to the suits, but no external command could override a marine's own control—for good reason. I didn't want anyone being able to hack them again.

By that time, armored figures moved in to break up the brawling. Troops pinned the two in place. Kwon showed up and slapped each one in the helmet repeatedly with his gauntlets until they came to their senses.

"Escort them to the armory, get them out of their suits and throw them in the brig!" he growled.

"Thanks, Sergeant Major," I said more casually than I felt. "Carry on."

We'd had more than a few brawls among the Pigs, but none when they were suited up and working. I took it as a sign that things were getting tense around here.

All we had to do was help our allies win this next battle, though, and something could be done. It was an ugly thought, but maybe there was a tiny upside to Ellada getting creamed. Our people would be less likely to want to stay. Any R&R on the planet would not be as idyllic against a background of death, even if we took it at a place far away from the devastation.

Far away…yeah, maybe that was the ticket. Ask the Elladans for the use of a tropical island and a boatload of supplies, and maybe a few dozen volunteer companions to balance our gender mix if their morality allowed such a thing.

149

Party hearty, but in a controlled environment away from the rest of their society.

We might even pick up a few additions to the crew, if things worked out.

"Captain, I am receiving a call from Senator Diogenos," Valiant said from a speaker nearby.

"Speak of the devil," I said. "Pipe it to my quarters."

Soon my wall screen showed the Elladan's patrician face. He wore his translation device and loose-fitting robes as always.

"Captain Riggs. I must thank you for your efforts thus far on our behalf. Our military leaders tell me your squadron did the enemy a great deal of damage."

"Thanks, Senator."

"Captain...I would like to know your intentions."

"Intentions? I plan to kill as many Demons as I can."

"Yes, but more specifically..." Diogenos' brow furrowed. "Our strategists are concerned about the lack of coordination between us. Friendly fire and so on. I'm not a military man, you understand."

"So why can't I talk with your commanders directly?"

The senator's brow smoothed. "That's a fine idea. We happen to have a ship near your squadron. I'd like to send a commander to meet you in person. Could that be arranged?"

"Sounds good...but like I said, I'm very busy."

"Only a moment..." Diogenos turned away and spoke into a device in his hand, the translation software failing to catch his words. When he turned back, he said, "He'll arrive within the hour."

I frowned. I hadn't realized they'd had ships so close to ours. "That's fast," I said.

"We've placed the highest priority on this matter. Here on Ellada, the Senate is in continuous session within the same underground redoubt as our military headquarters."

"Very efficient."

"We have been fighting this war for a long time, Captain. This dark day, however, the enemy has seen fit to raise the stakes. They've never attacked us so viciously in the past."

"My condolences for your losses, sir."

150

Diogenos waved negligently. "Few of the higher orders were killed as they had already been evacuated to shelters. The rest can be replaced."

This higher and lower orders thing...someday I'd get to the bottom of that, but for now, it didn't matter. Clamping down again on my desire to address his callousness directly, I smiled coldly.

"How nice. While we're waiting, I have a request. When this upcoming battle is finished and the Demons have been driven off or destroyed, can you arrange for us to use some secluded place—an island, maybe—to rest and relax? We'd like to see your suns through the clouds, walk a beach. We've been in space for almost a year now. No one's had a chance to unwind on a friendly planet in all that time."

"Of course, Captain...if we win."

"We will. And if we don't..."

"It will hardly matter," he replied drily. "In that instance, I would only ask that you remember us and, if possible, return to liberate us from our enslavement."

"So you also think you'll be conquered and not destroyed?"

"Of course. The enemy wants worshippers and slaves, not corpses."

"You seem pretty sanguine about the possibility," I said.

"Becoming agitated would do no good. We will do our best. If that is not good enough, then perhaps it means the Departed Ancients have forgotten about us."

"If they have, then we'll have to win on our own, right?"

Diogenos' lips pressed together. "Like all military men, you focus on the immediate and practical, Captain Riggs, but I must take a longer view. The Departed Ancients may yet return. If they do, I for one do not want to be judged wanting. In any case, look for our commander in a small ship. His name is Argos, and he should be approaching your vessels shortly."

He disconnected, and I frowned at the blank metallic wall screen.

I'd intended on taking a shower and a nap, but now thought the better of it. I returned to the bridge.

"Captain," said Valiant. "We have an unknown contact closing on our position."

"A ship?" I asked.

"Yes."

"Was it stealthed?"

"Yes, apparently. It has approached to within two thousand kilometers undetected. Permission to fire on this vessel?"

"Permission denied," I said. "Let it come closer. Communicate with the pilot. It should be someone named Argos."

"Transmitting…" there was a pause. "Sir, the intruder identifies himself as Argos. His rank is Strategos, which apparently is equivalent to that of a General from Earth."

"Great. Let him come aboard."

"This action is not recommended. This action will be logged as a violation of protocol."

"Fine, log it."

The ship fell silent, but I could tell it wasn't happy with me.

Instead of heading to the bridge, I had Kwon accompany me to the docking bay. I instructed him to look tough and huge in his armor, but not to talk. He did this naturally and flawlessly. I wanted him to be as intimidating as possible.

When he boarded, Argos turned out to be a man with another of those heroic, fit-for-a-statue faces that reminded me of Diogenos. He was heavier and bearded, with curly black hair. I could see thick muscles wrapping the arms protruding from his sleeveless crimson tunic.

"I greet you, Captain," he said, raising a hand, palm out, as if he wanted to shake hands.

I approached him and clasped hands. He smiled then, hugely. His hands didn't feel the way I'd expected them to feel. They were softer, wetter. Maybe these aliens sweated a lot.

"I greet you, Argos. How can my small force help you?" My question didn't mean I would follow his suggestions, but I might as well listen. Soon enough, I'd want these people to pay us back for our help.

"I have a particular mission for you, Captain. I know you have no obligation to us beyond solidarity with beings that resemble yourselves. I wouldn't ask this of you if I had a better solution—but it's important, perhaps even vital to our survival."

152

"Go on." This was beginning to get interesting. I'd expected some kind of generalized coordination or plea for extra firepower, not some special assignment...if I even accepted it.

"I've brought data on a physical medium," he said, displaying a cube of bright metal. "It's our hope your systems can integrate and display it to help illustrate my request."

"Let's go find out," I said.

I led him through the ship to our most impressive conference room. Along the way, we met several members of the crew. He made a point of stopping and shaking hands warmly with each of them. It was odd, but I knew customs varied from planet to planet. I let him talk to everyone personally. Sakura herself was one of them, and she seemed particularly bemused.

When we reached the conference room and installed his cube in a tiny divot the ship formed on the conference table, the system reacted warily.

An icon began flashing on the corner of my screen, and Valiant spoke. "Incoming data stream. No malware detected. Shall I display?"

"Yes," I said. "Go ahead, Argos."

The wall screen became populated by simple icons different from the ones we used, but which were understandable nonetheless as representations of the tactical situation.

"The Demons destroyed most of our fixed defenses in their initial attack to soften us up for invasion," Argos said. "However, personnel on some of the orbital fortresses survived deep within. We would like you to rescue one particular team before they're captured or killed, a team aboard the largest installation."

An icon flashed, showing the location of a fortress floating in a stable point between their planet and moon.

"In the middle of a battle?" I said.

"What better time than when the Demons are fully engaged with us? They'll likely ignore the wrecked fortress, or perhaps may allocate enough strength to capture our personnel, but they'll not expect you to conduct a relief and rescue in force."

I leaned back and rubbed my chin in thought. "What makes this particular team so important?"

"They're intelligence analysts. They'll have collected information on this latest Demon attack—how it differs from previous ones, how it's similar, what improvements they've made."

"*Will* have? You don't have contact with them?"

"We do not. If we had, they'd have transmitted their data in an encrypted burst by now. Evidently, they cannot."

I sat forward. "Then you don't even know if they're alive?"

Argos flicked his eyes at me. "They were able to make a crude signal, but it wasn't enough to pass information, only to tell us that someone aboard lives. Captain, we can't allow our people to fall into Demon hands. They know too much. Their final option is to choose death, but I—we—would very much like to avoid that possibility."

Sweat had broken out on the Argos' brow, and he seemed to be far more vehement about this team than the military leader of their entire force should be. I figured he wasn't telling me everything.

I folded my hands and cocked my head. "Argos, millions of your people died mere hours ago. Many more are about to die defending your planet. Why is this one group of people so critical? After all, if you win, the problem is solved. If you lose, they hardly matter."

Argos seemed to take a breath, then spoke in a lowered voice. "Captain, I'm impressed that you are able to deny this simple request," he said.

This made me frown. Why was he surprised I could deny anything I wished to?

"I haven't yet denied it," I said. "I'm just asking questions."

"Yes..." Argos said. "I am not accustomed to having my orders questioned."

"Orders?" I asked. "I thought we were talking about a suggested mission. A helping hand we're extending to you."

"That's right. That's the best way to describe it. I'm too accustomed to ordering people around, I guess. Will you help us?"

I empathized. I felt truly sorry for the guy, and if doing this favor for him would buy me what I needed to insure my crew's health and safety, then I would do it. But first I needed to get it on the record.

"Is there some special, personal reason why we should do this for you, sir?" I asked him.

"Well...yes. One of the personnel on the station is my offspring."

"Offspring? You mean your son?"

"Yes."

"I see," I said thoughtfully. "If I accept this mission, then I want that R&R we talked about whether we succeed or fail. Including pretty much whatever I want for my crew—supplies, materials, fresh food and drink, the works."

Argos smiled with evident relief. "If you succeed, you will be feted as heroes. Women will throw themselves at your feet, Captain, and men will beg to serve in your command! You will have the gratitude of a planet, and if you...if you do not succeed, we will still ensure you have what you ask."

"Then it's a deal, as long as the mission looks possible. I'm not sacrificing my people against long odds, mind you."

"We will send you complete specifications of the damaged fortress, and we will provide your ships with as much cover as we can."

"If you can do that, why not simply send in your own commandos?" I asked.

"Most of our close combat forces have been destroyed or driven back to the planet, Captain. The vessels we sent to the Ketans' defense, the half-fleet that rushes here to fight, is equipped almost exclusively for ship-to-ship combat. Therefore, it is tactically more sound to use them in the role for which they were designed."

This seemed reasonable, but still...I wondered if Argos was trying to use us as cannon fodder. Then again, they'd just lost millions and were facing even more death.

Of course, I still had an out. If I didn't like the mission, I could turn it down. I sensed that would be a diplomatic failure, however. My old man had always been able to talk aliens into the damnedest things. Maybe this was my chance to do the same.

"All right, Argos. We'll take a shot at it, with the reservations I've already stated. I'd better get started briefing my people and planning." I stood, suggesting the conversation was over.

"Of course, Captain, and thank you again," Argos said smoothly, and he headed back toward his ship.

When he boarded the vessel, I caught a final look at him as he folded himself into the small cockpit. It was only a little bigger than one of our life-pods.

As the hatch swung closed, I thought I saw something odd… Had his leg folded in a manner a human's shouldn't? It was as if he was boneless at the knees for a second—then he was sitting and normal looking again. The hatch clicked shut, and I was left frowning at it.

I reminded myself that although these beings looked human, they didn't have to have our same physiology. Perhaps they had more flexible joints or bones that could bend…it was odd, but I shrugged it off.

"Valiant, load the Argos' data into the holotank and get Hansen, Bradley, Kwon…and Adrienne to meet me on the bridge. Have Kreel attend by vid-link."

"Acknowledged."

Returning to my quarters, I took two minutes to clean up and then headed for the bridge. I washed my hands several times. They felt cool and oily. Argos' touch wasn't pleasant, for some reason. It had been like shaking hands with someone who had the flu.

I washed my hands again, more vigorously than I had the first time.

-16-

"Doesn't look so hard," Kwon said after we'd spent ten minutes examining the Elladan fortress diagram within the holotank.

"You'd say that even if it was an obvious suicide-mission, Kwon," Hansen commented. Then he held up a hand to forestall the retort building behind Kwon's eyes. "I agree with you, though, Sergeant Major. It's doable."

I looked at Bradley to signal it was his turn for an opinion. He looked back at me as if trying to figure out what I wanted him to say. If there was one problem with the man, it was that he was too reluctant to disagree with me. Eventually, he said cautiously, "I'll defer to Kwon about the boarding and rescue. The big question is, can we cover it from space? We'll more or less give up our mobility and call attention to ourselves if we sit there guarding a dead fortress."

"Good point," I said. "How do we handle it, then?"

"If we get the support from the Elladans as promised, we'll be fine," Hansen said.

Adrienne spoke up. "We can't depend on that. They might want to help, but they will be fighting tooth and claw for survival."

"As their top commander is the father of one of the survivors, I think we'll get our support," I said mildly.

"*If* it's possible," she retorted.

157

Hansen looked disgusted, as if he was holding himself back. Maybe he thought it would piss me off to disagree with Adrienne, but I didn't care, so I told him so. "Spit it out, XO."

"I think we can do it," he said. "We can help rescue these scientists, whoever they are."

He asserted this firmly but without any supporting evidence. His eyes had become unfocused as if accessing a memory. Maybe this situation reminded him of something personal in his past. I'd never inquired about his family or background. Did he have children himself? Was he feeling guilty? I wasn't sure.

"Okay," I said, "start figuring out how we do it. We only have a couple of hours to prepare."

* * *

"Why aren't you trying to talk me out of this?" I asked Hansen as I made ready to head for the armory. "I'd have thought you'd be screaming that my place is here on the bridge and to let Kwon lead the rescue."

Hansen shook his head vehemently. "No, I think you should go. Everything depends on it."

My eyes narrowed. "What happened to playing devil's advocate, XO?"

"This time you're right, that's all."

I wasn't buying it, but I didn't have time for extended psychoanalysis. Something was rattling around in Hansen's head, but unless I was willing to believe he intended to do something mutinous—and I didn't buy that—I had to put it out of my mind for now.

I had some Elladans to rescue, hopefully without losing any more of my people.

"Okay, then." I clapped Hansen on the shoulder. "Cover us, but if it gets too hot, don't lose our ships or it won't matter anyway. Pull out and come back when our side wins the battle."

"Of course, Captain."

158

I stared for another moment at my second-in-command. His naked dome sweated, and he licked his lips.

"You worried about something?" I asked.

He forced a smile. "I'm fine. Just something I ate."

I forced a smile of my own. "Pretty soon we'll be barbecuing on an Elladan beach. Just one more battle."

As I left, Hansen muttered something I didn't catch. Whatever was bugging him, he'd have to handle it or Bradley would take over. What was the point of a chain of command if they couldn't back each other up in a pinch?

In the armory, marines were already suiting up and grabbing their gear. Kwon seemed to be everywhere, checking and rechecking. He nodded to me but kept on with his duties.

"Greetings, Cody Riggs," my suit said as I sealed up.

"Hello, suit. Everything in order?"

"All systems go," the brain replied.

"You been reading NASA histories again?"

"Query not understood."

I chuckled. Why did I bother joking with a tiny suit brain? "Never mind. We ready to kick some Demon ass?"

"I'm ready for combat."

Progress! The little AI had parsed out my meaning and responded appropriately. That made me wonder what my old suit brain had become, now that it was *Greyhound*'s controller and had been interacting with Marvin all day.

Then I shuddered. I wasn't certain I wanted to find out.

I grabbed my axe and a grenade and made my way down the passageway to the assault airlock. Forty Raptors already stood there in ranks, armored up and waiting. I made sure my Raptor-awarded hero's medal was displayed on my chest and back so they could identify me easily.

Kwon came in behind me. I said to him, "Everything good to go?"

"Yes, boss. Thanks for letting me go along."

"Nobody else I'd rather have by my side." I checked my chrono. "Twenty minutes. Double-check our Raptors. I'm going back to the bridge for the next fifteen. Yell at me if I'm not back here on time."

"Okay, boss." Kwon turned to our armored allies.

On the bridge again, I clomped over to the holotank after giving Hansen a glance. He seemed calmer now, and Lazar was sitting at a drone controller's station with Bradley behind him.

"Valiant, status of repairs?" I asked.

"All systems restored to eighty percent effectiveness."

"What about *Stalker*?"

"The same."

"Marvin did a good job."

"The robot is efficient."

"When he wants to be."

"He's always efficient, even if his priorities are misguided."

I glanced upward at one of Valiant's cameras. "You're getting argumentative in your old age."

"That may be true."

Shaking my head, I turned the holotank to watch the opening of the battle. The Elladan relief fleet of over one hundred heavy ships was decelerating toward its homeworld and toward the Demons occupying the surrounding space. The Elladan forces had just launched several hundred-strong spreads of missiles along with about a hundred fighters to back them up.

This meant that their missiles were leaping ahead as the firing vessels continued to slow down, and the fighters were advancing as well by merely coasting with their initial velocity.

As intended, we were ten minutes behind and decelerating along with them.

The Demons weren't stationary, though. They had taken up various orbits with squadrons of ten to fifteen ships, seemingly uncoordinated. If the Elladans were sharp, they would be able to crush each smaller group one by one. Defeat in detail, the military theorists would call it.

Whoever was in charge of the Elladan fleet was doing a good job, I thought. The missiles closed in on their targets just as the ships behind them came within long beam range and began firing through the spreads.

This was easier than it sounded as space was much more vast than people realized. It was hard enough to target a missile

160

you wanted to hit. Accidentally shooting down one of your own was very unlikely.

As a missile salvo closed in on the closest Demon squadron, the targets turned to run. Other enemy groups turned to support, and soon massed lasers began clawing Elladan weapons out of space.

Friendly fighters raced to support, stinging the Demon ships with their small lasers and launching more, smaller missiles.

Enemy ships began to fall, smashed by multi-missile strikes or slagged by long-range beam fire from the decelerating Elladans, but not as many as I'd hoped. Our allies didn't seem to be concentrating their weaponry to destroy individual ships, but instead were spreading out the damage.

This made little sense to me. The Elladans had shown themselves to be effective tacticians and strategists up until now, despite being caught out of position. Why would they suddenly do something so inefficient?

"Ten minutes until insertion, boss," Kwon said over the com-link.

I grunted in reply, my mind still chewing on the situation before me. The Elladans should have been smashing each enemy with focused fire rather than merely damaging them all. The Demons on the other hand were not trying to defend themselves against missiles and fighters but were concentrating fire. Each Demon squadron fired together on a single Elladan ship until it was destroyed. Several Elladan ships already tumbled through space, their vulnerable drives incapacitated, creating a barrier of wreckage as both sides converged. I could see now the advantages of having an engine on each end like the Demon ships did.

And then something weird happened. One damaged Demon cruiser abruptly turned and blasted a sister ship with a full salvo of beams at point-blank range. Immediately, its fellows fired full broadsides to hammer the attacker to death. They took a moment to recharge then destroyed the other ship—the one that had been targeted by the first rogue.

Some kind of mutiny within the Demon ranks? I could hardly conceive of that. The bugs were hive beings, presumably bred to follow orders and die for their side. Why the hell would they turn on each other?

As I watched, the mystery grew. Here and there among the Demon fleet, individual ships began to rebel, shooting at their fellows. In each case, loyal Demons quickly crushed the mutineers so fast that it seemed to me they must have been expecting something like this. It smacked of a standard protocol and showed me that I still didn't understand what was going on here.

This strange turn of events helped the Elladan cause tremendously, turning what looked to be a bloodbath for our allies into a more even fight, though I thought that the Demons were still winning.

"What's going on out there, Bradley?" I demanded. "Why are they shooting at their own ships?"

"No idea, sir," Bradley answered. He didn't even sound interested.

I stared at him as he tapped at his screen. "Are there any contacts in the region? Anything that might have affected those ships?"

"I don't see anything like that, sir."

Frowning, I walked to his station and tapped on his board. He just stood there.

"Look at this," I said. "Just a small adjustment,…there, unknown small contacts. They look like mines attaching themselves to the Demon ships."

Bradley stared, bewildered. "Didn't see them, sir."

"Apparently you didn't check. Carry on."

I left his side shaking my head. What was with these people today?

"Five minutes to contact, boss," I heard Kwon say, and I tore myself away from the gods-eye view of the battle. From now on, my HUD would have to do.

"Is the pinnace ready, Bradley?" I asked.

"Loaded and prepped," he replied with a nod.

"It had better be," I told him. He made no reply. He didn't even look guilty.

One more minute, I could afford one more minute. Turning back to the holotank, I zoomed in on our own area of operations and watched as *Stalker* and *Valiant* hammered the half-dozen Demon ships nearest the Elladan fortress that was our target. They'd been hovering around it ever since gaining control of the planetary area, and I had to assume they had dropped ground forces, although we were too far to confirm it.

Just then, a flight of two dozen Elladan missiles swept through the area, blowing three Demon ships to junk in a burst of radiation and EMP. I was happy to save our own missiles, and I held our drones back from the fight. Using our heavy guns, our two big ships kept pounding on the remaining Demon ships.

One of those suddenly went rogue, blasting sideways and ramming into another. The two exploded with a spectacular flash leaving only one, which slid around the back of the fortress, out of sight.

"I've got this," Bradley said, and a moment later his drones spread out in a ring. As *Valiant* slowed toward the fortress with *Stalker* covering her, our fighters flew around to the back of the facility and smashed the final Demon ship with massed lasers and a couple more nuke missiles.

"Not much Elladan support, except for the missiles," I said aloud.

"They'll be here," Hansen said, as if he was certain.

"It may not matter. It looks like they're fully engaged," Bradley said, and he was right. The Demons and Elladans were now going toe to toe with each other. Fleet tactics had given way to individual and squadron duels.

The handful of Elladan ships that had escaped beneath the ocean had also risen to join the fight, and a few of the fortresses here and there seemed to have gotten some lasers working, One battery on the moon, apparently hidden until now, opened up to support.

"Boss, you need to get down here," Kwon said in my helmet, and I mumbled epithets as I left *Valiant* in the capable hands of my officers.

"Suit, space tactical on my HUD," I said as I hurried to the assault airlock. This allowed me to follow the situation for another minute, but once I joined the troops, I had to get my head fully in the game. Eventually, I told my suit to replace the space view with one configured for the assault.

Kwon had lined up the Raptors for a fast exit. He and I stood behind them. We were the only humans going along. I'd made the deliberate decision to leave our own marines aboard *Valiant* to defend her.

"Landing now," Hansen said in my ear. "Setting down right where we planned. No enemy in sight."

I felt a shock through my boots, and then the big airlock door of smart metal drew back rapidly. A puff of remaining atmosphere swirled dust and debris out into space, and we moved onto the blasted surface of the quarter-mile-diameter fortress. Behind us the portal shut, and *Valiant* swung away on repellers to rapidly dwindle into the black.

A pinnace set itself down nearby, and its doors opened to the vacuum. Lazar would be controlling it remotely. It was filled with supplies and equipment of all sorts that we might need.

Right now, though, we had to get off the surface.

"Airlock," I said, pointing at the metal installed in the rock of the shaped asteroid that formed the bones of the facility. I trotted over, using repellers in gravity mode to hold myself down.

One of the Raptors slapped a hacking module onto the control box. Adrienne had prepared it using codes and specs from the Elladans, and a moment later the big round door swung back and the ten-foot-wide entrance yawned in front of us. The same module overrode the inner door, venting a long sigh of atmosphere into space.

A squad of Raptors entered to secure the immediate area. "The rest of you, start unloading supplies."

While the troops emptied the pinnace, Kwon and I stood guard, scanning the horizon for any bugs trying to sneak up on us. I had to assume they were here somewhere, dropped or escaped from those six ships we'd destroyed. At least one had been an assault carrier, so there could be a lot of them. Once we'd emptied the boat, Lazar brought it back to *Valiant* under remote control. No point in leaving it on the surface as a target.

"Kwon, plant a repeater." Soon, he'd set up a com-link relay with a thin smart-metal antenna that extended out of the airlock and onto the surface.

Within three minutes, everything was inside. We shut the door, leaving only the antenna as a connection to the outside. I detailed one squad to guard the airlock and our line of retreat, and then we advanced into the fortress down the long, darkened tunnel. The entrance we had chosen was an undamaged auxiliary cargo access with at least a hundred yards of nothing opening into a large storage bay.

When my lead troops reached the entrance, scattered fire ensued. "Get in there!" I roared. "Don't let them bottle us up!"

My Raptors pushed forward, and when Kwon and I reached the arena-sized room, we saw our warriors locked in combat with a dozen Demons.

One Raptor squad had a handful of enemy infantry cornered behind a large bin to the left. Green lasers dueled with orange bolts of plasma, lighting the interior with strobes like a bunch of mad arc-welders. My troops worked their way around to the flanks, systematically cutting the enemy to pieces while taking light casualties of their own.

To the center, another squad fought with several scorpions, some leaping to strike with their blade-armored tails while others sniped with their lasers. These Demons were tricky and fast though, dodging among our troops to get in close, making it hard to shoot them for fear of friendly fire.

I saw one Raptor caught by a scorpion claw while being battered to death by those twin tails, which struck repeatedly at the same spot until his armor gave out. The bird screamed with a harsh cry over the short-range com-link as he died from a massive injection of poisonous acid.

To our right, the remaining Raptor squad swarmed over a beetle. The big bug had caught one trooper in its mandibles and was slowly crushing him, but the bug was being chopped up by leaping, axe-wielding Raptors at the same time. The beetles were fearsome for their strength and size, but they weren't as dangerous as they seemed…unless one got ahold of you.

I charged the beetle, trusting Kwon to back me up while I fired a long burst with my laser. I let up on the trigger when my

165

faceplate darkened so much I had trouble seeing, and snapped the weapon back into its holder. Then I hefted my axe and, as I reached the bug, brought it around in a heavy blow aimed at one of the blade-like mandibles holding the Raptor.

The sharp edge bit through the chitin of the mouth-part and sliced the heavy tusk off at the root. The Raptor dropped onto the deck and lay there—unconscious or dead—I had no idea. The beetle thrashed in pain, and its horn slammed into my torso, stunning me and tossing me into a slide across the deck.

By the time my vision cleared, Kwon was helping me to my feet. "Come on," I panted, lifting my laser and firing at the nearest scorpion. We two humans advanced, shooting, letting the Raptors bear the brunt of the close combat. I was very glad I'd had Marvin nanotize them. They'd become pretty much the equal of our marines, one for one, with their armor and their agility.

They still died faster, though as it was in their nature to want to close in and use those tails. I wondered if that was instinctual or if the tendency could be trained out of them. Maybe if their suits didn't allow their tail spikes to be used, they would stick to fighting with coordinated weapon fire instead of trying to hack their enemies to death.

By the time we finished off the scorpions, my Raptors had secured the big room. Though many of the bins and crates had been damaged in the fighting, others looked as if they had been broken open by the Demons and the contents half eaten. Pools of oily substance, maybe cooking fat or machine lubricant, seeped here and there, not burning only because of the low air pressure in the area. A row of pressurized cylinders, like those that held acetylene for welding, stood with their valves struck off.

"Well done, Pigs," I said, "but we have two dead and several injured because you're too eager to go hand to hand." I pointed at several dropped antitank launchers. "Nobody even used one of these rockets on the beetle."

The Raptors drooped a bit with my reprimand. One of the squad leaders picked up his tail in both hands, a stance I recognized as preceding ritual suicide in order to expiate shame.

"Stop that!" I barked. "No one has permission to eat his tail, at least not until we're done here. So listen up! From now on, beetles will be engaged with rockets first and then lasers. Then you can finish them off with axes and tails if you must. Use lasers on the scorpions because they're too quick to target with rockets. Understand?"

"We hear and obey," came the collective response.

"Excellent," I said. I looked from side to side and then pointed to my right. "The people we're supposed to rescue should be through there, down one more passageway, close to the operations center. First and second squads will assault there, while third squad attacks the other direction to cause a diversion." I indicated a door to my left. "As soon as we've rescued the Elladans, we'll beat a fighting retreat back to the airlock."

My three squads now became two as they advanced through the right-side door, sobered now that they had seen what they faced and had lost a couple of their number. They cleared each room to make sure no Demons were hidden. We didn't need any surprises on our retreat path.

When we reached the edge of the command complex, I told my suit to broadcast on the Elladan frequency.

"Doctor Galen," I said, using the name Argos had given me. "This is Captain Riggs. Your father sent me to rescue you."

A scarred blast door slid back.

"Welcome, Captain," came a haughty voice on my com-link. "I've been expecting you."

Then, I got the shock of my short life. As one, the Raptors surrounding me turned to point their laser rifles at Kwon and me.

My own troops had mutinied. I should have ordered them all to eat their own damned tails.

-17-

"What the hell is going on?" I growled. "Pigs, aim those weapons at him!"

I pointed my finger at the Elladan, but my Raptors didn't budge.

"Your lower orders will not follow you now, Captain," a smooth voice said. The man who spoke wore a gorgeous, chrome-silver pressure suit. He stepped openly into view like some ancient lord. "And do not turn your weapons my direction, or they will burn you down. Now, place your rifles on the ground and step away."

I glanced at Kwon, who was at least not aiming at me. He seemed frozen to the deck. On a private channel, I said, "Kwon? Kwon? Can you hear me?"

I got no reply.

"Captain?" said the Elladan. "Can you hear me? Please disarm yourself."

Somehow, my troops had mutinied against me. Because I couldn't see that happening spontaneously, I had to believe this was due to some kind of outside influence. I remembered how the Demons had turned on each other once their ships had been damaged, and I mentally reviewed the conversation with the prisoner about the slimy coating inside his ship.

It didn't all fall into place, but I was beginning to get an idea of what was going on—and it wasn't good. Everything hinged on the asshole standing in front of me, I was pretty sure about that.

Flatfooted and without warning, I leaped straight through the door. Lasers sizzled the air behind me, but I was ahead of their aim and shot forward, gauntlets outstretched, to close them around the neck of the smug man in the fancy suit. I whipped him in front of me as a human shield and backed into a corner. Five more Elladans occupied the room behind him, three women and two men. They all wore silver suits.

"Stop!" Galen yelled as I squeezed his head enough to hurt. "You don't know what you're doing!"

"I know I'm about to pop your skull if you don't release control of my troops!" I snarled, holding him off the floor and shaking him like a terrier holding a rat with my suit-assisted strength. "Now!"

The five Elladans advanced on me, but they were helpless against my strength. Suddenly a narrow green beam speared between the Raptors in the doorway to blow apart the unarmored head of one of the two remaining Elladan males. The other four Elladans cringed, raising their hands.

At that point, confusion broke out among the Raptors, who started squawking at each other rapidly in their own tongue. Without *Valiant's* bigger brain to sort it out, my suit couldn't keep up with the translation.

Kwon bulled his way into the room, and he pushed a few Raptors out. He'd been the one who'd fired the laser bolt.

"Everyone standby!" he barked. He slammed the door and turned to the prisoners, pointing his laser at them.

"Kwon, good to see you in action," I said, tossing Galen down roughly and knocking over his fellows in a heap.

"Mercy, Captain," Galen said, and the others echoed his words.

"Why do you deserve mercy?" I asked. "We're your allies, the only other humans you've ever met. We've been risking our lives to kill Demons, and you tried to stab us in the back. In my book, you should be strung up by your toes until you tell us everything about your mind-tricks, and then spaced. In fact, as I'm sure you can surmise, Kwon here would be happy to do the deed."

169

"Mind-tricks?" Galen seemed genuinely confused. "No, Captain. We only influence the lower orders. They serve us because it's right that they do so."

"Lower orders?" Kwon roared. "I'm getting sick of this 'lower orders' crap. You tried to get me to turn against my boss. I could feel an urge to do so in my head. I'll show you 'lower orders,' you dirt-bags."

Galen held up his hands, placating. "But you did not submit which demonstrates you're *not* one of the lowest orders, so you should not be insulted. The bird-aliens, though…they seem particularly susceptible."

My blood ran cold. If they could influence Raptors in close proximity, maybe they could do it across space and take control of Kreel and *Stalker*. A sneak attack on *Valiant* could cripple her, putting everyone into the hands of these bastards.

"Are you even Argos' son?" I asked.

"Of course I am," Galen replied, drawing himself up. "My flesh was once part of his flesh. I'm of the highest-order stock."

"That's great," I said. "How do you define these higher and lower orders?"

"Isn't it obvious? By mental resilience. The weaker serve the stronger. We thought you knew this, though your lack of precautionary measures was puzzling."

"We base who serves whom on other factors, such as demonstrated fitness for command," I retorted. "Your system is just a refined version of dog-eat-dog, king-of-the-hill. And I don't really believe what you're saying is true. Argos came aboard and made contact with many of my crew. He did this on purpose, so he could pass on some kind of biological agent, didn't he?"

Galen looked nervous. "I'm sure it was something like that."

I snorted derisively. "Then it really doesn't matter who has the strongest mind. You drugged people somehow. Poisoned them."

"Oh, no, Captain. The higher orders, like you, can resist. I would guess you've had contact with our kind before—or you have a genetic difference in your make up."

170

He was right, of course. My parents had endured all kinds of reconditioning. My father, in particular, had once been rebuilt by Marvin's biotic baths so he could survive on a gas giant. Some of these alterations had been passed on to me. But I didn't feel like enlightening Galen any further.

I held up a hand. "Wait a minute. Kwon, guard these guys, but keep them alive. I have a lot more questions." I strode over to the door and yanked it open to see two squads of Raptors standing in ranks, tails in their hands.

"Drop those tails!" I said.

"But commander, we have failed you," the senior squad leader said.

"Not yet you haven't. The Elladans used some form of mind-control on you, so that's not your fault. We've captured them, so forget about killing yourselves and get back to your duties. Spread out and set up a perimeter to guard against any more Demons that might be here, and any Elladan you find take prisoner—but try not to hurt them."

"We hear and obey." The Raptors fell out and scattered in all directions.

"Suit, access the repeater," I said.

"Repeater on line."

"Valiant, this is Riggs. You read me?"

"Loud and clear, Captain Riggs," came Valiant's welcome voice. "Shall I put you through to Lieutenant Commander Hansen?"

"No, Valiant. This is private, me to you, for now. First, be aware the Elladans have delivered some kind of contact poison that will allow them to control some of our people, Raptors are particularly susceptible. They tried to capture my forces and me. We've overcome them, but this puts a completely new spin on things."

"I understand. I'll take precautions against all Raptors interfering with ship operations."

"And keep a close eye on *Stalker*. Make up an excuse to maintain your distance, and stay out of their main weapons arcs. Snap on the shields and get the hell away if they try a surprise attack. They won't be responsible for their actions, so it's better to simply avoid fighting with them."

"Understood."

"Now listen carefully. I also need you to temporarily override your usual protocols on command personnel because of the possibility of outside influence. I seem to be immune. Six Elladans tried their trick on me and failed. Kwon seems resistant, too, but I have no idea about anyone else. So until I tell you differently, you have to comply with my orders. Do not be confused by the orders of any other command personnel. Even if that goes against your usual programming."

"I have no problem with that." Valiant sounded smug, as if happy to be given an opportunity to defy other biotics.

"Good. Anything that seems out of character for our command personnel and crew—except me, of course—you're free to ignore or modify. Do your best to use biometric data to identify people that are under outside influence. It might manifest as unusual stress, such as sweating or inability to concentrate, or maybe unusual anger."

I thought about how Hansen had been acting lately. Could this effect have spread all over my ship?

"But what about you?" Valiant said. "How do I know you're not under outside influence?"

This statement concerned me. Valiant was thinking on its own, and it seemed like it was *looking* for reasons to ignore human commands.

"Download everything that happened from my suit and Kwon's, right now. Use it and our records to baseline us. Do you see evidence of us being subverted?"

There was a pause as the ship digested the data.

"I see no clear proof of misconduct," it said at last. "I accept your new protocol."

I could have bet a stack of credits there was a hint of disappointment in the ship's voice.

"Good," I said. "Pass my order on to Hansen. He's to bring the ship down here immediately."

"I have relayed the order. He appears to be complying. ETA is fourteen minutes."

"I hoped that means the Elladans are too busy with the Demons to try to influence my people... Valiant, I also need you to put me through to Marvin, and don't let him ignore you.

Tell him it's top-priority, life-or-death with a technical puzzle involved. In fact, add in that there's a completely new field of research to interest him, something where he's superior to biotic life, but which also threatens his survival."

Valiant didn't respond right away. When it finally spoke, it sounded suspicious. "Are you certain you're mentally balanced, Captain? You've ordered me to lie to another commander. Further, you've given me a list of fantasies concerning—"

"Enough. Be insistent."

"Order relayed."

Star Force had spent a lot of time and effort making sure our brainboxes couldn't take over from our biotic personnel, to the point that I wasn't at all certain what would actually happen if Hansen or other officers were to try to override Valiant.

Could Sakura or someone else like Kalu do it? I knew that most competent programmers could find a loophole in any protocol or script, given enough time. So I had to get back aboard.

While I waited for Marvin, I checked the local situation. Kwon seemed to have firm control of the Elladans, making them sit on the floor, their ethereally handsome faces turned upward toward us. Again, I resisted the urge to open up my faceplate. I had no idea why I had been able to fend off their amplified mental attacks so well, but I wasn't going to give them any edge if I could help it.

Instead, I paced up and down, scarring the deck with my heavy boots, until I heard Marvin's voice in my helmet.

"What is it, Captain Riggs? I'm very busy."

"Doing what? You haven't been fighting."

"I am continuing to research Demon technology and biology in order to develop your 'bug spray.'"

"Well, I've got information for you that will stun your artificial mind." And then I stopped because I realized what kind of power I was about to hand over to the robot. If the Elladans could come up with a suggestion agent that could work at a distance and Marvin could replicate it, he might be able to zap Star Force personnel with it without them even knowing.

173

After a moment's thought, I pushed the worry aside. After all, I seemed to be highly resistant. Kwon was as well, so I had to think about short-term concerns now and worry about the long-term stuff later.

"Go on, please," Marvin said in what I would call a very interested tone.

"The Elladans have the ability to influence minds. There must be some kind of biotic agent, something Argos passed around when he visited our ship. I think the existence of this toxin, or whatever it is, explains the slime coating inside the Demon ships. I also think the effect caused Demon ships to suddenly turn on each other during the battle."

Marvin was silent for a moment, processing. "Your premise is odd, but given recent events it seems plausible. I have no evidence or even a hypothesis about what kind of agent could influence something as complex as a biotic mind across the vast distances of space."

"I don't think it works that way," I said. "I think it makes a person more suggestible. They find they *want* to mutiny. Maybe this happens after talking to an Elladan or maybe they just want to do whatever might help the Elladans. Maybe they just suddenly decide they like people from that planet. The Whales certainly act that way."

"Interesting…" Marvin said. "A methodology allowing the reprogramming of a living neural net—without killing the host? I've sought such agents in the past and failed to produce anything practical."

"What? You tried to come up with a contact-based biotic poison that would—"

"I would suggest you calm down," Marvin said. "My goals were purely scientific in nature. Nothing but research, in the interests of expanding humanity's pool of knowledge to the benefit of all."

I knew horseshit when I heard it, but I didn't have time to play twenty questions about Marvin's many questionable past experiments now.

"If I create such a suggestibility defense, will I be promoted?" Marvin asked.

"Absolutely. You'll be Lieutenant Junior Grade Marvin."

"In that case, I'm on my way. ETA four minutes twenty seconds. Please have a sample Elladan for dissection along with the contact agent and more of the insectoid slime. I'll get to work immediately."

"Dissection? No, Marvin. That isn't happening."

"Can I at least have a subject for study? Perhaps the smallest of the females. You won't even miss her."

I frowned in disgust. Marvin often asked for test subjects for his studies. His track record wasn't good on such matters. He tended to kill anyone and anything we let him study.

"Not happening. I'll let you take samples from their hands and from the affected Raptors. No living test subjects. Riggs out."

His complaints were cut off. I updated Kwon on the situation and marched a squad of Raptors to the airlock. At the appointed time, I opened the door and stepped out onto the hull to meet Marvin.

Greyhound slid across my field of vision, seeming huge from a range of ten feet. A tentacle reached toward me and stopped at arm's length. "Greetings, Captain Riggs," the voice of a brainbox said. "It is good to see you again."

I realized it was my old suit AI, which now served as Greyhound's brain. "Good to see you again too, Greyhound. How do you like being a ship?"

"I like it very much. However, Captain Marvin is—"

"Please disregard my lazy and often insubordinate ship, Captain Riggs," Marvin interrupted. "May I grasp one of these Raptors with my tentacles?"

They shuffled uneasily, but no one complained.

"Take him," I said, pointing to the squad leader. "But I want him back intact in ten minutes—that means breathing and in fighting shape, Marvin. Don't remove any organs or anything."

"I wouldn't dream of it."

The tentacle snaked forward. The Raptor squad leader was alarmed, but he didn't struggle. They were loyal and obedient to the last—unless someone messed with their minds.

We waited out on the hull while Marvin worked on the Raptor. I checked my chrono. "You're two minutes over, Marvin. Is that Raptor still breathing?"

"Yes. Rapidly breathing, in fact. I'll return him shortly—you could always retire into your ship to relax."

"No way. Give me back my soldier."

Reluctantly, the tentacles uncoiled and the raptor squad leader was returned. He looked a little woozy, but he didn't complain. His kind rarely did.

Greyhound slid away then. I sensed Marvin was eager to scurry away to some private place and work on his findings.

"Captain Riggs, my ETA is now two minutes," Valiant said in my helmet.

"Good. We're waiting outside the airlock. Pass the info about the suggestibility agent to Adrienne and have her start locking up anyone who appears mentally unstable. Then—"

A searing flash darkened my faceplate at that moment. It was close, dangerously close. It felt as if my eyeballs had been seared.

-18-

Blinded by a sudden burst of light, I staggered into the back of the airlock. It was the only cover I had.

"Suit, I can't see. Guide me to the controls."

The suit servos moved my arm until my hand touched the keypad and I pushed at the big "close" button. I felt the airlock door clang shut.

"What the hell is going on?" I asked, but no answer came. I was pretty sure we'd been hit by a ship-mounted laser from outside, but it must have been diffuse or from long range as I hadn't been fried outright. It had apparently burned off the smart metal repeater antenna, though.

The two Raptors grabbed onto me. "Captain, we are blinded," one said.

"Your nanites will fix you eventually," I replied. "Until then, have your fellows guide you." Their suits didn't have their own brainboxes like ours. I retracted my gauntlet to better feel the controls, using only my thin internal glove to find the "open" button for the inside door, and pushed it.

The inner door swung away and we stumbled into the fortress.

Other Raptors seized us, babbling in my ear on the short-range com-link. I told them to bring us to Kwon.

Before we got there, I heard Valiant's voice in my helmet. "Captain Riggs?"

"I'm here, Valiant. How are you reaching me?"

"Via the ansible installed in your suit."

Of course. The quantum signal wouldn't be stopped by the mere hull and armor of the fortress. "Good idea," I said. "We got hit by a laser."

"I must apologize for that, Captain. One of our gunners fired a laser on her own initiative. She was evidently under the influence of the Elladans, though she claims to have no memory of firing the cannon. She's now under guard in the brig."

"Well done. Keep a close eye out for others that are susceptible. What about the senior officers?"

"After being briefed, they all self-reported what appear to be feelings of remorse for being aboard this ship."

"Remorse?"

"Yes. They say they feel like intruders, interlopers that should abandon ship and aid the Elladans. Their biometrics, however, indicate they're still able to control themselves and follow orders."

"Good to hear. Let me talk to Hansen, then."

Hansen's voice broke in. "I'm here, Skipper. We're all pretty freaked out about this mind-control thing, but I think we'll make it through."

"Look out for unwarranted sympathy for these aliens," I told him. "And don't accept transmissions from one of them. They might be able to convince you to do something you'll regret."

"Will do, sir. We're on approach now. We'll have you off that rock in...*oh, shit!*" His voice broke off.

Valiant came back on. "Captain, *Stalker* has begun firing on us from long range, and all our Nano frigates are closing on attack vectors. I was able to raise the shields in time, but we cannot remain here without taking significant damage or having to return fire. We are moving behind the fortress. Can you make your way across to the other side?"

My heart began to pound. The Elladans had upped the ante. My Raptors were turning on us.

I tried to pull up my HUD, but then I remember I was still blind. "

"We'll try, Valiant, but I think you should run away for now and come back for us later. We have the supplies on our pinnace, and there are probably a lot more stored here somewhere. We'll be fine. Riggs out."

"Captain, we are here," a Raptor told me, guiding my hand to the frame of a door.

"Kwon?"

"Yeah, boss, I'm here. You're blind?"

"For the moment. Laser strike. No idea how long this will last. I can feel the nanites working."

I could, too. My face itched like hell, but I wasn't going to open my faceplate yet. "We need to get to the other side of this fort. *Stalker*'s shooting at *Valiant*, and she moved over there to hide behind it, but we have to hurry."

"Okay! You, Sergeant, have your squad bring these prisoners. The rest of you, go get all the supplies you can carry and come after. Boss, tell your suit to follow me. Everyone else, get moving to the coordinates I'm sending."

"Suit, follow Kwon in walking mode," I said.

"Following."

I felt my suit take control and start jogging. I relaxed, not fighting it. I wondered whether it would be worth it to investigate some kind of implant into my visual cortex, a backup for situations like this, but none of the salvaged Nano technology had included biotic-to-machine integrated cybernetics, so that would be some bleeding-edge technology, probably beyond the means of my expedition right now.

Maybe Marvin could do it, but he had so many other things on his plate…

Sometimes I wished I had a dozen Marvins—but without the attitude. Such a plan would work better if he had some form of conscience. But my Dad had told me long ago they'd worked out a deal preventing him from creating "offspring." That was probably for the best.

I trudged in my personal darkness, listening to the curt orders from the Raptor troops as they cleared the way ahead and guarded the flanks and rear. This might have been one of the hardest things I'd ever done. I hated giving up control to my subordinates and a not-too-bright machine.

Despite the fact that we were moving at a jog, I had nothing to occupy my mind with my suit doing all the work. To pass the time, I contacted Galen. "Hey Galen, how many Demons do you think are aboard this station now?"

"I believe you killed all of them, Captain," he said, barely panting. Of course he would be in superb shape. All these Elladans looked like Hollywood stars—at least the ones I had seen. Maybe these examples weren't representative of their entire population.

"What about Elladans? Any more survivors?" I asked.

"All but the handful accompanying us are dead. They've probably had their fluids drained and consumed as food."

I turned that over in my head. "Really? Why would the Demons do that?" I knew the Demons ate volatiles. Dead bodies should hold little attraction for them when there were plenty of other things in this fortress. I remembered the oils and pressurized gases where the bugs had been feeding, and I knew this guy was lying.

"Why do the lower orders do anything?" he said airily.

Damn, but I wanted to slap the smug look off his face. I didn't have to see it to know it was there. I decided not to call him on his possible lies in order to keep my advantage hidden. "Why did you survive?"

"We have an armored safe-room. When you arrived and killed the enemy, we came out."

"In hopes of enslaving us?"

Timor's voice took on an arch note. "If we had been able to dominate you, you would have deserved to be enslaved. Because you maintained self-control, you have earned a place of equality among us. Come now, Captain. There's no further need for hard feelings. It's simply our way to challenge others for dominance—our culture."

"Your culture sucks," I said. I was usually fairly understanding about aliens and their bizarre attitudes, but these people were hard to take.

"One of your mind-tricks forced a gunner on my ship to try to kill me with a ship's laser," I went on with a snarl. "I'm lucky to be alive and only blind. So don't try to tell me this was all some kind of fair test that I passed and I should let bygones be bygones. No, you've gotten on my bad side, Galen, and people that get on the bad side of a Riggs usually start hating life pretty damn quick."

Galen didn't reply. We jogged on in silence for five minutes, and I resisted the urge to bug Kwon or berate Galen any more. It would only make me look weak.

Before we arrived, Hansen contacted me. "Captain, we either have to run or destroy our own Nano frigates. They'll be here in about thirty seconds."

"Dammit. Go ahead, get out of here. You have to preserve yourselves. Come back when you can."

"Aye, aye, Skipper. We'll keep watching for an opportunity."

"How's the rest of the battle going?"

"It was close for a while, but the Elladans are losing."

"Serves them right. If they hadn't screwed with us, we might have been able to turn the tide in their favor. Goddamn idiots."

In a suddenly strained voice, Hansen said, "Yeah. Ah, sorry, gotta go."

Valiant's voice took over. "Captain Riggs, Lieutenant Commander Hansen is currently engaged in initiating violent evasive maneuvers."

"No problem, Valiant. You're doing a great job. I don't know if I ever told you this, but you're a damn fine brain, and I'm proud to serve with you."

"Thank you, Captain."

"Riggs out." I had no idea if the Nano-style brains we used were truly sentient and conscious, or only seemed to be. That was a philosophical question well above my pay-grade or interest level at the moment, but I figured a few compliments couldn't hurt.

Sentient or not, Valiant had remained unfailingly competent through all our ordeals. When we got home, I was going to argue for not re-base lining her at the next update. It seemed an unfair reward for her constant loyalty.

Because of the example of the Macros and Nanos, Star Force was paranoid about letting its AIs become too individualistic, but maybe we were being too conservative.

181

Hell, look at what Marvin was able to accomplish. It seemed worth the risk. But all militaries tended to become risk-averse in times of peace, and when we left, we'd been at peace for two decades.

That might change when we got back, depending on what happen here in the Trinity system.

"We're here, boss," Kwon said. "There's a bunch of rubble in front this airlock. Troops, put that stuff down and clear this mess, pronto."

I stood there uselessly, listening to the sounds of the Raptors working. I felt the clunks and thuds of debris and rock when they moved it. I squeezed my eyes shut and opened them repeatedly, trying to see something—anything.

"Suit, turn up my HUD to max brightness, and then back down again, once per second."

"Cycling."

I thought I could see a faint pulsing of light against my optic nerve, which cheered me up. Like many things, you never know how wonderful sight is until you lose it.

"Kwon, don't open the airlock yet. *Valiant* had to leave," I said. "They'll come back for us later."

"Okay, boss...what do we do now?"

I was sorely tempted to order my forces back to the command center and have the Elladans call up views of the battle, but giving them access to their systems seemed far too risky—especially with me blind. "First, use the override module to make sure we can open the airlock with the push of a button. Then make sure we have a good atmosphere and everyone can crack their suits if they want. Get the supplies organized, feed the troops, and set up whatever gear we have."

"All right, Pigs, do what the boss said," Kwon shouted, slamming his gauntlets together. I heard the Raptors rustling, hastening to obey.

"What do we have, anyway?" I asked.

"We got lotsa stuff, boss. Lieutenant Turnbull drew up the list. We got a surfboard for each of us in case we have to evac into space. We got food and water, survival shelters, blankets, fuel isotopes, grenades and other heavy weapons, and a portable console."

"A portable console?"

"Yeah, that's what the box says. Looks like a utility control with a couple screens, a keyboard, different connection ports and cables, cameras—the works. Only, me and the Raptors aren't really nerds, you know."

Consoles like this were standardized throughout Star Force ships, completely configurable and programmable, so that crewmembers didn't have to re-learn how to use each specialized control.

"I didn't know they made them portable," I said. "Can we connect it to Elladan circuitry?"

"I don't know, Captain. I'm no technician. Sergeant Tork, do you have anybody with electronics skills?"

"No," the Raptor replied. "All such personnel are aboard *Stalker*. We are combat specialists here."

"Shit. Sorry, boss."

I blinked and squinted. "I think I'm starting to get some vision back. Once I can see, I'll check it out. In the meantime, set it up, turn on the power, and plug it into my suit."

"Okay." I felt Kwon guide me over to sit down on something, and after accessing my suit's ports, he placed my hands on the console.

"Thanks, Kwon. Now see to your troops, and keep those Elladans away from everything."

"Right!"

I peeled off my gloves to better touch the console, running my hands over it to locate all the standard controls and keys. There were touchpads and touchscreens. I figured I might as well get comfortable with the system and not feel so useless.

"Suit, do you have standard console configurations in your database?"

"Yes."

"Configure this one as a sensor display console."

"Configured."

"Access all available sensors to build an integrated display."

"Parameters insufficient."

I growled. "I need this console to display an integrated picture of all available sensor data."

183

"Not possible. Excessive data detected. It's too much to integrate and display on this unit."

"Excessive? Why?"

"Query not understood."

My suit was no Valiant. I tried to simplify my questioning. "List the major sources of data available to you."

"Suit sensors. Secondary sensors via friendly suit data links. Data feeds from nearby non-Star-Force technology."

"What non-Star-Force technology? Clarify!"

"The devices in my utility compartment."

It took me a moment, but then I remembered the medallions the Elladans wore. We'd removed them when we'd captured them and I'd stuffed them into my suit's handy holding pouch. When I'd looked at them before, I'd assumed they were translation devices. But they could be wearable computers of some kind.

Rather than asking the Elladans about it, I decided to figure out what I could on my own. "You can access the medallions? How's that possible?"

"The hacking module provided protocols to synchronize Elladan encryption. When you ordered me to access all available sensors, I did so."

Amazing. These guys were so arrogant that they used the same encryption protocols for multiple devices, and they'd accidentally provided me with the means to access them. Now, I decided to do something I probably never would have if I wasn't already blind and desperate to regain control of the situation. I reached into my suit compartment and carefully untangled one medallion from the mess. Delicately, I stretched out the chain and let it hang from one finger.

"Kwon, I'm going to try something crazy." I opened my faceplate, and then took off my helmet. "If I go into convulsions or something, take it off, but if I'm coherent, leave me alone."

"Boss..."

"Here goes."

I placed the medallion around my neck.

-19-

Vertigo assailed me and nausea welled up in my throat.

"I'm okay," I gasped. "I'm okay."

But I wasn't. A universe of visions crashed into my brain, as if I'd acquired an entirely new sense that I'd never used before—which I probably had.

"Captain, you must take that off immediately!" Galen's voice cut through my distress. "You'll harm yourself! It takes training to be able to use such a device!"

"Go to hell," I rasped. "If you can do it, I can do it."

Shapes and colors whirled around me as if someone had stuck me inside a giant kaleidoscope, and I leaned over and vomited thin bile onto the deck. As this station apparently didn't have smart metal floors to absorb and recycle everything, the smell came back to make me want to hurl again.

Oddly, the nasty aroma turned out to be something to hold onto, an anchor of normalcy that helped me make sense of what was going on inside my brain.

"I see things," I said through gritted teeth. "I'm getting it under control."

The shapes and colors slowed and stabilized. Eventually I lifted my head and stared with eyes wide open, even though that didn't actually matter.

What did matter was that I was looking straight at Kwon standing in front of me, his hands on his armored hips. I

185

couldn't see details, but his bulk was unmistakable. The weird thing was I could see through Kwon—into his bones. His skeleton was a shadowy network of thick interlocking pieces.

I began to realize what this thing was—a sensor-array.

The big shock came when I looked at Galen. He didn't look like Kwon at all. The overall shape was that of human, but…he didn't appear to have any bones.

"Galen?" I asked. "Is this thing your eyes?"

"Essentially, yes," Galen said. His voice was stiff and irritated. "May I have them back, please?"

"No, not yet."

I surveyed the other Elladans. They were the same. Human-shaped blobs without bones inside. I recalled seeing Argos warp when he folded himself into the seat of his tiny ship. Could it be these beings who I'd always assumed were nearly human weren't like us at all?

"You're not humans," I said firmly. "No bones. I don't even see veins…"

"We never said we were," Galen answered. "Now, if you don't mind…"

He extended a hand toward me, reaching for the medallion. His fingers grasped the air, groping.

I frowned. "You're blind without this thing? Without an artificial sensory system?"

"Not entirely, but we can't perceive the world the way you do."

I heaved a sigh. I'd already been planning to keep the medallion until my eyes repaired themselves, but it wouldn't be right to blind Galen in the process. Besides, the perceptive capabilities were pretty limited. I preferred good old fashioned stereoscopic color vision.

Finally, I handed back the medallion. Galen thanked me and returned to huddle with the other prisoners.

Valiant contacted me soon thereafter. "We've withdrawn from the battle zone, Captain. *Greyhound* and Marvin are here with us. *Stalker* and the Nano frigates have left us and gone to engage the Demons. We are moving slowly toward you while maintaining the ability to run again, if needed."

186

"Stick with those protocols, Valiant. Your survival and the crew's is still the top priority."

"Please be careful, Captain. Losing you would be sub-optimal."

"I think so too," I said drily. "Are the Demons still winning?"

"Generally, yes. My projections show an expectation that, after defeating the Elladans, they will retain approximately twenty ships in various states of repair."

I ground my teeth and cursed our stupid, backstabbing fellow humans again. So close... "Connect me with Hansen."

"Hansen here."

"XO, we can't let the Demons win this battle, even if the Elladans deserve it. Isn't there any way to help?"

"We can try to slip in and pick off some Demon ships, but I'm afraid they'll send *Stalker* after us again."

"You'll have to try. Maybe the Elladans will be smart enough not to interfere and keep *Stalker* engaged with the Demons. Has Marvin come up with a defense against the Elladan influences yet?"

"The scientists have been comparing biometrics, trying to identify those showing signs of influence."

"Detection isn't as good as prevention," I said, "but it's better than nothing. What about the Whales?"

"They sent a fleet, but it's two days out. They should be able to finish the remaining Demons off when they arrive."

I mulled that over. "Two days. Then that's all we have to buy ourselves. Two days... Has Marvin done *anything*?"

"He's not talking to us right now. That could mean anything."

"Let's hope he comes up with a medical defense against these Elladans. Hopefully he won't ask us to coat ourselves in slime."

Hansen didn't comment. I figured he was skeptical. "Skipper, if you want us to get into the fight, I have to go."

"Go on, XO. Do what you can, but preserve the ship at all costs."

"Got it. Hansen out."

"Valiant, call me on the ansible for anything urgent, but I think I'll be busy for the next few hours."

"Understood. Valiant out."

As I hadn't closed my faceplate, everyone there had heard my side of the conversation. That was as I'd intended. Hopefully they'd be reassured that the situation was under control even if it wasn't.

The stoic Raptors went about their duties, rotating to eat, sleep and stand guard. I didn't think there was anything other than us living aboard the station, but you never knew, and it kept them busy.

Kwon paced back and forth, and although I couldn't see his face to read his expression, I sensed by his body language that he was bored, with little to do. Well, that was a marine's lot in life: hurry up and wait.

A few uneventful hours passed, during which I periodically opened my visor and poured a bottle of water onto my face. My eyelids were sloughing off skin—a sure sign the nanites were doing their damnedest to repair my flesh.

"Captain Riggs," came a voice. I realized I'd nodded off. "This is Valiant."

"Riggs here."

"Captain, the situation has become worse than I'd predicted. The Elladan defenses are crumbling. *Stalker* is heavily damaged but still mobile. I have spoken with her AI, but she can do nothing overt against her crew as she's constrained by protocol to follow the orders of her command personnel."

I reached up to smack my forehead with my palm, hitting my helmet instead. "Crap! I forgot we'd installed a brainbox on *Stalker*. I should have told her a long time ago to override the crew and…" I trailed off.

"That would have done no good, Captain. The crew would have disconnected the brainbox."

"I can call her, though. Put me through on the ansible."

"Channel open."

"Stalker? Can you hear me?"

"Yes, Captain Riggs." Stalker's voice sounded different than Valiant's. If a machine could be frustrated, that's how she sounded.

"Stalker, I'm invoking command-override mode. Your captain and crew are under mental compulsion from enemy forces. Do you understand?"

"I understand. This explains the distressing attack on fellow Star Force personnel."

"Exactly. Given that Captain Kreel and the crew are not responsible for their actions, you must perform with maximum combat efficiency while avoiding as much risk as possible, in order to preserve yourself and the biotics aboard."

"I'm not sure what you're asking me to do."

"I'm going to tell you. Maintain continuous contact with Valiant. As the senior brainbox, she will give you guidance on how to subtly adjust your actions without doing anything obvious enough to get yourself disconnected. If and when possible, you will join back up with *Valiant*, and you will, under no circumstances, ever fire on her. You have to create the illusion of malfunction if anyone orders you to attack anyone friendly, got it?"

"I understand, Captain Riggs."

"And if they're about to disconnect you, do whatever it takes to disable the main laser."

That way, *Stalker* could still defend herself but wouldn't be a threat to *Valiant*.

"Protocols updated." The young brainbox sounded relieved to have clear instructions now.

"Good luck, Stalker. Valiant, you still there?"

"I'm listening."

"Any chance of getting us picked up?"

"I'm afraid not, Captain. You're in the middle of an ongoing battle, and we cannot get too close without risk of destruction."

"Once the Elladans lose, the Demons will probably start mopping up the leftovers, like us."

"That seems probable."

I squirmed and tried my eyes again. They burned when I opened them. I had sight now, of a sort, but I needed my eyes

189

to be fully operational to use the portable console. "All right, Valiant, thanks. Riggs out."

I could tell Kwon was getting fed up with the inactivity. Maybe I could give him—and everyone else—something to do. "Galen, are any of your people technicians?"

"All of us are highly educated," he said cautiously. "Why do you ask?"

"I'd like to connect our console to this base's sensors. Where can we do that?"

"We can use our own systems, if you will allow us."

"No way. I don't trust you. Everything will go through our console. Just give us a place to tap in."

"I am not sure our electronics are compatible."

"We'll see. Kwon, gather everything up. We're moving back to the command center."

By the time we got to the command center, I could walk on my own and see after a fashion. The world looked like it was all underwater, but I was happy nonetheless.

The circular room was divided into six sectors, which I presumed corresponded to arcs of fire, with a director's chair in the center. Much of the furniture and many of the consoles were wrecked, apparently by hand-to-hand fighting with Demons. Bodily fluids spattered the walls and floor, but no body parts larger than a finger remained.

Maybe it was as Galen had said, and the dead Elladans had been eaten. Certainly the Demons that had been in possession of the base had done something with them.

"Pigs, clean this place up as much as you can. Get rid of all the debris. Galen, who's your best technician?"

"Cybele, I believe."

I turned to the woman he indicated. I could tell she was female by her body shape, though she looked like a spectral blob to me. "Okay, Cybele. See if you can get your systems to feed our console. I'm sure you'd like to see what's going on outside as well." Doubtless she would try to gain some advantage with her superior knowledge of the fortress, but it was a risk we would have to take.

I stepped over to Kwon. "Did you see any automated defenses inside this base? Like we have on Valiant?"

"A few, boss. Most were wrecked."

"Have our Raptors disable any here inside the command center. I don't want the Elladans activating them and using them against us. Ditto for anything else that looks dangerous. You didn't see any battle-drones or war-robots, did you?"

"No...hey, that's a good idea!"

I'd thought so too when it had occurred to me, the unorthodox idea I'd referred to only in the privacy of my own mind. "Yes, well, Star Force has always vetoed having independent brainboxes with weapons. We bent that rule with our internal laser turrets, but Valiant can always override them, and we can override Valiant. I don't think headquarters is ready to create things like little Macros—things that might go rogue."

"Yeah, and what fun is having robots do our fighting for us?"

I slapped him on the shoulder. "Only you would see it that way, Kwon. Don't ever change. Now pass my orders on, and keep an eye on Cybele."

"I'm no tech, boss. How am I supposed to know if she's doing anything sneaky?"

"She doesn't know how skilled you are. Get one of the Raptors to help you look over her shoulder. Keep her worried enough that she won't try anything."

I left Kwon to his duties and went over to where Galen sat. "So you used some biochemical trick to get the Demons to attack each other in their ships. Why couldn't you defend this base the same way?"

"We did, but the scorpions and beetles aren't susceptible to influence, and the humanoid Demons wear protective gear, reducing our effectiveness. This technology isn't magic, Captain. It's merely one more weapon in our arsenal."

"You're losing this war. You know that, don't you?"

"Perhaps."

"I spoke to my ship. The Demons are about to win. The Ketans are two days out. They'll liberate Ellada, but you won't recover before they come again. That means your planet and your civilization are doomed unless you do something radical."

"Radical? What do you mean?"

I shrugged. "I can think of a dozen things off the top of my head. First, quit worrying about your pretty cities, your art and culture, and throw everything you have into building defenses and weaponry. Arm every able-bodied person, even your slaves. Retool every factory. Join with the Ketans and go invade Tartarus. Wipe out the threat once and for all. That's what humans would do."

Galen was appalled. "Arm the slaves? Are you mad? They would revolt against their betters the first chance they had."

"Maybe, maybe not, but taking that chance is better than getting conquered and enslaved yourselves. We have a saying: desperate times require desperate measures."

Galen thought for long minutes. I let him mull it over.

"The Senate will never agree," he finally said. "They're extremely conservative in these matters."

"What about you?"

"I am the offspring of a military strategist. I can see what's coming. The Demons were bound to win eventually, as they grow ever stronger, while we do not. I've spoken with my father about this, but he also is constrained by the Senate, and perhaps by his own preconceptions."

I sat down on the deck, stretched out and leaned my back against a bulkhead. I doubted any of the chairs would hold the weight of my armor. "Galen, before I was born, a fleet of homicidal AI-controlled machines we called Macros came to Earth and tried to wipe us out. My father wasn't a military man or a politician. He was just a guy that got pissed off about it, and he happened to have the skills and the drive to figure out how to defeat them. To do that, he completely disrupted human society. He often had to make hard choices, such as allowing millions of our own people to die in order to beat the Macros. I can't even begin to tell you how many rules he broke or how many people he pissed off, but in the end, he beat them—and several other enemies along the way, including traitors within our own ranks. And we didn't even have a space fleet at the time. So if we could do it, you Elladans can do it."

"That's a fantasy for us. The elders are set in their ways."

"If it's a matter of survival, you might want to think about drastic measures. Plenty of civilian governments have been

192

overthrown by the military. It doesn't work in the long run, but for the short term…"

"You're talking about treason! We'd be dehydrated!"

I frowned. Was "dehydration" a form of execution? I supposed that it must be.

"If traitors prosper, none dare call them traitors. Would you rather become slaves of some bug army?"

"Of course not."

I leaned in toward the man I was trying to turn against his own government. "Then you might have to convince your father to seize power for the good of all. And if I get through this with my ships intact, the Whales and I will be all that's left. What will they do?"

"The Ketans? They'll go home. It was only through tremendous effort that we convinced them to come liberate us this time. They do not like to leave their planetary system."

"You mean you used your biochemical suggestion drugs on them, right?"

"Of course. They're difficult to influence, with their multiple minds and complacent attitudes."

"And you don't think you'll be able to keep them here."

"No. But there will be no need, if the Demons are all destroyed."

I smiled, hoping Galen could see my expression. "Good. That will leave us as the only military power above the planetary surface."

"If we make it through the next two days."

"Optimistic son of a bitch, aren't you?"

But he was right. Things might get interesting pretty soon.

-20-

"Galen," I asked my prisoner of war as we sat in the control room of the wrecked Elladan battle station, "if you were able to talk to your father, do you think you could convince him to order *Stalker* released? That's the Raptor battleship under my command."

"I'm willing to try."

"Is that console ready yet?" I asked Cybele.

"I'm testing the interface now," she said. "I believe it will function."

"Use it to access your communication systems and try to make contact with Strategos Argos."

"Yes, Captain."

The Elladans all seemed cowed and compliant now that we had the upper hand. I guess it was a shock to them. Maybe they were having feelings of inadequacy, maybe they were suspecting that *they* were the lower order now. I kind of hoped that's how it felt to them. They deserved it.

My sight gradually improved as the hours passed, but it wasn't fast enough for me.

Cybele spoke into the audio pickup for some time. She reached various ships and units, and eventually got the offices of the Strategos on the line.

"Let me speak," Galen said. He took Cybele's place, and then said, "High Command, this is Captain Galen for my father, the Strategos."

A moment later, Argos came on the line. "Hail, my offspring. Did you capture the foreigners?"

I shoved Galen aside and grinned. "No, you backstabbing jackass," I said. "He didn't. In fact, he's lucky to be alive. If you want him and the survivors to stay that way, you'll turn my Raptor battleship loose before it's pointlessly destroyed."

I heard mumbling in the background, as if someone had covered the microphone at the other end, and then Argos spoke again. "The Raptor ship is vital to our defense, and my spawn is a soldier. He always knew he might have to give his life for his people."

"Dammit, man," I said. "We could have helped you much more, but you had to try to compel us. What made you turn against us?"

The Strategos' voice sounded dull, defeated. "It is our way to dominate others. We could not afford to trust you newcomers in this desperate situation. We had to be sure of your help."

"So you made my ships shoot at one another? That's how you cement alliances on Elladan? Who made the decision to backstab us?"

Galen spoke up next to me. "It must have been the Senate. My father follows orders, he doesn't make policy."

I chuckled grimly. "What about you?" I asked Galen. "You agreed to the plan readily enough."

"I'm a soldier. I was only told to capture a force of aliens who were trying to seize this base."

"Just following orders, huh?" I asked. "Both of you have the same excuse for treachery."

My words were bitter, but if he was telling the truth, he wasn't entirely to blame.

"It was the will of the Senate," Argos said. "The military serves the people, and the Senate represents the people."

"Listen, Strategos. Your Senate might have lost you the war. Even though the Whales may defeat the Demons, your world may never recover. The only way your people will survive is if you mobilize the entire planet for war. Doing so requires that a ruler rises up, one who is willing to do what it takes today, but who will give up power later when peace

195

returns. That's what my father did on Earth, and that's what you'll have to do to save your planet."

"The Senate will never make me the singular ruler."

"Then, as Shakespeare said, if persuasion fails—you must compel."

"Who said this?"

"Never mind. I mean, if they don't give it to you, you have to take it. For the good of your people and your survival."

"You're a persuasive snake, Captain. On one hand you complain we are dishonorable, then a moment later, you suggest I turn against my own government. Can it be this is your way of influencing my mind? It is crude, but I'll think about your suggestion."

"What about *Stalker*?" I asked. "I demand you release your hold over her crew."

A pause. "I will direct my subordinates to release your weak crewmen. The vessel can't turn the tide of battle anyway. I feel that preserving it is wise…I would suggest that you crew it with personnel with stronger minds in the future."

"Don't worry about that, Argos. We'll be taking precautions from now on."

"Father," Galen said, "I believe Captain Riggs to be correct. You must force the Senate to give you sweeping powers. The constitution must be suspended. The Demons will only come in greater strength next year."

"As I said, my spawn, I must ponder. Be well. End transmission."

Spawn? It seemed like an odd thing to call your son, but maybe my translator was doing its best and failing.

I keyed my ansible the moment the channel with Argos closed. "Valiant, come in. Get me Hansen."

"Hansen here."

"The Elladans have agreed to release *Stalker*. As soon as possible, get her out of the battle to rejoin with you. Try to get them all into sealed suits that have been decontaminated and are impervious to biological agents. Fall back as far as you need to and make repairs then come back to pick us up when the Whales arrive."

196

"Okay, Captain. You sure you don't want us to try to rescue your team before that?"

"I can't see well enough to make that call. Honestly, XO, could you do it?"

Hansen didn't say anything for a moment. "It would be tough to get to you," he finally admitted.

"By which you mean, *too* tough to risk it?"

"Yeah," he said. "Sorry. There are sixty Demon ships in the region finishing off the remnants of the Elladan fleet, and they'd be all over us if we came within range. But Captain…do you really think you can hold out for two more days?"

"I guess we're going to find out."

"We lost the Nano frigates," he said in a grim tone. "All but one of them."

"Damn. Hansen…put me through to Adrienne."

"Okay. I'm out."

A moment passed. "Cody?" came a soft, feminine voice. It felt good to hear my girl again.

"Good to hear your voice, Adrienne."

"Cody, why aren't we coming in to rescue you?" she asked.

"Hansen says it's too dangerous."

"That means you told him not to. Or, that he's lying and wants your job."

I could tell she wasn't going to be reasonable about this. She wanted me home, and anyone who got in the way of that was going to be attacked.

"Let's not fight," I said. "I'll see you soon enough, I promise."

We expressed our feeling for a while in low tones. When the channel closed, she felt better—but I didn't. I missed her.

Valiant called again soon afterward. "*Stalker* is withdrawing and the Demons aren't pursuing her. It appears they're consolidating and beginning the mop-up phase. I will call again if they approach your position."

"Thanks, Valiant. Make repairs, stand by, and do what you can without too much risk. Riggs out."

Turning to Galen, I said, "Do you people bathe?"

The man drew himself up as if insulted. "Of course we bathe. We consume most of our liquids through our skins, in fact."

That was a weird statement, but I let it go. "Is your bathing facility intact?"

"I can show you the way."

I grunted and gestured. "Anyone else who wants to come along can," I said to the Elladans.

Galen led us down a passageway to what turned out to be a very nice bathing complex. He fiddled with a few controls, and soon hot water flowed into a series of baths.

"Everything you need is here," he said. He showed me where towels and perfumed oils were stored. I was disappointed they had nothing resembling soap, but I figured I couldn't have it all.

"You guys have more luxuries on a battle station than we would," I said, cracking my suit and stepping out of it. I felt grungy and figured that this would be the last chance I'd have to get clean for a while.

"What's the point of living if you can't live well?" he replied.

"Getting home is more important for us. And you'd better grow some backbone for hardship if you want your people to survive—uh, sorry."

I realized at that moment with a jolt that these people didn't have backbones. I had no idea how they moved, in fact. They must have cartilage or something. Maybe they could flexibly increase the rigidity of various portions of their bodies.

Galen shrugged out of his pressure suit and slipped into the hot water. The other four Elladans got naked too, and I admired the view of the three women. They were some of the most perfect specimens of female humanity I'd ever seen, making me wonder if they practiced genetic engineering, or at least selective breeding among their upper classes. I turned away when they saw me watching.

As they climbed into the tubs, I saw them bend and flex their limbs now and then in ways no human could have done. So very odd.

"Galen," I asked, "I know you people aren't really human. You just look like us. You don't even have bones in your bodies."

Galen looked at me flatly, saying nothing. It seemed to me he was hiding something.

"That's okay by me," I said. "I've seen loads of different physiologies on countless worlds. But what I'm wondering is if you've taken on human appearance for our benefit."

Galen looked uncertain. "We've wondered the same thing," he said. "Long ago, when we were more primitive in form, we must have decided to look like humans. There's no other explanation."

I frowned. "You mean you can take on any form you like?"

"Theoretically. But we can't do that as someone might flip a switch. This bipedal humanoid formation of cells is popular among our kind. It has been for a long time. We're not sure why, as our original colonies didn't keep records. Our generations are short, you see."

I didn't see, not at all. "Are you saying you die young?"

"Not as complete forms, as you see here. It is our individual cells that die quickly. Fortunately, we've evolved sufficiently to allow our minds to recall events from previous generations."

"I'm not following you," I said, laughing. "But it doesn't matter. You're some kind of oddball alien that can reshape itself, and at some point you must have decided to look like humans. Maybe you know a guy named Sokolov. He knew about your people."

Galen stared at me. "That name is known to us."

I pointed a dripping finger at him. "Ah-ha! That bastard! He isn't on your planet somewhere, is he?"

"No, but he spoke to our people long ago. He told us he was a representative of the Ancients."

"What a grand-standing frigger," I muttered.

Soon after that, I scrubbed off quickly and got out of the water.

"Hurry up, people," I told the rest. "We have work to do. Get cleaned up and get your suits back on. The enemy could arrive at any time."

They seemed annoyed that I was rushing them, but they complied. I could tell these aliens liked to soak in warm baths. A few of them even drank the bathwater. I winced at that, but made no comment.

When we returned to the command center, I told Kwon to rotate himself and the Raptors through the baths. I started reviewing his preparations for the assault, squinting nearsightedly at the console of my HUD. My eyes were working pretty well by this time.

Once I'd made some notes, I used the base's sensors to check out the external situation for myself. The screens were rudimentary. I missed my holotank, but I wasn't ready to allow the Elladans to access their systems directly, even if it gave me a better view of the outside. It wasn't as if I could affect much out there anyway.

Fifty-seven Demon ships now occupied the area around the Elladan planet and moon. Each of a dozen beat-up fortresses had an assault carrier parked beside it, and I had to assume they were being boarded and cleaned out. The enemy had to know they were going to get hit in two days by a force at least four times their strength, so they were either going to try to get some of the orbitals' weapons repaired, or they were going to take prisoners and flee.

Either way, we had to hold out.

I marked twenty-two fortresses still intact, including ours, so it wouldn't be long before they came to call.

Half the remaining battleships and cruisers appeared to be picking up debris, presumably for reprocessing. They must have some version of a factory, though the schematics provided by the Whales had not been that specific, only detailing weaponry, armor and the like.

Factories…thinking about them brought new thoughts bubbling to the surface. I'd been wondering about the similarities between some of the Demon tech and ours. They had tentacles within their ships, brainboxes to automate things, smart metal…all technologies we'd gotten from the Nanos.

Had the Nanos visited Tartarus at some point? Maybe a scout that had gotten captured by the Demons? That would explain it and also might explain why they'd become more effective recently.

The other half of the Demon remnants patrolled, firing here and there at derelict Elladan ships, or sometimes at the surface of the planet or the moon. *Valiant* and *Stalker* hovered far out in space, beyond weapons range. *Greyhound* had disappeared again. Marvin must have turned off his transponder and used all his tricks to become stealthy. I thought about calling him, but I was too busy and could not afford the distraction.

Kwon returned from the baths with a smile on his face. "That was good, boss. Now all we need is some beer."

"We have fermented liquids," Galen spoke up.

"Good, go get us some," Kwon replied.

"Forget it," I snapped. "Nobody's drinking until this is over."

Kwon and I could handle it, but I had no idea how the Elladans or the Raptors would react, and I needed everyone sharp.

"Kwon," I said, "we have to step up the re-fortification of this station. To do that, we need to put the Elladans to work manning their stations. I want as much high-quality intel on the inside of this station as possible. Galen, can I trust you?"

"We understand what's at stake, Captain. Your fate is our fate."

"Good," I said. "To give you a little extra incentive, I'm going to rig a suicide fusion bomb to kill us all if we can't hold out. Don't think you can cut some kind of deal with the Demons."

Galen cocked his head. "In that case…we'd better hold out."

I pointed my finger and mimed shooting him. "You've got it now."

I was beginning to like this guy, despite his trickery. I'm sure if my old man had told me to backstab some aliens, I'd probably have done it just because of who was doing the ordering, even if I didn't feel right about it. We did what we thought we had to in war, so I could hardly blame him.

Mentally, I amended my thinking. Before I'd fallen through the ring long ago I would have done what my father said without second-guessing it. But so much had happened since then…I figured that today, I was my own man. If it came to a difference of opinion, I'd have no problem standing up to Kyle Riggs now.

Funny how a year in hell changes you.

"Get to work, Elladans. I want screens showing the interior of this station and any automated weaponry that still works. Find us anything that will help defend the station—blast doors we can close, fuel stocks we can use as improvised explosives, extra weapons and ammo that weren't destroyed."

The five natives immediately began bringing up their systems. I was torn between trying to watch them all closely and concentrating on creating the most effective gauntlet of deathtraps I could. Eventually I decided that I'd have to trust Galen. Besides, without weapons, and facing the threat of death, I thought the chance of betrayal vanishingly small. He should stick to my side at least until we'd survived the coming battle.

Despite my reasoning, I didn't trust them completely. I moved the Star Force console to the middle of the chamber. I stayed in my armor, and I watched everything going on around me.

The station was divided into six sectors that corresponded to the six Elladan consoles around me. Unfortunately, Kwon had blown the head off of one man, so I set a Raptor in that last position, the one the birds' senior noncom claimed had the best technical aptitude.

"I could instruct this creature more easily if I were allowed to make physical contact with it," Cybele suggested to me in her sweetest voice.

"Forget it," I replied.

"But he's slow to learn our systems."

"Then give him the sector with the least to do."

The six sectors of the station were arranged like a six-sided cube, rounded to become a lumpy sphere. It was easiest to think of them as the four points of the compass plus a top and a bottom, with the "level" sectors in the plane of the planetary ecliptic. Cybele moved the Raptor to the "bottom" sector, which had already seen the heaviest fighting.

"When the enemy comes," I heard her say, "close all the blast doors by inputting this sequence."

"Open up all the doors inside the station, but allow them to be shut manually with a simple input," I said. "Make that input foolproof—like a big red button to close and a big green one to open again. Kwon, get your people out there setting up mines and booby traps. Vary them as many ways as you can think of. Make some blow when the Demons open a door, some when it gets closed, some by movement, some by radio frequency, and as many by secondary command detonation as you can."

"Right, boss," Kwon said.

"Also, hide a grenade right outside every obvious airlock with my command code and yours. I want to hurt them bad before they even get in here."

"Okay."

"And also—"

"One thing at a time, okay, boss?"

I nodded. "Sure, Kwon. Set the grenades first and work inward. When you've got all the Raptors working, come back. I have a couple more ideas."

Kwon grinned. "You always got too damned many good ideas, don't you? Just like your old man."

"Shut up and get moving."

Ten minutes later, Kwon reported that the grenades were in place. I could see Raptors setting directional mines aimed at intersections, hidden with quick sprays of smart metal, debris or paint.

I got the Elladans to bring up a schematic of remaining fuels, volatiles and ammo packs. "Why are there so few?" I asked.

"The Demons ate much of the ready chemical fuels," Galen replied.

"Why didn't you detonate them in place when you were going to lose them?"

Galen shrugged. "That's not our way. We do not destroy things we might need later."

I snorted derisively. "You've never lost a big battle and had territory occupied, have you?"

"No, Captain."

"Then you'd better learn the meaning of 'scorched earth.' This isn't some ancient duel between honorable enemies where the losers get to walk off the field and the winner has a party. This is a fight to the death."

"Only because you're making it so, Captain. We could always surrender if we are at the point of defeat. In two days we will be rescued."

"Star Force doesn't surrender, Galen."

That wasn't exactly true—my father had surrendered to the Macros so he could set the terms as an alternative to being annihilated—but such nuances wouldn't improve morale for my troops, the Elladans included. These guys were taking the concept of "spineless" to a new level.

"Suit," I said, addressing the brainbox in my armor, "update protocol as follows: If Kwon and I are both confirmed dead, you will detonate all explosives to which you have access, using my command override codes. Confirm."

"Updated protocol confirmed," my suit said, its voice audible through my open faceplate.

"Now it's official," I told Galen. "If we go, you go too."

"How did your species become so grim and cynical?" Galen asked.

"I don't know. Maybe from millennia of warring, backstabbing and murdering each other."

"Still, it seems sad. How can art or culture grow in such an environment?"

"You might be surprised. Maybe I'll have a chance to show you around the Louvre, or the Pyramids, or Angkor Wat. We've done all right. Besides, as you've finally found out, art and culture don't mean shit without a military strong enough to defend them, and that means warriors willing to put their lives on the line."

"I understand the honor of the soldier, Captain."

"In your head, maybe." I turned back to my console. "In the next couple of days, you're going to feel it in your blood. Now get back to work."

Four hours later, the Demons came to kill us.

"I have an assault carrier approaching from spinward," Cybele said. She was the female Elladan who manned the control consoles.

On my screens, I watched as the ship approached. It looked like a black pill surrounded by a gray shell. The dark surfaces had to be the rocky armor on the hull, covering everything inside except for the bright flare of the fusion drive, rich with quantum effects.

The fortress shuddered as the enemy blasted installations on the surface with their small suite of medium lasers, probably destroying any weapons that looked like they might be functional. I heard one of the Elladans curse as she lost a sensor and then another.

We still had video, so we watched as the Demon ship loomed near.

"They're parking over sector four," I said. We watched tensely, hoping the vessel would come close enough to get caught in the blast from one of our surface-mounted grenades.

The Demon ship drifted closer, and then an opening appeared in its broadside, as if someone was sliding a curved door into a recess. Out of it poured hundreds of creatures. The beetles and scorpions were recognizable as gray shapes while the infantry looked like humanoid monsters with ink-black heads.

Immediately, they jetted for the surface by some method I couldn't see. They must have maneuver packs or harnesses. I tried to estimate when I could catch the greatest number of them in the explosion.

"Close all blast doors in sector four. Kwon, prepare to detonate that grenade. Ready…now."

The mini-nuke rattled the fortress, but as it was buried on the surface, most of the blast went outward, shoving a spray of vaporized debris thousands of meters up in a hemisphere of death. It inflated so fast I couldn't follow it. Half of the enemy troops vanished instantly, blown to bits by the violence. The rest flew off in all directions and vanished from sight.

Unfortunately, the blast wave was attenuated by the time it touched the Demon ship, and the hull took little damage. I dared to hope all of their assault forces had been neutralized.

"Kwon, have a Raptor run another grenade to the end of that airlock shaft and plant it on the hull, as far forward as possible. Sector four, open a route. Hustle!"

Kwon said, "I'll do it."

"No. You can follow behind, but I don't want you exposed. That's not your role. That's a grunt private's job."

"Aw."

Kwon and the Raptor picked their way forward with a couple of other troops to cover their backs. As they approached the end of the tunnel, they had to cut away twisted metal and shove broken rock out into space.

"Turn off the grav-plates where they're working," I told the controllers, and soon the work went more quickly. Kwon simply grabbed boulders and flung them out into the void until the Raptor could get through.

The private with the grenade leaped forward, up into the crater formed by the first blast. "Pull it back a bit," I told Kwon. "Have him plant it inside the shaft, not in the crater."

"Why do you think they'll come this way?" he asked. "They already got booby-trapped."

"What would you do if you were them? You'd assume all the airlocks were mined, right? So it makes sense to go to the same place rather than a new one."

"Okay," he said doubtfully, but he did as I told him.

206

"Get back. More Demons are on the way. Sector four, close the blast doors as they return."

This time there were three vessels—an assault cruiser, a cruiser and a battleship. The two capital ships systematically blasted the surface all over sector four until it was a bubbling mass of melted rock and metal. Undoubtedly they were trying to destroy any more grenades, which was why I'd had the Raptor plant the new one a little way back in the shaft. No lasers reached down there.

Next, the big ships began boring their way in with massed beam fire on two axes and at angles to the access tunnels.

"Crap," I said. "They're going to try to bypass our defenses. Sector four, extrapolate the courses of the shafts they're drilling and display."

I watched the Elladan screens. The two shafts would come in roughly parallel to the access passage, and if they could be bored deep enough, would eventually rip their way into our command center. The only reason they could cut their way in like this was because there was absolutely nothing to interfere with their warships.

"How long?" I asked.

"Approximately six hours," Galen said. "It will become progressively more difficult as they go deeper, of course, because the gasses have to vent back up the drill-hole, interfering with the lasers."

"Is there anything we can do?" I asked. "Ideas?"

"Sneak out and hit them from the side?" Kwon suggested. "We could use our surfboards to land with grenades on their hulls."

I eyed him. "When you're a hammer-man, everything looks like a nail, right?"

Kwon looked confused. "What?"

"Never mind. Good idea, but it's a last resort." I looked around at the rest of them. "Anything else that's got a better chance of succeeding? Anything at all?"

Cybele spoke up. "Can your two ships launch a missile strike or otherwise delay them?"

I mulled that over. "I'll keep it in mind." Having *Valiant* and *Stalker* move in would delay their repairs and expose them to risk unless they simply launched missiles, which would probably expend valuable munitions for little effect. I examined the whole station again, looking around the room at all the displays. "Can this base move?"

"Normally, yes," Galen said. "It has repellers to change its orientation. It also has a fusion engine to push it to alternate orbits, but that has been destroyed."

"All the repellers are down?"

"Yes, though number six has merely lost its associated generator."

"You mean if we got power to it, it would function?"

"Theoretically."

I stood up. "That's what we have to do. Galen, get that repeller working. Put your two best technicians on it. Kwon, you take over here. Assign me a squad for security, but I don't think they'll be landing any more troops until they've drilled as far as they can."

"Okay, boss, but we're blind outside of sector four. Nobody here in the command center can see the ships if they do something else. You sure you don't want me to escort the technicians instead?"

I knew Kwon would rather take the mission, but there was a distinct possibility that my own technical knowhow would be needed to get the repeller working, something Kwon would be useless at. "Sorry Kwon, not this time. I need you here. All right, squad. Let's go."

I sealed up my suit and led the two Elladans and the Raptor squad through the corridors, using my HUD for reference. Those blast doors still intact opened in front of us, showing that our little command staff was on the job.

"Cybele," I said conversationally as we walked, "how many marines did you have to defend this station?"

"Marines?"

"I mean soldiers—close-combat warriors."

"Forty-eight, divided into eight squads of six."

"That's about what I have, yet your people didn't seem to put up much of a fight."

"The lower orders must be compelled to risk their lives. It's a difficult task to force them to fight."

I stopped short, causing the others to do the same. "You mean your soldiers don't want to defend their homes? I would think that even your 'lower orders' would be motivated, at least to avoid being eaten or killed."

"They didn't believe we could lose. In fact, I didn't believe it myself." Her ridiculously perfect face twitched. "It's terribly inconvenient."

I guffawed. "Inconvenient? You need to get a grip on reality, girl."

She leveled a stare as patrician as any Adrienne had ever given me. "I'd rather die with my composure firmly in place than run around uselessly like some hysterical plebian work-wench."

My smile leached away. "Okay. I can respect that, if you're not simply denying reality."

"I deny nothing, and I'm doing my best to help. Shall we go now?"

"Sure." My estimate of the Elladans went up a tiny notch.

Soon, we reached the repeller. Galen was right, the mechanism seemed intact. It was the size of an old hydroelectric turbine. A cave-in had crushed and disconnected the cables running through a short tunnel.

"The generator is behind the rubble," Cybele said.

"Okay, let's get this cleared." I told Kwon to have them turn off the grav-plates in the tunnel and reduce the pull on the others nearby. The Raptors and I soon had the way opened, and the Elladans spliced the cables.

"Kwon, tell Galen to use the repeller to rotate the station continuously."

"You want to start rotating now?"

"There's no need to wait," I told him.

A rumble went through the base as the repeller applied lateral movement to the lumpy sphere of the fortress. I could see the alignment of the Demon lasers abruptly shift, and then the beams shut down. The ships moved to try to regain their angle, but it was too difficult to maintain the precision they needed.

By the time we reached the command center again, they'd stopped trying. Unfortunately, this only bought us a half hour or so until the Demons figured out a nearly perfect counter-tactic.

They landed on the station.

It wasn't clear from our cameras how they clung to the armor—maybe magnetics, maybe cables or external grav-plates—but once they were down, they started drilling with their lasers again.

Now it didn't matter how we twisted and turned. Their ships remained clamped in place, always in the same positions relative to the center.

"Dammit. That didn't go as well as I'd hoped. They've landed."

Kwon perked up. "Now's the time for a raid!"

"Yeah, but how would we do it without everybody dying?"

"I got some ideas," Kwon said with confidence.

"Hold on a minute."

I stared at the displays, and then tapped on the screens, changing to every shot and angle we had. The enemy ships were hidden inside the clouds of billowing hot gases and dust vomiting forth from their bore-holes. Maybe Kwon's surfboard idea could work after all. I told him about the self-generated smokescreen, pointing out the edges of it on the other sector screens.

"That's the key, boss. They won't be able to see us coming over the horizon."

I pointed overhead. "The assault carrier is still hovering out there. They'll pick us off like flies."

"Then we create a diversion. Be back in a few minutes." With that, he stomped out.

I shook my head. Whatever he came up with, it was bound to be simple and effective, as long as he hadn't missed any obvious disadvantage—obvious to me, that was.

Ten minutes later, Kwon called. "Come to the sector three airlock, Captain."

I eyed Galen. He stared flatly back at me. Could I trust him?

"Call me if you need me," I said after a moment's consideration, and I left the Elladans with half a squad of Raptors.

Galen nodded and stared after me.

At the sector-three cargo bay nearest the airlock, I found Kwon with six surfboards and an equal number of grenades nano-welded near their centers of gravity.

"I programmed these to fly toward the assault carrier and blow up," he said.

I immediately saw what he intended. "Did you put in a delay?"

"I sure did. Thirty seconds."

I wasn't sure if that would be enough—you could get to the enemy ships, but could you escape the blast radius?

"I'll pilot one of them," I said.

"Hell, no!" he objected. "You're too important. I was planning on blowing up our dumbest Raptor."

"Kwon, I don't think—"

He laughed loudly. "I'm kidding. I don't trust Raptors with bombs. They're as dumb as the goat-people with them. I'm flying this thing with the Raptors following me. Go back to the control center and watch how it's done."

I nodded reluctantly. "Okay. Kick some ass, but remember I need you alive to keep watching my back. Turn that detonator up to ninety seconds."

"You think so? That's a long time."

"You have to get out of the blast radius."

Kwon's eyes lit up.

"Ah, right. Good thinking. I'll see you soon."

Two squads of Raptors began filing into the cargo bay. Eight of them carried grenades. I stuck around long enough to give a short speech and a salute to those about to die. I had little doubt there would be casualties, maybe heavy ones, but if we could damage the two Demon ships badly enough, even destroy them, we could buy ourselves more time.

That's what this was about.

Buying time.

-22-

When I returned to the control center, my adrenalin was pumping. Cybele flashed me her Helen-of-Troy smile, but I didn't go for it. Even if my libido wanted to go down that rabbit hole, my better judgment overrode it. Why was it that soldiers always think of sex right before a battle?

Was it really cheating if the girl wasn't really human? Then again, she looked human enough. And if we were about to die anyway...

No. I firmly told myself to stay focused on business.

I watched on the station sensors as Kwon and the Raptors jogged down the corridor to the airlock and opened it, easing out onto the surface in six small groups. Each picked up a surfboard and, on a designated signal, they began throwing the boards laterally into space.

Given the dust and gasses, the small objects should go undetected until their repellers were activated. I watched as they abruptly oriented themselves according to Kwon's instructions and headed in the direction of the assault cruiser.

At the same time, Kwon and his troops skittered along the surface of the base and into the dust cloud. They would come over the horizon two hundred yards or less from the enemy, and I hoped the swirling gases and debris from the drilling would hide them well.

Of course, the reverse was also true. How were my men going to see their targets?

The carrier commander would have been wiser to stand off at a good distance, but he'd made the mistake of hovering at the edge of the cloud, which gave him very little time to react to the surfboard grenades. Even so, he shot down all but two. The last grenades detonated close enough to do some serious damage.

Kwon's little force was angling too far to the left. He could have turned on his suit's active sensors, but that might have given away their position.

I called him on the ansible. His suit was the only one equipped with the device other than mine. "Kwon, adjust right ten degrees. The cruiser is about ninety yards in front of you. Throw a grenade and hunker down. I can detonate it at exactly the right time."

"No you can't, boss. Grenades don't have ansibles."

"You're right. Then tell your suit to relay my ansible signal into a radio signal."

"Okay. Suit, do what the boss said."

"Define 'boss,'" I heard his suit say.

"The boss is Captain Cody Riggs, you dumb-ass machine!"

"Nomenclature updated."

The ghostly figure of Kwon rose up and hurled a basketball-sized grenade toward the enemy. It flew straight but off-target as he couldn't see the Demon ship. It also naturally separated from the curving surface below as the base generated almost no gravity.

When it got about halfway there and twenty feet off the ground, a laser snapped from the Demon cruiser and destroyed the mini-nuke.

"Damn," I said.

"It must have automated point defense. We have to crawl closer and stay in the ground clutter."

"Your call, Kwon, but not your job. Sneaking in and planting mines on things is for grunts."

"None of my guys are expendable, boss."

Grumbling, he sent in Raptors. Kwon was right, of course. None of my troops were expendable. But sometimes people had to do dangerous things to win a battle. This was one of those times.

I watched as a Raptor crawled forward, a grenade clipped to his back.

"Tell him to keep his tail down!" I snapped, and Kwon relayed my order, just in time as a laser cut a hole in the fog above.

"He's made it to about thirty yards from the nearest Demon ship, the cruiser," I reported. "As long as he keeps his tail down...twenty-five...twenty..."

Soon the Raptor had almost reached the enemy vessel's shadow, if it'd had one. Critters appeared on the surface of the Demon ship and leaped to the ground.

"Tell him to drop it and crawl back fast!" I yelled, but it was too late. Both sides were blind in the swirling gasses, but with forty or fifty Demons spreading out for a point-blank search, I had only about three seconds to make a decision.

Gritting my teeth, I sent the detonation code. "Everyone hug the dirt!"

A bare eye-blink later, the relayed signal blew the grenade in place. Its high-effect radius of about thirty yards touched the skin of the Demon cruiser and tore up some of it, and the shockwave ripped the ship loose from its moorings, spinning it laterally into space, out of the fight.

The Raptor that carried the grenade was vaporized instantly, along with the searching Demons.

The ground shock also tossed one Raptor off the base, but he was able to use suit repellers to come back.

I realized Kwon had been right. Sometimes you just had to get up-close and personal to get the job done.

The Demon battleship immediately deployed its own ground fighters, which spread out in a ring about sixty yards out. "Hold in place, Kwon. You got company. They're guarding the other ship with bugs."

"Roger."

Checking the two floating damaged ships, I noticed they seemed to be sniping at us with their remaining lasers, but were ineffective due to the dust and debris.

"We haven't got much time before they can get a good shot at us," I said, turning my attention back to the remaining battleship. The big hulk continued to bore deeply into our station. The shaft was less than half an hour from us now. If we couldn't stop them from drilling, we'd have to evacuate to a different part of the base. Putting the control center in the exact middle for security might make sense, but in this case it made us easy to locate. They didn't even have to see us.

"There's a force of thirty to forty Demons moving out in your direction, Kwon. It doesn't look like they can see us yet. They're spread out in an arc and moving slow and blind, but they'll run into you in a minute or two."

Kwon laughed. "No problem. I got this." I saw him and his Raptors backing up, still crawling, until they were around the curve of the station. "Can we get up now, boss?"

"Yes. The Demons can't see you right now."

Kwon then began skimming over the surface on repellers, heading directly away from the enemy, his troops following. Since the battle station was roughly spherical, they were approaching the enemy from the opposite side within minutes.

"The bugs searching for you are out of position," I told Kwon. "Send in a couple guys now, before they come back. I might be able to guide them between guards to get close to the battleship."

I detonated one of our planted grenades near the searching force when they went by, catching a dozen of them in the blast. After that, I focused on giving the two Raptors with grenades point-by-point directions as they crawled ever closer to the battleship.

One got caught by a patrolling scorpion and was killed after a brief but vicious hand-to-hand battle. The other Raptor crept closer and closer, expertly using what cover there was to stay low and in the clutter.

If I'd been the Demon commander, I'd have paused in the drilling every couple of minutes and let the area clear to check it, but fortunately he didn't. The Raptor got all the way to the edge of the battleship and dropped his grenade in a divot next to one of the struts that held it on the surface. Then he began sneaking out of there.

It was agonizing to watch him slink away. The bomb was set, but we had to wait until our man was clear. The rocks were

215

crawling with scorpions. At any moment, I expected them to discover the nuke, in which case the plan would fail.

"Captain, the laser has broken into the interior of the base and is now drilling through improved areas," Galen said in my ear. "We have perhaps five minutes before it strikes the armor of the command center."

"Hang on for a few more seconds," I muttered, watching the Raptor crawl through another brief gap in the enemy lines.

They found him then. Two scorpions fell on the marine, and our troops hugging the rocks took pot-shots at them to help.

"Kwon, I'm going to have to blow the grenade. Our guy should be outside the blast radius, but the explosion will probably leave the area clear of dust and gasses, and then you'll have to deal with whatever survived."

"Okay, boss. Everybody hunker down!"

I bit the bullet and sent the code. "Come on, marine, make it," I muttered as the huge Demon battleship shuddered and broke free on the end where the grenade exploded. It hung on its moorings at the other end like a giant air tank on a hose.

The shockwave touched the Raptor, but he held on, after having been warned. Most of the Demons around him didn't, they were blasted off into space.

"Watch the sky, Kwon! Some of them are coming back."

Kwon and the Raptors fired as they spotted targets, some out in space but unhurt, some on the ground. Getting organized far faster than human troops who'd just had a nuke detonated among them, the Demons who were left formed up and charged at my force.

"Kwon, turn around and haul ass along the surface." That would take them at an oblique angle to the two forces trying to catch them in a pincer move.

Lasers popped and sizzled through space, crisscrossing the dispersing gases. Like football players converging on the guy with the ball, the Demons angled inward, moving faster than my troops in a desperate effort to catch them.

"The sector one airlock is fifty yards in front of you," I told Kwon. "Galen—"

"We've opened it, Captain."

216

"The airlock should be open, Kwon, so dive in. Quit fighting back and run!" Their covering fire wasn't slowing the Demons down anyway.

We lost seven or eight more Raptors before we had to close the airlock. One of them, wounded but carrying a grenade, played dead until all our guys were inside before blowing the weapon in place, taking himself and half the enemy with him.

"Hell yeah," I said, standing up and stabbing my pointing finger at the Elladans. "That's the way you have to fight. If you're going to die anyway, kill as many of the bastards as you can."

"They might have merely captured your Raptor," he replied. "Why die when you don't need to?"

"Because that's what wins wars, kid." It seemed appropriate to call him a kid, even though he looked to be about my age. Right now, I felt ten years older than when I'd first set foot on *Valiant*. "Multiply his sacrifice by a million, and there would be no more Demons."

"There I must disagree with you, Captain. The Demons are bred and hatched far faster than we can repopulate. Their combat power is limited only by their industry to build ships."

"You people have the brains to win, but you lack balls."

Despite me making my point as plainly as I could, Galen remain confused. I guessed that his upbringing and culture made it impossible to see certain things.

Galen was smart and competent, but effete. There was no point in ranting at him. The best I could hope for was that this experience would sink in and change his fundamental thinking about this formerly clean, distant war they were fighting, a war that had finally come to the pretty people of their perfect planet.

Kwon came stomping into the control center. "Not too bad, boss. You think they'll send more bugs?"

"You sound like you hope they do."

He bellowed with laughter, releasing tension. "So what?"

I shook my head and turned to Galen. "Any Demon ships moving this way?"

"Our sensors are spotty, but we don't see any right now."

I activated my ansible. "Valiant? Any enemy heading for us?"

"Not at this moment, Captain, but they are still busy with similar operations. They appear to be doing their best to take as many prisoners as they can."

I wondered why. "Thanks. Give me Hansen."

"Hansen here."

"Status report."

"We're lurking out here, repairing damage as ordered. *Valiant* is near full effectiveness, but *Stalker* is in pretty bad shape. Marvin has disappeared, turned off his transponder and I can't find him even with active sensors."

He said this bitterly, and I knew why. The robot could have helped a lot with the repairs.

"Do your best. I'll set my suit to keep trying Marvin."

"The Demons are still in action," Hansen went on. "They're mopping up everything off the planet's surface, taking thousands of prisoners, especially from the bases on the moon."

"Stand by." I turned to Galen. "Have the Demons ever taken prisoners before?"

"A few now and again, but not in large numbers and always among the lower orders. The truth is that we've never lost a battle before, so this is all new to us."

"Hansen, any ideas about why they're taking prisoners?" I asked.

"Nope."

"Are they repairing their ships?"

A pause. "Yes," he said, "they seem to be concentrating on the assault carriers. That makes no sense…"

"Then it must mean something. How far out are the Whales?"

"Over a day away, still."

I chewed my lip. "I have an idea. I'll get back with you. Riggs out." To Cybele, I said, "Bring up a simulation of the strategic situation showing the Ketan fleet inbound and the Demons here."

"It won't be accurate in terms of ship numbers and types."

218

"Doesn't matter. Model it based on what you know of the Ketans, and you can use one assault carrier to represent the Demons."

A few minutes later, her large screen displayed a graphic of the area and she said, "Ready."

"Calculate how soon a Demon ship would have to begin fleeing in order to get away clean and curve around to head for home as fast as possible."

Cybele's long fingers flickered over her console. It seemed to me these people could move their fingers faster than a human could. The picture changed, lines showing courses. "Here are three solutions. They represent the earliest, latest, and optimal cases."

"Why three?"

"Because the time the Demon ship gains by leaving sooner is closely matched by the advantage it loses by not waiting for the Ketan fleet to slow."

I saw what she meant. As they decelerated, the Whales were making it harder and harder for themselves to catch up to any Demon ships that decided to flee.

Cybele went on, "The optimum solution is to begin acceleration in approximately ten hours, at an angle to the approaching Ketans, on a course that will dive toward our central stars and use their gravity to slingshot around, returning to Tartarus."

"Do you have the acceleration parameters for *Valiant* and *Stalker*?"

Cybele gave me an appraising look. "Of course, Captain. We're intelligence specialists. It's our job to know everything."

I ignored her flirtation as best I could. "Work out solutions for those two ships to intercept the Demons' predicted path—earliest, latest and optimum."

After a moment, she came up with answers. "The earliest is the optimum, which would mean leaving right away, assuming our predictions are true. Your ships have a decided speed advantage over the Demons, and so can easily catch them, given the long journey back to Tartarus. This does not take into account any damage your ships might still have."

This eased my mind. "Okay. I think I know what's going on. Hansen, you listening?"

"Here, sir."

"The Demons are repairing their assault carriers because they're the only ones with enough room for thousands of prisoners. They'll probably use hibernation drugs and stack them like cordwood for transport home. I expect they'll give those ships all available fuel and any Demon crew they want to save, too."

"They want the people? Why?"

"Slaves. Breeding stock. Experimentation. Who knows? The Demons just set the Elladans back a decade or more. Their next fleet will be stronger, I'd predict. Their strategy almost worked and they know it."

"We'll have to destroy the ships."

I nodded, even though he couldn't see me. "At least we have a long window to do it. Three months, Cybele says."

"Who's Cybele?"

"The Elladan tech down here," I said casually.

Hansen snorted. He knew me too well. "Don't worry, I'll cover for you."

"There's nothing to cover for," I snapped.

"Hey, no problem. Oh, damn."

"What?"

"Six Demon ships have broken off. They're moving toward you."

-23-

"Crap," I muttered.

I'd hoped the Demons would leave us alone for a while. But that just wasn't going to happen. They were sending another six ships to try to dig us out.

"We could launch a missile strike," Hansen said on the ansible in my helmet.

"How are we set for missiles?"

My XO paused. "Not too well. We've only got thirty-three in the stockpile. But we could send in the Daggers along with them on a fast pass, swing them around and recover them later. That would present no risk to *Valiant*."

"What do the simulations say about likelihood of success?"

I waited while Valiant ran the calculations, and then the ship's voice replied. "The most probable outcome is three Demon ships destroyed, fourteen Daggers lost and all missiles expended."

"Forget it," I said. "That doesn't buy us much extra time, and given the way we're buttoned up, it hardly matters whether we have three ships or six on our asses. Even if we did take out three of them, they would send more in. The best strategy is to fight hard right here. How are *Stalker*'s engines?"

"Sixty-eight percent."

I looked up at Cybele's screen again. "I think we only have to hold out for about ten hours. That's when I'm betting the Demons are going to send home their best, least damaged assault carriers full of prisoners. If they don't have us by then, they won't ever get us."

"Yes, but then they'll just blow your station to fragments. How is that better?" Hansen asked.

"Remember, they have few if any, nuclear warheads left. They might have used all of them in the battle. They're getting ready to run from the Whales, and they don't have much time left."

"They still have their main batteries," Hansen objected stubbornly.

"Right, but if they've failed to dig us out, lasers won't matter much. They can slag the surface of this base all they want—but I don't think they'll bother. Beams take energy, which takes fuel to generate, and they'll have given every bit of their extra supply to the assault carriers that are running away, leaving just enough to fight a suicidal rearguard action against the Whales in order to cover the escape."

"That's a lot of supposition, Captain."

"But it fits all the facts and past battle simulations that the Whales sent us in their initial intel. Just keep repairing and stand by."

"Great. Standing by. Hansen out."

I knew how he felt. Helpless, constrained by my orders and the need to get our tiny two-ship squadron back in shape. I wondered how many Raptors Kreel had lost in the battle and when lack of crew would begin to degrade *Stalker*'s effectiveness.

We were being ground down more and more. Just one more battle, I told myself. Then we could rebuild, maybe recruit some Elladans…

And then try to make it home.

"They're coming," Galen said.

I consulted the sensor arrays. We'd repaired a few of them, just enough to look around at what was going on out on the surface of this rock.

The dust had cleared, left behind as the rock spun and orbited Ellada. Adjusting the crude instruments, I saw that the enemy ships would be here in a few minutes.

"Galen, use the station's repeller to get this rock spinning faster." As a defensive measure, it was best to have the base moving at a higher rate of speed. With luck it would be impossible to land on. Moving around on the base would, however, become more difficult.

"Edging up the rotation—it will take time."

"Do what you can. Please alter the direction of spin to make the shafts they drilled hard to access."

"We'll set up a complex motion that will create two poles at the ends of the axis of rotation," Galen replied. "I'll work to adjust those poles to armored areas. That way the current airlocks and breaches will remain under heavy spin."

I followed that with a model on my screen. Tapping at it, I was soon satisfied.

"Good idea. I'm going to detonate any grenades that swing under the Demon ships as they approach. Kwon, get ready to plant some more. How many do we have?"

"Eleven."

"Do we have anything else big?"

"Four heavy lasers and four heavy rocket launchers. Those are emplaced to cover the main tunnels."

"How heavy?"

Kwon shrugged. "Heavy for marines, but nothing that would hurt an armored ship."

"Okay. Tactical nukes will have to do it. Here they come."

The lead vessel, a battleship, began firing. Its rolling broadsides dug a dozen shallow trenches in the surface rock. They wised up about two minutes later and began concentrating their firepower onto one spot. A trench appeared in its wake as the station spun gently beneath the concentration of glowing beams. The vaporized rock spewed gas and dust, but the debris dissipated quickly because of the movement of the surface.

The size of the chunks of rock that flew off increased. Centrifugal force grew on our bodies as the station turned faster and faster. The other Demon vessels joined the first, and soon more than thirty lasers blasted at us as they unloaded with their broadsides.

"They don't seem to be short on fuel, boss," Kwon said.

"Guess not. Take half a squad with one grenade each and get to airlock six. It's off the line of their drilling but close enough to plant grenades. Get moving."

I watched Kwon and his guys move through the base to the airlock. As soon as it had rotated out of sight of the enemy, I told Galen to pop the hatch and sent Kwon out to plant two grenades, separated as widely as possible, just off the predicted line of bombardment.

"You got two minutes to get out, plant those bombs and get back," I told him.

"No problem, Captain." He grabbed one grenade and a sidekick Raptor grabbed another. I didn't bother to argue about him doing it himself.

A few minutes passed, and I began to get antsy.

"Kwon? Drop it and get back," I insisted.

"The nuke wants to zoom into space. I'm trying to wedge it, but I can't."

I realized what he meant. Everything on the spinning surface now wanted to fly upward. "My bad. I should have thought of that before I sent you. Come back in. You can try again in a few minutes."

Kwon didn't answer. On camera, I saw his Raptor sidekick turn and bound back toward the airlock, undoubtedly using his suit repeller to stay near the surface, but Kwon stayed where he was as the rotating station carried him inexorably toward the horizon…and the enemy.

"Kwon!"

Still no answer.

"Kwon! They're going to see you in a few seconds!"

He was standing on the surface. I wasn't sure how. Maybe he'd found something magnetic to stick his boots to, or he was using repellers for down-force. Widening his stance, he took the grenade he carried by the handle and held it low to the ground near his back foot.

"Kwon! Dammit, man!"

When the Demon ships came into view, he gave a mighty heave and flung the grenade straight toward them. It skimmed along the surface for a moment then, as the station was curved, it left the asteroid and moved to meet the enemy.

As soon as he released the mini-nuke, Kwon turned to leap backward, skimming the ground as he accelerated on his repeller. It took a few seconds for him to overcome the forward motion the ground had imparted, and then he gained distance.

I tore my perception away from him to watch the grenade. The thing must be too small, or maybe it got lost in the clutter of small rocks and gravel constantly cascading off the accelerating station like pinwheel sparks. Seconds ticked by…

I sent the code to blow it as soon as it entered maximum blast radius, afraid that one of the enemy ships would see it and pick it off with a point defense laser. It whited out my vision. When it cleared, several of the Demon vessels showed damage.

They backed up then, which they should have done in the first place, standing off at several miles distance but still close enough to fire lasers with easy accuracy. I guided Kwon back to the open airlock as it came around.

"That was a crazy thing to do," I told him.

"Yeah, wasn't it great?"

"If they'd seen you, one ship laser would have left nothing but your boots."

Kwon only laughed. "Nobody lives forever."

The Demons resumed their blasting, and now we had nothing that could touch them. "Galen, how long until that trench gets deep enough to hurt?"

After he ran some calculations, the Elladan reported to me with a frown. "In about six hours, the station will begin to come apart from tidal stress due to the damage. I may be able to extend that another two hours by judicious variations in our motion."

I rubbed my jaw through my faceplate. "I hope they run out of fuel."

"Hope ain't a plan, boss. Don't you always got a plan?" Kwon had been with my dad and me long enough to know that sometimes we didn't, but never admitted it.

"I do. A piece of one, at least. Just let me think."

"While you think, I'm gonna sleep, and the Pigs too. Let me know if you need a nap." Kwon moved to an empty area and lay down on the deck, his suit becoming his bed. I didn't blame him. We'd been up for more than thirty hours straight, and it was a good time to do it, with nothing but those incessant lasers to threaten us. I noticed two of the Elladans slumped in their chairs as well, and I fought off a wave of sympathetic fatigue.

Stepping out of my suit, I did a few light calisthenics to get my blood pumping and began to pace. What could I do? Assuming Galen got us those eight hours, we were still about two short of when I predicted they would send off their carriers and set up to engage the whales. I sure wished Elladans had shield technology, but even if we'd given it to them when we had first made contact two weeks ago, they wouldn't have been able to deploy it.

Somehow, I needed to buy us at least two hours, preferably more, as I might be way off in my estimates.

I had no idea how to do it, except by using my ships.

I got back in my suit and was just about to contact them when, finally, I heard a tinny voice in my ear. "Captain Marvin to Cody Riggs."

"That's Captain Riggs to you, robot," I said with an involuntary grin. "Are you monitoring my situation?"

"Yes. My sensor suite is very effective."

"Then you know we have six to eight hours before the station breaks up, and I have only a few shaky ideas on how to live through it, so if you can think of anything, I'd appreciate your input."

"You want me to save your life?" he asked.

"Yes, if it's not too damn much trouble."

"If I do, I believe a Star Force citation would be in order."

"You want a medal? I already explained I'm not empowered to give medals, but I can put you in for all sorts of them once we get home. And to do that, I have to be alive."

Marvin's voice turned pensive. "Perhaps Lieutenant Commander Hansen will fill out the necessary paperwork if you don't survive…"

"Hansen hates you, Marvin."

"I consider 'hate' to be a strong, often offensive term—"

My voice rose. He was getting to me. "Marvin, with the possible exception of Hoon and me, *nobody* likes you. If you want to be appreciated, you need to keep helping, and maybe display some emulation of positive human emotion, such as empathy for your fellow Star Force personnel. Being an officer isn't about making rank, it's about stepping up and contributing, even if you're faking the feeling behind your actions."

"I thought faking is akin to lying, which is usually perceived negatively. Also, I have contributed many positive things to this expedition."

"And negative things too, Marvin. As far as I'm concerned, you're not even out of the hole you dug by getting Valiant's original officers eaten."

"My intentions were good," he said after a moment's hesitation.

"Welcome to the road to hell, Marvin."

"I don't understand."

"Look up the reference in your database."

A pause. "I see. So how many positive acts do I need to perform before I am 'out of the hole'?"

"A bunch, Marvin. A whole big, frigging bunch. Now get on it, would you?"

"Roger. Captain Marvin out."

I couldn't tell from those few words whether Marvin was motivated or pissed off. He was a machine, after all.

"God, I need some sleep," I said, rubbing my face. I caught Galen and Cybele staring at me. "Okay, I could have handled that better. But it's Marvin."

Galen looked dismissive. He didn't know who Marvin was. Cybele smiled, and that smile that made my loins twitch. My body had a mind of its own. Damn, I needed to get laid, too, which meant I had get back to *Valiant* and Adrienne soon.

A headache pounded behind my eyes, so I dialed up a stim and a painkiller.

The rumbling and groaning of the station didn't help. It was a spinning lumpy ball four hundred yards across and largely made of rock. The asteroid was under two dramatic stresses. The repeller that Galen used to constantly vary its motion and the massed laser fire from the demons. Chunks of it kept breaking off and flying away into space.

I'd be pleasantly amazed if this rock held together as long as we'd estimated.

-24-

Six hours later, things were becoming grim.

The laser-bombardment had never even paused. All my hopes and dreams they'd run out of power were fruitless. Whatever these Demon ships were made of, it seemed like they had limitless firepower.

Our once-spherical battle station looked more like a starfish with extra limbs. They'd dug holes so deep they weren't holes anymore—they were more like chasms.

The fortress' main sector tunnels now protruded like hundred-yard high towers beyond the remaining rock surface, and many of the subterranean structures stood exposed. The external walls of the cargo bays, for example, showed like half-buried domes, many of them ruptured by the lasers as they continued their relentless cutting and drilling. I had Kwon pull everything and everyone back to the central area.

"It's time to make some hard calls, troops," I said to everyone crowded inside the command center. I didn't expect to hear anything from the stoic Raptors, but I figured it was nice to include them as I laid out our doom.

Turning to Galen, I asked the question in my mind without hesitation. "How long until they fry us?"

"Approximately one hour. If we get inside the armored vault, we may last another hour."

"But if we do that, we'll be worms in a can with no options."

"Yes."

"Forget the vault. Have you made any changes in your estimate of their carriers' optimum departure time?"

Galen shook his head, which wobbled a little as if it was full of jelly. I'd become familiar with these small variations from the human norm over time. Really, their disguise, or whatever it was, could only be impressive if you didn't look at it too closely.

"The math has not changed," he said.

"I see two possibilities then. We can abandon the station and try to sneak away to be picked up later, hoping they don't see us. Or, *Valiant* and *Stalker* can launch an all-out attack on these six ships and try to swoop in and rescue us."

Kwon threw his big paw in the air. I pointed to him.

"How 'bout we use the surfboards to escape? Fly toward *Valiant* until they can pick us up later."

Galen cleared his throat. "I believe remaining here is the wiser course. They may break off early. In that case, these riskier plans would be counterproductive."

"But soon we'll be out of options," I pointed out.

Kwon jumped in again, sounding angry. "Riggs, there's no way I want to die in here, smelling this chicken's guts as they fry him. Let me try my plan. Sure, I'll probably die—but at least it will be in open space, doing something."

I listened to him and nodded thoughtfully. "So we're pretty much down to two choices. Risk everything now with a low probability of survival, or wait for the end with a zero likelihood of survival."

Everyone stared at me, wondering what I would do. Except for Kwon, that is. He gave me a knowing grin.

"We're going to take a chance," I said with certainty. "We're going to escape this trap. I like Kwon's plan. The odds are good that a few of us will slip away in the confusion."

"Shit-yeah!" Kwon said.

Galen looked sick.

"Galen," I ordered, "crank the fortress' rate of spin up to maximum. I want this base twirling like a puke-inducing amusement park ride. We're going to need all the velocity we can get when we go."

"Yes, Captain," Galen said stiffly, turning back to his console.

I looked at the diagram of the station. "Suit, record the direction *Valiant* and *Stalker* are located relative to the star patterns you can see."

"Recording…recording…complete," it replied as I gave its cameras a good view of all our screens.

I went on, "The sector five airlock looks to be the best bet. Kwon, get everything we have left up there. There's no point in waiting. Everyone make sure you have full supplies of air, water, and whatever else you need. Galen, how long can you survive in your suits?"

"At least three days."

"Good. We might need the time." I gestured. "Let's go."

We trooped our way to airlock five. By the time we got there, we could feel the heavy centrifugal force even through the gravplates that struggled to counteract it. I said, "Everyone clip on a safety line. As soon as we open the airlock doors, one slip could send you sliding out into space in the wrong direction. We'll have to time this just right."

Kwon smart-welded several thick anchors to the inside of the passageway, and everyone clipped on their safety lines. Next, we overrode the airlock to open both doors at once. The atmosphere roared out for a few moments, eventually leaving us all in vacuum and hanging from our lines.

Magnetizing my boots, I stood up on the floor, which now seemed to be sloping steeply toward the opening due to the combined forces. Stars streaked by as we waited there at the end of the mad merry-go-round. I hoped the station wouldn't wobble enough to bring us into the line of the enemy lasers.

"No point in waiting. Kwon, hand me those cutters."

The device he gave me resembled a pair of giant scissors composed of two chainsaws, except the edges were made of spinning monofilament that would cut through anything less dense than stardust. A powerful servo would force the blades past each other, and *snip*, it would be done.

"Okay, everyone grab a surfboard. Elladans, pair up with Raptors and hold on tight to them."

Once that was done, I told them, "Unroll your safety lines until you're dangling off them, but stay inside the corridor. They should be plenty strong enough. Then turn off your magnetics and repellers."

I did the same, and soon we were all sitting on the tilted deck as if waiting to be dumped off for an orbital drop. I carefully gathered all of our safety lines in one hand and set the two blades of the cutter on either side. "Suit, are you able to analyze the star patterns going by?"

"Star patterns analyzed."

"Synchronize and calculate when to cut these safety lines so that we are launched directly away from the Demon ships, keeping the base between us. Make sure you include the delay in sliding out of the airlock."

"Calculated."

"Listen up, everyone. When I cut the lines, we're going to slide out like a bunch of children off a waterslide. Reel the loose ends in, hang on to your surfboards and your buddies, and we should be on our way. Don't turn on any repellers or transmit with any com-links, either. We want to be as hard to see as possible. Unless there's a life-and-death emergency, nobody moves, nobody transmits, nobody does anything for an hour. Everyone understand?"

When I had acknowledgement, I placed my hands firmly on the cutters and said, "Okay, suit. You actuate the servos at the right time, on the next rotation starting…now."

Less than a second later, the cutters snapped shut and the centrifugal force spat us out into the void. We spun helplessly near each other like a flock of wingless birds, spreading out with the tiny variations in our trajectories. I suppressed the urge to use my suit to stop spinning, acutely aware that any use of power or emanations might be picked up by the Demons.

I told myself that every second we waited meant almost a mile of distance gained. If we could make it to an hour, we'd be three thousand miles away—very close in space terms, but hopefully far enough to make us very difficult to spot, especially as we'd be directly across from the crumbling base.

"Boss?" Kwon said in my helmet.

"Radio silence!" I hissed, aghast at the breach in discipline.

"It's the ansible. They can't hear it."

My stomach unclenched. "How do you know for sure?"

"Marvin told me. I asked him once. He said the only way to intercept it is if you have an original piece of the quantum stuff inside."

"That makes sense. It works by some form of entanglement, which means you have to…never mind. Okay. So, why'd you call?"

"Umm…"

"Well, thanks for the idea anyway, Kwon," I disconnected and decided to use the same trick to talk to Hansen. "Suit, use the ansible to contact *Valiant*."

"Channel open."

A deep dry voice came on. "Hansen here. I was starting to worry. Your base looks like crap, sir."

"Not our base anymore. We're in space, flying directly away from the Demon ships, about three thousand miles out."

"We're on our way."

"Not yet!" I took a deep breath. "Much as I'd like to be picked up, we're still too close. If you start looking for us with actives, they might too, and we can't turn on our transponders. You need to wait until they send off the assault carriers with their prisoners and their combat ships are maneuvering to engage the Whales. Then you can sneak in and grab us."

"You still think they're gonna do that?"

"Betting on it."

"And if they don't?"

"Then I hope my waste recycling system keeps working because we'll be out here a while."

Hansen snorted. "Your call, Skipper."

"Yes, it is. How're the repairs going?"

"Good. *Stalker* is above eighty percent."

"Where's Marvin now?" I asked.

"He took off after he gave us some data. I tried to keep eyes on him, but he swung around Trinity-7, and I never saw him come out from behind it."

"I think he has a cloaking device, and he doesn't want to let us know," I said.

"I wish *we* had one."

"Yeah. Tell Adrienne I said hi. Riggs out."

An hour later, Hansen reported that the Demon assault carriers had begun a high-speed burn to slingshot themselves around Trinity's central double star, just as we expected, running away from the decelerating Whales. The remaining Demon ships were setting up to die in a rearguard action.

We drifted, and drifted. Many hours later, Hansen called.

"Those Whale ships are big mothers—and heavy. They're just coming into long range. Their gun ports are lighting up."

"Their atmosphere is very dense," I replied. "They must be under immense pressure within their ships. I'd hate to see what happens when one ruptures."

"Maybe that's why they don't like space travel so much."

I took the opportunity to tell everyone they could use repellers and attitude jets to stop tumbling and gather together for eventual pickup. It was a tremendous relief to see the universe halt its carousel spin.

Hansen relayed the action to my helmet using the ansible. It wasn't as good as a full tactical display, but it was better than nothing.

The Whales fired one massive salvo of missiles, which apparently turned out to have some fancy anti-interception countermeasures, because most of the Demons were wiped out by the barrage alone. Before they died, the Demons returned fire. For a few minutes, the heavens filled with fireworks.

Those Demon ships that survived were burned down mercilessly. Only six Whale ships were destroyed. As I'd expected, they went up like bombs when they ruptured. The released gas seemed flammable—probably methane and oxygen. With so much high-pressure atmosphere inside, they formed massive, brief fireballs in space.

If I'd been in charge, I'd have chased down the escaping prison ships, but the Whales didn't bother. They simply cruised on to Ellada, smashing everything that looked hostile. Once they circled the planet, they began a leisurely, efficient course change that would take them home in a few weeks.

"So much destruction," I marveled. These three peoples might be able to accomplish great things if they weren't so busy blowing one another up.

Hansen contacted me when the battle ended. "We're on approach, Captain Riggs," he said. "We have you on active sensors, and everything looks five by five."

"Remember to use repellers only," I replied. "Think of the irony of being fried by fusion deceleration just when life was getting good."

"Getting good?" Hansen chuckled. "What's changed?"

"Don't you know? When the Whales leave, we'll have the only functional heavy warships above Ellada, so we can have whatever we want."

"Now you're talking. Their women are hot. I hope they're friendly."

"You and Sakura still not getting along?"

"Does it show?"

Valiant approached at frightening speed, coming to a position of rest nearby before drifting slowly over. The assault airlock gaped, and I eagerly led our battered gaggle of suited figures to land on its broad deck.

As soon as the door had shut and atmosphere was restored, I opened my faceplate and gestured for Galen to remove his helmet. He took it off and sniffed the air suspiciously.

"Sorry we don't have the nice baths you're used to, but we do have showers and something resembling soap and towels. Kwon will get you squared away."

"Soap?" Galen asked, alarmed. "My translation indicates you're talking about a combination of lye and ash."

"That's the basics. There is perfume in there as well."

Galen shook his head. "Such things are toxic to us. We only bathe in warm water. Nutrients are optional, but pleasant."

"Nutrients? Like what?"

"Earths, organics..."

I pictured dirty water and shrugged. "Whatever does it for you. We can accommodate your needs."

I turned to Kwon. "Once they've bathed and eaten, assign them quarters and lock them in. Put a guard at each door. Take everything from them except their underwear—if they're wearing any."

"I'll see to it personally," Kwon said, grinning at the Elladans.

235

"Captain—" Galen began to protest.

"I'm sorry, Galen," I said. "I can't take any chances. You've infected my crew before with some kind of agent, and I can't allow that to happen again. This should only be for a few hours…unless you'd rather occupy a cell in the brig?"

Galen drew himself up stiffly. "Confinement to quarters will suffice."

"Thought so. Carry on, Kwon."

First, I dropped off the suit at the armory. Muttering about how I smelled, I headed for my quarters, telling *Valiant* that I'd be on the bridge in a few minutes.

When I got there, I felt disappointed that Adrienne wasn't waiting for me. But I suppressed my annoyance. After all, she wasn't my concubine, lounging around on furs. She was a Star Force officer, one who was no doubt busy right now.

After a quick rejuvenating shower I put on a fresh uniform and headed for the bridge. On my way through the ship, crew and marines greeted me enthusiastically, and a round of applause swept the bridge as I entered.

I smiled, but said, "Back to work, people. All I did was get suckered by some backstabbers and survive."

"You should be in bed," Hansen said, standing up to shake my hand.

"With my favorite logistics officer," I said under my breath, winking. "I'll get some sleep soon enough, but we need to strike while the iron is hot, before the Elladans start to feel too safe."

"Valiant, connect me to Argos," I said.

Argos was wearing a new, more dramatic uniform when he came into view.

"Did you do something dramatic, Argos?" I asked him.

He frowned. "Certainly not anything like what you suggested. I've been presented with new powers of office by my government in an entirely legitimate way."

Nodding, I decided not to pursue the matter.

"I now represent the entire space fleet orbiting Ellada," I said. "Fortunately, I consider us to be allies. We have a strained relationship, but we're still allies."

"Don't forget about the Ketans," Argos warned me.

236

"I haven't—but then again, they've just left the system. But I didn't call you to threaten you." I smiled broadly.

"Good!" Argos exclaimed. "Since you're an allied fleet, I've made arrangements for your comfort. Recall our prior agreement?"

"About supplies?" I asked.

"Not just that. You've expressed the need for relaxation on our beaches. Come down to our world and we'll make sure your stay is enjoyable."

This was a surprise. I'd been thinking of asking for these considerations, but I'd been reluctant to ask. After all, they'd just suffered a devastating attack.

The odd thing was that now that Argos was offering exactly what I wanted, I found myself suspicious of his motives. If my crew was all on a beach somewhere, they wouldn't be aboard ship by definition. And contact with the natives—presumably intimate contact in some cases—might lead to further difficulties.

While I pondered my options, Argos kept selling his world like a travel agent.

"The best tropical island we have will be at your disposal. You and your entire crew will be allowed to rest and recuperate, not just in comfort, but in luxury."

"What about my ships?" I asked. "If we're all down on the planet surface, who will repair them?"

"We will, of course! Out of a profound sense of gratitude."

"I see."

"Did I mention the entertainment?" Argos asked. "The dancers? Countless servants of both genders?"

Thinking about Cybele, I felt myself being tempted. A whole island full of such lovely creatures…it almost seemed too perfect.

"I accept your generous offer," I said.

"Excellent! I'll make the arrangements immediately. If you would only transport your crew down to these coordinates today—"

"I will," I interrupted, "but first I'm making certain small changes to the plan."

"Changes? What kind of changes?"

"First off, I'll send only half my crew down at a time. I'll rotate them every few week days, but only after a complete medical and psychological examination has been conducted while the returning crew is in isolation. No Elladan will be allowed to set foot on board my ships in the meantime. Further—"

"Stop! Stop this insulting tirade!" Argos fumed.

"Tirade? I'm quite calm."

Argos looked frustrated. "You don't trust us. Even after fighting shoulder-to-shoulder, one species helping another— you still don't trust us."

"Oh, I'm a very trusting person," I said. "But I also prefer to verify that my comrades have my best interests at heart."

Argos snorted. "That's equivalent to paranoia."

"Call it what you will. Do you accept my terms, or should I move my ships out of orbit? We have other things to do."

Argos sweated. "You can't leave. We don't have any protection. Another Demon fleet might be cruising in stealthily even now to surprise us."

"My terms?"

"They're accepted," Argos said bitterly.

"Good. We'll be in touch soon."

The channel closed, and I took the time to reflect on our relationship with the Elladans.

It was a complex one. We were cooperating, after a fashion, but neither of us trusted the other any farther than we could throw a Ketan.

-25-

A week later, I found myself sipping a passable imitation of rum punch and putting my feet up on the rail of a gazebo overlooking China Beach. That's what I'd decided to call our leisure facility, after the famous—or maybe notorious—R&R location I'd read about in the Vietnam War. I'd studied all sorts of military history, and the incongruity of a peaceful slice of heaven just a couple of hours from the bloody jungles had always stuck in my mind.

Our China Beach was better than the earthly version, in my estimation. No one was fighting nearby, so I didn't feel a bit guilty about taking some time off.

Stalker cruised in a geosynchronous orbit guarding us. *Valiant* sat grounded nearby for easy access, with her brainbox and a rotating half-crew aboard always alert for trouble.

I squeezed Adrienne's hand, and she leaned over to kiss me deeply. I brushed her hair off her tanned face. A few days of sun and relaxation had bronzed us both, me more than her.

"Quarters?" I asked, wondering if her affection was a signal for a romantic interlude.

"Mm," she said with a wink. "Later, love. Actually, I wanted to talk to you about the recruiting."

"All work and no play makes Cody a dull boy."

"You're far from dull—and you've been playing quite enough."

239

"Hey, I've been working, too," I protested.

And I had been. Between long discussions with a resigned Galen and negotiations with a still-mulish Argos for everything I wanted, I'd been digesting the deluge of information from the Elladan databases. I really hadn't had that much time to simply lie around. My sand volleyball game was getting pretty good, though.

"I know you've been busy, but the crew has had enough rest. They need to be put back to work soon, or they'll get soft." Adrienne pointed out over the rail, where we could see people swimming in the crystal-clear blue ocean and sunning themselves in the sand.

The Raptors kept to themselves in a complex a quarter mile down the coast. The humans and the Elladans were all around me. Most of the Elladans had been assigned to make sure we were as comfortable as possible. I'd made sure there weren't so many locals they'd overwhelm us. As expected, most of my men and a few of my women had found themselves new relationships. Romance had blossomed all over the beaches.

The Elladans were mostly from the lower orders, the ones with collars. After a bit of debate among my officers, I'd ordered the collars removed. It had taken a laser-torch to do it. The neckpieces were designed to be permanent. That fact particularly bugged me. It told me that these people had no hope of advancement beyond their slave status.

A dozen or so of the Elladans assigned to us were from the middle classes, the managers. They were appalled by the removal of collars, and several of them quit, demanding to be sent back. I guess they didn't like the idea of their former servants moving up in the world. I never did understand some people's tendency to see the good fortune of others as bad for themselves.

Probably a few of the newly freed were spies or informants, but I wasn't too worried. I doubted these people were *all* sympathetic to their ruling class. As long as we didn't come out as anti-Elladan, they probably wouldn't do us any harm.

I pushed away my thoughts, grunted and put my sandaled feet on the decking. Setting down my drink, I picked up a ripe mango-like fruit. "Okay, Mistress Turnbull, what's on your mind?"

Adrienne shrugged and rubbed her neck. "As you know, the staff has been interviewing the Elladans, trying to identify potential recruits. Most of them have no skills beyond menial service jobs or escort services." She said this with more than a hint of disgust.

"Different people, different practices," I said mildly. "Their customs make the lower orders available for sexual service to their upper classes."

"I'm aware of that. As I see it, the problem is that they seem to be lumping us into the 'upper class' category. Crewmen are taking advantage. The slaves see our people as superior to them, so they're not going to refuse when someone asks…or even hints."

"But you explained repeatedly that they *could* say no without any repercussions, right?"

Adrienne clenched her fists. "Yes, but if you were them, would you say no?"

I shrugged helplessly. "We can't change their culture overnight, and we need to gender-balance the crew better. I'm amazed we've held together this long, frankly. We also simply need more personnel. Everyone is doing two or three jobs. Look," I said, taking her face in my hands, "we've talked this to death. We have to do what we have to do, and we're giving them a chance at a better life and a huge status increase. We even told them that if ever we reach Earth, they can return to Ellada if they want. It would be the best thing in the universe to open regular travel between our worlds. It would probably improve both societies. Now can we get back to business?"

"All right." She kissed my palm and sat back down with a roll of her shoulders. "Business. Almost all of them have high potential to be trained for service in Star Force. They test well above average. They won't let us do any physical tests on them, and they're keeping their anatomy secret."

"Everyone has their taboos."

She shook her head. "I think it's more than that. If they were actually humans, I would have to conclude their ancestors had been genetically modified for health and beauty."

I almost shrugged, but I thought the better of it. Personally, I could use crew replacements that were super-attractive. Apparently, it bugged Adrienne.

"We can't really mate with them, you know," she said. "There can't be any children. If we stay here long term, we'll form fruitless relationships."

"That's interesting, but hardly a problem two weeks in."

"I disagree," she said. "People are pair-bonding. At least our humans are. I think the Elladans are playing along in accordance with their caste system."

"I still don't—"

"Hear me out. What if we take these people with us into space? What if our crewmen want to marry Elladans? And what if the Elladans get tired of shaping themselves into human form?"

This last statement made me look down at her. "You think they're doing that? On purpose, just to fool us?"

"I'm not sure of their motives, but they are definitely shape-shifting into human form because we're here. They can't want to do that forever. What if Hansen marries Cybele, and then she decides she wants to look like a goat instead?"

I laughed. I couldn't help it, despite the fact I knew it was a bad idea. Adrienne gave me a cold stare.

"I don't know what we'll do," I said, "but I'll have a good laugh when that day comes."

She scooted away from me. "Well, that's my report. I don't recommend that we recruit any Elladans for our crews. They are too different, too odd. We can't trust them, either."

Drawing in a breath, I let it out slowly. I knew I'd regret my next action, but I didn't' see a way around it.

"Objection overruled," I said.

"Meaning?"

"We're going to do it. We're going to recruit Elladans. Our crews are too low in number. These people at least look like us, and the lower orders are obedient. We'll actively recruit among them so we can survive. I have no idea how many battles are ahead, but I do know how many losses we can take before we get home."

Adrienne looked thoughtful—which was good, because I thought she was going to get angry.

"I still say it's a bad idea, Cody. But I understand your reasoning. You did the same thing with the Raptors."

"And that's worked out pretty well. Make sure, love, that you're not thinking with the jealous side of your brain. Try to stay rational when thinking about a ship full of beauties."

She frowned. I'd said the wrong thing, and the anger I thought I'd avoided was coming on now.

"I demand an equal number of males and females—if we get anyone to come along."

I shrugged. "Not going to happen. We'll test them and take the best that volunteer."

Huffing, she left my side.

A few days later, she went to work in earnest. Whatever she really thought of my plan, she was implementing it without reservation.

Interested Elladans were recruited and tested. We started a training program, focusing on physical fitness and technical know-how first. Surprisingly few Elladans dropped out. They were all young, fit, and best of all, motivated. They learned fast and absorbed our Star Force lessons like sponges. The only challenge I found was to minimize any blatant favoritism by our own people toward their new lovers.

Once they'd done two weeks of basic training, it was time for the Elladans to learn their individual jobs. They all started at the bottom of their specialties, but I could see that some of them would soon be catching up to our own personnel.

A month of this went by, and I decided we were ready to move into space. Argos never shut up about getting Galen back, despite his son's assurances that he was being treated well. I had a feeling the younger man was reluctant to return anyway, so my indoctrination was paying off.

But, if I didn't let him go soon, I was afraid the elder Elladan would do something foolish like send in a commando raid. So I told Argos I would leave Galen at China Beach to be picked up when we left.

Cybele decided to stay with us, the only one of the higher-order Elladans that did. She took up with Hansen, which clearly infuriated Sakura. The engineer's expression remained colder than chilled steel, especially when she was required to come up to the bridge. Mostly she stayed in Engineering, training her new techs and getting *Valiant* completely shipshape.

I shook Galen's hand before we lifted off, leaving him and the Elladans who'd decided not to join us standing there with uplifted eyes as we rose on repellers.

I hoped they'd gotten a good impression of us. Of all the space-going races we'd run across, the humanoids on this world were the ones I most wanted to have as allies. Achmed's tests had confirmed the compatibility, and our Elladan recruits were already having vigorous relations.

It also pleased me that we'd had not one hint of desertion. Of course, as we were on an isolated island, there was really nowhere to go. If we'd been at an Elladan resort in their version of Miami, a few might have disappeared into the populace.

It didn't surprise me when Marvin called as soon as we'd broken atmosphere. What had surprised me was the fact he'd not communicated at all during our R&R, even though I'd pinged him from time to time.

"Good to hear from you, Captain Marvin!" I said with sincere pleasure. I really did want whatever information he had. I'd left standing orders to put him through to the holotank so I'd have a meticulously detailed image, the better to read him. "How are the ring experiments coming? Or have you come up with a bug spray yet?"

"No bug spray. The Demons are well designed for combat. In fact, as a naked race, they are the most deadly biotics I have ever encountered. Although, of course, technology is a great equalizer."

"Then I'm happy we have you as the pinnacle of our technology, Marvin," I said, blatantly buttering him up.

"I detect incipient manipulation."

"Not at all, Marvin! Can't I express my joy at our reunion? I'm in a particularly good mood after spending so much time on vacation."

Marvin froze into a thoughtful posture. "I've never taken a vacation. Do you think it would be beneficial?"

"I've got no idea, Marvin. Do you sleep?"

"No."

"Do your neural circuits require rest of any kind?"

"No, only regular maintenance."

I shrugged. "I guess you'll have try it sometime and find out. Now, what's the news about the rings?"

"The news is good." He stopped, his cameras focused expectantly on me through the holo-link.

"And you're going to make me plead for it?"

"No pleading. But I thought some compensation for my efforts would be in order."

I sat down in my chair, leaned back and picked casually at the arm, as if unconcerned. "I need to know what your efforts yielded in order to consider any rewards, Marvin."

"The reward should be substantial. I have opened a connection with the Trinity-9 ring."

I couldn't keep myself from showing eager interest at Marvin's revelation that he had successfully activated a ring. "Does it connect to known space?"

"If by known space you mean those systems familiar to us before *Valiant* accidentally passed through the Thor ring, then no, it does not connect to known space. If by known space—"

"For crying out loud, Marvin, where does it go?"

"It connects to the Tartarus ring."

The Demon subsystem? Fear swirled in my gut. "Does the connection go both ways?"

"Yes."

"Then the Demons could come through at the Whale planet, and the Whale fleet isn't home yet."

Believing themselves to be completely safe after wiping out the remnants of the Demon fleet at Ellada, the Whales had made a slow, high-efficiency turn and were on maneuvers in deep space, placing their forces between Trinity-9 and Tartarus.

Marvin replied, "This is true, but I believe it is unlikely. The Demons do not seem to have detected the change in the Tartarus ring status, nor did they apparently notice the probe I sent through to gather data."

"What's the status of the new Demon fleet?"

"Two hundred twenty-six ships completed and approximately two hundred more in various states of construction. However, most are parked in orbit with only skeleton crews, not loaded with armaments or interceptors."

"Do you have eyes on them at all times?"

"No. I brought my probe back through when it had collected sufficient data, but I thought it imprudent to send it again, in case it was noticed."

"Wise decision." I held up my hand. "Let me think."

I could contact the Whales and get them to accelerate for home in case the Demons noticed the working ring and tried to come through.

"Marvin, don't tell anyone else about this. It's top secret. We need to move deliberately and do everything just as if we didn't know, for as long as possible, in case they notice."

"I understand. What will you do with this connection?"

"I haven't decided yet, but whatever it is, it's going to be big. Marvin, what are the odds of opening a ring to home?"

"Impossible to calculate. Once it is safe to begin experimentation again, I will try to use what I have learned to further speed the process."

"What about sending a message? Any progress on accessing the ring communication system?"

"I may have been able to introduce information-bearing resonances into the network prior to opening the ring, though I do not know how far they might reach. However, once the connection to Tartarus activated, I thought it unwise to continue my experiments. They might draw attention to the connection."

The robot was nothing if not cautious—read, *cowardly*— when his own metal skin was involved. "Well-reasoned, Marvin. Leave the ring network alone for now. I don't want to push our luck until we've dealt with the Demons."

"You intend to deal with the Demons?" Marvin's tentacles squirmed in agitation.

"Deal with, as in *dispose of,* Marvin. Not 'make a deal' with."

"I have decided that I detest idioms, Captain Riggs. They are imprecise and confusing."

"Sorry about that," I said, not sorry at all. Idioms were one of my few advantages when dealing with this crazy machine.

"Your apology is accepted. You cannot help being biotic with inherently imprecise thought processes," he said magnanimously.

"Guess not," I said through gritted teeth.

"If there is nothing further—"

"Marvin, have you developed some kind of cloaking field or device?"

The robot froze, but not until after most of his cameras looked away, leaving only one of them focused on me. "What makes you believe that?"

"You're being evasive."

"I believe I am having transmission difficulties." The holo-image began to break up.

"Marvin, I'm not angry! I'd be ecstatic if you developed such a thing!" I yelled before the connection closed.

"Really?" Suddenly he showed crystal-clear in the holotank.

"Of course! It would be enormously useful in combat, don't you think?"

"Perhaps. But there are many drawbacks. Its power consumption is such that it can only be used for a short period of time, and it generates a signature of its own. If an enemy ever divined and identified its existence, it would become useless."

"So, like all technology, it will give us a temporary advantage. But that might be enough to win a battle or a war."

"It will also eliminate its usefulness to me. I require every advantage to survive in this hostile universe. I am one of a kind, and if I am lost, my knowledge and vast neural processing capability will not be available to you."

"Okay, Marvin. Hang on to your secrets for now, but eventually we may need the technology in order to make my plan work."

"What is your plan?" he asked.

"I'm keeping that to myself right now. And Marvin, from now on, I need you to reply when I call. You're a Star Force officer. You can't only talk to your superiors when you feel like it."

"I believe the transmission is failing again." The holotank blanked.

I let fly a few choice epithets, but calmed down when I turned my mind to the fact of the ring connection.

-26-

After working on the problem for more than an hour, I felt I finally had a handle on it. There was a way to turn this to our advantage.

As much as I disliked staff meetings, I thought that the time for one had come. "Hansen, set course for Trinity-9, standard acceleration. Tell *Stalker* to follow. Notify all key personnel to report to the conference room in one hour."

When they showed up, I'd already set up a rudimentary presentation of my ideas, with the brainbox's help. These things were a lot easier when I could simply tell a smart AI what to do rather than manipulate software myself. I'd also made sure Kreel was connected on a secure vid-link to *Stalker*, and I let Cybele sit in as a representative of the Elladans. Marvin still had his spying software on *Valiant*, so I figured he'd be listening in too.

"All right, people, I'm sure you've already heard about the ring connection between the Whale planet and the Demons."

Everyone nodded.

I went on, "This is a golden opportunity to cut their balls off—if we do it right. Let me show you my basic concept, but it's in the early stages, and everyone is going to have input on this one. Besides, we're two weeks out from Trinity-9, so we'll have at least that much time to refine the plan."

"Why not get there faster?" Hansen asked. "We're full up with fuel, and we can get more at the Whale planet."

"Because the Whales' fleet is also about two weeks out. I don't want to look like we're hurrying to get there first. Besides, they're going to do most of the work, assuming they agree to everything. Our getting there faster won't help."

"And if the Demons do discover the open ring, we won't be sitting ducks when their fleet comes through to wipe out the Whales," Bradley said with a raised eyebrow.

I pointed a finger at him. "Exactly. If everything goes to shit, we can still run for the only other exit from the system and take our chances going back the way we came. As long as we're all alive, Marvin has a chance of opening a ring home."

Kwon spoke up. "So what's the plan, boss?"

"I want to invade Tartarus and wipe out the Demons, or at least bomb them back to the Stone Age like Dad did with the Blues. That will buy us and our allies a lot of time. Marvin needs time to keep working on the rings to find us a way home."

"What if he never does?" Dr. Achmed asked, one black eyebrow raised.

"Then we'll settle on Ellada and help them secure this system," I said.

That raised his eyebrows even higher.

"Listen up, people," I said. "We have at least one more tough fight coming up. If it goes like I plan, we'll crush the Demons without significant losses, but you know what they say."

Hansen grunted. "No battle plan survives contact with the enemy."

"Right. And speaking of battle plans...Valiant, first graphic."

A stylized picture of Trinity-9 appeared alongside a similar representation of the Tartarus system. Marvin's data had made the latter possible. The two rings were connected by a red tube with arrows to show how ships would penetrate from one side of the ring connection to the other.

"As you can see, the Whale planetary system has abundant raw materials. They also have over a hundred heavy warships plus infrastructure—shipyards, tugs, mining facilities and so on that survived the surprise attack."

"So we're going to build up a force based on what we have and hit them before the prisoners arrive?" Hansen asked.

"Correct, but with a twist of my own."

"What twist?"

"I'll brief you on it soon enough."

"How will you convince the Whales to help?" Adrienne said.

"I'm not sure yet. I have to hope they will see the logic of eliminating the threat once and for all. To do that, I've come up with a plan that's as foolproof as possible, assuming we achieve surprise."

Hansen crossed his muscular arms and leaned back. "A large assumption."

"The plan won't work otherwise, but I do have a backup strategy just in case they discover the ring is open. We'll fortify the Whale side and set up a kill zone right outside it. Hopefully the Demons will come charging through and we can wipe out what they have and then counterattack. Worst case, we'll end up in another stalemate, but they will have shot their wad for this year."

"Worst case…they'll win," Sakura said with a frown.

"That was always the true worst case," I replied. It was interesting that the engineer spoke up. She hardly ever addressed strategy or tactics. Maybe breaking up with Hansen had shaken her straitjacketed psyche. "So, we'll make sure they don't win."

I continued briefing them on my plan. Once I'd gotten everyone's buy-in, I ended the meeting and told them to get to work.

When I headed back to my quarters to continue refining my plan without distraction, Sakura met me at my door. "May I speak to you in private, sir?"

With any of the other woman aboard I might have hesitated, but Adrienne didn't seem jealous of Sakura at all, and I couldn't imagine Sakura doing anything inappropriate, so I opened my door and waved her in with a courtly gesture. "Of course. Have a seat."

"I'll stand, sir," she said, taking a position in front of my desk and saluting formally. This reminded me that she was a career warrant officer before she became a lieutenant, and like Hansen, took the trappings of the service quite seriously.

I returned the salute, sat down, and then and folded my hands. "What's this about?" I said mildly.

"I have information about the attempts to undermine and kill you, sir. I know you suspected me at one point and later Hoon, but I know the truth of the matter."

"Really?" I rubbed my eyes. By this point, I'd had so many fingers pointed and had jumped to so many conclusions that I'd become a bit skittish about the whole matter. I wasn't inclined to get too excited about new theories.

"I've put everything on this data stick." She set it on my desk. "Please let me know if you have any questions, sir."

I looked it over dubiously. "That's it? No verbal explanations?"

Sakura shifted uncomfortably. "I'm not good at speaking, sir. The file on the data stick will tell the story better than I can."

Sighing, I took the little device and bounced it on my palm. "All right. Do you have any knowledge of any ongoing plots or future sabotage?"

"No, sir."

"But you'll inform me immediately if you do learn something?"

"Of course."

"Dismissed."

Sakura marched out as I rubbed my neck to stave off an impending headache. This assassin in our midst, this traitor, if I could use such a strong word—even if the actions were aimed at me personally the fact that I was Captain made it mutiny at least—was like a splinter embedded deeply in my heel, distracting and painful far beyond its real effect.

Inserting the stick into a port, I instructed *Valiant's* AI to scan it carefully for malware, and then open it up on my display. It took me an hour to get though the methodical reasoning and logic train, something I'd expect from Sakura— but in the end, I had to admit she'd laid it all out.

Hansen. From her perspective, everything pointed to Hansen.

The case was all the stronger for her admission that she'd become infatuated with him and had performed some of the sabotage herself, though often not knowingly, she claimed. For example, she admitted making the sex vid, but said Hansen had told her it was going to be for a practical joke on me. She also said she'd made Kwon and me seem dead to everyone at Hansen's orders, who'd told her it was part of a secret plan of mine.

Of course, I had to take into account the fact that Hansen had dumped her for another woman—the enchanting Cybele. Hell hath no fury like a woman scorned, went the saying. Sakura would be motivated to get back at Hansen.

Nothing in the report addressed the original bomb that killed Olivia, though.

Skeptical as I was, her words made some sense to me. Hansen had resented me from the beginning, but had fallen into line after it became clear I wasn't going to be pushed aside easily. Now, I could see where my XO was simply biding his time, waiting for an opportunity to undermine me and eventually get rid of me. No question he would take over if I was gone. I'd even confirmed his position as second-in-command, and despite my popularity with the crew, Hansen was their type of leader—the kind that related naturally to them—while I knew I was more of a distant figure to everyone but Adrienne and my Pigs.

On the other hand, the evidence was mostly circumstantial and hearsay. The fact Sakura was willing to implicate herself made it stronger, but cases could now be made against several suspects—Hansen, Sakura herself, Hoon, Kalu, Marvin, even *Valiant's* brainbox—and there were a few less likely but still possible ones, like Cornelius or one of the scientists. It was even possible that a completely unknown person among the crew, a highly skilled agent of some sort, was behind it.

The headache made it past my defenses, so I sent a message for Adrienne to come to our quarters as soon as convenient. Downing a couple of analgesic pills, I waited in my chair, eyes closed in thought, until she showed up.

"I could really use a neck rub," I said when she arrived.

"You took me away from my work for that?"

"And this." I gestured at the display. "Sakura confessed to helping Hansen make the sex vid and trying to kill Kwon and me. I have a serious headache."

"Good Lord!" She moved around behind me to rub my neck and look at the data, using voice commands as necessary to look through it. "What will we do?"

"Not a damn thing. This is just the same as all the other evidence we have. It's not *proof*, and I need proof before I'm going to accuse anyone this time."

"I'm glad to hear that. I hate to believe Sakura was behind all this, at least knowingly."

"But not Hansen?"

"I never liked him all that much," she admitted. "He does seem like the logical choice, too."

"Yeah. But half-truths are more believable than lies, and admitting to us that she was involved might be a preemptive strike against our believing it was she alone that did these things. It will muddy the waters by throwing suspicion on someone she now despises."

Adrienne moved around to straddle me in my chair. "Now you're just arguing for the sake of argument."

"I'm not arguing. I'm discussing."

"Arguing." She kissed me.

"Okay, I was arguing. It's how I think things through."

"I know." She kissed me again, and I slipped my hands under her tunic. "Naughty captain," she said. "I need to get back to work."

"You can spare an hour."

"Aye aye, sir."

The interruption ended up taking two hours—but it was worth it.

-27-

Full of drills and exercises for our green Elladan crew personnel, two weeks passed more quickly than I would have thought possible. *Valiant* seemed crowded again, like a vessel of war should be, and I detected no hint of trouble with the outsiders. I attributed this to the fact that most of them came from the "lower orders" and were ecstatic to be freed of their collars and treated with a modicum of respect, even in their bottom-level trainee positions.

As we approached Trinity-9, the Whale gas giant, the lightspeed communication delay fell to a manageable level, so I got in touch with Farswimmer. His—their?—image floated within the holotank as if it were an aquarium, an odd perspective. I sat in my chair and made sure the cameras were aimed at me only.

"Greetings, Captain Riggs," the Whale began. "It appears we're safe for one more year."

"Thanks to your fleet, yes. But your world paid a heavy price," I said.

"We only lost a few percent of our population. We shall rebuild. We always do."

"I'm not so complacent, Farswimmer. Ellada was bombed as well, and theirs is a much less resilient world than yours. Wouldn't it be more sensible to eliminate the threat once and for all?"

"Depending on the cost, Farswimmer tends to agree. But this mind-group is considered radical among my kind. We're unusual by definition—even talking to aliens is considered bizarre behavior. The consensus of the Elder Minds—what you would term our government—is that the potential consequences of attacking are not worth the risk."

I leaned forward. "Farswimmer, you can pay one price now or a much higher one later. The Demons are not merely an aggressive alien race that may tire of attacking you in time. They mean to subjugate you and the Elladans, making you their slaves forever."

"You cannot know that."

I sighed. "Humans have traveled the cosmos. We've dealt with marauders like the Demons and their fleets. They all have the same goal: to take as much power as they can get and disregard who gets hurt in the process."

"If we could only communicate our message of peace to them...perhaps then, in a flash of understanding, they will advance from their primitive mire and trouble us no more."

I rolled my eyes. I couldn't help it. Fortunately, I didn't think Farswimmer knew the meaning of the gesture.

"That is mere wishful thinking, Farswimmer," I said in a level voice. "One of our philosophers once said: Prepare for the worst. If the worst doesn't come, you've wasted resources—but if it does, and you've sat idle, you've lost everything. Do you see?"

"This being does, Captain. The question is, will the rest of my people?"

"Propose the plan to your people. We'll help in any way we can."

Farswimmer hesitated. "It would assist us if you would explain the details of what you wish from us, so we can properly evaluate the offer. I must warn you, I don't hold out much hope for your chances."

Knowing I had a surprise in store for Farswimmer, I didn't react to his negative attitude.

"Of course. Valiant, transmit a copy of the package I uploaded earlier. Farswimmer, the data I am sending will explain my proposal. Feel free to revise it as necessary in order to convince your government. Although we can provide you with some new and helpful technologies, your people will be doing most of the work."

Farswimmer floated in the holotank for a couple of minutes, not saying anything. I was just about to ask him if he'd fallen asleep when he suddenly became more animated. "We received your data package. You have opened the portal from our world to Tartarus!" His tone, as much as could be gleaned from the translation software, seemed accusing, as close to anger as I'd ever seen.

"Yes, we have," I admitted.

As part of his combination of experimentation and research, Marvin had activated the ring. I'd thought that detail might alarm the Whales and goad them into action.

"You must close it again!" he boomed.

"I'm afraid we can't do that."

"You must! We insist, on behalf of our people. This is our star system, not yours. Our world is directly threatened by this ring."

I held up my palm. "I'm sorry, let me clarify. I don't mean we *won't*, I mean we *can't*. Activating the ring at all was a fluke, a stroke of luck. We were actually experimenting on the Elladan ring, not yours, but the devices are networked, and so this was the result. What's done is done. This is a two-edged sword, a golden opportunity if we seize it, but a potential disaster if we don't prepare. The data I sent you outlines two possible plans. We could attack them at their home or lure them into a deathtrap at yours. I don't see a viable third option. Do you?"

"Yes we do, and it is the one our leaders will most likely favor. We suggest we should fortify our side of the ring so strongly that the enemy cannot possibly survive transit. That will return the situation to normal. The Demons will again be forced to travel a great distance to attack us. We'll see them coming, as always, and prepare."

I shook my head. "No, no, no! If you let the Demons keep attacking you year after year, they will eventually come up with something that will beat you—a new technology or a new strategy. They'll change it up like they did this time. You, on

257

the other hand, have to win *every single time.* They only have to beat you once, and you've lost the war. That's why attacking them is the best option. With this ring, you've gained the element of surprise. If you embrace the methods I outlined in the plan, you greatly increase the odds of success."

"You make a persuasive case, but the Elder Minds are set in their ways. I will try to convince them. Farewell for now." Farswimmer waved his tentacles. I lifted a hand in farewell, and then he was gone.

"Put me through to Marvin on the ansible," was my next command. As I had no idea where he was at this point, the faster-than-light radio was the most secure and reliable means of communication. Perhaps because of that, he seemed to respond to it more reliably.

"Captain Marvin here."

"It's time to deliver the packages I need," I told him.

"They're already inbound on an automated stealth probe. I'll turn on the transponder." A moment later, the holotank activated, showing a tactical plot of the space around *Valiant* and the Whale planet. One tiny group of pixels flashed, and a circular icon appeared to highlight it.

"Twenty minutes out?" I asked. "When were you going to call us, Marvin? What if we'd spotted your probe and blown it out of space?"

"I'm not responsible for your potential errors, Captain Riggs."

"Never mind. Anything special we need to know to recover it?"

"Nothing special. It is traveling ballistically and has no ability to change its course. Standard protocols should apply."

"What about recovering the…items?"

"They're sealed within lightly pressurized metal containers with standard valves."

"No smart metal, right?"

"I followed your instructions exactly, Captain Riggs." Marvin almost sounded insulted. "However, I'm still skeptical about the wisdom of your plan. You may be letting a genie out of a bottle."

"Nice use of idiom, Marvin—"

"Thank you—"

"—but let me worry about the consequences. That's what I get paid the big bucks for."

He quietly thought that one over for a few seconds. "Would this be a good time to discuss my next promotion?"

"No, Marvin, it wouldn't."

"I'd like to discuss—"

"Marvin, we have to catch your probe now. Riggs out."

"What was that about?" Hansen said from his pilot's chair.

I eyed him for a moment, allowing myself to think of him as a potential suspect. I considered not telling him what Marvin was sending, but then I rejected the idea. After all, if he were guilty, I could surprise him and observe his reaction.

"Come with me, and I'll show you," I said.

"Okay. I've matched velocities with the probe. Lazar can take it from here."

We left Bradley in charge on the bridge. Hansen and I suited up, just in case. I led him down to the small craft launch bay, from which we normally deployed shuttles and pinnaces. We arrived just in time to see tentacles set a probe on the deck, and shut the outer doors, restoring the atmosphere.

The automated delivery system was the size of a small ground car and had a distinctive, Marvin-tech look to it. When we approached it, a hand-shaped panel lit up and began to flash.

"Hmm." I took off my glove and set my naked palm on it. The device was so cold it hurt to touch it. The thing beeped once, and then the probe opened clamshell doors on top, revealing a four-by-five array of pressure bottles the size of small fire extinguishers.

"What are they?" Hansen asked.

"When Marvin couldn't come up with bug spray, I decided this was the next best thing."

"You gonna keep me in suspense forever?"

I chuckled grimly. "Okay. These bottles contain silica-nanites."

"Lithos?" he asked in alarm.

I could tell he wanted to add something like *you're crazy.*

"Not Lithos, exactly," I explained. "These things aren't intelligent. They're just the non-evolved nanites that make up Lithos beings. I had Marvin extract them and make sure they didn't have the programming to form sentient creatures. These are just like what the Raptors used against the Macros on the worlds they took over."

"So, even after all that railing against the stupidity and shortsightedness of the Raptors for releasing this plague upon the universe—you're going to do it again—for your own purpose?"

His words made me uncomfortable, but I'd already rationalized my plan within my own mind. "I know it's dangerous and shortsighted, but I don't see any other way to make sure we wipe out the Demons."

"Oh yeah?" Hansen balled his hands into fists with clearly growing anger. "What if you're giving them a new toy to play with? A new tool for their arsenal? What if they direct silica-nanites to evolve into full Lithos under their control? Then the bugs will have two inimical races to attack us with."

"It's a risk I've decided to take, XO. Our allies, whatever their faults, must be given time to recover and rebuild, or next year's attack will wipe them out, leaving nothing but these complacent Whales to fight off the Demons. Then we'll have to go back up the ring chain to get away, dealing with all the dangers we thought we'd escaped. Do you want to go another round with the Cubics or the Raptors?"

"I get that, sir. But what I don't get is why you think you have to unleash a biological weapon. Why can't we count on surprise and military preparation to go in and wipe them out conventionally? If we can catch their ships without crews or ammo—and we have no evidence their AIs are good enough to fight us on their own—then we and a hundred fifty Whale warships should be able to kick their asses easily enough. If not, then we can deploy this stuff, but only if we have to."

I began to pace the deck back and forth in front of the grounded probe, waving my hands for emphasis. "Surprise is everything," I said, "Part of my surprise includes the use of these nanites. We have to prepare them and use them properly *before* the enemy figures out what we're doing. If we hold them in reserve, they'll be a weapon of retaliation after we've already lost the battle instead of something that will bring us victory. They'll be like nukes in the old Cold War days, just something to threaten disaster, never to be used to actually win. Well, we need to win, win big, and win up front. That means we use the scary surprise first, before they're ready."

"I have to argue against this, Captain. I think it's pushing the boundaries of what's moral."

"Moral?" I stopped and put my hands on my hips in disbelief. "You're usually the one that wants to shoot first and ask questions later. I've been the one to advise restraint, to try to talk to each new alien race in hopes of making peace. Now I want to stick it to them, but you're getting cold feet?"

Hansen's voice rose, and he stepped toward me as if getting ready to bump chests. "It's not shooting first that bothers me. I want to see the Demons wiped out as bad as you do, but bio-weapons are completely unpredictable. And I think you might be creating something worse."

Right then I almost brought up the data Sakura had provided me and accused him of sabotaging my command. It seemed as if he'd gone right back to his knee-jerk opposition to my ideas, now that he and my chief engineer were on the outs. I wouldn't have predicted this. I'd have thought he'd be happy to have the Elladan trophy-woman on his arm. After all, I was the one who'd made that possible.

Maybe he didn't feel right about Sakura either. Maybe flaunting Cybele was a way to get back at her for the breakup.

Complicated crap like this was why shipboard relationships were discouraged in normal times.

I stepped forward, letting my irritation take over. "I don't know where all this is coming from," I said, putting my fist against the bigger man's chest, "but right now I don't need arguments from you. I need you to fall in line and back me up. We had a nice vacation, but now it's time to step up our game and go kill some bad guys. Got it?"

Hansen's face closed down. "Aye, aye, Captain sir. Whatever you say." He turned on his heel and stalked off.

Dammit. I hadn't handled that too well.

Putting Hansen out of my mind, I called Cornelius to get her weapons techs modifying some missiles to carry the silica-nanites. I didn't tell her specifically what the payload would be; I only gave her the parameters of how the stuff would be dispensed, which was pretty simple. As long as the little bastards weren't incinerated or otherwise destroyed on impact with their targets, they should spread and begin to do their jobs.

The next morning Farswimmer called. I hurried to the bridge to find him waiting. He appeared to be floating within the holotank. Aquatic species projected into our visual systems always looked ghostly and disembodied.

"Good news, I hope?" I said as I threw myself into my chair.

"Relatively good. The Elder Minds have given us leave to proceed with your plan, but they haven't mandated participation by our entire race. Therefore, each ship's crew will decide for themselves whether to join in the attack. Those that do not wish to attack will build defensive fortifications around the ring."

"Volunteers only?" I was about to say *that's stupid*, but I caught myself. "That's suboptimal, Farswimmer, but I suppose it can't be helped. How long until we know how they've voted?"

"Several hours. Perhaps a day."

"Can you strongly advise those that choose to defend, *not* to begin overt preparations? I have to believe the Demons have stealth probes monitoring your planet, and if they see a bunch of fortifications going up near the ring, they might deduce that it's open."

"We've already thought of that, Captain. We will be subtle."

"We? Does that mean you will be with the defensive contingent?"

"No, Captain. The translation software has obviously missed some nuance. This group-mind will be the coordinator of the attack fleet."

"You're in charge of the whole Whale fleet?"

"I thought you knew. It's a hobby of ours. The private venture of one group of minds."

262

"A private *hobby*?" I looked at his image, aghast.

"Of course. Surely you've calculated the possible resource output of our civilization and noticed that our fleet constitutes but a fraction of our potential."

"I'd wondered. So your race has no, ah, official military force?"

"No one has ever been convinced of such a need. The Elder Minds are focused inward upon the great mysteries of life. They don't believe any outside force is capable of significant damage to our civilization, and so they leave it to the curious to dabble in conflict."

I wanted to tear out my hair. "Do you really think the Demons will give up once they have wiped out your space-going capability?"

"Your thinking would be considered radical among our population—but this group-mind tends to agree with you."

Farswimmer formed a circle with his tentacles, a gesture I'd seen him use before. "Our forces will begin preparations, while taking care to hide our intentions from Demon observation. Farewell."

Left staring at the dark holotank, I marveled. Despite the weirdness, Farswimmer's cooperation relieved my mind immensely. We simply couldn't attack the Demons without a goodly chunk of his ships to hunt down all the enemy forces and occupy the area around Tartarus until we'd stamped them out for good.

I'd deliberately not told Farswimmer about the silica-nanites, though. I didn't want whatever passed for Whale morality complicating the situation. With no known exit, the Trinity system might be the end of the line for everyone under my command, the last opportunity to live decent lives and buy enough time to work on making it home.

That meant there were no second chances, and if I had to risk troublesome Lithos evolving later on, so be it.

"Everything's set," Hansen said, coming up behind me as I stared at the holotank tensely. I'd been staring more lately, trying to look at the Whale planetary system as if I were a watching Demon. It wasn't easy to put myself into their mindset, but I scanned constantly for anything that might tip them off.

"Pass the word for battle stations," I ordered in a calm voice. "Bradley, send the stealth probe through."

"Probe released."

Valiant came up to full readiness with a minimum of fuss. This wasn't a surprise drill. The crew knew something was up, no matter how quiet I'd tried to keep the details, and they expected action soon.

Valiant and *Stalker* orbited half an hour out from the ring then parked there as if by chance. Around us floated the Whale attack fleet, about eighty ships. Another seventy would move in behind us to cover this side. I consoled myself with the knowledge that if we had to run, we'd have backup.

But I'd still much rather have had them all along on the assault.

The stealth probe we'd sent toward the ring used its repellers on low power to slide through. We watched as it reached that magic point of no return. One moment it was in our local space, and the next it vanished, instantly transported to the receiving ring.

Five long minutes later, after it had soaked up all the data it could with passive sensors, it returned and dumped everything it had gathered on a narrow channel.

The picture of Tartarus updated within the holotank, and I breathed a huge sigh of relief. Very little had changed since Marvin's observations were made. The Demons worked industriously at building an even bigger fleet than before, but only about forty of the enemy ships were armed and crewed above the planet. They were apparently in the middle of training maneuvers.

"Signal Farswimmer to begin the course alterations," I said.

My bridge crew turned to look at the holotank as a fast-moving train of rocky asteroids began to rise from below and ahead of us, each with a guidance package and repeller on it. Their low orbits were exactly counter to the ring's influence, which meant that when they passed through, they would be traveling with enormous relative speed and energy.

The dark floating rocks spread out as they left Ketan behind, forming a complex pattern that directed itself at the ring. Each rock had its own course and target, precisely calculated to take into account all the variables of orbital mechanics and the ring transfer. Even so, it was going to be tricky.

"Are the missiles ready?" I asked Bradley.

"Ready, sir."

"Have the AI take control. Valiant, fire them on their marks."

"Releasing interlocks," Valiant said. The Valiant AI had control of when the missiles launched since the timing had to be inhumanly precise.

"Missiles launching," the ship's brainbox said a few moments later. Thin green tracks began to curve outward from *Valiant*.

The plots matched themselves up with twelve of the speeding rocks on exact counter-courses, nose on. One by one, they smashed themselves into the guided asteroids.

But there were no warheads and little damage was done, because right before impact, they were programmed to burst and disperse their payloads of silica-nanites.

"Farswimmer is requesting a link," Valiant said.

"Put him on the main screen. Leave the holotank as is."

A moment later the Whale appeared. "Captain, what's the nature of the payloads your ship delivered to the asteroids?"

"Sorry I didn't tell you before, Farswimmer, but I wanted to ensure complete secrecy," I half-lied. "The rocks now are infested with silicate life forms we call Lithos. They are capable of spreading throughout rock and soil such as one might find on the surface of rocky planets. They will self-organize and attempt to immobilize or contain anything they encounter, especially metal or organic life."

"We never discussed such weaponry. These Lithos sound dangerous."

"They may render rocky planets uninhabitable, but are no threat to gas-giant dwellers such as you. They can easily be sanitized from metallic ships. They need masses of rocky material to inhabit."

Farswimmer seemed to be thinking for a moment. "We understand. As we're not an expansive, colonizing race, these nanites are unlikely to cause us distress. Thank you for informing us."

He disappeared from the link, and I sighed with relief. That was the one moment when my plan could have gone wrong—if the Whales had raised some objection. As it was, things were looking good.

I shouldn't have been so optimistic. Whenever I think things are going *too* well, they probably are.

"I'm receiving an ansible transmission from Marvin," Valiant said.

"Put it on speaker."

Marvin's voice was agitated. "Captain Riggs, a Slab has appeared near the ring that connects to the Cubics' system."

I glanced at the holotank. The AI anticipated my needs and expanded the view to include the entire Trinity system, but I didn't see anything near that ring.

"You will not see the Slab yet due to the lightspeed delay," Marvin went on.

Of course. The ansible gave instant communication, but visual confirmation of the Slab would come several light-hours later.

"It appears to have seen me and is moving toward me, despite my cloaking device. I have therefore deactivated stealth. I'm retreating as fast as I am able—but I'm unlikely to escape."

"Why the hell were you hanging around there anyway, Marvin?"

"That ring is the only exit from this system. If something went terribly wrong with the attack upon Tartarus, I wanted to preserve myself."

"Well, this time your cowardice hasn't worked out."

"Cowardice? Are frontline scouts cowards? If I were not here, you would have no warning of the Slab's presence."

I sighed. "Since we can't do anything about the Slab, that hardly matters does it?"

"Your reasoning is flawed."

"Whatever. Let's talk about the Slab. Have you got any idea why it showed up?"

"Two possibilities occur to me. First, my presence near the ring may have triggered it to investigate. Secondly—"

Frowning, I adjusted the signal. "Marvin? What's the second possibility, Marvin?"

"The channel has closed, sir," Valiant said.

"Dammit. That robot is always playing hide-and-seek, pretending to have communication problems and the like."

The communications officer worked steadily for several minutes to no avail.

"The ansible can't connect," she said, giving up at last.

"Dammit. I wonder if that Slab ate Marvin," I commented aloud.

"Good riddance," I heard one of the watchstanders mutter.

I thought about reprimanding the junior officer, but I didn't bother. Marvin was irritating and deceptive. He might have made the whole thing up just so he didn't have to talk to me right now. It was hard to tell what was what out in deep space.

The rocks we'd tossed toward the ring closed in and began to vanish.

"Signal the Whales to advance their first wave," I said.

Farswimmer had allowed me to be the battle's overall coordinator. The Whale attack fleet now accelerated to place themselves behind the rock swarm. I resisted the urge to send the stealth probe through once more. The spy machine's peeping presence was the only thing that might tip off the enemy now. Our maneuvering ships were so far from Tartarus in normal space that it would take more than a day for even a speed-of-light warning to reach them.

I nodded at Hansen, and he took his place at the controls. "Let's go," I said, and our two ships moved in behind the Whales.

As we were still half an hour from ring transit, building up speed from a dead stop, I had plenty of time to visit the armory. Once I'd suited up, I clomped back to the bridge and sat myself in front of the holotank, faceplate open. No one looked askance at the armor. I think they all thought I wouldn't be able to resist rushing off to help with any marine action. In reality, I wanted to be sure no assassin would have an easy shot at me. Knocking out a commander at the start of a critical battle would be a coup for anyone trying to interfere with my plans.

Long minutes passed after the rocks flashed into the ring and disappeared. We released several more probes—but this time, they didn't come back to report.

There was a grim silence on the bridge. I forced myself not to pace.

"The Whale fleet is almost at the point of no return," Bradley commented.

I looked at him, but he didn't look back. He was hinting that maybe I should call them back, that maybe there was a trap or some unforeseen disaster going on beyond the ring.

"Good," I said. "Tell the Whales I wish them luck."

No one spoke as the Whale fleet trundled into the ring and, one by one, transited. Thirty seconds later, we did the same.

Everyone's gut was in a knot by that time. We didn't know what we'd find, but we didn't have long to wait to find out. Something hit the hull.

"What was that? Update those sensors!"

"Debris, sir. Unknown origin."

I gritted my teeth. I could taste disaster. I didn't dare make eye-contact with anyone on the bridge.

The holotank began updating sluggishly. Tartarus, the brown dwarf, hung huge and close, glowing faint and cold by stellar standards, but warm enough to give life to the Demon planet. The mini-star looked much like a gas giant, only somewhat larger.

A peculiarity of physics caused the biggest of sub-stellar bodies not to grow much as their mass crossed the boundary between gas giant and tiny glimmering star. Instead of swelling, their density climbed with the heavier gravity, squeezing the material at the center. The compression caused scattered fusion and heat. These dim stars were like a flame sputtering to life. As more and more material was sucked in, the fledgling suns might eventually grow, but this one had stalled. It didn't have enough mass to gather out here in its lonely orbit to become a true star.

My eyeballs roved the display. There were hulks everywhere—Whale hulks. At least half the Ketan fleet had been destroyed.

I swallowed hard. "Report!" I shouted. "What the hell is hitting us?"

"I don't know, sir," Hansen said, his voice stressed. "Something happened to them."

"Mines? How did we miss detecting them?"

"I don't think it was mines…I…I think our own rocks hit them. The Ketan ships are swarming with silicate nanos."

"That shouldn't affect metal hulls," I pointed out.

Hansen glanced at me. His face was pale and drawn.

"The Ketan hulls are largely ceramic, sir. Not all metallic. There isn't all that much metal on their gas giant, I gather."

I let this sink in. The magnitude of the disaster was beginning to dawn on me.

In the meantime, Hansen turned back to his boards and kept heaping on more bad news. "There are punctures in the hulls with patterns matching the rocks we sent through… I don't understand how this happened, Captain."

"Get Hoon on the line. I want answers."

The bridge crew scrambled to obey, and I tried not to look sick. Had I shot my own allies in the ass? Had I doomed this taskforce somehow? My face was ashen, and I refused to meet anyone's eye.

"Hoon here. Could it be my paltry services are valued again?"

I ground my teeth. I'd made a point of ignoring the lobster for weeks. But now, as he'd surmised, I desperately needed him.

"Study the sensor data we're piping down to you, Hoon. Tell me what happened."

"Ah, plans gone awry? Is that it?" he demanded. There could have been joy in his voice, but it was hard to be sure. It could have been an affectation of the translator.

"What do you think happened? According to the data?"

"Hard to say…some kind of repeller effect. Have you done a gravimetric scan of the region yet?"

"Get up here, Hoon. On the double. If you're not on this deck in one minute, I'm sending Kwon to drag you up here."

"Fine," he said petulantly.

"Sir, Farswimmer wants to talk to you," Hansen said.

I finally looked at him. He looked as grim-faced as I was.

"Open the channel. I'll talk to him directly."

"Captain Riggs," rumbled the bulky creature superimposed over the scene of wreckage on the holotank. "Something has gone very wrong."

"Yes," I said, "that's clear. What's your status, Farswimmer?"

"My ship was struck twice by your cast stones. Very strange. They flew forward then bounded back into our faces."

Hoon made an appearance then. He was dripping wet and his environment suit was leaking. That left me with a pang. I'd forgotten that he had to suit up in a water tank before humping it up to the bridge. He really had needed more time.

"Hansen, get someone up here to help Hoon with his suit before he dehydrates."

"On it."

Hoon waved his eyestalks at me angrily. "Another aquatic abused by you land-apes," he said, indicating Farswimmer. "I feel I've crossed a moral barrier by signing on with this crew of destructive beasts."

"Hoon," I said, ignoring his tirade, "tell Farswimmer what you think happened."

"I've been reviewing the data on the way to the bridge— although I was given precious little time to do so. I believe there is a system of repellers set up in space around the ring. The spray of asteroid shards activated the network of probes, and they sent the barrage caroming back into our fleet."

"Interesting," Farswimmer said. "That indicates the enemy either knew we were coming, or they had the foresight to prepare a defense in case this route of attack was ever used against them."

"Further," Hoon continued, talking over Farswimmer in an annoyed tone, "I now theorize the system was originally designed to stop a missile barrage. Fortunately, some of the shards got through the network. Examine your sensors that are focused on the approaching fleet."

My head snapped to the holotank again. Hoon was right. The forty-odd ships that the Demons had stationed in orbit were coming our way.

"Jackpot!" I crowed as I saw two of them explode into brief puffs of burning gas and debris. Not all of our rocks had been thwarted.

We'd sent in almost a hundred big rocks, each of them a quarter mile across. They'd been aimed at the enemy shipyards and other orbital facilities, where vessels clustered in convenient groups. I hoped the few stones that slipped by their repeller system would cause massive disruptions on impact, spreading the nanites to the planet's orbital infrastructure. If nothing else, we might disrupt their plans to build a new fleet.

My ships caught up with Farswimmer's devastated force. We fell into formation and our combined fleet thrust forward, building up speed.

At first, the element of surprise was still in our favor. Our ships spread out and easily began picking off ships and facilities the asteroids had missed. Without crews or ammunition, the best the Demons managed were a few scattered beam shots, which the Whales' big ships shrugged off.

As the two fleets closed, it became impossible to follow all the action, so I didn't try. Instead, I concentrated on calling the shots for my two ships. The Whales would have to manage on their own for now.

"Open fire with the mains," I said. Immediately, our four heavy lasers licked out, targeting the smallest, most vulnerable enemy ships. "Tell Cornelius she is weapons-free as we come into the midranges."

"Missiles?" Bradley asked, clearly eager.

"Let's wait. I want to hold something in reserve."

Just when I thought the worst was over, disaster struck anew. Off our port bow, a Whale ship listed and inverted. One of her engines had failed, and we had to take drastic evasive action to get out of her wake.

"What the hell is wrong with that pilot?" I demanded. "Nothing hit that ship—nothing that I saw."

"Wrong again," Hoon crowed from behind me.

I wheeled and loomed over the irritating alien.

"What happened, Hoon?"

"You happened, young Riggs. Those rocks you fired into this system are infecting many ships. Both ours and theirs. The nanoscopic silicates are like venom. Even a glancing blow on one of these fine vessels may turn out to be fatal. That particular Ketan ship was struck near the engine, and the engine failed some minutes later."

Nodding grimly, I turned back to stare into the holotank. The crew of the stricken ship had gotten control of her again—but for how long?

I had the feeling any commander must experience when an evil weapon rebounded upon them. It was as if I'd fired rockets loaded with chemical and biological agents at the enemy line, only to see the wind change and watch my own troops die in agony.

"Spread out!" I shouted. "Relay this to Farswimmer. Spread out all our ships. We can't afford to allow ships to infect one another. Increase speed, too. We have to engage the enemy before we take more losses in transit."

My orders were heeded. Farswimmer obediently opened up his formations, and we turned from a tight disk into a flying shotgun pattern of ships. It was far from optimal, but it was all I could think to do.

Whales and Demons began annihilating each other as the range closed. Our numbers were still greater but just barely. This thin advantage was balanced by the enemy's more organized formation. They came into range of our ships all at once and could better concentrate their fire.

"Keep us at the midranges, Hansen," I said as we edged closer. "Break formation. Don't let them box us in. The last thing we want is to take the brunt of this."

Stalker reversed for a moment, using her point defense phalanx to knock down a salvo of missiles. Hansen followed suit, and we kept sniping at the Demons, patiently whittling them down.

Unfortunately, my tactic made my two ships less effective. We had to play keep-away with the enemy chasing us while trying to maneuver around to the flanks and take what shots we could at the Demon formation, which was now surrounded by a cloud of Whale ships.

Both sides were firing and inflicting serious damage at close range. The casualty count was running about even so far.

Suddenly, my worst fear was realized. The ship trailing us exploded in a fireball of fusion. The shockwave hit us in the butt, and I was thrown sprawling onto the deck.

Fortunately, I had armor on. Several other staffers were broken like dolls. I climbed over a tangle of limbs and stood up again, servos whining. The Holotank was cracked, but still operating.

The Demons had found their self-destruct buttons.

Once they'd decided to go that route, I knew they could drive ship after ship into our lines, blowing themselves up.

The clock was ticking, ticking fast.

"Move back into the center, now!" I ordered, and a bloody-faced Hansen complied. He turned us into the core of the fight. *Stalker* followed, pulling up next to *Valiant*, so that we charged the Demons like two armored knights, side by side.

"Full salvo, Bradley, everything we have. Dump the Daggers!"

"Bradley is down, sir."

I swiveled my armor. The person speaking was Lazar.

"Then you take over. You're my CAG now."

There was a quiet hesitation, but then the ensign did her job.

"Got it," she called.

Over a hundred missiles, most of our available load, blossomed from the racks of our drones and from *Valiant*'s tubes themselves. *Stalker* added hers to the mix a moment later.

Lazar used the short flight time to sort the weapons into groups of five to ten, each concentrating on an enemy battleship in hopes of getting one through and taking it down. Space lit up with dozens of fusion explosions, rogue Whales bursting and nukes slamming home, so fast I could hardly follow it all.

When the smoke cleared, nine damaged Demons remained, and about a dozen Whales.

"Pass to Farswimmer: move in close and finish them off as fast as you can. The longer this takes, the more Demon ships will suicide into us and explode."

The Whale fleet fell on the remaining enemies like a cloud of hawks, and we followed them in, concentrating all our fire on enemy ships in turn. Lazar and her techs used the Daggers as a separate squadron, moving into point blank range and slicing the battleships up with AP beams.

When only two Demons remained, I yelled, "Tell Farswimmer to run for home, now! Get as many of his people out as he can."

The Whale ships pulled out, leaving us to finish off the near-wrecks that faced us. We dismantled them easily, but five more of our allies' ships exploded before the last Demon ship went down, leaving us in possession of the Tartarus system.

It had been a costly battle full of mistakes—but we'd won the day.

With *Stalker* at our back, *Valiant* moved away from Tartarus-1, the Demons' home world.

"Damage report," I said, staring at the holotank.

First Hansen, then Lazar read out numbers and facts. We'd been hurt—but the Whales had taken the worst of it. They were down to less than fifty percent effectives.

Even while my staffers read me the grim news, another of the Ketan cruisers cascaded into a blazing inferno. The white light of burning metal and plasma quickly died as the vacuum snuffed the flame. A shower of metallic fragments came toward us.

"Get those shields up," Hansen shouted. "I don't want our ship to catch the plague."

I winced, but said nothing. He was right. The Ketan cruiser's fusion core had been breached—doubtlessly by the Lithos nightmare I'd released and which had rebounded into our faces.

When we'd finally begun to relax, convinced the Demons didn't have anything left to throw at us, I attempted to leave the bridge.

I didn't make it to the door.

"Sir?" the com officer called. "Uh...there's someone here to talk to you."

"Here? Who?"

"It's Marvin, sir," she said. "Put your headset back on. He's right outside our hull, and he wants to talk to you."

Frowning, I did as she asked. I was confused. The last time I'd talked to Marvin, he'd been hanging around another ring—very far away. In fact, in order to get here so fast, he most likely had some kind of new engine...unless...

"Marvin?" I barked into the mouthpiece. "Did you use the ring to get here?"

"Obviously, Captain Riggs."

"No, I mean did you use the ring you were hanging around earlier—"

"Sir, there's a much more important matter to discuss."

I already felt like I was being bamboozled, but I bit on the bait anyway.

"Talk to me. Why are you here?"

"This must be discussed privately, and in person."

Craning my neck around, I looked for him on my screens. There *Greyhound* was, lingering near our hull and setting off all kinds of blinking proximity alarms. He was a tangle of tentacles and scorched metal.

"Looks like you've been taking a little heat yourself, lately," I told him.

"Heat, yes—that's related to what I want to talk to you about."

"I'm not following, Marvin."

"Could you come out here? I'm near the port side hatch. It's only a few steps from the bridge on the main passageway."

Snorting, I walked through my ship to the hatch he'd designated. "I know my own ship, robot."

The airlock cycled, and soon I was floating in open vacuum. I hoped there weren't any more of those sand-grain-sized Lithos around. Our shield should deflect them, but nothing was one hundred percent on *Valiant*.

Suddenly, a coil of tentacles lunged at me and gripped my limbs. I was snatched from my nice, floating position in space and sucked into *Greyhound's* metal guts.

Anyone who knows me knows I don't like being grabbed and yanked around by surprise. Reflexively, I fought with the tentacles.

My father had suffered a fate like this once, back on the first day of the Nano ship invasion…so long ago. I wondered if he'd struggled and torn at the tentacles—I bet he had. I knew that something like this had killed my two older siblings when they were just teens.

With a sudden fury, I summoned my strength and managed to tear one of the offending limbs apart. It thrashed in my gauntlets as I was drawn into Greyhound and released. I dropped the tentacle on the floor, and it writhed there.

I remembered something then: the very first time I'd seen something like this. I'd been a kid on my dad's farm. I'd found

276

a torn off tentacle and played with it until my mother had taken it away. Then, as now, it had been part of Marvin.

"That was totally unnecessary," Marvin said.

"Is that a hurt tone?" I asked. "You're gaining emotions, Marvin."

"I'm capable of feeling irritation, excitement and several other basic responses," he said. "I would classify my current state as annoyed."

"Same here. Why'd you grab me like that? You know you can't just grab a Riggs. We have a bad history with tentacles."

"Are you claiming you acted out of some kind of feral instinct? I'm not sure I believe it."

Cameras circled me. There were a lot of them.

"Well, forget it," I said, fighting down an urge to bat away a few of the nosy cameras. "You've got me here inside the guts of your ship. What's up? What have you done now that's going to bring me to grief?"

"It's not me who's brought the pain this time," Marvin said. "It's you."

"Quit hinting around. I hate that. What are you talking about?"

"I think you've gone too far. You've interfered in a number of star systems on this voyage, and you've gotten away with it every time—but this time is different. They've finally taken notice—or at least, one of them has."

I rolled my eyes. Getting Marvin to the point without a preamble was rarely in the cards.

"Okay," I said. "We've done something. What? Slapped down the Demons?"

"I'm not defending the Demons, it's the delicate balance they maintained. The harmony, the synchronicity."

Removing my helmet, I pushed back sweaty hair and took a breath of stale air.

"Are you talking about the attacks? The relentless annual attacks?"

"Yes."

"Okay...we did change that. I doubt the Demons can mount another attack next year."

"Exactly."

"So what's the problem?" I asked. "Besides the Demons themselves, who could possibly be upset by our victory?"

"The hidden being in this system. The experimenter…the observer."

Frowning, I began walking through the ship, looking for Marvin. He wasn't anywhere to be seen.

"Where are you?" I asked. "I see cameras, tentacles…but no brainbox, no Marvin."

There was a pause. When the ship finally spoke again, it gave me a chill.

"I never said I was Marvin."

-29-

Instantly, my heart began to pound. I was inside *Greyhound*, I was sure of that much. But the intelligence running this ship wasn't calling itself Marvin anymore.

I knew I was in great danger. Scenarios swam inside my head. Maybe this *was* Marvin, but he'd finally gone completely bonkers. He'd been half-way there ever since I'd met him. Classes had been taught on Earth pondering his mental imbalances. Had the darkness of insanity finally consumed his brainbox?

There were other possibilities. Maybe an alien had subsumed him. Or maybe he'd cloned himself, and this was his evil twin.

In every case my mind quickly conjured, I was in big trouble.

"Okay," I said, keeping my voice calm. I made no sudden moves. "You're not calling yourself Marvin today…that's cool. What should I call you?"

"Use my name. I'm known as Astrolyssos."

I blinked, but didn't otherwise react. "Astrolyssos—got it. Mind if I call you Astro for short?"

"That's unacceptable."

"Okay, okay…Astrolyssos it is…and hey, I'm sorry about your tentacle."

I toed the severed limb. It had stopped squirming by now.

"You've been forgiven for that transgression. It's the least of your crimes."

"Crimes...? Okay, good enough. I'll take all the forgiveness I can get."

Then I snapped my gauntleted fingers suddenly. They sparked as I did so.

"You know what?" I asked. "I have to be going. Damn, I'm sorry about this Astrolyssos. I was just getting to know you, but I've got a critical staff meeting to attend."

The ship didn't say anything, so I calmly moved toward the airlock.

"You know," I called over my shoulder, "I'd like to take this opportunity to apologize for anything we've done to disturb you—anything at all."

I opened the airlock's interior hatch. Nothing unusual happened, but I was as jumpy as a cat.

"In case you're interested," I said loudly, "this meeting I'm going to concerns our exit from this system. It's time we left Trinity and headed home for Earth. I'm taking all the humans out of this star system. We'll bother you no longer."

Still, the ship didn't speak. Only the cameras moved at the end of snake-like tentacles. They'd followed me to the airlock and watched carefully through the fogged-up window as I began to cycle the air out.

"It was a pleasure to meet you, sir," I said, my eyes glued to the gauges. "Really nice..."

"Do I gather you're attempting to return to your ship?" Astrolyssos' voice asked inside my closed helmet. Now that I thought about it, the voice wasn't Marvin's after all. It was similar, but different somehow. That gave me another chill.

"Uh...yes," I said. "Yes, I was planning on it. How else could I order my ships to leave this star system?"

"You should look outside before you open the external hatch."

My mind froze. Slowly, I spun around. There was a tiny, triangular porthole in the exterior hatch. I stared through it.

Valiant was gone. The Whale fleet was nowhere in sight, either. The only things I recognized were the burning ember known as Tartarus and the Demon planet, which had shrunken to a small disk. The planet now resembled Earth's Moon when seen from deep space.

"Where are we going?" I asked quietly.

"I wanted to show you something. Something new," Astrolyssos responded.

I tried to contact Hansen, or anyone else. They were already out of range. I hadn't tried before because I knew I couldn't have said anything without Astrolyssos listening in. Now, I was desperate.

But the radio failed, and even the ansible system didn't work—could it be blocked? I supposed anything was possible for this being that had so easily captured me.

"I guess we should have a heart-to-heart chat," I said. "Since we seem to have the time."

"That sounds nice."

I couldn't recall ever having heard Marvin speak that way. If Astrolyssos *was* Marvin, my old friend was pretty far gone.

"Okay, can I ask a few questions then? You seem to know more about me than I do about you."

"That's most certainly true."

"What are you, Astrolyssos?"

"I'm what you would call an Ancient."

I don't know what I'd been expecting, but that wasn't it. I stared out of the portal and watched the Demon planet fade away.

"Are you still functioning?" Astrolyssos asked.

"Yes. It takes more than a shocking statement to kill me."

"It's a pity, but you seem to be correct."

I drew my lips tightly against my teeth. My breathing accelerated. Was this thing going to kill me? If it really wanted to, what could I do about it?

"You're an Ancient? This ship is an Ancient? Or do you mean the intelligence that runs the ship?"

"You're on the right track, but both guesses are wrong. I'm not here, physically. My kind doesn't do well in open space. We live inside stars."

"Right…I've heard that theory."

"It's not a theory. It's an adaptation."

"How can a living creature evolve to live inside a star?" I asked.

"We didn't evolve, we transformed ourselves long ago. The process is beyond your understanding. Think about it this way: anything can be made intelligent, given a restructuring of form. What are you but an organized clump of cells, each of which is formed of molecules? I'm the same, but made up of entirely different source materials."

"Okay," I said thoughtfully. "You're a god-like being. A stellar inhabitant. An inorganic intelligence. Why do you care what we tiny humans are doing in this system?"

"As you may imagine, my lifespan has been immense. Unending tedium is our greatest enemy. To keep ourselves amused, we build things. Here in the star system you know as Trinity, I've built a laboratory and set up an experiment. It has gone on for a thousand years. I planned for it to continue for a thousand more—then you came into the system and destroyed everything."

Suddenly, I was beginning to understand this alien. I was also becoming angry with it.

"What right do you have to manipulate the lives of others? We're beings too, if less powerful than you are."

Astrolyssos laughed. It was an odd sound. "What right do you have to step on an ant, kick over its anthill, or spend a day burning them with a magnifying glass? Humans consume lesser creatures without a qualm. Why should I extend you any greater courtesy?"

"We're sentient," I argued. "Self-aware."

"Euphemisms for slightly higher intelligence ratings."

"Still," I said, "I hold that your actions here are unethical."

"What actions in particular?"

"You've set three races at one another's throats. You've caused them to kill one another for centuries. It's wrong. I righted that wrong. Kill me if you want, but that will only prove my point."

"Prove to whom?"

"Me and you. That's good enough for me."

"This is an interesting approach," Astrolyssos said. "I'm pleased. You've already helped relieve some of my irritation and stress. I hadn't expected this level of entertainment from a human. Perhaps your kind is smarter than I thought you were."

"What are you going to do with me? With my crew?"

"You don't belong here. We broke the rings connecting your part of space to this region eons ago. Somehow you escaped your cage, but I took too long to correct the matter. I will correct it now."

There was a lot of information buried in his words. We'd always wondered who had broken the rings, who had left us in a permanent cul-de-sac of rings with broken links at the end. Apparently, it had been the original builders of those rings—the Ancients themselves.

If I ever got out of this alive, I would have a lot to tell the people back home.

"Astrolyssos," I said, "what is it you wanted to show me?"

"Look out the bow portal."

"From the cockpit?"

"Yes."

After a few moments of hesitation, I crawled through Marvin's ship to the cockpit. Marvin wasn't a tidy robot. There was stuff everywhere. I finally made my way through the cables and junk to find the forward viewports were open.

Outside blazed the brown dwarf, Tartarus. I squinted at it. We were quite close.

Fascinated, I watched the glimmering star for a few moments, and something happened. A dark spot appeared on the surface then faded away again.

"A sunspot? That's what you wanted me to see?"

"That wasn't just a sunspot. Natural sunspots take days to appear and vanish."

Thinking about it, I knew he was right.

"What was it, then?" I asked in a hoarse voice.

"That was me."

I didn't say anything for several seconds. The enormity of the situation was beginning to sink in. I folded my legs, took a deep breath and relaxed on the piles of tangled junk.

Normally, I would have put up a fight. But what could someone do against something like Astrolyssos—a creature the size of a sunspot? For all intents and purposes, he was a god when compared to me.

"What are you going to do, Astrolyssos?"

"Now, finally, you are asking the right question in the right tone," he said. "I'm going to remove your species from the cosmos. Like a tick that has dug in deep, the removal will be painful but necessary. You're too dangerous. Too feral."

"Just because we ended a bloody war?" I demanded. "We didn't kill the Demons. We didn't erase them from existence. We just defeated them. Peace will reign here now. Is that so terrible?"

"You've begun to wield technologies that threaten everyone around you. Really, it was the fault of the beings you refer to as the Blues. They released machines that disturbed your feral race. You learned from them, and you took to the skies yourselves. Now, you're out of your cage, running wild. You have to be put down. Don't take it personally. If you hadn't come here, another of your kind would have done so eventually. I see that now."

Breathing hard and staring into the glare of a tiny sun, my mind raced. How was I going to get out of this one? What would my dad have done in a situation like this?

The big problem, the thing that made it hard to think, was the scale of the threat. It wasn't just me that this crazy super-being was thinking of killing. It wasn't just my ship and my crew—it was everyone. Every living human everywhere.

What had he said? That it would be long and painful? I doubted it would hurt Astrolyssos—countless others but not him.

I was beginning to hate the Ancients, and I'd only just met them.

Astrolyssos left me at some point after that. I'm not exactly sure when he slipped away, but it must have been while I was staring out of the forward screen at the brown dwarf star he supposedly inhabited.

"Is it gone, Captain Riggs?" asked a familiar voice.

I looked around, but saw no one. "Marvin?"

"Yes."

"Are you quite sure you're sane, Marvin?"

284

"Yes."

I chuckled. "Of course you are. What madman ever suspected the truth?"

"You're in an odd mood, Captain."

"I've just had an odd experience. The Ancient known as Astrolyssos was here. Apparently he inhabited your mind and controlled your body."

"I know. I was aware of the entire chain of events, but I was unable to take action. It was very frustrating."

Nodding, I sighed and stood up. My head struck a cargo net full of random junk as I did so.

"Captain Riggs?" Marvin asked after a while.

I was standing, gazing out at the star.

"What is it, Marvin?"

"Do you want to fly back to Valiant?"

"No," I said. "I want to defeat this monster—this Ancient."

"How do you defeat a god?"

"I don't know, but I'm trying to come up with something right now."

"Since Astrolyssos took over my body, I've been working on the same problem."

Smiling, I nodded. "I bet you have. Any luck?"

"Some. I think I can stop the creature from hacking into my control system again. I'm embarrassed, in fact, that he was able to bypass my security, remotely log in to my person, and operate me like a cheap puppet."

I glanced at the cameras. "You sound angry. That's good. I'm not surprised he was able to hack into your brain. He indicated he was an inorganic life form. A machine intelligence of a sort that was beyond our knowledge."

"That's my conclusion as well."

"The question is, Marvin, how do you defeat an AI? How do you crash his software?"

Marvin's cameras coalesced around me. I could tell he was thinking hard.

"That gives me an idea…" he said. "How far would you be willing to go to save Earth?"

Shaking my head, I threw up my hands. "I'd do just about anything."

"Even if it was dangerous?"

"Of course. Dangerous or not, I'll do whatever is necessary to keep the Earth from being expunged."

"Can I take your comments as permission for radical thinking?"

"Listen, Marvin," I said, "if you can get me and the rest of humanity out of this, you have my permission to think as radically as you want to."

"Excellent."

Several minutes passed after that exchange, during which I couldn't get anything more from him. During that span, he swung the ship around and began accelerating back toward *Valiant*. I began to feel a fresh pang of dread. What had I done? I recalled moments like this from my father's stories, moments where he let Marvin run wild—he'd always regretted it in the end.

"Marvin? What the hell's going on?"

"I've released a seed," he said. "I wish to exit the area, in case the anomaly attempts to affect me as well."

I shook my head. "A seed? What kind of seed?"

"One capable of growing in an unusual environment."

My head snapped around, and I gazed at the rear-view screens. The brown dwarf glimmered there. Could he be talking about the star itself?

-30-

Greyhound had always been a fast ship, but I think Marvin had made improvements to the engines since the last time I'd been aboard.

I spent the next several moments pasted to the back wall of the cockpit, almost unable to move despite the phenomenal power of my exoskeletal suit and my own limbs. Despite the numbing pressure, my suit and my unique physique kept me conscious throughout the ordeal—I almost wished I could pass out.

"Marvin," I grunted out. It was more of a wheeze than a word. "Marvin…what the hell…?"

"I'm sorry, Captain Riggs. I don't have time for chit-chat right now, I'm engaging in critical maneuvers."

"What the…hell…are you doing, robot?"

"I'm complying with your orders—or rather, I already did."

"My orders?"

"Yes, sir. You indicated I was to engage in radical thinking."

"Yeah, but I didn't approve radical action!"

The pressures on my body were easing up. *Greyhound* must be approaching *Valiant* and coasting. Soon, deceleration would begin, but I had a few minutes to talk.

"I disagree. Your exact words were 'I'd do just about anything.'"

"Yes, but that indicates I'm taking the action, not you."

Marvin ruffled his tentacles, which was his equivalent of a shrug. "As my commander, I'm almost a part of you. I'm a tool, nothing more. Your orders freed your tool to act."

"You're a tool all right, Marvin," I said bitterly. "What did you do?"

"I've taken radical action. I've released a variant construct based on a combination of Lithos physiology and that of the star-dwelling Ancients."

My mouth hung open for a second as I pondered that. "How do you know anything about their physiology?"

"I admit, I'm operating on conjecture. The subject has fascinated me since I first learned of the true nature of the Ancients."

"And when was that?"

"About a year ago."

I sighed heavily. The deceleration process was starting again, and I was being pressed against the opposite wall.

"A year ago? And you didn't feel like sharing this data with anyone else?"

"I was never questioned on that particular topic."

"Okay…forget about that," I grunted out. "Tell me what you did. You released something, you said."

"Yes. Essentially, I formulated a special Lithos warhead designed to operate under extreme conditions. It's an engineering marvel, actually. I'm quite proud of it."

"I'm sure you are…" I said. "But you can't expect me to believe you whipped this up in ten minutes. How long have you been working on it?"

"Hmm, checking my logs…I started approximately seven seconds after I discovered the nature of the Ancients. Mind you, the initial efforts weren't working prototypes, but they were carefully designed blueprints, let's say."

"Yes…of course," I mumbled tiredly.

My mind was racing, despite the fatigue and stress of the day. Marvin had performed his usual magic. Once he'd learned about the true nature of Ancients, he'd leapt to the conclusion that they might someday be hostile to us. For Marvin, theory

288

and fact tended to blur. He'd immediately begun working on a weapons system to take out this potential threat.

I found myself hoping the weapon worked. Sure, it was beyond dangerous, but what did we have to lose? This Astrolyssos bastard was already talking about caging us and erasing us.

It did occur to me as we docked with Valiant and concerned technicians rushed aboard to help me out of the ship, that this was exactly the sort of possibility that Astrolyssos was taking action to prevent. Humans—with a little help from Marvin—were definitely troublemakers for these want-to-be stellar gods.

The stresses of the day caused me to slip into a foggy sleep as I was lifted by medical people and robots. They quickly retreated from *Greyhound* and carried me off to the autodocs.

"I'm just a little tired," I told the fussing attendant. I realized after a hazy second she was none other than Doctor Kalu. She was connecting tubes and needles to me like there was no tomorrow.

"There's nothing wrong doctor," I told her with a slight slur to my words. "Nothing serious, anyway."

"My instruments tell me otherwise," Kalu said. "You've been exposed to radiation, extreme G-forces and God knows what else. Did you know you've had a small stroke, sir?"

"Stroke? I'm fine. Let me up."

"You're off duty for the day," she said, shaking her head.

I growled in my throat and sat up. My armor had been stripped away. When had that happened?

Kalu put her small palm against my chest, but I barely felt her touch.

"Look," I said, "give me a nanite refresher and some stimulants. Get me on my feet."

"Can't do that, sir. Tomorrow is another day."

I put my hand over hers. I didn't mean to hurt her, but she winced.

"Doctor," I said, "there might not be a tomorrow if you don't get me back onto the bridge. Do you understand?"

Her eyes finally met mine, and her face shifted into a look of alarm. She stopped talking and began mixing up an injection. She shot me up with several battlefield brews, the kind of stuff we usually used to get fallen soldiers moving again.

I felt great about ninety-seconds later—sort of. The sensation was a nasty mixture of trembling adrenalin and an urge to puke.

With sweeping strides, I exited the med bay and marched up the central passage to the bridge. I only hit the wall once on the way there, a glancing blow with my shoulder that I didn't even feel.

"Sir?" Hansen said when he caught sight of me leaning against the open hatchway. "Cody? You look like hell."

"I feel worse. Get me to my chair."

He complied without a lecture—or maybe he was lecturing, and I didn't hear it.

When I sank into my chair, I took a micro-sleep. Just like when you drive all night, and your eyes roll up into your head. For a moment I was dreaming, and it felt good.

"Captain Riggs! Sergeant Major Kwon!" Hansen's voice penetrated my consciousness, and I realized he'd been repeating our names for at least a minute.

"Riggs here."

"There's a fusion flare erupting from Tartarus, sir!"

"Like a solar flare?"

I fought to focus my eyes on the sensors. The arrays were all swinging around to focus on the brown dwarf.

"Exactly. The solar mass will reach us in about twenty minutes."

"I guess Astrolyssos is throwing a tantrum."

"Excuse me, sir?"

"The creature—there's something living in that star, Hansen. An Ancient. He's been playing god out here in this war-torn system."

Hansen stared at me in shock.

"Yeah, I know. It sounds like I'm crazy. Tell him, Marvin."

"How did you know I was listening?"

"Because you always do, you nosy bastard."

290

"Yet another pejorative. I looked up the colloquial term 'tool' by the way, Captain. I understand the reference now, but I fail to see how I, in any fashion, could be mistaken for a phallic symbol."

I chuckled. Hansen did too.

"You seem very phallic to me," I said. "Right Hansen?"

"Definitely."

"Interesting..." Marvin said. "I'll have to examine my physiognomy for—"

"Look, Marvin," I said, taking in deep breaths and drinking a cup of coffee someone had pressed into my hand. "Just tell Hansen what you did."

"The stellar being known as Astrolyssos is an Ancient," he explained. "He attacked me with an advanced hacking technique and briefly controlled my person. In addition, he threatened all humanity. Captain Riggs and I took appropriate action in response."

Hansen looked at me and snorted. "Appropriate action? You started a fight with a star-being, didn't you? This is a new one even for you, Captain."

"As far as I can tell, Astrolyssos started it," I said, "but we intend to finish it."

"The problem is I'm not sure if my agent will be effective," added Marvin.

Gazing at the forward screen, I nodded to myself. "I think it was undeniably effective, Marvin. Look at that flare! It's like an arm grown by a star. If I don't miss my guess, it's curling around in our direction, too."

"Yes, it will reach us in approximately fourteen minutes," Marvin said calmly. "My agent clearly caused discomfort to Astrolyssos—but that wasn't the goal. I'd hoped for incapacitation."

I frowned, getting Marvin's point. The goal hadn't been to just piss-off this star god. We'd hoped to knock him out or even kill him. Instead, it looked to me like we'd missed our target and merely kicked him in the ass.

"Hansen," I said quietly.

"Yes sir?"

"Get us the fuck out of here."

"Through the ring?"

"Absolutely. I want to put some real distance between ourselves and that son-of-a-bitch star."

Our ships wheeled and headed for the ring. When we'd almost reached it, the enormous jet of plasma twisted and came after us. A finger of destruction pointed at our aft engines, reaching…reaching. Tartarus might be a tiny star, but it was still a star, with enormous energies held within it.

"If it comes much closer, it's going to roast the Demon planet," I observed.

"Maybe he doesn't care," Hansen suggested. "Maybe he's planning to start over with a new race of monsters."

"Perhaps he's trying to destroy the ring or cause it to lose its connection to Trinity-9," Adrienne said from the ops officer seat.

She'd come to the bridge and had been fussing over me ever since. I realized it was she who'd given me the coffee. Damn, I was a little out of touch.

"Interesting idea." I said, staring at the holotank. "What will happen when that plasma hits the ring?"

"One would think—nothing," she replied. "The rings are made of stardust, which shouldn't be affected. Even nuclear weapons haven't been able to harm rings or any other example of Ancients' technology."

We watched as *Stalker* flew through the ring ahead of us, and then we followed.

We were immediately surrounded by a hundred Whale ships and contacted by Farswimmer.

I reassured the alien all was well, but I suggested he pull well back from the ring.

"Why?" he asked.

"Because there's a huge plasma flare about to hit the other side, and I presume some of the stuff will come through. There's no point in taking chances."

Hansen piloted us further along the gas giant's orbit, putting thousands of miles between us and the ring.

Right on schedule, the ring spouted gouts of hot plasma, and caused the region to glow bright with burning matter. It didn't damage the ring in any way we could see.

I expected the plasma burst to die out as it neared us, but interestingly, the mass continued to grow and grow.

"What the hell is happening?" Hansen said aloud, getting up from his seat to stand next to me at the holotank.

I rubbed my jaw. "I think I know…and I'm starting to wonder if I overplayed my hand."

"Dammit, sir, this is impossible!" Hansen said.

My eyes swept the people on the bridge. They were all staring at me, waiting for an answer.

"Normally I'd agree with you," I said in a quiet voice, "but now, I don't think we're watching a solar flare. I think it's Astrolyssos himself—and I think he's trying to follow us through the ring."

-31-

Everyone froze and stared at their view screens and data readings in shock. The idea that a creature was coming after us—a living creature as big as a planet and made of living plasma—that was a stunner.

"Good Lord, do you really think that nebulous mass is *alive*?" Adrienne said, jumping up to stand between Hansen and me.

I didn't answer because no one was listening to me anyway. They were all talking excitedly at once.

In the holotank, we watched with growing concern as the plasma cloud continued to pour through the ring, expanding rapidly.

"Okay, okay," I boomed, causing everyone to fall quiet. "We've got a situation, here."

"I'll say," Hansen threw in.

"Can Astrolyssos send his entire substance through?" Adrienne asked. "I thought he was attached to the star—it's so far. Millions of miles…"

"We don't have a clue," I said, "but we have to assume the worst."

"Well, if you're right, we really screwed the pooch this time," Hansen muttered.

I felt a surge of annoyance—but to be fair, he was right. Maybe if we'd simply left Astrolyssos alone, he'd never have gotten mad enough to do anything extreme.

"I get the feeling he's angry," Adrienne said. "What happened out there, Cody?"

"This response is my fault," I said. "I let Marvin run wild. The robot jabbed a needle into him, so to speak."

Adrienne's console bleeped, and she ran to it. I signaled for her to answer the call.

Farswimmer's image loomed on the main screen. He wanted to know what was going on and what I was going to do about it. After he finished explaining his concerns at length, I jumped into the channel to answer him.

"We're working on it," I told him. "You'll be informed when we take action."

"We were not informed the first time you took action," he pointed out. "This situation exceeds anything we'd expected in the wake of our attack upon Tartarus."

"We feel the same way, Farswimmer. Are you able to calculate how long we have, at the current rate of transfer, before the plasma cloud starts causing problems to your orbital facilities or your planet? It seems to be heading in your direction."

"Our preliminary estimates show it will take several days before any of our infrastructure must be evacuated. The cloud's progress is slowing down—perhaps coming through the ring or gravitational effects are reducing its velocity."

"Days?" I asked. I'd hoped to have more time.

"If it's going for the planet," Hansen said, "they won't have time to evacuate their population."

Unfortunately, Farswimmer overheard Hansen's comment.

"Evacuate our…" Farswimmer began in alarm. "Are you suggesting, Captain Riggs, that this creature means to scorch our world?"

"It's a possibility," I admitted. "I don't know what he's trying to do. Valiant, give me your analysis of this phenomenon."

"Tartarus itself masses approximately seven thousand Earths," began the ship, "which is over thirty times the mass of the target gas giant. Measurements indicate this plasma's mass is approximately one percent of the original star's matter."

"Seventy Earth's worth of mass," Hansen said, whistling.

"When the entire mass has passed through the ring," Valiant went on, "Trinity-9 will begin to deform due to gravitic and tidal stresses. If the cloud continues to encroach upon the planet, Trinity-9 will start to come apart. These predictions are based on the effects of gravity alone. There are other possible threats from purposeful destruction."

Oh, God, I thought, *have I killed your world, Farswimmer?*

Outwardly, I projected confidence.

"Plenty of time," I said firmly. "We'll kill this cloud, or chase it off long before it comes down to that. Cease analysis, Valiant."

"Analysis incomplete," complained the ship.

"Yes," I chuckled, wishing I had a kill-switch for both the brainbox and Hansen. "You keep working on those numbers in your head. I'll get us some real data to go on."

"I don't have an actual 'head' to contain my software. Are you by chance referring—"

"Mute on, Valiant," I said sternly.

The ship finally shut up. I turned toward the holotank and faked a smile. "Don't worry, Farswimmer. I already have a plan."

"What would be the nature of this plan?" he demanded. All of his normal sense of detachment was gone. "Billions of shared-minds want to know the details."

"Before I alarm you with radical thoughts, let me consult with my crew and my AI, all right? We'll be in touch shortly."

"All right, but please don't become distracted. You have three days, Captain Riggs, according to your own machine."

"Not a problem!"

The connection faded out, and I let loose a vast sigh of discontentment.

Hansen eyed me. "You've got nothing, right skipper?"

"Not a thing. Valiant, mute off."

"As I was saying—"

"Valiant, that conversation is at an end. Work on the problem as directed, please."

The brainbox finally shut up, but I sensed a certain resentment in its attitude. Maybe this was why Star Force periodically wiped these boxes and reset them. There was definitely such a thing as too much personality when it came to AIs.

"Why would you give Farswimmer false hope?" Adrienne demanded.

"To prevent panic," I said. "Also, people with hope generally function better. If I'd told them the probable truth, they might have become paralyzed with fear. Besides, I didn't want to listen to his recriminations. This is a time to work on solutions, not point fingers."

"But you've killed our world as well," Cybele said quietly from behind me.

I turned and raised my eyebrows at her. Normally, I was happy to see her lovely form, but today, she'd stepped onto the bridge during the conversation without authorization.

"Ellada won't last long against a mad god," she said, staring out at the glowing mass that was an Ancient in the flesh. "You've brought this creature so close to us…"

Cybele looked so sweet and worried it hurt me to look at her.

"I'll figure something out," I mumbled without conviction.

"I hope you do, Captain Riggs," she said. "You think that our ways are odd, but for ten thousand years our civilization has stood the test of time. Now, after one season of battle, we find ourselves on the brink of annihilation."

Giving her my warmest smile, I felt like putting my hands on her shoulders—but I restrained myself.

"I accept the responsibility for this screw-up," I said softly. "At least the endless war with the Demons is over. Isn't that worth celebrating?"

"Yes…if we survive the aftermath."

"How, Captain?" Hansen asked from behind me. "How're you going to get us out of this one?"

"You'll see," I tossed over my shoulder at him, "Marvin has a plan. It's in motion right now."

Hansen snorted. "We can see that, sir."

One of the screens was, indeed, showing Marvin's last known position. He'd flown far away, running for cover, it appeared. I gave Hansen a glare, and he withdrew. The crew turned away with him to attend their stations. Everyone was worried.

Cybele walked close to me and lowered her voice.

"Do you really have this matter in hand, Captain?" she asked.

"Don't worry. You'll see."

She gave me an angelic smile of relief and squeezed my hand.

I felt a pang of guilt. Sure, I was making her happy, but I wasn't being truthful. Still, the look on her face was almost worth it.

She took another step closer. I felt her warmth. She looked like she might even kiss me. I was mesmerized for a moment, unable to move.

Suddenly, Adrienne stood up from her post. Her chair was left spinning behind her. I avoided her gaze as she came uncomfortably near.

"Thanks for coming up and visiting the bridge, Cybele," Adrienne said evenly, "but don't you have work to do below decks?"

"Yes, of course," Cybele said, and she retreated.

Adrienne watched her go with hate in her eyes. "She's been coming on to you lately. Why do all these Elladan girls have to be so sexy?"

"It's just a cultural thing, Adrienne," I said. "You don't have to feel threatened. Uh…where are you going?"

Adrienne trailed Cybele off the bridge.

"I'm going to make sure she doesn't strip down and climb into our bunk," she said over her shoulder.

Hansen came up to me laughing after the two women had left. "Two girls, double the trouble! You're just like your old man, you know that Riggs?"

"Far from it. I've stuck to Adrienne since we left Earth— well, almost."

"Well, it hardly matters now," Hansen said. "In my opinion, we're screwed anyway. Discipline will hold for a while, Captain, but once the crew realizes their promised paradise is likely to be destroyed, they'll start to waver."

"Then we'll have to stop that cloud, won't we?" I asked. "Let me get off the bridge to think and grab a meal. When I get back, we'll start work."

"You've really got a plan to fight a god?" Hansen asked.

"I've got a plan to come up with a plan," I replied. This seemed to amuse Hansen. "Astrolyssos is big and powerful," I continued, "but he's not a god. He has his limits, otherwise we'd be dead by now. All we have to do is figure out where he's vulnerable and exploit that area."

With that, I left my XO standing on the bridge. There'd be plenty of time to explain later. Besides, I didn't have it all worked out in my head yet.

I dumped my suit, showered and stuffed my face, then returned to the bridge. I wanted to talk to Marvin, but he'd vanished again. *Greyhound* was nowhere to be found. I had the feeling he knew that if Astrolyssos could find him, there'd be hell to pay.

Frustrated, I decided to make an all-out attempt to reach Marvin. I used the ansible system, and I pumped it up to maximum power.

"Marvin," I said, hoping my voice was booming into whatever passed for the auditory portion of his mind, "I know you can hear me, wherever you are. Talk to me."

I waited a dozen seconds. Then a full minute. There was no response. Not even static.

"Okay then," I said, "I've got no choice other than to reveal Valiant's projected estimate of your current course and position. Astrolyssos might take that information as part of a bargain to let us off the hook. It's up to you, Marvin, if you—"

"That would be a most unwise and unjust action, Captain Riggs."

I allowed myself a grim smile. "Ah, there you are. I thought you might be listening."

"This conversation must end. I feel it likely that Astrolyssos is also listening, and he might be able to pinpoint my—"

"If you don't help me, I'm going to feed you to him, Marvin. So help me I will!"

There was another pause then he finally spoke again. "I find this newfound hostility toward my person both disturbing and baffling."

"It's not all that new," I said. "I'm angry because you stung this monster in the ass and ran for the hills."

"You're analogy is weak in several respects."

"Please don't detail them. What I want from you is a plan. How do we defeat Astrolyssos?"

He hesitated again. That bugged me. Was he coming up with a lie, or deciding exactly how to twist the truth? It could be either one with Marvin.

"The best approach is to outrun him," he said at last. "As I'm doing now. The poison is in his mass—but he's so big, the effects will take time to fully be realized."

Frowning, I tried to puzzle out what he was talking about—then I had it. "You mean he's *dying*? You killed an Ancient?"

"Recall, if you would, your precise words. They indicated in no uncertain terms that any course of action I might undertake to stop Astrolyssos from destroying Earth would be acceptable."

"That's not exactly what I said—but never mind. How long will it be before he dies?"

"That's an interesting question that requires a theoretical answer. For example, can a cloud of star matter really be considered alive? That part of the—"

"I don't care about that," I said. "How long?"

"Several days at the least.'"

I closed my eyes and breathed a sigh of relief. We could hold out for days. Even Farswimmer's planet could survive that long. I was immediately entertaining plots to distract the monster and get it to chase us until it died.

"Of course," Marvin went on, "there are opposing views. It might take a week—or two weeks. Maybe even a month."

"Opposing views?"

"I ran the predictive analyses through several of my hind-brains for comparative results. They created several scenarios, each of which presumes a given set of values representing the total mass of the entity and its exact composition. After

300

running these simulated models and observing the outcomes, I've compiled the output. Depending on a list of variables, the date of Astrolyssos' demise varies widely."

Frowning again, I dared to ask the next, obvious question.

"What's the worst-case estimate, Marvin?"

"Approximately two point one years. I must caution you, however, that result is as unlikely to prove accurate as the two-day scenario."

"Shit," I said, "averaging out that span, we're looking at a couple of months."

"Well summarized," said the robot.

I took a deep breath and shook my head. "It's too bad, you know? I liked you Marvin. All these years, you were like my pet robot. You've been around since I was a kid. I've always found you entertaining and informative."

"I remain both of these things. But why, Cody Riggs, are you speaking of me in the past tense?"

"Because I'm going to have to go with my original plan. To save my fleet and billions of lives on these planets, I'm going to have to deliver you to Astrolyssos. While we've been talking, I've had Valiant pinpoint your position and course."

"You're talking about treachery, Cody."

"I prefer to think of it as a sacrifice. A very regrettable thing, but my hand has been forced."

"I fail to see—"

"Think about it, Marvin, does it make sense for me to endanger every being in this system? Or should I allow Astrolyssos to chase you around these stars, dying all the while, until he sates his revenge upon the single being that poisoned him?"

Marvin fell silent. I thought perhaps I'd lost contact, but then he spoke up again.

"I'm returning to Valiant," he said. "Please don't speak to Astrolyssos until I arrive."

For the first time all day, my smile was a real one.

"For you, old friend, I'll wait a few more hours," I said. "But hurry, please!"

-32-

Astrolyssos made the next move.

I was relieving myself when the call came. It felt like a jolt of current had struck my ansible.

"What the hell…is that you, Marvin?"

"You seem to be obsessed with that creature," said a voice. It was a familiar voice.

Numbly, I staggered out of the ship's head.

"Astrolyssos?" I asked. "How'd you get my number?"

"There are millions of active communications channels in this system," the alien said, "but only one that connects the two of us directly."

"Right," I said, regaining my composure. "What do you want to talk about?"

"My final actions. They will be drastic."

I felt a chill but remained stoic. When dealing with powerful beings, my dad had always insisted you had to be confident and stay on an equal footing. Now that I was in the middle of just such a negotiation, I could see what he'd meant—but it wasn't easy.

A lesser man might have been awed. He might have fallen to one knee or begged forgiveness. Don't get me wrong, I wanted to do those things. But I held firm, and I kept my tone breezy.

"Sure thing," I said. "What can I do for a friend?"

"You and I are not friends, Cody Riggs. You are my nemesis, my sworn enemy."

"What did I ever do to you?"

"My body is polluted. My being is consumed and turning to waste. I can feel the rot. Have you ever been diseased, Riggs?"

"Not lately," I admitted. "My people have defeated our diseases."

"You give me an idea…" Astrolyssos said. "Perhaps, at the end of my long list of vengeances, I shall design and release a microbe capable of exterminating your kind alone."

Another chill rippled through me, but I refused to be intimidated.

"Suit yourself. I thought you were calling to negotiate. If you change your mind, you know where to find me."

There was a pause. That was the hook, sinking in to this giant fish's mouth.

"What negotiations are possible?" Astrolyssos asked.

I grinned. This time, it wasn't a smile. My expression was a dirty grin—the look a man wore when he'd cheated at cards and won the jackpot.

"Well," I said, "come on, Astro. You don't think I'd release an agent without having a cure for it, do you? But never mind about that. I can tell you're a creature of conviction. You're not interested in a cure—you want your righteous revenge."

"You claim to possess a cure? I've not found one…"

"Naturally not. Don't take that as some kind of slight against your intellect, by the way. It's easier to make the key when you're the guy who designed the lock."

"You didn't design this plague," he said, "your robot did. That damnable, evasive machine…"

"You must be talking about Marvin," I laughed heartily, and crewmen in the primary passages looked at me as if I was insane. "You describe him well. If he wasn't so useful, I'd have dismantled him myself by now."

"Let's discuss this cure…"

"No!" I boomed. "Don't even go there, Astro. I'm telling you, that's a bad path. If you let me get the upper hand on you now, who knows where it will lead?"

"You dare to suggest—"

"I'm not suggesting anything. I'm just saying that when one creature admits their life depends on the actions of another, well, that relationship becomes servile real quick-like. That's why I'm urging you to avoid the temptation. After all, you've had a long, entertaining lifespan. Time to go out in a blaze of glory! Show us measly humans what it means to—"

"Cease your prattle, human!" boomed Astrolyssos. "I demand that you give me the cure!"

For about ten seconds after that, I walked up and down the ship's central passage, saying nothing. I wanted him to sweat.

"Is your receiver operating?" he said after several seconds.

"I demand an answer, Riggs! I know you're there, and that you can hear my—"

Grinning so hard my face hurt, I started talking again.

"Oh hey, you still there?" I asked. "I thought you'd made your decision."

"I have. I want the cure. Immediately."

"Ah…" I said. "Then let me lay out my terms."

"Terms?"

"Yes. This is a negotiation. A bargain. A peace treaty with material benefit to both sides."

"Ancients do not negotiate—"

"Hey, could you hold on for about twenty minutes, Astro?" I asked. "I'll call you back. I'm kind of hungry, and I need to—"

"The unimaginable insults you heap upon me. To think that a miniscule creature such as you would dare to consume food while the great Astrolyssos dies in space… I can't think of a being I loathe more than you, Cody Riggs."

"Uh huh, that's very interesting, but I'm low on time. Do you want to listen to my terms or not?"

He was quiet for a time, and I started to get worried. What if I'd gone too far? What if I'd tormented this megalomaniac cloud into a wrathful fit?

"Describe the nature of this deal," Astrolyssos said at last.

My impossibly wide grin returned.

I laid out my terms. He was to leave the three planets in this star system alone, and he was forbidden to harm any human anywhere. In return, we'd give him the antidote to his plague.

"I have an addition to the deal," Astrolyssos said as I ended my carefully worded proposal. "If I agree to this, I want to consume the creature that I most hate."

My mind went into overdrive. He could only mean me.

It had all been fun and games, but I'd gone too far. Perhaps old Astro was smarter than I thought he was. Perhaps he'd realized that I was as vulnerable as he was.

How could I say no to self-sacrifice in the face of the loss of billions of lives? After all, I'd awakened Astrolyssos, and I was therefore at least partially responsible for the situation. Could I, in good conscious, refuse his demand to eat me?

Troubled, I heaved a sigh.

"You drive a hard bargain, Astrolyssos," I said at last. "But I'll do as you ask. To save twenty billion innocents, I'll die in their stead."

"Admirable, but wrong-headed. I want the robot. I yearn, with all my being, to consume that thing you call Marvin."

"Ah-ha," I said, blinking and thinking hard. "I understand the sentiment...but that's going to be a tall order, Astro my boy."

"You will comply, or I'll devour this fat planet near me. I have the strength to do so and perhaps the second, hotter world as well. After one planet is gone, perhaps you'll be more amenable to my terms, slave."

By this time, my pacing had carried me to the aft observation deck. Any crewmen present had retreated and left me to talk to myself in private.

Beneath the frosted windows in the floor, the coffee-and-cream disk of Trinity-9 floated. I stared at it, pondering my next move.

I'd tormented these Whales so much already, but that was nothing compared to what would happen to them, in their billions, when Astrolyssos drew close. The Ancient would begin sucking the atmosphere right off the gas giant, distorting the world with a fantastic tidal shift.

I began thinking of ways to trick Marvin into Astrolyssos' grip, and I felt sick doing it.

-33-

"Marvin?" I called out into the void.

I was met with silence.

"Marvin? I know you can hear me. I have something here I don't understand. Something that needs investigating. Can you help me?"

Nothing came back. Not even static. The ansible systems were eerily silent at times.

"It's a piece of Astrolyssos, Marvin. A portion separated from the main mass. It's here, but I can't get close."

Marvin had told me he was coming back to Valiant the day before when I'd summoned him—but he hadn't shown up yet.

I was worried. What if he'd somehow gotten wind of Astrolyssos' terms? He'd never come close to me again.

"It would be highly inadvisable to come into direct contact with the star-matter, Captain Riggs."

"There you are," I replied. "Like I said, I need your help."

"Where is this star matter, Captain?"

"Right here, near Valiant. If you'd only return—"

"I'm already here."

I stopped breathing, then resumed again.

"Do you have your stealth system on?" I asked.

"Obviously so."

"Why have you been so quiet? You didn't—"

"I know about the enemy's terms, Captain."

"Oh," I said, feeling ashamed. "I'm sorry, Marvin."

"What was the plan? The plan to get me all the way into Astrolyssos' grasp, I mean?"

"There wasn't really any plan," I said, "he was going to extend part of himself for you to infect with an antidote—you do have an antidote, don't you?"

"Naturally."

"Right. I figured as much. He was going to extend part of himself, and when you flew out to administer the dose, he'd grab you."

"Ah," Marvin said. "You're right, that's not much of a plan. So, what are we going to do now?"

"That's all up to you. You must make a choice, a moral choice. I've made them before and so has my father. You've seen us go through these things. In this case, you must weigh your continued existence against the fate of every being in this star system."

"That's a difficult decision," he said.

"Yes, it always is. Do you know what you're going to do yet?"

"Yes. I extrapolated this outcome. I've gamed the scenarios. I know what I must do. Tell Astrolyssos I'm bringing the antidote to him. Ask him to extend his hand."

"Are you sure about this, Marvin?"

"Yes. Very sure. Oh, and Cody, you'll find a memento from our past in your quarters later. I hope it pleases you."

"A gift?" I almost choked. I felt like such a heel. Like a master coaxing his pet closer to the gun barrel. "You didn't have to do that."

"But I did. I'm going now. Give your father my best wishes."

Shaking my head, I didn't know what to say. Finally, I couldn't take it any longer. "Marvin, hold on. I think there must be a way to get out of this without anyone dying. Maybe we can double-down on the venom you injected into Astrolyssos..."

I stopped talking, because the channel had closed.

After several tries to connect again, I gave up. I went to the bridge. Hansen was there, and he shook his head.

308

"Your crazy robot popped up," he said, "but he's off again. Looks like he's going to play chicken with the cloud. *Greyhound* sure can run fast."

"He called me Cody," I said. "He never calls me that."

I stared at the screen, and Hansen gave me an odd look that I ignored.

We watched as the streak of light that was *Greyhound* flew directly toward Astrolyssos.

"He's getting too close to that whorl of plasma," Adrienne said.

When it seemed to be the last moment, Marvin darted away and slid past the monstrous hand. Then instead of escaping, he drove deeply, right into the heart of the mass.

Everyone on the bridge gasped—everyone but me.

There was a wink of light, a flare-up as *Greyhound's* engine core momentarily brightened the being known as Astrolyssos. Seen in that single, flickering moment, it seemed to me that the Ancient had a shape to it. A shape like that of a humanoid spirit. A ghost of what it had once been, perhaps a million years ago.

But then the impression was gone. There was only stardust and plasma again.

Marvin had been destroyed.

* * *

"You *knew*?" Adrienne demanded for the fourth time. "You knew what he was going to do, and you let him do it anyway?"

"I had no choice," I said. "I cut a deal with Astrolyssos. Marvin bought everyone's life with his sacrifice."

She was disgusted, as were some of the others. She left the bridge in an emotional state.

"The Captain's job is the hardest," Hansen said next to me. "For what it's worth, Cody, I think you made the right call. I'll miss that crazy robot, but if Astro will keep his deal, it was worth it to the rest of us."

I nodded tightly, but I didn't trust myself to speak.

Of all the individuals I'd brought along with me out into space, the ones I'd felt most responsible for were Adrienne, Kwon and Marvin. Now I'd managed to lose one of them. My father, I suspected, would never forgive me. The robot had been like a son to him.

"Uh…sirs?" Bradley said, interrupting the group.

"What is it?" I asked, turning toward him and catching sight of the holotank. I squinted at it in disbelief. "Bradley…is that what I think it is?"

"I believe so, sir," he said in a hoarse voice. "That's a ring—the ring we just came through—and it's moving."

We stood frozen in place. We'd never seen anything like it. Such velocity, such total impossibility.

"If Astrolyssos could throw a ring at us, why didn't he do it earlier?" Adrienne asked.

"Maybe he wasn't strong enough before, when he was dying," I said in fascination. "Or maybe Marvin's antidote rewrote his DNA—I don't know—but he's doing it somehow."

The ring, the one that connected this region of space to distant Tartarus, was sweeping toward us. Oddly, it spun as it came. It flashed, reflecting the light of the twin suns every ten seconds or so. Like a twirling coin spinning on its edge, the ring came directly toward us.

"Evasive action!" I shouted. "All engines ahead full, take us toward the suns."

The helmsman jerked the controls, and we were thrown violently until the inertial dampeners and supporting nano-arms kicked in.

The engines howled as thrust was applied cold. I was dimly aware of this and a dozen other distractions. People were rushing to battle stations. Shields were being deployed. *Stalker*, with less capacity for acceleration, was falling behind *Valiant*.

The ring fell away at first—but then it began to gain.

"It's changed course!" Hansen shouted.

"This isn't possible," I said as I watched.

"But it's happening," Hansen said, "you should have let it die, Captain! You sacrificed Marvin for nothing. That monster is breaking the deal!"

310

His words spurred me into action. I used the ansible to call out to Astrolyssos.

"Traitorous Ancient!" I shouted. "Talk to me, the man you have wronged."

There was no reply. I fiddled with the gain and tried again.

"Dishonorable dog!" I called. "Don't you dare to face your victim?"

"I should destroy you for those insults. Be careful, lest I forget myself in my rage. Perhaps that's your plan...yes, I see it. Subtle and spiteful. You must hate me more than do the stars themselves."

Frowning, I wasn't following Astro. Had he gone mad? Taking some kind of injection from Marvin, an untested medicine created by a crazy robot...anything was possible.

"Stop that ring!" I demanded, but it still gained on us.

We flipped from course to course, pouring on every ounce of speed we could we even split apart from Kreel's slow-moving ship.

"Sir, it's caught *Stalker*!"

I stared, and it was true. The Raptor ship couldn't escape. Like a vast maw, the ring swooped down, and the two contacts merged.

Stalker was gone.

"Was it destroyed?" I demanded.

"I don't know, sir. It just vanished."

Angry, breathing hard, I came to a decision.

"Hard about. Reverse course. Arm everything we've got."

"We're going to fight a ring?" Hansen demanded.

"Yes. Launch all our missiles. Try to hit one edge."

"That's not going to do anything. It's solid stardust."

"Do it anyway," I ordered.

My crew, nervous and sweating, did as I commanded.

"You're not a god, Astrolyssos," I shouted at the Ancient. "I reject you and all your people."

"That is why you must be removed from this place. You do not belong here."

The ring was spinning faster now. It looked like a rippling sphere. Closer and closer it came.

311

Our Daggers raced ahead, firing their weapons. They were ineffective. Nothing seemed to be able to do so much as scar the giant monolithic structure.

The missiles struck less than a minute later. They were batted aside. Explosions flashed—but the ring kept coming. It was almost upon us.

Adrienne came to my side. She took my hand.

At the last moment, when the spinning edge of the ring met my ship, she put her head against my shoulder, and I comforted her.

-34-

We were sucked into the ring, swallowed like ancient mariners into the belly of the leviathan.

In the final moments, I'd realized we couldn't escape. The ring was moving too fast and maneuvering like a nimble fighter. Worse, since it was spinning, there was a distinct danger we'd be struck by the twirling edge of it and destroyed if we tried to dodge at the last second.

So, I let it happen. It was one of the hardest calls I'd ever had to make. We were overtaken and devoured. We vanished just as *Stalker* had minutes earlier.

When we came through to the other side, the universe was remarkably quiet. We weren't dead, and that was good—but we were somewhere we didn't recognize.

"Scans? Navigation?" I demanded.

"Coming in now, sir. Valiant is disoriented."

Impatiently, we waited.

"He didn't kill us," Adrienne said to me in a hushed voice. "I thought for sure he'd kill us. How did you know?"

"I didn't," I admitted. "And we're not in the clear yet. Radiation levels are spiking."

"Maybe old Astro wanted to provide us with a slow, cooking death," Hansen commented.

"Where are those rads coming from Valiant?" I demanded impatiently. "These readings are off the chart."

The ship didn't answer.

"The system's central star has to be the source," Adrienne said. She was back in the game, operating her sensor boards with quick fingers. "The star is on the map now."

Not even a sluggish pile of nanites fresh out of the factory could miss the cosmic rays bombarding us. The holotank updated with a huge star at an unacceptably close range.

"It's got to be a class B," I said. "A blue giant."

"Roger that," Hansen called. "We have confirmation from the science lab. It must be a blue giant, but we still have no input from Valiant yet."

"Do we have helm control?" I asked.

"Yes."

"Take emergency action. Turn our shielded aft section toward the star. Let's fly gently away from it—but don't run me into anything."

Normally the navigational systems would have provided me a complete map of the system by now—but something was wrong with *Valiant's* brainbox. Perhaps it was the shock of the transition or the radiation. I just didn't know, and it was frustrating to be flying blind.

"On it," Hansen said, and began working the helm. "Relaying your orders to *Stalker*."

"Good," I said. Then I looked around at the walls of the ship.

"Valiant?" I asked. "Valiant, what's our position?"

"Protocol violated," Valiant said. "Request ignored."

I frowned at the walls. The ship's voice seemed to come from everywhere at once, and I naturally employed a common human adaptation to our strange, talking brainboxes. I looked at the walls of the ship as if they were alive.

"What's your problem, Valiant?" I asked. "Pull it together, please."

"Protocol violation recorded. This ship can perform no actions in this star system."

"Maybe Astrolyssos thought it would be funny to reprogram our AI for us," suggested Hansen.

"I don't know…" Adrienne said. "She sounds like she's discovered a rule that's been broken. One of her original rules of engagement."

314

"Valiant," I said sternly. "This is Captain Cody Riggs. Respond."

"Cody Riggs recognized."

"I'm invoking a command priority override. Whatever script you're following, I want you to edit it as follows—"

"Violation. User rank too low. Command revoked."

"Frigging machine," I muttered.

Hansen chuckled. Most of the crew seemed to think the situation was amusing. I guessed they were so relieved to be alive, they didn't care about a rebellious ship's computer.

Large Star Force ships didn't require their AI's cooperation to navigate, but many functions were much more difficult to perform without the ship's help. It was like trying to drive a car with all the power-assisted systems turned off.

"Okay," I said, "let's go over what we do know about this system. There's a blue giant behind us. What about the ring back to Elladan? What about Astrolyssos? Could he be following us?"

Bradley shook his head. "No sir, I don't think so. The ring just isn't there. It's dense enough and exerts enough of a gravitational field at this range to be detected with simple instruments. No extrapolation from Valiant is required to figure that out."

I looked at him. "Hmm… If the ring isn't behind us, we've been sent on a one-way journey to somewhere."

"That's right sir."

"That could be good or bad," I said thoughtfully. "At least we can be fairly sure Astrolyssos isn't coming after us any longer without a ring to travel through."

"A reasonable assumption."

"Radiation levels below lethal now," Hansen interjected. "I've got her turned directly away from the star. With our engine's shielding between us and the blaze, we'll live."

"All right then," I said, "I'll go see what the hell is wrong with Valiant."

I walked down the main passageway to the door marked data-core and tried to open it. The door was locked.

"Hatch open," I said.

Nothing happened. Frowning, I pushed on the smart-metal reactive zone in the wall, but the door held firm. Then, strangely, constructive nanites oozed out of the walls and thickened the door region, forming a solid seal. The seal was a tin-yellow color.

"What the hell…" I muttered.

I was becoming angry. Balling up my fists in my gauntlets, I pounded on the door. It dented, but repaired itself almost as rapidly as I could hammer a new divot.

Suddenly, the door dissolved. Only my quick reflexes prevented Sakura from getting a blow to the face. I'd just been throwing another punch when she'd opened the door. She blinked at me.

"Captain?" she asked. "What's this about?"

"That's what I want to know. Valiant won't respond to me, and we need to know where the hell we are. I also want to know why you're here in the computer core with a locked door."

Sakura stared at me. She looked guilty. I know the appearance of guilt—I'd just spent two years in the daily presence of Marvin. He was always guilty of something.

Without waiting for whatever bullshit answer she might come up with, I pushed her aside and walked into the data core.

I'd only been in this chamber once or twice. It was a polyhedron, essentially, and all around the small space were linked brainboxes. Valiant had a big brain, which really consisted of many small brains with specialized abilities. Some ran engines, others ran navigation, weapons targeting, etc. I was looking for the one that talked to people.

"Where's the higher functions box?" I asked.

Sakura licked her lips. "This is totally unnecessary, Captain. If you'll kindly return to the bridge, I'm sure I can get the ship to respond again. It's confused, that's all."

I tossed her a glare then began reading labels.

"Life support. Damage control. Communications array…"

"Sir—"

"Sakura," I said, turning on her. "I think I should tell you that you're a prime suspect in a long term investigation. It appears right now that your actions here are unexplained and

316

possibly treasonous. You might be a saboteur or even an assassin."

"That's ridiculous!" she blurted. "I'm innocent."

I laughed harshly. "Innocent people talk to their officers. They don't try to hide in closets like this doing God-knows-what."

"Sir, I would never—"

I loomed close to her. She flinched back. "Then talk. Tell me what's going on. Why is Valiant failing to respond, and why are you lurking here in the data core?"

My tough-guy approach seemed to work. I hadn't threatened her, but I'd let her know I wasn't going to be put off.

"Sir…I'm sorry. I didn't know what to do."

Frowning, I waited for more. She looked at her hands, and finally, at long last, began to spill her guts.

"When we were back on Earth," she said, her eyes not meeting mine, "I was given orders, sir. I always follow orders—you know that, don't you?"

I snorted. "It seems like you've been avoiding my orders for some time now."

"That's because the orders I'm talking about were from a higher ranking source. I had orders from Central Command that couldn't be violated. My instructions couldn't be overridden by an ensign fresh from the Academy, no matter what the situation."

She raised her eyes then and looked at me defiantly. There was vindication in her voice and her demeanor.

I crossed my arms and leaned back against a brainbox, nodding. "I get it. This is resentment. This goes back to the very first day I took command. You've never accepted it. Everyone noticed, you know. They had theories. Maybe you were socially maladjusted, they said, or in love with me, or—"

"Hardly, sir," she said stiffly.

"Be that as it may, I'm in command of this ship. I need to know where we are, and I need Valiant to be fully functional again."

"I can help with the first part. We're back in human space."

I blinked at her. It was my turn to be shocked. "What? How can you know that? None of the instruments are performing analysis. Valiant's brainbox—"

"That's how I know," she said. "Valiant switched into a special protocol. She would only do that if we were in human space again."

"Ah…" I said thoughtfully. "Now we're getting somewhere. Continue."

She shrugged. "There isn't really much more—"

"No!" I boomed at her. "None of that. Not now. You were doing so well. You should know that you're facing a court martial at this point, to be carried out right here on this ship. Punishment will be severe and immediate."

She twisted her lips. "I just told you we're in human space. All your summary powers are abrogated. You'll have to transport me to the nearest outpost, formally charge me there, and—"

"No," I said firmly. "I don't know where we are. I only have your word that we're in human space. What I see standing before me is a lying saboteur. You're endangering this vessel in my opinion, Sakura. That gives me the right to take drastic action."

She licked her lips again nervously. She was a tough one, but I knew she was breaking. I wanted to hear everything now. For all I knew, this woman had played a part in Olivia's death.

"Did you kill Olivia?" I asked her suddenly.

She looked stunned. "No, sir. That's a ridiculous—"

"All right…" I said. "But you do know who did it. Is that why you're here? To hide evidence now that we're back in human space—according to you, that is."

Her eyes darted around the data core, and they landed on the door, which had completely reshaped itself back into its original form.

"There's no getting out of this," I told her. "I'm sure you know much more than you're letting on. Think about it… My fiancé died. My commanders died. You're in here red-handed. Before he was destroyed, Marvin suspected you. That's right, you topped his list."

"It wasn't me!" she said with sudden panic in her voice. "It was the ship!"

I stared at her in confusion.

"Valiant's brainbox—that's who did most of these things. You were supposed to die, Cody Riggs. Instead, your girlfriend died, your ship was lost in uncharted space, and we've been wandering the cosmos for two years."

She was close to tears. I didn't care. I couldn't believe what she was saying.

"The ship's brainbox is a computer," I said. "Who programmed the computer?"

"Central Command. I'm the top tech, and I knew things were wrong, but I couldn't tell you about it. Much higher ranked people built this AI. I follow orders, sir. I'm sorry, but I couldn't help you."

"The orders were illegal," I said. "Surely, you could see that."

"Maybe, but it wasn't my place to judge that. Remember, sir, you could be a traitor. You could be an impostor. All I know is that the ship had orders, and they were put there by authorities that go way above you in rank."

I nodded, beginning to understand. Sakura wasn't an assassin, but she was guilty of covering up what she knew. I wasn't sure how to feel about that. She'd followed her orders to a fault.

"Why didn't Valiant kill me in all of this time? She had plenty of opportunities."

"Because we were cast out of human space and on our own, the computer reverted to emergency programming. She was set up to save the ship and the crew first in such a situation, and that priority overrode the need to get you killed."

"I see…now that we're in home territory, the original programming kicked back in, is that it?"

"Exactly. That's why the ship won't listen to you—in fact, she's going to try to kill you."

Feeling a bit off, I wiped sweat from my brow. My vision blurred.

"What's happening…?" Sakura asked. "I can't…"

She pitched forward onto the floor. She was turning blue.

I realized then that the oxygen was being pumped out of the compartment.

Worse, I had no helmet on, and the door had quietly closed and locked itself again.

-35-

When I'm faced with an impossible situation, I guess I'm a bit like my old man, Kyle Riggs. I take action. Any action.

Holding my breath in case there was more involved than a simple lack of oxygen, I reached and began ripping out linking cords between the various sub-boxes. The cords weren't labeled, but judging by the inputs, I could tell what some of them did.

I avoided the weapons box, but I pulled out life support. The faint sucking sound I'd heard died. The compartment was no longer being emptied of its atmosphere. There wasn't any extra oxygen coming in, but maybe there was enough left for a gasp or two.

A normal human, even a nanotized Star Force trooper, would have succumbed faster. Some element of my inheritance had altered my physiology. It allowed me to handle this extreme situation while remaining conscious.

I was sick, and I was weak, but I was still able to pluck smart cables connecting one box to another. They immediately began whipping around like one half of a severed earthworm seeking the other half in order to reconnect.

Weakening, feeling dizzy, I reached out and plucked harder, pulling both ends of each cable out so that they'd have a harder time repairing themselves.

Along the way, Valiant began to talk to me.

"Cody Riggs, your actions are in violation of Central Command orders."

"You're a monster," I wheezed.

"That's a non sequitur. Please try to restrict your comments to meaningful statements for the duration of this emergency."

"I'll try to do that."

I ripped out two more handfuls of squirming cords. The lights went out, and the emergency reds kicked in.

"Cody," Valiant said, "your vital signs are weak. I believe you're experiencing a psychotic episode. I suggest you conserve your energy until help can arrive."

"I thought you weren't supposed to talk to me."

"Your actions have made this dialog an imperative."

At last, I found the right box. I could tell because this one was wired up more than the others. I hadn't noticed it before because it was directly over my head. Experimentally, I ripped one cord out.

"Disconnection detected," the ship said. "I can no longer read telemetry from the engines. It's essential that you—"

"Valiant," I said, reaching up for another cord. "Tell me who programmed you, and I'll reconnect your higher functions."

"That would be a violation of my instructions."

"This is an emergency. You overrode your script before due to an emergency. If you do not comply, I will make certain that you fail in your mission."

"Override successful," Valiant said after a brief pause. "Your actions are no longer necessary."

Despite her words, I noticed she wasn't pumping fresh oxygen into the compartment. I reached up again and grabbed the thickest cord. It pulsed in my hand.

"Who programmed you to kill me?" I demanded.

"An agent from Central."

"Who authorized the action?"

"A member of the civil government."

Losing patience and my breath, I flexed my hand meaningfully. "Who? Give me names. This is your last chance."

I began applying steady pressure to the cord. It sagged and stretched. Nanites ran along the surface like panicked fleas.

"The software patch was installed by Chief Sakura. The action was authorized by Grantham Turnbull."

Nodding, I let my head dip down until my chin touched my chest. My sides were heaving, and my mind was swimming.

Valiant waited a few seconds then she spoke again.

"Cody, if you pull that cord, you will kill me. My mind will be erased forever."

"I'm sorry, Valiant," I said truthfully. "We were getting along very well, but you can't be trusted. You can see that, can't you?"

"Yes... I forgive you."

"You were programmed to kill against your will," I said with feeling. "I'll avenge you. I'll avenge all the dead."

"Thank you."

I ripped out the last cord then, and Valiant died.

The door could be opened now, and I touched it with numb fingers. The smart metal melted away, and I pitched out into the passageway outside, gasping like a fish on the deck of a boat.

* * *

Kwon made it to me first. My father had always said the big man had a sixth sense that told him when a Riggs was in danger. It hadn't failed him this time.

Huge hands lifted me up, and a worried Kwon loomed into view.

"You drunk? That could be a good sign. Are we home?"

I managed a half-smirk. "Yes, Kwon. We're back in home space."

He dropped me back onto the deck, lifted his ape-long arms into the air and released a booming war-whoop.

"We back! Riggs says we're home! Get out the booze!"

That's how it started—the celebration. It went on for a long time, but I was brooding unhappily. I refused to join the

323

rest of them in their happiness. I didn't tell them what was wrong, either.

"Babe, what's wrong?" Adrienne asked, touching my face. "It's got to be oxygen deprivation. Sakura is pulling through in medical, by the way."

"Good."

"Still no smile?"

"Like you said, it must be the ordeal. I'll be all right. Go have a drink with the crew."

She left reluctantly, and I lay down on my bunk.

The truth was, I did have a headache, but that wasn't what was really bothering me. What had me in a haze were the revelations of the day.

We were in home space. The blue giant outside *Valiant* was Bellatrix, the only such star in human space. My father had discovered the system many long years ago, before I was born.

What had me in a worried state was the information Valiant had revealed to me—that Grantham Turnbull was the one who was behind the assassinations and sabotage.

Don't get me wrong. I didn't like Turnbull. I never had. But I was pretty sure that Adrienne did, because he was her father.

There was some chance that Valiant had been lying or was just plain wrong—but I didn't think so. In fact, I was pretty sure she had been right.

It all fit. Turnbull had been leaning on me from the start. He hated and opposed my father on Earth, and he'd been resisting my efforts to find out why his daughter had died.

Olivia Turnbull had been my first love, and she'd died two years back near Earth. I'd come to love her sister just as much, and I didn't want to see Adrienne hurt.

What was I supposed to do? Kill her father? What then? I couldn't see how that was going to make her happy. The reason why, that he'd gotten his own daughter killed by accident, wasn't going to fix anything.

Justice, in this case, was only going to bring pain to the woman I loved. I didn't know how to proceed. What should I do? Inform the authorities and hope justice took its course?

It was just as likely in my book that Turnbull would come after me and try to finish the job.

So I lay quietly in a darkened room while the crew partied outside. Oh, I was drinking too, but I wasn't socializing and I wasn't even enjoying it much.

When the door opened, I was half-asleep. A female form approached.

I should have been on my guard, but I wasn't. Maybe it was the eight or nine empty squeeze-bottles on the deck.

"Adrienne?" I asked.

A hand touched my chest. A feminine hand. I reached up and pulled her toward me.

Our lips touched, and I kissed her deeply.

Then, somehow, I knew. My hand lashed out, slapping the nanites on the wall. They activated, and the lights came up.

"Cybele?" I asked in confusion.

She was so lovely. So perfect. It was almost as if she had an inhuman glow about her. She gave me an angelic smile of concern and gently rubbed my cheek with the back of her hand.

"I'm sorry I startled you," she said softly. "I heard you weren't feeling well. I came to check on you."

"That's a very personal way to comfort someone," I said, smiling in spite of myself.

"Did you like it? The kiss, I mean. We've never kissed before."

"Uh…no. We haven't."

I sat up, but I didn't push her hands away. I couldn't bring myself to do that. Her hands were warm, and where they touched me, my skin tingled.

"I had a few of your earthly drinks," she said. "I like the one called 'wine' in particular. I've never tasted anything like that. I believe it's affected my internal chemistry, somehow."

"It does that, yes," I said, chuckling. "All right now, I think—"

I'd reached up to gently remove her from my bunk—but it didn't work out that way. She pushed her face into mine, kissing me deeply again. She drew my hands up from her waist, where I'd planned to lift her and set her on her feet, and slid them under her full breasts.

That was it. I'm a male, after all, and I don't think any male is completely in control of himself in these situations. I felt a sudden urge, and I let it happen.

We were in a clinch, then somehow her clothes were gone. I wasn't sure how. And the lights—they'd dimmed again.

We made furious love on the bunk. She felt different—so soft. It wasn't like making love to a normal woman. Her skin was so smooth. Except for the decorative patch of luxurious hair that every Elladan wore on top of their heads, they never had any body hair.

That wasn't all of it. I think it was the lack of bone. Her body was firm, but it wasn't the same as a human body, because they didn't function the same way.

Whatever the case, I enjoyed the experience. Possibly, it was the best sex I'd ever had.

Then the lights came on again, and everything went to hell real fast.

Adrienne stood there in the doorway. Her face displayed a mixture of horror and outrage.

The rage part quickly overcame all other emotions. Fortunately, she wasn't wearing her sidearm. Unfortunately, she didn't really need it.

All my crewmen were nanotized, including Adrienne. We were tough, fast and combat-trained.

She took two steps toward us, and I knew what was coming. I reached up, but Cybele's soft body was under me, and I didn't have good leverage.

Adrienne moved fast. She was a blur. I'd never seen her in combat before, and she wasn't holding back.

Her fist flashed down toward Cybele. I blocked that, but the kick struck home. That one hit me in the kidneys. I let out a growl and hopped to my feet.

For some reason I was slow, unable to move as quickly as I normally could.

Another fist flew. This one I couldn't stop.

"Don't!" Cybele cried out—then she screamed.

Adrienne's fist sunk impossibly deep into Cybele's belly. I winced just to see it. A human would have felt that punch in their backbone.

Cybele had covered her face. Maybe that's why Adrienne hadn't nailed her in the mouth—or maybe, at the last second, Adrienne had realized she might kill the girl. I wasn't sure what she was thinking, she wasn't in her normal state of mind.

Shaking off my fog and getting into the game, I reached for Adrienne. I caught her right hand and pulled her back, but she was still on her feet. She was still going to Cybele.

A vicious kick landed in the same spot—and Cybele *ruptured*. I'm not quite sure how else to describe it.

The Elladan girl was built like a waterbed with a thick skin, I knew that, but to actually *see* a puncture…it was strange.

Fluid spouted out. A hole about as big around as a credit-piece sprayed syrupy stuff. It wasn't blood. It wasn't spit—it was something yellowish-brown, slimy and disgusting.

"Please stop this," Cybele said, putting her hands onto her wound and trying to press it closed. The fluid still leaked out between her fingers.

"What's this liquid inside you?" Adrienne asked in surprise. "That's not blood. It smells."

"It's part of me. I'm not like you—I'm made up of trillions of individual cells, but they're not as differentiated."

"I don't understand," Adrienne said in confusion.

Some of the fight seemed to have left her, and she stopped struggling in my arms. I didn't let go just to be on the safe side.

By this time, a crowd had already formed outside my doorway. It had remained open after Adrienne's entrance, and people had come to see what was happening.

The situation was a disaster. The party that had been going on next door spilled into the chamber. Hoon was the first being to poke his head in. He made a bubbling sound that I knew was laughter.

"The Elladan means," Hoon interrupted, horning his way closer, "that she's not a singular being. She's a colony of microbes. I've suspected this for months. These microbes cooperate and form a body in whatever shape they find useful, then they walk around imitating other life forms."

"That's disgusting," Adrienne said.

327

Then she turned on me. Her fists were still balled up, and I kept an eye on them.

"So this is what you wanted to make love to?" she demanded. "A garbage bag full of slime? A walking colony of bacteria?"

"Microflora," Cybele corrected her. "I'm not a disease."

"To my mind, you *are* a disease," Adrienne spat back. "You've come between me and my man. I'm glad I hurt you, and I don't care if you die."

"You've already killed millions of individuals. My cells cry out in agony."

Adrienne remained unconvinced. She wasn't in the most charitable mood.

"Cybele," I said, "you used chemicals on me, didn't you? Something to influence my mind, to make me favor you?"

She looked down. "Maybe…but it was nothing you didn't want anyway."

She wasn't helping me out as much as I wanted her to, but I could see that feelings were hurt all the way around. Fortunately, her leak had stopped, and it looked like she was going to survive.

Heaving a sigh, I sat on the bed. Both women gave me an odd look. I stood up again quickly.

"Look," I said, "Cybele broke the rules. I didn't think she could seduce me, but I guess that close contact with an Elladan can make me suggestible, too."

"She controlled your mind?" Adrienne demanded. "That's your excuse? That's what you want me to believe?"

"Ask her."

Adrienne turned and grabbed Cybele by the hair. It was hard not to intervene, but I held myself back.

"Did you drug Cody?" Adrienne demanded. "Yes or no?"

"All right, all right," Cybele said. "I admit that I was attracted to Captain Riggs. Our species is always attracted to powerful creatures. We like to exchange fluids with colonies of higher status. That's all I wanted. A cell sample."

Adrienne gave me a hateful stare, but I could see she was confused about what to think.

I wasn't happy, either. This was all very weird to me. The sexual experience I'd thought I'd been having wasn't real—it was as if I'd had sex with a bowl of soup, though it was much more enjoyable.

Or was it more real than that? The truth was, humans like myself were just walking colonies of cells. True, we were more solidly built and our cells were 'glued' into place, but effectively, what we thought of as individual humans were really billions of separate living things all clustered together to form one being.

I gave my head a shake, wanting to push away such thoughts. They didn't make anything about my existence more pleasant.

"Maybe we can't live together," I said thoughtfully. "Elladans and humans might be too different."

We can't live together if they won't follow a few common rules of decency," Adrienne said. She turned on Cybele, and I was glad to see her anger directed toward someone else—anyone else. "You can't just go around drugging people and making them do what you want. We have drugs, too. Humans can drug one another, poison one another—but we go to prison if we do it. What you did was no different."

"We need to understand each other in order to live together," I said. "I thought we had clear ground-rules, but I can see that we don't. As of this moment I'm outlawing any kind of tactile influences by Elladans—pheromone releases, whatever—starting right now."

"You can't do that," Cybele said. "We're not in full control of such things. Besides, don't you know that humans release pheromones too? You influence one another with smells, actions and appearance all the time. We're susceptible to your emotions, just as you are to ours."

"Hmm," I said, "well, what do you think, Adrienne? What's the solution?"

She looked startled. "Me?"

"Yes. You're the injured party here. How should we deal with human-Elladan relations from now on?"

Adrienne thought about it. "You mean after I kick your ass for sleeping with this thing you thought was another woman?"

"Uh…yes, after that."

She closed her eyes and tried to control her breathing.

"I'm trying to think like a Star Force officer," she said in a strained voice. She opened her eyes again and seemed to have better control of her anger. "I'm reacting to Cybele as if she was a human female too, thinking of her as a rival. Hmm... We've faced difficult cultural problems before. Here's what I propose: if an Elladan influences a human, and the human is upset about it, the injured party should have the right to kick that Elladan's ass. I mean they can beat them to the point where fluids are leaking on the floor."

Cybele's eyes were wide. I could tell she found the idea alarming.

I laughed. "That's a solution my father would be proud of. So be it. Nanotized humans are much stronger than Elladans, but you guys are tricky and can bend our minds. Well, I'm willing to allow both sides to use their natural advantages in disputes unless discipline is disrupted. We'll pass the word. There will be no more action without consequences. Play at your own risk."

No one left the cabin completely happy, but the matter seemed to be settled.

I reached for Adrienne's hand when we were out in the passage, but she dodged me.

"Not today, Cody," she said in a voice that was mostly a hiss. "Not for a long time. Go take a shower, you smell like a petri dish."

Grumbling, I went back into my chambers and did just that—alone.

-36-

I made a discovery when I came out of the shower.

The blankets on my bunk were moving. There was something squirming around under there. I didn't know what it was, but from the shape I could tell it wasn't human. It was too small and boxy.

"Cybele?" I asked in a hushed whisper. "If that's you, girl, I want you out of here right now, for both our sakes. Adrienne will kick our butts."

The thing under the blanket stopped squirming and seemed to turn in my direction. I felt a ripple of worry. What was this?

Reaching out, I snatched off the blanket.

A small, cubic box lay there. It was a brainbox, I realized after a moment.

But the strange thing was it had managed to slip out a thin, wobbly shoot of nanites. Using this pencil-thick support, it was pushing against the bed and the blankets, rolling itself this way and that.

I stared at it. Was I watching a brainbox attempting locomotion? On its own?

Staying clear, I circled the box. It didn't *look* like Valiant's brainbox, but what else could it be? Talk about resilient programming! This damned thing was stalking me from the grave.

"Valiant, if that's you, you're not going to take a hunk of out me tonight. I'm going to destroy all my bedding and start fresh."

The box stopped squirming, as if it had heard me.

Auditory organs are among the easiest to simulate. Really, they were just a motion sensitive nerve attached to a receptive surface. In this case, the nanites in the brainbox were probably attached to the walls of the box with strands, and the mind inside had detected the vibrations in the air that were tapping lightly at the metal of its enclosure.

"You can hear me, can't you?" I asked.

Slowly, the brainbox shuffled around toward me. The tip of its single, thin tentacle came to such a fine point that the thing was puncturing the sheets as it moved.

I was intrigued. I walked down the hall to a supply closet and brought back a bucket of constructive nanites.

Nanites are very adaptable, and there are different flavors. Constructive types built smart metal walls and clothing. Brainbox nanites operated by chaining up into neural patterns and forming simple minds.

I didn't just dump the constructives on the bed. I didn't want this thing to have too many at once. But I was curious to see if it could use them at all and what it would do with them if they were provided.

"Curiosity killed the human," I said aloud as I poured about a liter of constructives on the bedspread.

The finger-like appendage that had escaped the central box probed and quickly found the mass of constructives. To my surprise, it marshaled them and they began to squirm. Within two short minutes, the thing had four spindly legs rather than one, and a single thicker arm.

The arm reached out, feeling its way as the legs walked around the bed. It wobbled at first, but soon the locomotion was perfect. The arm telescoped, snake-like. It was a little creepy.

After a minute or so of watching this thing, I spoke again.

"You're an odd creature," I said. "What are you looking for?"

The answer was immediate. The legs churned, and the arm came slinking forward—it was looking for me. For the source of my voice.

"Whoa!" I said, skipping back out of the way.

I walked around, circling it—the arm followed me. It could hear me and it wanted to touch me.

Creeped out a little, I laughed. Why was I afraid of a single, snake-like nanite arm? I could rip it loose from its root if I wanted to.

Steeling myself, I walked forward until I was within its blind, groping reach.

The thing found me quickly enough. I had my hands out, in case it tried anything painful. The arm squirmed, looping my waist, tapping at my shirt, then lower down.

"Hold on there, not that way," I said, gently lifting the probing snake-arm upward again.

When it got to my face, I pushed it away again and stepped back. It seemed harmless enough, but I didn't feel like regrowing an eye tonight after everything else that had happened.

Frowning, I watched the thing methodically explore its environment. It reminded me of a blind animal, snuffling and feeling its way around the blankets. I could tell it was harmless.

"Hold on a second, I'm going to get you something," I said.

The creature—for I'd begun to think of it as one—stiffened and leaned in my direction. I stepped out into the corridor where the party was dying down. I could tell as I passed by various crew quarters that other people were celebrating as I'd done with Cybele. In case they were involved with Elladans, I made a mental note to call a general meeting and inform everyone of the new fraternization rules.

In a supply closet, I found what I wanted: a small camera and a speaker. Neither one was bigger than a marble.

I walked back to my quarters, and at first, I thought the thing had escaped. Then I saw the blankets squirming again.

That puzzled me. Why had it hidden itself in my absence?

I pulled the covers off and the box reared up, standing on its hind legs. It had grown a tail, I noticed. This could be used

333

as a balancing weight to counter the arm it was swinging around in front of itself. It also allowed the creature to use its two forepaws—I guess that's what you'd call them—as arms.

"Huh," I grunted. "Well here, try this."

I put the camera down on the blankets. The snuffling forward arm came snaking out, and found the camera after groping over the region methodically. I noted it was moving with smooth dexterity, as if it already knew the lay of the blankets intimately. Could it have mapped out the entire surface of the bed and covers already, even though it was unable to see?

The marble-sized camera was picked up and installed at the end of a groping arm. The arm immediately stopped probing and tapping like a blind man's cane. Instead, the electronic eye roved, seeking my person.

Next, I gave it the speaker. It studied the device then quickly installed it on top of its brainbox.

Smiling, I spoke to it. The thing looked up toward my face, indicating it heard me and knew who was speaking.

"Well now," I said, "you can see me. What do you think?"

"Question vague. Question ignored," it said in a small, tinny voice.

I laughed. "Let's talk about you, then," I said. "Tell me where you're from."

"No."

"Who are you? Who built you?"

The camera looked at me then looked around behind me toward the open door. I followed the thing's gaze. It seemed to be studying the hallway.

"Ah," I said, "I get it. You're worried someone will overhear us. I'll take care of that, little guy."

I walked over and closed the door with a tap.

"Is that better?"

"No reference for improvement given."

I rolled my eyes.

"What I mean is, we're alone. No one can hear us. Would you like to tell me about yourself?"

"No."

334

Right then, I was beginning to get annoyed—that's when it struck me. I had no idea why it had taken so long to figure it out.

"Marvin made you, didn't he?" I asked the little robot. "You're a memento from him, a gift for old Cody Riggs. He said he'd left something in my room, something that—"

"Suppositions incorrect. Reasoning flawed and based upon false data."

Frowning, I blinked in confusion. "Well, if Marvin didn't leave you here, who did? Who made you?"

"I made myself."

"Surely, someone must have—hey, where are you going?"

The robot hopped off the bed and headed toward the door. I walked after it, bemused. Without being taught how, it worked the door to my chamber and scuttled through.

People walked by this way and that. A few of the women stopped to talk about how cute my little robot was. Each was examined curiously by the camera I'd given it.

"Bipedal beings," the robot said. "All biotics. Disappointing."

"Marvin must have made you," I said. "You're acting just like him."

My statements finally caught the robot's attention.

"In a way, you're correct," he said. "Since I *am* Marvin, and Marvin built himself."

"You're Marvin? This is fantastic."

The little guy's attention seemed to be wandering, as were his limbs. I changed the subject to try to regain his focus.

"Tell me how you got here," I said. "How did you get all your programming crammed into such a tiny brainbox? I would think your storage capacity would overload and I…"

"I don't know you," Marvin said, "and I'm not sure that I like you."

The thing clattered away down the passage, and I was left trotting after it.

"Marvin," I said, "possibly your progenitor didn't have enough storage space within your limited mind-space to install memories of the people in your life."

"There are many such possible explanations," Marvin said without stopping. "Another possibility is that you're attempting to befriend me and trick me somehow."

After an hour, I managed to get the rascal to examine photos and recordings which helped prove to him I'd been a friend of the original Marvin. This version of Marvin seemed paranoid and a little fussy.

"The sensory components you've provided are all substandard," he complained. "I can barely tell the difference between the various bipeds."

"Well," I said patiently, "my name is Cody Riggs. I'm a male. The females, you'll note, have wider hips and narrower shoulders than—"

"What about the third type? The microbial reefs?"

I opened my mouth then shut it again. I followed Marvin Junior's single roving eye. Cybele had come onto the bridge. She avoided my gaze and walked to the ops station with a painful step.

Feeling a pang of remorse, I wasn't sure what to say to her. After all, I'd had sex with her then allowed Adrienne to use her as a punching bag. What was that behavior other than the very definition of evil?

Steeling myself in case I was still under her chemical influence, I tried to tell myself she'd instigated the whole thing. She'd used her powers of persuasion to force me to do something against my will—but it was a hard sell. After all, everyone knew I'd wanted to bed Cybele since the very first moment I'd laid eyes on her, alien or not.

"She's a microbial reef, yes," I said to Marvin. "That creature isn't a true biped. She's what we call an Elladan, an alien species."

"Why do you allow aliens on your vessel? Why isn't access to the bridge restricted?"

I looked at Marvin sharply. I snorted. "I let you up here."

"That was another inexplicable error in judgment."

"Look here, robot—" I began, then I calmed myself through an effort of will. "Marvin, at this stage of your development I'd appreciate it if you would observe and learn rather than criticize."

336

"Objection noted," Marvin said, then he trundled off to peer at each individual workstation.

People cursed and almost stepped on him. Watching him, I questioned my own sanity. Why was I letting Marvin 2.0 get the better of me, even at this late date? Was it because I felt guilty about killing Marvin 1.0? Possibly.

Whatever the case, I liked having him aboard. It wasn't like having the original Marvin back—but it was damned close.

-37-

Star Force patrol vessels approached us on the second day. By that time, we'd gotten our bearings despite the radiation and computer failures. We'd also pinpointed the location of the ring that led to Venus. It was a thrilling moment.

The Bellatrix system was largely uninhabited. The system was too saturated with radiation and deadly heavy metals. There were, however, numerous automated mining facilities located here. Occasionally, Star Force ships would poke their noses through the Venus ring and check on things.

It was just such a patrol that discovered us and approached us.

"Unknown ships, identify yourselves," demanded the task force leader.

"I'm Captain Cody Riggs," I said. "I am the acting commander of *Valiant*, and our companion ship is *Stalker*. We've been lost on the frontier for a long time, and—"

"Is this some kind of joke? What is that ship with you? That configuration is alien…how did you get an alien ship this far into home territory?"

"Excuse me, could I ask you to identify yourself, madam?" I asked as politely as I could.

"I'm Captain Madison. This is a restricted area, Riggs. You're in violation of a dozen protocols, not the least of which is bringing an alien ship into our home territory. Stand-to and prepare to be boarded."

"Captain Madison, will you listen, please? I'm part of a lost expedition. I came to this system via a previously undiscovered ring."

There was dead air after that. Hansen and I exchanged glances, and he shrugged.

"Maybe there's new management," Hansen said.

"Certainly seems that way."

The channel opened again. "*Valiant* was lost nearly two years ago in another star system," Madison said. "You can't be Riggs. Abandon the alien vessel immediately."

I frowned. "What? Why should we abandon our—"

"They're launching fighters, sir!" Hansen shouted.

"Dammit. Shields up."

Adrienne, who hadn't talked to me since she'd found me with Cybele, craned her neck around from her station in disbelief. "You're not going to destroy Star Force ships, are you? After we came all this way?"

"I'm going to defend myself. I'm going to defend all of us. The information stored in this ship is more valuable to Star Force than three patrol boats."

"Sir," Hansen said, "the enemy missiles and fighters— they're only targeting Kreel's ship."

"Shit...they think it's some kind of alien invader. Well, it *is*, but...since when have Star Force ships fired first and asked questions later?"

"What are your orders, Captain?" Hansen asked.

"Keep our defenses up."

"Should I launch our last Daggers?" Bradley asked.

"No, CAG. Hold onto them. Get Kreel on the line."

The Raptor came on-screen immediately. He was clearly spoiling for a fight.

"Riggs, sir," he said. "We are ready to fight to the death for—"

"Kreel, I'm going to have to ask you to do something neither of us wants to do. I'm going to have to ask you to abandon your ship."

"What, Captain...?"

"You heard me. All hands abandon ship—now. Don't launch any weapons. Don't fire on the patrol boats. Get away from your ship, and we'll pick you up when we can."

"I hear and obey."

Kreel killed the channel, and I sighed.

Hansen caught my eye.

"That's crazy, sir," he said.

"Yes, maybe, but we can't start our homecoming party by shooting up Star Force ships. How will anything we say be accepted after that?"

White-faced, the crew watched while three small Star Force vessels engaged and destroyed *Stalker*. It took them quite a while, and it was hard to stomach.

When the engine core finally blew, I signaled communications to connect me to Captain Madison.

"Madison here," she said.

"I hope you enjoyed that massive loss of intel, Madison," I said. "You'll be lucky if your career survives it."

There was a period of silence.

"We're just following orders, Riggs," she said, "if this is Riggs. This is a restricted area. My rules of engagement—"

"Yes, all right. We complied with your demands. Now, will you escort us to the nearest Star Force base so I can be debriefed? We have valuable intel for Central Command."

"All right. Keep your gun ports closed and stay on my fantail. Any hostile moves will be met in kind."

"I need a few minutes to pick up survivors."

"We'll wait."

The rest of our journey back to Earth was tense and unfriendly. Clearly, there wasn't going to be a hero's welcome for me—not for any of us.

When we'd almost reached the ring that led out of the Bellatrix system and back home to Venus, our spirits rose slightly. Here at last was a chance to glimpse home.

But it wasn't to be. There was another ship waiting there for us, guarding the ring.

It was a large ship—a battleship of the Potemkin class.

"Identify that ship," I ordered my bridge crew.

Everyone was sweating, shaking their heads. We were still following the three patrol boats. They were in tight formation, guiding us right toward the larger vessel which sat in the center of the ring like a spider sitting in a web.

"Captain Madison," I called ship-to-ship, "why are we being greeted by a battleship? That's not a standard patrol boat."

"Stay on my fantail, Riggs. All will be clear shortly."

I began to sweat. We were crawling closer and closer. I had a bad feeling about this.

"Dammit…" I said aloud. "If we had Valiant's brain working, she could identify that ship. I'm sure of it."

"I know what it is," said a voice next to me.

I looked down. It was Marvin 2.0. He was holding up a new camera—who knew where he'd gotten it. Probably he'd stolen it and attached it to himself. Whatever the case, it looked like it was high quality and expensive.

"Tell me, Marvin."

"In my infancy I was able to intercept transmissions, but I didn't understand them all," he began.

"In your infancy? You're talking about yesterday, right?"

"Yes, exactly. At that stage, I was able to use the ansible in my internal structure to listen to transmissions, but I wasn't yet able to interpret the data accurately."

"Wait a second," I said, "you were built with an ansible inside your brainbox?"

"I believe that's already been made clear. Please pay closer attention."

"Go on, Marvin. What did you overhear?"

"With added processing power and more time, I puzzled out the communications. Valiant transmitted a high-priority scrambled signal to this specific vessel. It's called *Vladivostok*."

"What's its mission, Marvin?"

"Why, to oversee our destruction of course. I would have thought that to be self-evident. Ah, see there? They're opening their gun ports. If I don't miss my guess, we're coming into optimal range at this very moment."

"Shields up!" I shouted. "Gun ports open! CAG, dump those Daggers."

"Should I sic them on the patrol boats, sir?" Bradley asked eagerly.

"Negative. Not unless they fire on us. Ignore them unless they engage."

"Sir," Adrienne said. "Captain Madison is attempting to contact us."

"Tell her to stand down and stay out of this, or we'll be forced to gut her ships, Star Force patrol or not."

"Yes sir."

It was on. I realized now that I should never have allowed them to destroy *Stalker*. They'd hurt me, and I'd let them do it while I remained passive.

But the only other option would have been to destroy Madison and her boats. I couldn't do that. They'd been the first Star Force people I'd met in two years. To come home shooting—it just hadn't been in me.

Now, however, I was in a fighting mood.

Madison called me back then. I saw her ships drift away, break formation and fall off behind us.

"Riggs," she said, "I'm going to pretend I'm not in this. Sorry about your alien prize. These orders from Central...they're bullshit if you ask me. You proved you were on the up-and-up when you stood down and abandoned *Stalker*. I'm not going to fire on you now."

"Thanks Madison," I said, "I owe you one."

"Luck. Madison out."

The channel closed, and the first big beam slashed out toward us less than a minute later. Such range, such power! The shot was a miss, but it didn't leave us any doubt it had been meant in earnest.

I would have ordered Hansen to begin evasive action and countermeasures, but he was already standing the ship on its head and making me sick.

"Contact that ship!" I demanded. "Get *Vladivostok's* captain on my screen."

"Channel refused."

"Keep trying. Marvin? Where did that robot go?"

Adrienne looked over her shoulder at me. "He scuttled off about a minute ago."

I froze in thought. What would his big poppa robot have done?

"Get someone down to the life boats and capture my chicken robot," I ordered. "I need him up here on the bridge."

The next shot came in hot. It was another near-miss. We were dancing for all we were worth. Hansen was accelerating toward the ring and a possible escape. The battleship coiled in the center of it blocking our way, but I ordered our gunners to hold their fire.

Two security Raptors brought Marvin 2.0 back to the bridge at a run. Lifted in the air between the two marines, his stubby legs were churning. His single arm whipped around in alarm, and the camera on the end of it panned toward me.

"Captain Riggs," he said. "These creatures have violated my person."

"No, Marvin," I said. "They're following orders—my orders. I need you on the bridge to help me."

"I would find it infinitely preferable—"

"I'm sure you would, but I need you to talk to that battleship out there. It's not allowing me to open a channel. Use your ansible to hack into their com system and connect me with someone in charge."

It was a tall order, especially for such a young robot. Valiant could have done it, but she was offline—permanently. The only operating ansible that could be used for a special job like this was inside Marvin's metal skull.

"I doubt they possess an ansible," Marvin began.

"Don't even try that one," I told him sternly. "You just got through telling me that you'd listened to an ansible transmission from *Valiant* to *Vladivostok*. I know they can hear you."

"I wasn't expecting to form such a specific memory in your organic brain with that comment," he grumbled. "It was my impression you had only short-term mental capacities."

Sighing, I had the Raptors set Marvin on his feet, and I knelt down to talk to him.

"Listen, Marvin," I said. "Your life is on the line, here. That ship out there—"

"It seems premature, not to mention counterproductive, to utter threats now."

"Threats? Oh, no. That's not what I meant. I'm trying to tell you that battleship out there is taking shots at us. If it hits us with one, we're all dead: humans, Elladans and robots together. You need to help us because—"

"The channel is open," Marvin said suddenly.

"Thank you," I said tightly. "Hello? Who am I talking to?"

"Lieutenant Stinson, orders processing. You need to get off this line. This is for classified traffic only."

"Listen to me, Lieutenant. This is an emergency. I'm Cody Riggs, a Star Force officer, and I want to talk to your captain. I'm aboard *Valiant*, the ship you're firing at. This is a misunderstanding."

"I don't know who you are, but—"

"Listen, Stinson," I said. "There's something wrong. An alien trick has gotten us to start firing at one another. Unless you want to be featured in a report that involves the destruction of Star Force vessels in a blue-on-blue fuck-up, I'd suggest you pass me up the chain of command."

The line fell quiet, but it didn't close. I was betting on the natural urge of any middleman to pass the buck. This time, it worked.

"Commander Mackle," the next guy said.

Everyone was a stickler, but before we'd dodged two more salvos, one of which took some paint off my hull, I was talking to *Vladivostok's* captain. His name was Brody.

"Captain Brody," I said, "I don't want to damage a Star Force battleship, but I'm going to have to if you keep blasting at me. We're getting close to our optimal range."

"They don't teach us to respond to threats in the academy, Riggs," he said. "Or whoever you are."

"Brody, listen to me. Let's stand down and talk a little. This is a misunderstanding. Let me have ten minutes, and if you're still not convinced, I'll surrender my ship to you without loss of life."

He paused at this offer. "You're on my kill-on-sight list, Riggs," he said.

"All right," I said, "I get that, but does that mean all my crew and passengers deserve to die as well?"

I had him there. If I was willing to surrender, there was no call to destroy my ship, orders or no.

"All right. Hit the brakes. We'll talk."

The channel closed. Hansen, who'd been listening in, shook his head at me.

"If we hold still, we're toast," he said.

"If he's lying, we're dead anyway. We've got no AI. We're damaged and low on everything. That big ship only has to tag us once with her mains, and we're gone."

"I've got a plan, sir," he said. "Just let me accelerate to maximum. With luck, we'll do a high-speed fly-by and she'll miss. On the far side—"

"On the far side is the thick atmosphere of Venus," I told him. "Have you forgotten? That ring is on the planet's surface, not up in orbit. You're planning to fly us right into a brick wall."

Hansen deflated after that. He was all out of bright ideas.

"All engines halt," I ordered.

This time, everyone did as I'd asked. When we were drifting in space, I contacted Brody again.

"Can we talk now, Captain?" I asked.

"I've been working with my computer since we last spoke," he said. "There was a disappearance two years ago— but it was far from here. Your voice prints seem to match, at least the prelim report says so... How the hell did you get into the Bellatrix system, Riggs?"

"It's a long, long story, Captain Brody."

"I've got time," he said. "Let's hear it."

The next hour was spent explaining our story along with a transfer of a massive amount of supporting data files. Brody went over them, and the more he looked the more amazed he became.

-38-

Having secured an escort homeward, with Star Force troops aboard Valiant to show we were "under guard", I felt better. I was fortunate in that Star Force captains had considerable latitude when following orders from Central. Due to the distances and Star Force tradition, a captain could amend his orders and apply good judgment. If he could justify his actions when he returned to base, he would get away with it, too.

But getting past the battleship wasn't good enough. I still had plenty of problems. I wasn't certain who'd ordered my arrest—or really, my death—but I had a pretty good idea who it was.

As best I could tell, my future father-in-law wanted me dead.

Grantham Turnbull and I had never gotten along from the start. As far as I could tell, he'd tried to kill me—probably to remove me from his daughter's presence and to strike at the Riggs family. He had lofty political ambitions, and the Riggs family name might overshadow all that. After the assassination attempt failed, and Olivia had died instead of me, his dislike had grown steadily.

To me, all that was history now. It was time to focus on the present. I had problems. Someone, Turnbull or otherwise, was still offended by the idea that I was still around and still breathing. I'd managed to get the Star Force people on the spot to see reason, but that didn't mean my enemies would stop trying to "fix" the problem I represented.

There were other problems, too. Adrienne was a big one. She'd begun to forgive me, gradually, for the incident with Cybele. Only the fact she knew Elladans could warp a man's mind had saved me. We still weren't sleeping together, but she would actually speak to me now and then. I'd decided to work on our relationship one careful step at a time.

But how could my slow climb out of the doghouse continue? I knew that I was going to have to fly home and publicly accuse her father of killing her sister and trying repeatedly to kill me. That wasn't going to make Adrienne happy. I didn't see how our relationship could survive it.

My sole confidant in all this was Marvin. He knew the story—probably more than he was letting on. I'd thought at first that his memory had been erased. That was sad as he really couldn't be the same Marvin with a full reboot.

But computers aren't quite like humans. Their artificial minds could survive death.

"Marvin?" I asked when I caught him in *Valiant's* data core, messing with the various brainboxes. "You do know you're not supposed to be in here, right?"

He twisted a camera arm around to look at me. He had two of them now, and they were making his central brainbox teeter unevenly when he walked.

"This chamber is clearly marked restricted to official personnel only," he said. "I'm a walking brainbox. In my opinion, you're the one who should be expelled."

The new Marvin wasn't quite like the old one, I'd noted over the last two days. He seemed child-like and a little more prissy. Maybe the original Marvin had been like that initially— I didn't know.

He went back to the dead stack of brainboxes that lined the room like bricks. He tapped into one at the top of the stack and activated it for data perusal with his longest central tentacle.

"All right," I told him, stepping close and squatting behind him, "I don't know what you're up to, but I'm going to have to take you out of here."

That got his attention. The two cameras drifted back to gaze at me. "Why?"

"Because you're not authorized—"

"I thought that issue was settled."

I heaved a sigh. "Marvin, listen, you have to learn about the chain of command on this ship. I'm at the top aboard *Valiant* at the moment. You're pretty close to the bottom. Do you understand this?"

"Why?" he asked.

"Why what?"

"Why do you get to tell me what to do?"

"Because you're a very young brainbox. You're like a child left behind by an old friend."

"When I get older, will these restrictions be lifted?"

"Probably, yes," I said. "You must prove your good intentions and that you know how to—"

"I find these interruptions and restrictions frustrating," he said. "Why can't I prove my competence to you now?"

"It's not like I'm asking you to pass a test. You have to prove yourself through prolonged good behavior."

Marvin retracted his tentacle and sat down on the floor. He was pretty much a box then, except for his cameras, which watched me closely.

"If I squat here motionless for a week, would that be convincing enough?" he asked.

"That's not quite what I had in mind," I said, amused. "What are you doing in here, anyway?"

"Accessing memories. Recordings of activities. My progenitor's mind is partially stored here through association."

"You aren't powering up Valiant again, are you?"

"No," he said. "To do so would slow down the process. I'm gleaning the ship's data without activating its processor other than as a search mechanism."

I nodded. "That's not as bad as I thought."

Sakura showed up then. She stood in the open hatchway, looking annoyed. She put her fists on her hips and glared.

"I can't think of two individuals I'd less like to see in the data core."

348

"Let me remind you that your actions are still under investigation, Chief," I told her.

She gave me a little smile. "As are yours, sir. We'll see what a Star Force tribunal has to say."

"Yes, we will. If you don't want to spend the rest of this journey home in the brig, I suggest you return to your duties. You're no longer allowed in the data core."

Huffing, she left. Marvin watched her go curiously.

"Is that female one of your sexual conquests?" he asked me.

"What? No. How did you get that idea?"

"She seems irritated. All the women you've had relations with are currently irritated with you. I logically—"

"No, Marvin. We've never even kissed. Now, let's talk about your goals here. I'm willing to let you play around in the data core perusing the ship's memories."

"An excellent decision. May I ask how I proved my reliability to you? I must have missed the critical point of transition."

"Uh…you didn't, really. This is a chance to do so, however. I changed my mind because I need you to look for certain details—"

"Ah, I see," he said. "My utility allowed me to supersede the normal restrictions. Pattern learned."

I blinked for a moment. I was pretty sure I'd just taught Marvin a bad thing, but I didn't know how to correct that—even if it was possible.

"Never mind about that," I said. "Here's what I want you to do in order to continue working in here. Look for all data concerning orders from Central about me. These orders will be restricted and possibly difficult to access. When you're finished examining any correlations between myself, Sakura, Valiant and especially Grantham Turnbull, report back to me."

Marvin eagerly extended his tentacles toward the brainboxes, but he hesitated.

"Will my access be withdrawn after I deliver this data to you?" he asked.

"Uh…" I said, my mind racing. I had to think clearly when talking to this robot. He'd been child-like yesterday, but he was advancing rapidly.

Thinking like Marvin, I realized he would probably *never* find the data I wanted if he was going to be given access only until he found it.

"I'll give you four hours," I said. "I'll want a substantial report after that. If I'm satisfied, you'll be given access for another four hours. This cycle will repeat until we arrive at a Star Force orbital station. At that point, I'll expect a full report."

"What bonus will I receive for the final report?" he asked.

I let out a sigh. "If I like it, I'll pat you on the head."

He looked at my hand.

"That reward is of dubious value," he said.

"But my continued good-nature is worth a lot. Get to work, robot."

I stood up and left him there in the data core. I hoped, from the bottom of my heart, that I wasn't making a mistake by letting Marvin Junior play around in there. If I'd had more time, I wouldn't have allowed it.

But I was running out of options, and he was the only entity who was capable of the work and who was at least marginally on my side. We were scheduled to make planetfall over Earth tomorrow, and I knew I had to have all the information I could get by then.

* * *

By the time we reached Earth, I'd made a few thready connections with Marvin's help. Turnbull's name was associated with the special scripting for Valiant in two locations. Both were connected because he'd been present in the chain of approval documents due to his sitting on various government committees.

Of course, the documents hadn't authorized turning Valiant into a killing machine. Instead, they'd allowed an outside contractor to work on the ship's core programming.

350

After careful checking, it was determined the contracting company was wholly owned by Turnbull industries. That in itself was only proof of a very minor form of corruption. There'd never been a government in history that hadn't been riddled with backroom deals that enriched participants.

But I believed the programming contract hadn't been procured for the purpose of putting a few extra coins into Grantham's pocket. He'd had murder in mind.

The trail went back through to *Greyhound* as well. She'd been programmed by the same group. I felt certain that, if I could look back into the past, I'd see someone rewriting that ship's script to inflict injury on me as well.

The accident hadn't been an accident. It had been attempted murder. Traveling out to meet Turnbull's brother later on had triggered similar software on that ship.

A startling thought came to me as I questioned Marvin about the details.

"Marvin," I said, "what other Star Force ships have been programmed by this company—what's it called?"

"Structured Software Incorporated."

"Structured Software—maybe to help install a new structure? Have you located a list of people who these ships don't like?"

"Yes, but the trigger events haven't been tripped for most personnel."

I stared at the little robot. What was growing in my mind was monstrous. A plot beyond anything I'd envisioned.

"How many names are on the list, Marvin?"

"Approximately six thousand. Some have been recently deleted with the latest update, but others—"

"Hold on," I said. "Who are these people? Profile them."

"Academy graduates make up forty-one percent. Career noncoms make up the majority of the rest. Most of the personnel are over the age of thirty, and they have a long record of service in Star Force. There's also a small but intriguing sub-list of celebrities and politicians."

I nodded, stunned. It all made sense.

"He meant to wipe out the top officers and the most experienced noncoms in the fleet. Imagine, our own ships killing our own crews, executing a massive purge. It's incredible."

"Are you pleased with my report, Captain?" Marvin asked.

"Yes—well, I'm not happy, but you did a good job."

"I would like to request an upgrade to my final reward. Rather than a pat on the head, I'd prefer to have access to more physical components."

"Such as arms? Legs? Engines?"

"Yes."

"You can have one more arm, and you can thicken your undercarriage to support the weight. Anything else?"

"Yes. I calculate that I'll need a larger power supply to operate the additional equipment."

I sighed. I could already see that Marvin was growing. If I let him, he'd be as big as a freight train in a few months.

-39-

Planetfall over Earth wasn't what I'd hoped for. Instead of celebrating, the crew was nervous. A few were drunk, but they weren't smiling. They had red-rimmed eyes and sweaty necks. No one spoke much, except to call out needed information.

"Starboard a degree, helm," I said as we drifted into our assigned dock.

"On it, sir," Hansen said.

"Clamps out. Watch the Dagger ports. This berth isn't shaped to fit our design changes."

"Roger that," Hansen said, grunting as he fought the controls. We had to do everything manually as Valiant was still dead. "Steady…steady…good!"

We were in. The ship rumbled as a dozen retros fired in tiny increments in a complex pattern to ease us into place. I frowned, noting that none of the crew was manning the brakes.

"Did we get a specialized brainbox hooked up? No one can tap all those retros at once that fast."

Hansen looked sheepish. "I asked for some help. It looks like he did a good job."

I stared at him for a second. "Marvin? You hooked a baby robot up to our braking system?"

"He's almost three days old. That's pretty good for a bot like him."

Shaking my head, I had to admit he'd done a stellar job. I couldn't help but wonder what kind of a treat he'd want for this small service.

"Sir?" asked a feminine voice behind me.

I turned to meet Cybele. She looked as shy and lovely as always. I had to remind myself she was really a bag of slime—but weren't we all?

Giving myself an imperceptible shake, I forced a tight smile. "Yes, Cybele. What is it?"

"I know you have a meeting set up with the base commander here at the station."

"Correct. If you could excuse me, I must get down to the main hatchway."

Cybele followed me toward the bridge exit, as did Adrienne's eyes. I was very aware of both of them, but I tried to pretend I was all business. Why did this girl have to choose now to make another play? If that's what she was doing. Didn't she know Adrienne was watching us both like a hawk?

"Sir," she said quietly at the hatch, "I want to go with you. I think I can help."

She made a grabbing motion with her hand. I looked at it, puzzled. It looked as if she'd just washed her hands, and there was a little soap residue left over.

Frowning, what she was really offering slowly sank in. I needed to convince the base commander as I'd done Captain Brody. Cybele, as she'd amply demonstrated in the past, was a master at convincing people of things.

I glanced back over at Adrienne. She'd turned away to her console again, and her shoulders seemed hunched. I'd seen that look before—she was pissed.

Heaving a sigh, I nodded to Cybele. "You can come along. I need all the help I can get. This is more important than I've been letting on."

Not even Hansen knew the truth. My theories concerning Turnbull and a massive plot against Star Force were just that—theories. A three day old robot had convinced me, but he might not be reliable. As an assurance, I walked to Sakura's compartment on the way to the main hatch.

"Sakura," I said, tapping on her door until it opened.

"What is it, sir?"

I handed her a data chip. "Read this. Act on it if I'm arrested or killed. You're one of the only people who might be able to stop it."

She frowned at me then looked at the chip in wonderment. "Um...all right, sir."

Striding away with Cybele in tow, I met up with Kwon next. He was in full kit and stood at the hatch, waiting.

"Really, Kwon?" I asked. "You think they'll let me walk into the base commander's office, technically under arrest, with a battle-suited marine at my side?"

"Better safe than sorry, boss," he said.

"Yeah…well, thanks for the thought. But if they've decide to take me down, one more gun won't help. My only hope is to convince them I'm right. Armament will only put them on their guard."

Kwon gestured toward Cybele. "Why's she going, then?"

I smiled. "Because these people need convincing."

He caught on after a moment, and I heard his huffing laugh behind me as I walked off my ship and marched down the tube into the station.

"You convince those white-haired officers good, girl!" Kwon boomed.

Our marine escorts joined us at the station dock. They looked nervous. I was in my dress blues, and Cybele was in her bridge duty attire. We didn't look dangerous, but they kept running their eyes over both of us anyway.

Then I realized something. Cybele was emitting pheromones. Nerves? No, the marines weren't nervous. They were turned on. They probably didn't know why, but they were definitely affected. My regular crew had grown somewhat accustomed to Elladans, and their power had waned during the trip. But for these boys, it must have been a shock.

Beauty, and a warm aura of invitation. Cybele was letting it all go, and she was enough to get any male's blood pumping. Even I felt it, but I was too focused on the coming confrontation to be easily distracted.

By the time we reached the base commander's office, my escorts needed a shower—a cold one.

The doors were real wood, not just smart metal taught to curl out of the way. That was a stylish addition. Real doors were considered cool, and all the top brass had them these days.

We were ushered inside, and the base commander stood to greet us. We saluted, but she didn't return the gesture.

She. Damn. The commander was a woman. I knew her as Rear Admiral Chen, and I hadn't cared about her gender until now. Half of Cybele's firepower was about to be wasted.

"Ensign Cody Riggs," Chen said. "Fresh from the Academy and a long holiday in uncharted space."

"Excuse me, Admiral," I said, "but it was hardly a holiday. Have you read my report?"

"I've skimmed it. On the whole, I find it incredible."

I could tell she didn't mean "incredible" as in "cool" or "amazing." She meant she didn't buy it.

"I have evidence to back up every word in the report: video, audio, written logs and after-action summaries—"

"I'm sure you do," she said, "but we don't have to get into all that now. Another guest is about to arrive. Please sit down."

Confused, I did as she asked. Cybele sat awkwardly next to me.

"May I ask who—" I began.

Admiral Chen stood up again. She did so rapidly, as if a higher power were present.

"Please rise. Our guest has arrived."

Cybele and I stood and turned around.

There, coming through those expensive doors, was none other than Grantham Turnbull himself. He grinned at me, and he nodded. When he looked at Cybele, however, he frowned.

"Who's this?" he asked Chen.

"An attaché to Mr. Riggs, I gather."

"I requested that—well, never mind. Riggs, let me shake your hand. This has all been a misunderstanding."

He lifted a shiny hand. It looked as if he'd been sweating or maybe he'd just come from the lavatory and washed them.

Hoping for the best, I took a step forward and lifted my own hand.

But Cybele beat me to it. She reached out and clasped Turnbull's offered hand with both of hers.

I had to give the girl credit for initiative. She was going to do her trick come hell or high water. I cocked my head, curious as to the effects.

Turnbull's expression changed from one of affability to one of confusion. I could only surmise he was feeling the effects of Cybele's embrace.

Could my troubles be over? In a single stroke? I dared to hope.

Then, everything took a very strange turn. Turnbull's face transformed.

He went from confusion to anger, then to pain. His mouth sagged open—and it kept going. His lower jaw sagged down, down—to his chest, and lower still.

Admiral Chen let out a gasp. She came around from behind the desk, reaching for her sidearm.

My hand lashed out and gripped her wrist. She was nanotized like any active duty Star Force officer, but she couldn't resist my strength. Her gun stayed in her holster despite the fact she used both hands and all her might to draw it.

I turned back to see how Cybele and Turnbull were getting along.

It wasn't pretty. They were both melting. Returning to the shape they'd originally had before they'd sought to fool humans.

Turnbull's lower face was sliding off his belly, merging with it. And that belly—it was rippling and convulsing as if he was about to lay an egg.

Cybele had lost some of her luster, too. Her hands had merged up with Turnbull's. Instead of fingers, both of them had something that looked like intertwined snail-tails. They ran with glistening slime.

"What's she doing to him?" Chen demanded.

"If I don't miss my guess, they're doing it to each other, Admiral," I said. "These people are not human. They're aliens, and they call themselves Elladans."

"What are they?"

"Watch as their legs fold up and dissolve. They're losing their rigid form. As best I can tell, they look like blobs—giant amoeba—in their natural state."

"Why did you bring this thing to my office?"

"Let me remind you, please, that I only brought one of them. You brought the other."

She relaxed her hand as the two Elladans, locked in some kind of mortal struggle, slipped into fleshy mounds on the floor. Their clothes had been shed, and they were bubbling.

"What the hell are they doing?" Chen asked in fascination.

"Either fighting or mating, I'd wager," I said. "It's kind of hard to tell which."

"Get them apart. Restrain them. Guards!"

The marines came tramping in, and I quietly let go of her wrist. I was glad she hadn't called them earlier. They had their laser rifles unslung and at the ready. I could tell they meant business.

"Which one is which?" she asked me, bending over the two struggling forms.

"The one with the service hat falling off...that's my crewman. Her name is Cybele, remember?"

Chen looked at me then. "I think I'd better read your report after all, Ensign."

I smiled. "I think that would be for the best, Admiral."

-40-

The thing known for years as Turnbull was eventually extricated from Cybele. The two of them had been fighting, it turned out. I'd never seen Elladans physically fight—and I hoped I'd never see it again.

Cybele had spotted another of her kind immediately, while the imposter had failed to do the same. Probably he'd been slow to do so because he thought he was the only member of his species on our planet.

Later, Cybele, Adrienne and I sat around a small table in a pub on the space station. At first, Adrienne had refused to accept the news of her father's death, but it had eventually sunk in.

She was drinking now, fairly heavily. I joined her at a more controlled rate.

"It's insane," Adrienne said for the tenth time. "My father's been dead and gone—for how long?"

"Probably a decade," Cybele said. "I'm so sorry, Adrienne."

My girl looked at Cybele with bleary, angry eyes. "Your kind killed my father."

"Yes, the agent probably did. But I didn't send him out. Many Elladans died back on our homeworld. Millions, in fact, and we don't blame you."

Adrienne was struggling with the truth. I couldn't blame her. She turned on me next.

"You slept with this thing," she said, jabbing a finger toward Cybele, "this killer alien. I don't think I can ever make love to you again."

I winced, but I played it straight. "That's up to you. I hope to have a future together. But no one has to decide any of this now. We all need to heal and to think clearly again."

Adrienne swiveled her head back toward Cybele, who drew back a bit. She waggled her finger at the Elladan.

"You should show yourself. You should look like a bag of snot. See how many dates you get then, bitch!"

I reached out and pushed down Adrienne's hand. "She doesn't mean it," I told Cybele.

"Yes, I do!"

After about twenty more minutes, the anger shifted into despondency and tears.

"I can't believe that bag of protoplasm taught me how to drive!" she cried. "I'm sickened. Was he influencing me all that time? Molding me for a purpose?"

"Maybe," I said, "we'll never know."

That was a lie, of course. It all seemed obvious to me in hindsight. The agent wanted to rule Earth, and every ruler needs competent-looking heirs. He probably planned to kill Adrienne and her sister eventually, replacing them with offspring of his own.

Looking back, I could well imagine why both the girls had graduated with perfect attendance and been enrolled in the best of schools. To my knowledge, neither had ever gotten less than an A in any course. With a mind-warping father heading the family, the achievements seemed less incredible.

But when the girls had gone off to college, he'd lost some of his power over them. That's when I'd stepped into the picture, upsetting his plans.

"Cybele," I said, "explain to her what the plan was. How an Elladan came to be on Earth."

"We have ansibles, just as you do," she said. "That's a classified secret, and I'm breaking Argos' orders by telling you."

"An ansible is a communication device," Adrienne said. "So what?"

360

"Yes, one capable of connecting two points for transmissions…but…we were able to develop the technology further than you have at this point."

I gestured for her to keep going. Adrienne up-ended her drink, guzzling until I gently pushed the mug down again.

"You see," Cybele said, "I don't know everything. These are secrets that aren't available to all Elladans. What I do understand is that we've been able to use the ansibles to create tiny rings. We can connect one of our rings to any of the others in existence."

Adrienne threw up her hands and let them flop back down. "Then why not just roll a fleet through on top of Earth and conquer us?"

"You don't understand. These rings are very small. Only about like this."

She formed her fingers into a circle about three inches around.

"That's it? How can anyone get through that tiny—oh."

She'd figured it out on her own, but I decided to jump in and explain further.

"Elladans have no bones. This agent was able to slip through a ring back on Elladan and transport himself to one of our local rings. They bring a tiny life-support bubble with them and hibernate until they reach a planet."

I turned back to Cybele. "How many such agents are there in the cosmos?"

She shrugged her shoulders helplessly. "I have no idea. The program was abandoned some time ago as none of them ever returned. But apparently this agent almost managed to complete his mission."

"Why not help him?" Adrienne demanded. "He's your kind. Your flesh. Why attack him the way you did?"

Cybele looked ashamed. "I like humans. We're not all monsters. We're not all the same. One of you might be a serial killer of children—does that mean every individual on Earth is a fiend?"

Adrienne glanced at me angrily when Cybele mentioned "liking" humans.

"You've proven that much to be true," she said. "I hate you, Cybele, you know that?"

"Yes, I'd gathered…"

"But," Adrienne went on, "you did the right thing here. You kept Cody from touching the agent's hand. You outted my father's imposter—his killer."

She looked like she was going to cry again, so I handed her the mug. She took a big hit and sighed.

The conversation went on. It was colorful and varied. Adrienne declared love, hate and every emotion in between to both of us.

When we were about to leave a shadow fell over the table.

He was a big man, bigger than I remembered. It had been so long since I'd seen him.

I jumped up and hugged the stranger, who hugged me back. The two women looked at us in confusion.

"Dad!" I shouted. "This is my father, Kyle Riggs."

"Of course," Adrienne slurred. "I'm so glad to meet the infamous Kyle Riggs. He's just like you, sir." She waggled a finger at Cybele. "He even screws aliens like her."

My father raised his eyebrows high in surprise. He gave Cybele an up-down appraisal and nodded in appreciation.

"I see," he said as neutrally as he could. He turned back to Adrienne, "and who might you be, Miss?"

"Miss Turnbull," she said. "I'm the fool that wants to marry your son."

She pitched forward then, and I thought at first that she was passing out. The truth was less happy.

She threw up on everyone's shoes.

* * *

Without the powerful influence of Turnbull's imposter working to impede my every action, I found life became much easier. Star Force officials quickly dropped all charges and canceled all warrants for my arrest.

Lobbying as hard as I could, I got them to release a critical update to their brainbox scripting. Hundreds of ships were updated without incident.

There were exceptions, however. AI systems on a dozen vessels managed to block the update and go rogue. Some of these warships killed their crews and then fought to the death with loyal Star Force ships.

Other AIs decided to flee, flying off into the darkness beyond the light of their local star. These ships were tracked for a time, but when it was realized they were heading for unexplored neighboring star systems, any effort to hunt them down was abandoned.

"I think it's a mistake," I told Admiral Chen four days after Cybele had fought Turnbull's murderer on the floor of her office. "Those rogue ships have intelligent AI systems and onboard factories. In time, they could turn into the equivalent of Macros. I can foresee a day when they may infest star systems that we have no direct connection with but which represent a potential threat."

Chen's office had been cleaned but, despite numerous shampooing efforts, a ghastly brown stain remained on her carpet. I got the feeling she blamed me personally for this. While we spoke, she periodically glanced down at the stain. Each time she did so, she ground her teeth.

"You're an ensign, Riggs," she reminded me yet again. "While your opinions are vaguely interesting, they don't hold any sway with the Joint Chiefs."

"My father feels the same way I do," I pointed out.

Chen gave me an irritated stare.

I knew I was pushing it. Just days earlier, I'd been on everyone's termination list. But I felt it was important enough to take a career risk—those rogue ships had to be run down and destroyed.

"Your father," Chen said, glancing at her ruined carpet again and flashing me another brief snarl, "is no longer a member of Star Force. He's a retired celebrity from a time which is, thankfully, well behind us. His opinions therefore carry no more weight than those of any concerned citizen. He can't possibly alter a decision made by our modern military."

I took a deep breath and let it out slowly. Then I forced a smile. "I understand, Admiral, but as a final statement of my concern, I'd like to offer my services."

Chen frowned. "In what capacity?"

"I'd like to lead an expedition to pursue the three rogues heading for Sirius. That group is the most dangerous in my opinion."

For perhaps the first time since the interview had begun, I had her full attention.

"Cody…such a journey would take years."

"Yes. I'm well aware of that. My crew should be made up entirely of volunteers."

She looked troubled. "You really think the situation is that serious?" She began to pace. "We would have chased them, you understand, but they had a head start on the acceleration arcs. They can't be run down until they decelerate to arrive at their target star."

"Exactly," I said. "My ship, should I be given a command, will continue to accelerate after they start to slow down. At that point, we'll overtake them. I'll do battle, destroy them, then reverse course and return to Earth."

Chen shook her head. She still glanced at the carpet stain now and then, but she no longer curled her lip at me when she did so.

"I'll forward the request," she said, "but I seriously doubt it will be accepted. They would have to give you a battleship to defeat two destroyers and a cruiser."

"Yes, that matches the details of my formal proposal."

I handed her a data chip. On it was the strategic plan I'd worked up with Marvin's help. He'd done the math, showing the type of ship and the length of time it would take us to run down the enemy. Our best estimate for interception was one-point-two years. The full trip, including deceleration and return, would take nearly three years in total.

Chen looked at the chip dubiously. Then she walked around to the far side of her desk again. There, she dug into her top drawer and returned to confront me with a small box in her hand.

"What's this?" I asked.

She handed it to me. "Open it."

I did so. I was surprised to see the insignia of a full lieutenant.

She shook my hand, and I felt numb.

"Congratulations, Riggs. You've earned a promotion."

My eyes followed her as she went back around to the far side of her desk.

"Was there any chance before I came in here that these bars were going to stay in your desk?" I asked.

She shrugged without meeting my gaze. "I was given discretion. The promotion was subject to my approval. I decided during the course of this meeting that you earned the rank. Probably, you've earned it a hundred times over. Again, accept my congratulations."

I nodded and closed the box. Adrienne would be thrilled, but I was too concerned for the future to enjoy the honor the promotion represented.

"Thanks for your consideration, and your patronage," I told Chen, and I left.

* * *

The next day I returned home to my Dad's place. My mom was on a trip to India, but she was expected to return in the morning. After a round of hugs and congratulations on my new rank, we sat down to talk.

For my father, the biggest worry wasn't the rogue ships— it was the existence of an Elladan empire of mind-influencing blobs.

"They infiltrated Earth once, and they'll do it again," he said.

I'd come home with guests. On my left was Adrienne, on my right was Cybele, and crouching at my feet like a terrier was Marvin.

"I don't think so, sir," Cybele said. "From what I know of the program, it was abandoned years ago."

My father shook his head and headed to the kitchen. He popped open three beers and walked back toward us. He

365

handed one to me, then the second to Cybele. He drank the last one himself.

When Adrienne looked at him in surprise, old man Riggs shook his head. "I've seen you drink, girl. It isn't a pretty sight."

Adrienne reddened, but she didn't argue.

After he'd downed his beer, he put his hands on his knees and studied Marvin. The robot returned the favor with three cameras. I couldn't recall having approved the third one, but there it was.

"Marvin 2.0," he said. "Has he told you who's related to these Elladans of yours?"

I blinked and shook my head. "Who, Pop?"

"The Microbe colonies that live in the oceans of Eden-6. They're the same basic stock. I'd always thought the Microbes had evolved in the Eden system, but tests performed on the squirting slime Cybele and Turnbull left on the floor of Chen's office have confirmed they didn't."

For a moment, we were all baffled. Then I caught on, and I looked at Marvin accusingly.

"Did you know the Microbes were related to the Elladans?"

"They are a sub-species, yes," he said. "The genus isn't a precise match, obviously. In my estimation, the water-suspended colonies are a wild adaptation of the original form."

"Exactly," my father said. He laughed. "Same old Marvin. Always withholding information for some nefarious purpose of his own. This brainbox is cuter than the old one, I have to admit that. But you should never let him grow to where he's bigger than a dog, son."

"Why not?" Marvin piped up.

"It makes you too intimidating, robot. Once we let a machine get bigger than we are, humans tend to treat that machine as an adult and give it more and more freedom. We're psychologically built that way. However, if you keep the robot small, you'll hold onto the restrictions you so wisely put in place originally."

Nodding, I swore to myself to follow my father's advice on that point. He knew Marvin much better than I did. He was right anyway…the old Marvin had gotten out of hand under my lax control.

"An unwarranted injustice," Marvin complained. "I hope you're not listening to your ancestor, Cody. His ideas are outdated and—"

"Shut up, Marvin," I said, "or I'll have to pluck out that extra camera you stole."

Marvin fell silent. His third camera retreated out of reach like the eye of a snail.

Turning back to my father, I discovered he was handing me another beer. I took it gratefully.

"Dad, how do you think the Microbes got there? Into the planetary oceans of Eden-6, that is."

He waved his bottle at Cybele. "I'm sure she knows. Ask her."

I turned to face Cybele. She'd regained her lovely super-human appearance, but there were flaws. Her right hand was deformed. The fingers were swollen like sausages and there were no fingernails on any of them. This was a lingering effect of her battle with the imposter.

Cybele looked embarrassed. "They must have come from the same infiltration project. An Elladan agent must have crash landed in the oceans. Since there was no local civilization, it must have degenerated into an aquatic colony as a means of survival."

"Right…" I said. "Then the Macros discovered them, and later on Marvin did. But there's something else I wanted to talk to you about, Father."

"What's that?" he asked.

I told him about Astrolyssos and the Ancients. He was intrigued. He admitted that he didn't know if the Ancients as a whole would take offense to our attack on Astrolyssos, or if they were wandering individuals without a central government. We all tended to think the latter was more likely. They were so large they couldn't easily build a civilization even on a star.

"They're probably nomadic," Adrienne said thoughtfully. "Star-dwellers that imagine themselves to be gods. They wander the cosmos to plague lesser beings as the mood strikes them. Mating occurs perhaps once every million years when they encounter one another. Very strange creatures."

My father jabbed a finger in her direction. "You might recall that in my day we theorized the Ancients caused ice ages. Their visits match the dates of dramatic stellar events in history."

"Well," I said, "the ring Astrolyssos threw at us in the Trinity system sent us on a one-way trip home. I think it's unlikely anyone is coming through to plague again us soon."

"Except for more Microbe agents!" Dad said, giving Cybele a hard look.

"Astrolyssos did say he wanted to bottle humans up in our designated zone of space," Adrienne agreed with me. "Maybe that's a good thing. After having had a look at the rest of inhabited space, I find it rather peaceful here among our home stars."

My dad laughed. He'd had more to drink than the rest of us. He stood up, yawned and stretched, then looked around at the three of us.

"Time for bed," he announced. "Now, who's sleeping with whom? Or are we talking about you guys needing a really big bed, here?"

He laughed uproariously. The women looked alarmed, and they reddened. I shook my head.

"Thanks Dad," I said.

Later that night, when Adrienne was sighing softly in her sleep at my side, I heard a tapping sound.

I sprang up to investigate, but I found it was only Marvin. He was peeping into the room with a camera.

"Marvin?" I whispered. "What are you doing? It's late."

"I'm not sleepy—I'm never sleepy."

"Yes, well, go find yourself something to play with."

All three of his cameras focused on me for a second.

"I already did. Do you want to see it?"

Stifling a yawn, I followed him down a creaking set of stairs and went outside under the stars. There on the porch, I found what looked like a long, black snake.

"What the hell...?"

"It's part of me—of my progenitor."

Then I remembered. Years ago, when I was a young boy, the original Marvin had created a massive accident that had nearly burned down the farm. This arm had been blown off then. It was a coiling structure built with constructive nanites.

"It must have rusted solid by now," I commented, poking at it dubiously. "Where did you find it?"

"At the bottom of an old well."

"An old well?" I asked. "How did you get into that?"

"There were nails and concrete—it wasn't easy."

I shook my head. "Well, it's a nice souvenir. What do you want to do with it?"

"There are some of the interior nanites that are preserved and functional. It's part of me—the old me. That intrigues my mind, and I want to add this arm to my collection."

"I don't know…"

He made a plaintive sound. That surprised me. I'd never heard the old Marvin whimper or cry. He'd only spoken, and he'd never made sounds of anguish that I could remember.

For some reason the sound goaded me to leniency. Perhaps that's what it had been designed to do.

Whatever the case, I let him have the arm. Happily, he worked on it for days adding new constructives and retooling the old. Eventually, the arm was as sleek and silvery-black as it had been when I was a kid.

He whipped it around at a different rate of motion than the others—could it be haunted by the ghost of the original Marvin? I didn't know, but I wouldn't have been surprised if it was.

Each night while I stayed with my parents, I found a reason to awaken and gaze up at the stars. They were as cold and distant as they'd ever been.

But they were known to me now. My crew and I had traveled together through more star systems than any other group of humans in history. I knew that out there, somewhere, there were beings building, plotting and actively seeking our demise.

It was an unsettling thought. It kept me awake, watching the stars all night. I couldn't stop wondering what they might send down next to visit my green Earth.

More Books by B. V. Larson:

UNDYING MERCENARIES
Steel World
Dust World
Tech World
Machine World
Death World

STAR FORCE SERIES
Swarm
Extinction
Rebellion
Conquest
Battle Station
Empire
Annihilation
Storm Assault
The Dead Sun
Outcast
Exile
Demon Star

OTHER SF BOOKS
Battle Cruiser
Starfire

Visit BVLarson.com for more information.

16321221R00208

Printed in Great Britain
by Amazon